I0691787

DENVER CITY JUSTICE

Praise for J.v.L. Bell's Fiction

The Lucky Hat Mine, filled with period detail and real-life pioneers such as Mountain Charley, Green Russell and the Tabors, is a spirited...tale.
—Sandra Dallas, *The Denver Post*

J. v. L. Bell has written an unusual murder mystery with a romance angle set during the Civil War period. The dialogue and narrative, which is humorous at times, fittingly captures life in a gold mining town. The inclusion of strong female characters, such as a freedwoman, adds to the appeal of the story...The novel is an entertaining read.
—Waheed Rabbani, *Historical Novel Review*

The Lucky Hat Mine combines murder, mystery, gold mining and life on the early frontier in a perfect blend of fact, fiction and diversion. J.v.L. Bell has certainly done her research of the times and written a story that was hard to put down...I recommend this book to young and old, mystery and historical readers, and those who just enjoy a well written book.
—*Readers' Favorite*

JvL Bell's recipe for a great story, simmer a heroine in danger, add a dash of history, and spice with humor.
—HL Miller, author of the *PT Thomas Series*

An intriguing, fast-paced mystery lovers of westerns and coming-of-age tales alike will love.
—Andrew McFadyen-Ketchum, poet-editor

The Lucky Hat Mine is a fun historical romance set in the 1860s in Colorado...The book was a good old western delight...I would recommend it to those who like a fun read, enjoy early US western style tales, and like a little romance in the story they read.

—Rosie Amber, *NetGalley* review

I really enjoyed this historical mystery-romance. It is a clever tale of greed, murder and suspense with a good dollop of romance and humour.

—Inishowen Cailin, *Just Book Talk* blog

Our protagonist, Millie, is the most badass woman ever. Not in an assassin kind of way but she is stubborn and firm in the best way. She is independent and won't let any of the (many, *many*) men who try tell her what to do.

–Fiona, *The Bookworm Who Lived*, blog

Denver City

Justice

A Novel

J.v.L. Bell

HANSEN PUBLISHING GROUP, LLC

This is a work of historical fiction. All of the characters, organizations, and events portrayed in this novel are either a product of the author's imagination or are used fictitiously.

Denver City Justice
Copyright © 2019 by J.v.L. Bell

All rights reserved. Except for brief passages quoted in newspaper, magazine, radio or television reviews, no part of this book may be reproduced in any form or by any means, electronic or mechanical, including photocopying or recording, or by an information storage and retrieval system, without permission in writing from the publisher.

23 22 21 20 19   10 9 8 7 6 5 4

ISBN: (PAPER) 978-1-60182-340-3
ISBN: (EBOOK) 978-1-60182-341-0

Cover design by Nikki Rasmussen
Cover photograph Copyright © 2019 Clifford M. Conklin
Book interior design by Jon Hansen

Hansen Publishing Group, LLC
302 Ryders Lane
East Brunswick, NJ 08816
https://hansenpublishing.com

Author site: www.jvlbell.com

For my family, John, Tess, and Corrie
Thanks for supporting me
through this crazy writing dream.

In memory of June Pausback and Carol Douglas,
two strong and amazing women
and my wonderful father, Cleve Bell.
I miss you all.

DENVER CITY JUSTICE

ONE

January 3, 1864

A Winter Wedding

Mayhem poured out from the Beebee House dining hall as Millie peeked in and sucked down a breath. Oh Lor'! The hall was crowded with every man, woman, and child who lived in Idaho Springs. The townsfolk were packed shoulder to shoulder, as tight as a can of sardines, with children hanging from the rafters and men hollering as they sipped from their flasks. Everyone was dressed in their Sunday best—the men in faded flannel, patched buckskin, high ankle boots, and slouch hats, while the women wore sprigged calico dresses with paisley shawls.

They were all waiting for her to marry Dominic Drouillard. Or more likely, for the free meal after the ceremony.

Millie backed into the shadows and leaned against the rough wall, taking several deep breaths. Icy air seeped through the holes between the boards as her stomach fluttered and her heart raced. She wanted to marry Dom. She loved him.

But did she really know him?

Just minutes ago, Widow Ferris had burst into her dressing room and insinuated Dom had a secret in his past. Something so appalling he'd paid Mr. Ferris blackmail gold to keep it quiet. Millie had heard that many of the men

who'd come west during the Pikes Peak gold rush were running from something, but surely not Dom.

"No use hiding in the shadows." Widow Ferris' high-
pitched, nasally voice pierced Millie's unease. "Procrastinat-
ing won't change a thing." She gave Millie a shove, and they
both tumbled into the candlelit, raucous dining hall.

"There she is!" someone hollered, and the noise dropped
from a roar to a low rumble.

Millie straightened her skirt, regaining her balance if not
her dignity. This was her wedding. No way she'd let Widow
Ferris ruin it. She glared at the woman before turning to
face the crowd, forcing herself to smile.

"Thank goodness you're here." Mrs. Beebee, the propri-
etress of the Beebee House, squeezed through the mass of
bodies and hurried to Millie's side. The matron's normally
impeccable gown was wrinkled, and her calm demeanor
was replaced by wide eyes and jerking hand gestures. "The
menfolk are getting restless," she whispered, her voice shaking slightly. "They're starting to take more than a nip from
their flasks, eyeing the food table like a wake of vultures.
And the smell!" She waved a gloved hand in front of her
face.

Reflexively Millie sucked in a breath and then wished
she hadn't. Idaho Springs was deep in the Rocky Mountains, and bathing was considered optional by most miners,
especially during the winter.

Mrs. Beebee took Millie's arm and pulled her forward.
"Make room! Let the bride come through."

The crowd shuffled and jostled until a narrow aisle
formed. "That'll work for me," hollered Widow Ferris,
knocking Millie and Mrs. Beebee aside. Dragging an easel
and carrying a canvas and charcoal, Widow Ferris strutted between the audience like the bride-to-be. "I'm hired
to sketch this wedding," she announced loudly. "I need a
front-row seat."

"You hired her to sketch the wedding?" Mrs. Beebee whispered, sounding incredulous. "Can she even draw?"

Millie had not hired Widow Ferris to sketch the wedding. She'd been touching up her hair, trying to calm her nerves, when Widow Ferris burst into her dressing room and announced Dom had a shameful past. The pinched-face Widow Ferris wanted one of Millie's tear-shaped gold nuggets, "just like my husband used to get," to stay silent. Before Millie could find her voice, Widow Ferris insisted she'd sketch the wedding, "so your payment looks legit."

Trying to hide her annoyance, Millie brushed a stray hair from her face and said politely, "Thank you, Mrs. Beebee, for allowing me to have my wedding here." Her Southern accent stretched each word. "Widow Ferris is…" Her words petered out. The aisle had widened, and Millie caught sight of Dom. Her future husband looked, well, downright elegant. He towered over the crowd, his broad shoulders filling his white linen shirt and weskit. He wore his new slouch hat at a rakish angle, and his blue eyes glittered like jewels.

Oh Lor'! Millie blew out a long, slow breath. She was really going to marry Dom.

Drawn like a moth to candlelight, Millie stepped between her neighbors, forgetting Widow Ferris, Mrs. Beebee, and the rowdy miners around her, but halfway to the altar, the noxious stench of unwashed bodies made her gag. The place smelled worse than her outhouse! Covering her nose with her handkerchief, she hurried on, her watering eyes glued to Dom's clean-shaven face, wavy black hair, and mesmerizing eyes.

"Ain't seen this much skin since my last visit to Tit Bit's crib," muttered someone beside her.

The crowd erupted in laughter as a different voice said, "Bet there's a line at Tit Bit's crib tonight."

Millie froze and glanced down at herself. In the flickering candlelight, the shadowed lace encircling her waist shimmered like a deep evening sky. Folds of ornate, hand-tatted lace trimmed her sleeves and neckline. Dom had given her the dress as a Christmas present, just before he proposed, but now the neckline seemed just a tad low. Resisting the urge to pull it up, Millie hurried to the altar and took Dom's outstretched hand.

A familiar bleat made her look down and groan. Buttercup!

Last summer, Millie had answered a wife-wanted ad and traveled to the Colorado Territory. En route, she'd been given Buttercup by her traveling companion. The little goat was the size of a knee-high dog and had bulging eyes, floppy ears, and a strange habit of fainting whenever she was startled. The goat had been Millie's sole companion for months after she'd arrived to find her intended husband, Dom's older brother, dead.

Millie loved Buttercup, but she'd specifically told Dom a wedding was no place for a goat. Buttercup poked her head out from behind Dom's legs; green leaves from the altar's Kinnikinnick decoration hung from her mouth.

Millie glared at Dom, but he didn't seem to notice. Grinning like an excited madman, he released her hand, slipped his arm around her waist, and pulled her against him for a toe-curling kiss. "You kept me waiting," he whispered, his warm breath caressing her cheek.

Around them, the crowd erupted in hoots and hollers, stomping their feet until the floor shook. Millie stepped back, resisting the urge to fan her warm face. "Mr. Drouillard! We are in public and it is improper—"

"I need a better angle," interrupted Widow Ferris. The pinched-face woman moved her rickety easel over, bumping into Millie as she passed. "You there, bring my stool and charcoal." She fussed about as she seated herself beside Millie like the matron of honor. Once she was settled, she nodded to the preacher. "You can start, Brother Bunce. I'm ready."

Buttercup butted Millie and rubbed her head against Millie's beautiful skirt, leaving a line of goat drool. Millie ground her teeth. This was not the wedding she'd planned.

"Dearly beloved," began Brother Bunce, his deep Southern accent making his words sound smooth. "We are gathered here in the sight of God and before this community to join together this man, Mr. Dominic Drouillard, and this woman, Miss Permelia Abingdon Virginia, in holy matrimony."

Brother Bunce's sermon wasn't loud enough to block the noises from the shuffling, impatient crowd, but as the minister's voice rose and fell, Millie felt her beating heart calm. She glanced sideways. Dom stood beside her, beaming like a child at Christmas.

Millie loved him. She couldn't imagine life without him. Surely Widow Ferris had lied. The unpleasant woman was just sore because her husband had been a murderer, and Millie had fired the shot that caused him to fall to his death. Widow Ferris was just trying to get even and ruin Millie's wedding.

Dom hadn't paid blackmail gold to Mr. Ferris, had he?

"Holy matrimony is ordained by God and should not be entered lightly," Brother Bunce said. "The nuptial union between a man and a woman is one of the strongest bonds in nature, second only to that of a mother to her child. As is written in Matthew 19:6, a…"

"Like she ain't already with child." The drunken voice interrupting the sermon made Millie cringe. She tightened her hold on Dom's arm as he dragged her around to face her least-favorite, former suitor, Mr. Turck. The man, his beard braided into two stringy ropes, shoved through the crowd. The man's massive fists clutched each braid, squeezing them in a motion that reminded Millie of the milking of a cow.

"Millie's a lady and our relationship has been entirely

proper," Dom snarled. "And you, Turck, weren't invited to this celebration."

"Course, I were," said Mr. Turck, a drunken slur in his words. "Only reason you won is you got an unfair advantage over the rest of us. You been living with her for months. She probably gots to marry you now." He stared at Millie's abdomen, as if looking for swelling.

Mortification added to Millie's other jumbled emotions. "Dom was my guest!" she insisted.

Some of their audience nodded their agreement, but others looked dubious. Dom had arrived last fall and, after learning of his brother's death, moved into Millie's cabin insisting he wouldn't leave until he found his brother's murderer. In order to rid herself of this unwanted guest, Millie had unraveled the crime and discovered Mr. Ferris was the killer. But in the process, she'd fallen in love with Dom.

"Let the lassie have her day and marry in peace." Mr. Shumate, the town blacksmith, wrapped his thick arm around Mr. Turck and slapped a hand over the drunken man's mouth. In a strong Scottish burr, he added to Millie, "Brother Bunce still has a thing or two to say. You might want to get on with it, lassie, before your wee goat eats the altar."

Millie spun around, pulling Dom with her, and grabbed Buttercup. Half of the green-red Kinnikinnick leaves were gone while others had suspicious bite-shapes. Pulling Buttercup against her, Millie ignored the goat drool and scowled. "Please, Brother Bunce, can we finish?"

Brother Bunce lifted bushy eyebrows and continued, appearing to be in no hurry. He added a bit of fire and brimstone to his sermon before speaking at length on how a wife should honor, obey, and serve her husband. Millie didn't interrupt the man of God—she just wanted to be married—but it took all the control she possessed. If Dom ever expected her to honor, obey, and serve him, a sordid past would be the least of his worries.

Finally, the minister wound down and said, "Please face each other so we may begin your marriage vows." Dom turned to Millie, his expression melting her exasperation. Her heart swelled as he vowed to love and protect her for as long as he drew breath. Her own voice shook as she made her own promise.

"If any hath reason why these two shouldn't be married," said Brother Bunce in a thundering crescendo, "speak now, or forever hold your peace." The minister drew in a breath, and Dom released Millie's hand and reached into his weskit pocket, removing the golden band he'd forged with Blacksmith Shumate's help.

"A ring," began Brother Bunce more quietly, "is the symbol—"

"I...I got an issue," slurred Mr. Turck. Shaking off Blacksmith Shumate, he knocked over several guests as he rushed the altar. "She should be mine." He sprayed spit and drink out with his words. "I saw her first. Dom jumped my claim!"

This isn't happening, Millie thought as Dom thundered, "Turck, you ass. Millie wouldn't marry you if you were the last man alive." Dom punctuated his words by releasing Millie and roughly poking Turck's chest with Millie's wedding band.

"Course she would. She ain't picky. She's marrying you." Drunkenly, Turck knocked away Dom's hand and stumbled forward, bumping into Dom.

Dom fell back and his heel caught Buttercup. He threw up his hands to regain his balance, and Mr. Turck gave him another shove. Like a felled tree, Dom went down knocking over two guests before he struck the ground with a resounding thud.

Buttercup's eyes bulged out, and the little goat fainted.

Millie's shock transformed to fury. She narrowed her eyes and opened her mouth, but before she could get a word out, Mr. Turck grabbed her arm and spun her around toward Brother Bunce. Dragging her forward, Mr. Turck took Dom's place at the altar.

"H…hitch us up, padre," he burped loudly.

TWO

January 3, 1864
A Gross, Unpardonable Insult

Hitch us up?!" Millie jerked free and waved away Mr. Turck's foul breath. "An ox is hitched up, you muttonhead. A lady is married."

"W…where's a lady?" Mr. Turck looked around confused.

"Millie's a lady!" Dom scrambled to his feet, grabbed the drunk's shoulder, and spun him around. "And don't you forget it." None too gently, Dom shoved Mr. Turck forward, and as the crowd scrambled out of the way, Blacksmith Shumate opened the door. "I need to finish getting married," Dom said as frigid air blasted into the room, "and you need to leave."

"S…she's 'pose ta marry me!" Mr. Turck whined. He whirled around, and his flailing fist clipped Dom's chin.

Millie gasped as Dom's head jerked back and his face turned dark as a storm cloud. She knew that expression and the trouble it boded. "Dom, no!" she shouted, but it was too late.

Dom bellowed like an angry ox and rammed into Mr. Turck, knocking him back through the crowd. Slow moving wedding guests were bowled over, and Millie watched with horror as the town's founding father, Elder Griswold, tumbled to the floor. Mrs. Beebee in her fashionable crimson gown landed indecorously on top of him.

Dom disappeared as the crowd closed in, hollering encouragement. This couldn't be happening. Not in the middle of *her* wedding! Spotting Sheriff Reynolds, Millie pushed through the crowd and grabbed his arm. "Do something!"

The sheriff's shouts of encouragement died, and he sheepishly straightened his slouch hat and slapped the shoulder of his hollering deputy. The two lawmen, with the help of brawny Blacksmith Shumate, broke up the fight and bodily tossed a screaming Mr. Turck out the door.

The room quieted, and spectators shuffled as far from Millie as they could get, giving her a clear view of Dom. His weskit was torn, and blood oozed from his lip and dripped onto his white linen shirt. He looked like a belligerent saloon brawler.

"You're not yet married, lad." Blacksmith Shumate brushed dust off Dom's back and handed the groom his slouch hat. "Best return and finish before raising any more Cain."

Dom glanced at Millie and his eyes filled with guilt. Feet dragging, he walked toward her, looking like a six-foot tall schoolboy facing a strict schoolmarm.

Millie blew out a breath. This was Dom, the man she'd fallen in love with. His edges were rough, but he'd only been trying to protect her. Sighing, she stepped forward, straightened the horsehair stock around his neck and led him back to the altar. "Have you lost my ring, Mr. Drouillard?" She used her handkerchief to wipe the blood from his face.

Dom patted his weskit pocket—his knuckles oozing blood and deflated a bit more. "I must have dropped it in the scuffle."

There was a mad scramble, and the town shopkeeper, the man everyone called Old Shakespeare, hollered triumphantly. Holding the ring aloft, he rushed the altar. "The course of true love never did run smooth," he said as he handed the ring to Dom.

Dom took Millie's hand and gently removed her glove, slipping the ring onto her finger. He left a streak of blood on her sleeve, but nonetheless, Millie stared at the symbol of their marriage and felt her heart expand. She was wearing Dom's ring.

"I now pronounce you man and wife," Brother Bunce boomed out.

For better or worse, for future brawls or anything inappropriate he might have done in his past, Millie was now Dom's wife. The room erupted as miners clapped their hands and stomped their feet, shaking the floor.

"Kiss the bride!" echoed through the rafters.

Dom let out a wild whoop and swept Millie into a bear hug, kissing her with such enthusiasm she forgot about wedding brawls and improper behavior. She even forgot the impropriety of Dom's very public kiss or the fact he was getting blood on her dress. Her toes curled, and she felt a tingling through every part of her body. *She was Mrs. Dominic Drouillard.*

"Food!" someone hollered, and men stampeded toward the food table.

"Aye, and a dram of whiskey." Blacksmith Shumate led another charge toward the drink table.

"At least one dram," said Elder Griswold, rubbing his hip. "More likely several."

"Never seen Dom look like that." Mrs. Griswold sighed and pushed her slightly tilted bonnet back on her head. "He's grinning like a weasel in a hen house."

Much later, Dom led Millie out for yet another celebratory dance and when they finished, they found Mary—Millie's closest friend and neighbor—tightly gripping Dom's horsehair stock which now rested around Buttercup's neck.

"I be heading home with Buttercup," she said, beaming at them, her wiry black hair bouncing as she nodded her head. "I keep her and her babies for a night or two. Newly-weds need time *alone*."

Brother Bunce hurried over, but the man of God froze when he spotted Mary. His face betrayed his censure as he thrust a paper at Dom. "Your marriage certificate." Giving Mary one last disapproving glance, he stiffly walked away.

"Don't worry none about him, Miss Mary." Dom pulled Mary into a warm embrace. "We appreciate all you've done. You've been a good friend to both of us."

Millie nodded, proud that Dom didn't have the prejudices of Brother Bunce and many of the prospectors in town. When Millie first arrived in Idaho Springs, Mary had been an outcast, censured because of her ebony skin. Despite Millie being a Southern belle from New Orleans and Mary a free black from New York City, Mary had generously helped Millie survive those first few difficult months. As their friendship grew, Millie insisted Mary be included in all town functions. Eventually, even the three most powerful town matrons—Mrs. Beebee, Mrs. Griswold, and Mrs. Gilson—had come to accept Mary.

"I can't thank you enough, Miss Mary. You want us to walk you home? It's late." Millie gave her friend a hug and kissed her on both cheeks.

"I fine, Miss Millie." She patted a bulging pocket. "You made sure of that. Now remember what I tol' you 'bout tonight." She waved and dragged a bleating Buttercup outside.

"What about tonight?" Dom asked, his grin vanishing.

Millie turned to her husband. The knot in her stomach tightened, although her indignation was as great as her fear. "Mary and Doc Noxon visited me before the wedding and both told me about tonight." Their visits had caused Millie's pre-wedding anxiety to escalate significantly and that was before the visit from Widow Ferris.

"They told you about wedded bliss?" Dom asked uneasily.

"Sort of." Both of them had been short on details, except for emphasizing that even proper ladies participated in wedded bliss. "Doc Noxon described the last wedding he attended. While he visited with the bride's mother after the wedding, the young bride rushed from her bridal couch, half-dressed, and fell into her mother's arms. She said her husband had offered her a gross, unpardonable insult." Millie narrowed her eyes. "Mr. Drouillard, if you do anything improper tonight...Well, I have a six-shooter and I know how to use it. I think..." She paused as Widow Ferris scurried toward them.

"I sketched exactly what I saw," said Widow Ferris excitedly, her face more rat-like than ever as she unrolled her canvas and held it up for Millie and Dom to see.

Millie glanced at the parchment and fumed, despite Dom's laughter. "You really are quite talented, Widow Ferris," he said.

"That is not the part of the wedding I wish to remember." Millie angrily glared at the sketch. Widow Ferris had drawn a lifelike charcoal image of Dom—his face a mask of rage—striking Mr. Turck. Behind them stood Millie, dressed in her wedding finery with her gloved hands covering her mouth. Surrounding the brawl were the faces of the townsfolk cheering Dom on. Even Buttercup and an annoyed Brother Bunce were included.

Widow Ferris smirked. "I ain't done yet. Still got a few details to add before Blacksmith Shumate covers it with a fixative. Wouldn't want it to smudge since you're paying me so well." She spun around clutching the drawing and darted away.

"Paying her to sketch the wedding was kind. It's one of the things I love about you." Dom pulled Millie to him for another of his mind-numbing kisses. "We'll hang the sketch in the barn."

Tomorrow, after she survived wedded bliss, Millie would tell Dom the truth and ask about his past, but now it was time for another dance and Elder Griswold was calling for a toast. An hour later, Mrs. Beebee hurried over, her gown stained with what suspiciously looked like goat drool and her hair disheveled. "Mr. Drouillard, Miss Millie. It's time you left." She glanced at the rowdy crowd. "If these miners get any more liquored, they'll tear my place apart. If you leave, I can send them on to Diefendorf's Saloon."

Amid hoots of good will, Dom helped Millie don her winter coat and heavy boots. Her heartbeat raced and her mouth felt dry as they headed out into the night. Snow crunched under their feet and frigid air bit into Millie's exposed skin. The noise from the Beebee House diminished, and Dom asked, "So, what did Mary tell you about tonight?"

Millie had been raised by Catholic nuns in New Orleans. They focused on discipline and proper behavior and had never once mentioned the wedding couch. Probably they hadn't understood wedded bliss any more than Millie. Mary, though, had once been married, and her words of explanation still made Millie blush.

"Mary said, well…" Stars twinkled overhead and cold seeped through Millie's warm coat. She shivered as they carefully crossed the icy, rough-hewn bridge over Clear Creek and climbed up the other embankment.

"Cold?" Dom wrapped his arm around her.

"No, it's just…Mary said…" Millie exhaled and forced out a sentence in one quick word. "Shesaidwewouldremo veallourclothesandyou'dwantto…" It was too awful to say.

Dom's eyes glittered in the moonlight. "Maybe we should discuss this at home." He increased his pace, causing Millie to breathe hard as they began the climb up Spring Gulch. She didn't want to wait until they got home, but Dom was walking so fast she couldn't catch her breath. They passed through a dark stand of trees and emerged into a moonlit meadow. Mary's cabin on the far left looked dark and quiet, but Millie's cabin had light seeping through cracks and between the shutters.

Dom turned, gave Millie another mind-numbing kiss, and scooped her up, carrying her across the meadow and into the cabin, setting her down once they were inside. A roaring fire blazed in the fireplace—Mary had stopped on the way to her cabin. It illuminated the living area and kitchen, creating red reflections on Millie's prize Charter Oak cookstove, but it wasn't the stove that held Millie's attention. Mary had moved their two rocking chairs to one side and made a cozy bed of quilts in front of the fire.

Millie swallowed.

Dom began to unbutton her coat, his face averted as he spoke. "Millie, we're married now. Marriage bliss is…well, it's what a man and a woman do after they're married." He hung her coat on a hook and bent down to untie her boots, avoiding her eyes as he continued. "Even proper married ladies, ah, do what we're going to do. After they're married."

Millie narrowed her eyes and began tapping her now bootless toe. "What exactly are we going to do, Mr. Drouillard? Doctor Noxon said I wouldn't like it, and Miss Mary's description sounded highly improper. In fact, it didn't sound possible."

Dom took off his own coat and boots, finally looking at her, his eyes reflecting the flickering firelight. "It's not improper and it's, ah, quite possible. Maybe demonstrating married bliss is better than talking about it."

Millie remained suspicious but allowed Dom to lead her to their quilt bed. She didn't resist, much, when he pulled her into a tight embrace, his eyes set in an expression that made her both uneasy and caused her stomach to flip-flop.

He ran a hand gently across her face and through her hair, removing hairpins as he untied her hair knot. Her long, thick red hair fell off her shoulders, and Millie shivered as his fingers followed it down, coming to rest on the hook and eye at the back of her dress. He fumbled with the hook, then froze. "Millie, where's your six-shooter?"

"Mary borrowed it. Wanted it for her walk home." Dom exhaled audibly and the next instant he'd deftly unhooked the top hook and eye of her dress. "Mr. Drouillard, I..." His fingers caressed her bare neck and Millie's mind went blank.

"Yes?" Dom asked, running his hand down her arm. His fingers left trails that made Millie shiver. His touch made her feel warm all over.

After a long kiss, Millie's heart was racing, and she felt strange. Dom lifted his head and Millie had to hold onto him. Her legs felt like rubber.

"It's very warm in here," she said, a bit dazed.

"Yes. Why don't I help you out of your dress?"

Before Millie could object, the dress slipped off her shoulders and puddled at her feet. When had he unhooked the rest of the hook and eyes? Before she could ask, or object, he lowered his head and kissed her again. She felt his hands brush back her hair and slide down her back. She closed her eyes, her heart racing, but when he fumbled with the hook on her petticoat, she pulled back.

"Mr. Drouillard! What are you doing?" Her formal address didn't seem to faze him. In fact, his eyes were glazed, and his face looked feverish.

"You look awfully warm, Mrs. Drouillard."

Mrs. Drouillard. Millie shivered. She was married. She was Mrs. Dominic Drouillard. Her petticoat slid down to join the dress at her feet.

"Dom, I—"

Another kiss convinced Millie the removal of one petticoat wasn't so bad. After all, she'd worn four over her chemise. A second petticoat slid off, and when she leaned her perspiring forehead against Dom's chest to regain her balance, she found her corset puddled around her waist and Dom's shirt and weskit at her feet.

He smelled so good Millie rubbed her cheek against his chest, groaning at how the motion made her feel. She shook her head, trying to clear it. "I'm sure this isn't proper. Of course, we can't sleep in our formal wear, but you must keep your trousers on."

"Sure," Dom said, breathing hard. "Why are you wearing so many damn petticoats?" Millie felt the third slide off her hips.

Several minutes later, Millie's long hair was tangled around them both. Her bodice, skirt, corset, undersleeves, and all her petticoats were scattered everywhere, intermixed with his weskit, shirt, undershirt, and trousers. Dom pulled her tight against, him and through the thin fabric of her chemise and his heavy woolen drawers, Millie felt every inch of him.

"Dom," she asked breathlessly, "why don't you put your six-shooter on the floor. It's poking me."

"Millie, honey, that's not my six-shooter."

He ran his hands down her hips and pulled her closer, his words gasped out between his harsh breaths. "Honey, do you remember caring for little boys and their—"

An unearthly yowl broke the silence.

"What's that?" Millie jerked backwards.

Gunshots rent the night air. Yells, shouts, and loud clanging broke the silence. Millie spun around, lurched to the door, and dropped the slat into place. "We're surrounded." She gasped, wondering how many savages were attacking. Rushing back to the quilts, she grabbed a petticoat and slipped it on. In an instant, the hook was back in the eye and Millie was reaching for a second one.

"No!" Dom groaned as Millie deftly added another layer of clothing.

Millie stared at him. He stood wearing nothing but his drawers, looking disoriented and confused. "Indians are attacking, Dom. Listen to the red devils howl. Put on your clothes and pull out your six-shooter!" She dragged on her dress and began hooking up the back.

"Nooo!" Dom repeated. Turning toward the wall, he banged his head against the wood.

Millie stared in horror. They were under attack and Dom had gone soft in the head. She strode over, spun him toward her, and slapped him smartly across the face. His glassy eyes sharpened, but he still watched her stupidly.

"Oh Lor'!" She drew back her hand. "Dom, we need to defend ourselves."

"We're not under attack," Dom said, grabbing her hand before she could slap him again. "That's the townsmen here for our shivaree."

"Our shivaree?" The ungodly hullabaloo outside grew louder. "What's that?"

"A frontier tradition," Dom said glumly, releasing her and reaching down to pick up his pants. "I forgot." Dejectedly, he slipped into his shirt, running a hand through his thick, black hair. "After a wedding, menfolk come calling. If we don't have sweets, drink, or some kind of offering, they'll kidnap me."

"*Kidnap you?* But…we don't have any of those. You eat everything. This morning, I took all the food I'd hidden to the Beebee House."

"Come on out, Dom," hollered Doc Noxon. "Remember when you threw me in poison ivy on *my* wedding night. Too bad we have so much snow, but I did find a nice sized cactus."

Dom groaned and looked around. "You sure we don't have any peppermint candy? Cakes? Anything?"

"No!" Millie said shrilly. "You threw Doc Noxon into poison ivy on his wedding night?"

"Open up, Dom," hollered Mr. Payne who owned the only fiddle in Idaho Springs. "Remember my shivaree? You made me stand waist-deep in the river and give you a violin lesson. I just made a nice big hole in the ice. Right over a deep pool. It's time for another lesson, but this time *you're* getting wet."

Dom rubbed his face.

"You made Mr. Payne play his violin in a river?"

"It seemed funny at the time."

"What will they do to you?"

"Between Doc Noxon, Mr. Payne, and your former suitors…" He shuddered and looked at her bleakly. "I may need some serious warming when I get back."

THREE

January 4, 1864
Trouble

Dom slathered Millie's strawberry preserves on a warm slice of sourdough bread, devoured it with gusto, and pulled Millie to him for yet another kiss. Marriage, Millie decided, was just fine, but when Dom tried to coerce her back to the quilts for a bit more marriage bliss, Millie pulled away, grabbed her boots, and carried them to her chair.

Not that she wasn't tempted.

Last night, Dom had returned from the shivaree soaking wet, his lips blue, his hands shaking, and his feet so cold he couldn't feel his toes. His condition so frightened Millie she'd ignored proper behavior and helped him remove his wet clothing—all the way down to his skin. When his violent shivering continued, she'd banked the fire, but when that hadn't helped, she'd become seriously worried.

She hadn't put up any kind of a fight when he'd pulled her under the covers and snuggled against her, drawing heat from her body. Only later, after he'd passionately introduced her to marriage bliss, did he sheepishly admit his shivering might have been exaggerated.

The man could be as devious as the devil.

Still, devious or not, Millie had discovered Doc Noxon

was wrong. Marriage bliss was, well, wonderful—although the thought of being unclothed in front of Dom still made her blush. This morning, though, she had other concerns.

"Where are you going?" Dom asked, his expression pitiful.

"To talk to Miss Mary." Millie slipped on her coat, gloves, and bonnet. "I'm not ready to have babies."

"Babies." His face brightened. "Our own children." His smile grew alarmingly big. "I'd like that."

"No!" Millie said anxiously. "We don't want children yet. They change everything. Look at Nanny and Nanko." Buttercup's daughters, named after President Lincoln's goats, were barely two weeks old, but they'd already eaten two of Dom's socks, jumped on the table and stolen the bread three mornings in a row, and broken two jars of carrot jam. Millie didn't know how to teach them manners and was ready to move them into the barn.

When she'd first arrived, Millie had permitted Buttercup to live in the cabin—she'd been so lonely those first few months and Buttercup's presence had been a comfort—but now she believed Mrs. Beebee and the other Idaho Springs matrons were right.

Goats belonged in the barn.

"A son would be swell," Dom said, a faraway look on his face. "I could teach him about minerals and crystals. How to assay ore." His expression grew more animated and excited. "We could go into business together. D&D Assays. He'd be smart. Probably discover an aquamarine vug or—"

"No!" Millie interrupted, raising her voice. When she'd been fifteen, the nuns had hired her out to the LeGrand family as a cook, servant girl, and nanny. Seven years later, it had been the LeGrand's four spoiled children that had driven her to answer a wife-wanted ad and come to the Colorado Territory. Probably not all children were horrid—she had met one or two well-mannered ones—but she was certain all babies were smelly and messy.

"I don't want children. I want to explore the Colorado Territory with you." She looked at Dom to see if he understood, but he wasn't even listening. He sat staring into the fire with an alarmingly dreamy expression.

"We could have a daughter." Dom's grin turned loopy. "She'd call me Pa and be real sweet. I'd buy her a dress with a—"

"No!" Millie shouted.

Dom's silly smile turned down as he turned to Millie. "No?"

"No! We can go rock hunting together, and I'll find you an awkward marine vug. If we had a baby, we wouldn't be able to do anything. I'd have to stay home. Babies are messy. They cry and always get sick." She searched for an argument that might sway him. "You do gold ore assays all over the territory. I want to go with you, but if we had a baby, I'd have to stay here." She shrugged. "You'd be alone. Without marriage bliss…"

His distressed expression made her turn and cough into her apron.

"You're right! I hadn't thought of that."

"It's best if we don't have any. At least not right away." Even as she said it, she felt a twinge of guilt. Millie's heroine, Florence Hartley, advised ladies in her book, *The Lady's Book of Etiquette,* to "occupy yourself, if you can, with children; their freshness, their joyful unconsciousness, the elasticity of their spirits, will sustain and draw you from yourself." Growing up, Millie had always dreamed of being a lady and normally she followed Florence Hartley's advice to the letter, but children…Millie shuddered.

"But…" Dom interrupted her thoughts and rubbed his chin. "With the tear-shaped gold nuggets we found in our mine, I don't need to travel and do assays. We can stay here. I'll work the mine and do local assays." His expression brightened. "That way we can have marriage bliss and a daughter."

Millie's chest tightened. She clearly remembered the awful screams of Mrs. LeGrand during the births of her children and the bloody mess she cleaned up afterwards. Worse were the memories of two other orphaned girls whose mothers hadn't survived childbirth. Looking up at Dom, she said quietly, "Women die during confinement."

Dom knocked his chair over in his rush to her side. "That's why you don't want children?"

Millie nodded, feeling like a coward.

"I don't know what I'd do if anything happened to you." He hugged her tightly. "I don't need children. Just you. And marriage bliss."

Millie rested her forehead against his and drew in his strength. She snuggled closer to him, enjoying the intimacy, finally pulling away only to find Dom had unbuttoned her dress almost to her waist. The man was incorrigible! Adjusting her clothing—ignoring his smoldering eyes—Millie slipped into her coat.

"Hurry home," Dom said gruffly. "I think I'm catching a chill." He gave an exaggerated shiver.

"When I get back, Mr. Drouillard," Millie said, walking to the door and swinging her hips in a most unladylike fashion, "I'm the one who'll need warming." His groan filled the cabin as she opened the door and freezing air burned her exposed skin. She turned to face him and blew him a suggestive kiss.

Yes, marriage was just fine.

Bright sunshine blinded Millie as she adjusted her bonnet, stepped outside, and pulled the door shut. She turned toward the meadow and a scream gurgled in her throat. A horse's nose was so close, it almost touched her shoulder.

On the mustang rode the most vicious-looking savage Millie had ever seen.

The horse stretched out its nose and nuzzled Millie's

neck. Yelping, Millie jumped sideways and landed off balance on the uneven whipsawed boards that made up her porch. She fell forward, throwing up her arms, and wrapped her fingers around something solid. Solid and warm.

Struggling to regain her balance, Millie found her fingers wrapped around a deerskin moccasin. Her eyes looked upward, following leather fringed buckskin leggings, a breech cloth, and a loose fringed tunic. Finally, they reached the penetrating gaze of a tall brave. She was so close she saw the intricate design of porcupine quills, animal teeth, and stone beads on his buckskin shirt. A heavy buffalo robe covered his broad shoulders and beneath it protruded the butt of a rifle and the sheath of a hunting knife—a knife that had surely scalped many an innocent settler.

Millie screamed and jerked backwards, but the Indian grabbed her arm and pulled her body against his muscled leg.

"Dom!" Millie cried, struggling against the Indian's hold.

Abruptly, the brave released her and Millie tumbled backwards, sinking up to her armpits in the snowdrift beside the porch. The Indian didn't move, but Millie had read enough newspaper accounts about scalpings, murders, and Indian depredations to have her heart pounding like an ore stamp mill. "Dom!" she screamed.

The door to the cabin opened and Dom laughed when he saw her. "Take a tumble in the snow? Come inside and I'll help you out of those wet clothes and warm you right up."

Millie glared at him. No gun. Marriage bliss had made them both fools.

The Indian said something, a guttural sound, and Dom turned, catching sight of the man. Like at the wedding with Mr. Turck, Dom bellowed and charged.

Millie watched in horror as the Indian vaulted from his horse and the two male bodies collided with an audible thud. She held her breath, expecting to see the glint of the Indian's bowie knife or worse, the red explosion of blood.

"Héébee, Woonbisiseet," Dom hollered.

"Héébee Kooníini'ííni, Niibeeseitit Wox."

Millie's heart thundered, but confusion quickly replaced dread. Dom and the Indian gave each other fierce hugs and slaps that would have sent a small man flying. When they turned to face her, each had an arm thrown lazily over the other's shoulder.

"Millie, this here's Woonbisiseet. Calling Thunder, or something like that in English. I call him Thunderhead when he is in a temper." Dom laughed and dragged the Indian forward, extending his hand to Millie. "Woonbisiseet saved my life a year or so ago. We ran into a rabid wolf. Woonbisiseet shot the insane animal just before he jumped me."

Dom grasped Millie's hand and pulled. Millie sailed out of the snowdrift and bounced off her husband's chest. He kept her from falling again by wrapping his free arm around her and pulling her close. The Indian's hand brushed against her neck and Millie jerked away.

"In '61, Chief Little Raven and a bunch of other Cheyenne and Arapaho signed the treaty of Fort Wise at Bent's Fort. Woonbisiseet's Little Raven's second cousin." Dom paused and shrugged. "Or something like that. His tribe usually winters out on the plains, but they visit our hot springs a couple times each year."

Dom knew the savage? They were friendly? Millie couldn't hide her revulsion. Since coming to Idaho Springs, several of Millie's early beliefs had changed, especially because of Mary. Still, despite her skin color, Mary felt familiar. There was nothing familiar about this brave with fierce eyes and long braided hair.

Like all women settlers, Millie feared Indians. Most of that terror came from the gruesome details included in newspaper stories. In '62, papers described the Sioux massacre of hundreds of settlers in the Minnesota River Valley, detailing all too clearly burned homes, mutilated bodies, and scalped remains. There'd been other massacres, but the stories that scared Millie the most were from women captured by Indians. Newspapers said they'd been beaten, or worse, were handed from man to man in what the newspapers delicately described as "passed over the prairie."

Dom interrupted Millie's frantic thoughts by saying "Netesih'e," adding in English, "My woman."

Woonbisiseet thumped Dom's back with a blow that knocked him out of the way and before Millie realized the brute's intent, the Indian stepped forward and pulled her to him, enveloping her in his buffalo robe. Her senses reeled as she inhaled male mixed with horse, smoke, leather, evergreen boughs, and fresh earth. The hard butt of his buck knife pressed into her side.

Millie jerked free and backed away, but Dom didn't seem to notice her fear. Instead he began an animated conversation with the Indian using hand and finger gestures, guttural sounds, pantomimes, and the occasional English word. Glancing at Millie, he said, "Why don't you go visit Miss Mary? Woonbisiseet and I have some catching up to do. Good thing you made that second loaf of bread."

"Visit Miss Mary?" Millie repeated. "But. You're not...I don't want it in my cabin!"

Dom turned, his eyebrows rising. "It? Woonbisiseet's my friend."

"I don't want a savage in my home."

Dom's face darkened into an expression Millie had never seen aimed at her. His voice dropped to a harsh whisper. "Woonbisiseet's *my* friend and he's welcome in *my* home." He glared at Millie a moment before twisting around and looping an arm over the Indian's shoulder, leading him onto the rough porch. "He also understands English!"

Dom led the Indian inside and slammed the door.

FOUR

January 4, 1864

Miss Mary's Advice

illie glared at the closed door and stomped back
onto her rough porch, ready to give Dom a piece
of her mind. She grabbed the metal door latch
but paused. This was no longer her cabin. She was Mrs.
Dominic Drouillard. What would she do if Dom insisted
someone she cared about—someone like Sara Ouellette,
the friend who gave her Buttercup—wasn't allowed in their
cabin? Sara was rough, poorly educated, but she had a good
heart.

Could this Indian have a good heart? Millie tried to
imagine such a thing, but she couldn't. Once, while she
crossed the plains in a covered wagon, she met a native
face-to-face. That Indian had saved a girl's life, but he'd terrified Millie. Not only were his looks and dress strange, he
insisted on payment for his good deed. Millie had thought
she'd be the payment—or her scalp—but in the end he'd
taken only the bottom half of her braid.

Dom said this Indian had saved his life.

Millie narrowed her eyes. It didn't matter if the Indian
was good or bad. Dom had slammed the door in her face!
The freezing latch stuck to Millie's fingers, forcing her to
pry each finger loose as she released it. She shook out her

cold, stiff hand and took a step back. Later she'd have it out with Dom. Now she needed Mary's advice.

Spinning around, Millie came face to face with the mustang. "Out of my way, Mr. Horse."

The mustang's big brown eyes gazed at her without blinking.

Huffing, Millie stomped into the snow, but as she passed, the mustang nudged her with its nose. Millie again toppled back into the snowdrift. Using several improper words—all learned from Dom—Millie crawled onto the trail behind the horse, shook her damp skirt, and marched toward Mary's cabin.

The clear, blue sky and bright sunshine did nothing to soothe Millie's temper as she crossed the meadow, mumbling about cantankerous men, savages, and the evils of marriage. Storming into Mary's cabin without knocking, Millie slammed her friend's door so hard the tin plates rattled.

"Mr. Dom let you out of bed?" Mary asked, grinning.

"He's entertaining an Indian. I'm so mad I might offer to hold him down while the savage scalps him!" Millie clapped a hand over her mouth, horrified by her awful words and burst into tears.

Buttercup and her daughters, Nanny and Nanko, rushed to Millie, knocking into Mary's stout frame as they passed. They butted Millie in the thigh and looked up at her with bulging, concerned eyes. Millie bent down and hugged each animal, sobbing against their long, floppy ears.

"Come, honey. You tired. Bet you didn't get no sleep last night." Mary pulled Millie against her and patted her back, her wiry hair tickling Millie's face. "Now, who visiting Mr. Dom?"

"A…horrid…Indian." Millie gasped out each word, pressing her face into Mary's ample bosom. "D-Dom'll turn his back and t-the savage will kill him."

"Now, now, Miss Millie. Mr. Dom know Injuns. This one surely be friendly."

Millie sniffed and wiped her eyes. "How can he be friendly? He's an Indian. They're all savages."

"Course they ain't."

Mary's casual statement caused Millie to pull free from her friend's embrace. "Miss Mary, Indian attacks and savagery are reported in every newspaper we receive. Of course, they're *all* savages!"

Mary casually turned to her kitchen table. "I just reading this December 23rd *Weekly Commonwealth*. Mrs. Beebee give it to me yesterday. Ain't no mention of Injun massacres, but looky here." She stabbed an article with her finger. "This one 'bout the Utah Treaty. It say," she reads slowly, stumbling over words, "'The people up here, think it a pretty good thing to extinguish Indian titles to one-third the area of our Territory, including all our gold mines.'" Pausing she flipped to another page. "Here another one."

INDIANS DISAPPEARING

A GENTLEMAN, WHO HAS RECENTLY TRAVELED THROUGH THE CROW, BLACKFOOT AND FLATHEAD COUNTRY SAYS: "THE GREAT MASS OF THE WHITES, WHO ARE NOW FAST SETTLING UP THE COUNTRY ONCE OWNED BY THESE INDIAN TRIBES, HAVE VERY LITTLE CONCEPTION OF THE AMOUNT OF DISEASE AND MISERY THAT ARE RAPIDLY DECIMATING AND HASTENING THEM HOMEWARDS TO THEIR FATHERS."

Mary turned back to Millie and shrugged. "Maybe them Injuns got reason to kill white folk."

Millie took a step back, unable to mask her horror. "*You* like Indians?"

"There be good Injuns and bad. Just like whites and coloreds." Mary patted a chair. "Now come, sit. Tell me 'bout this Injun."

"Dom called him Woon something. Thunderhead." Millie dropped wearily into her seat and rested a hand on Buttercup's head. The dog-sized goat pushed her head into Millie's lap, leaving a line of drool.

"Woonbisiseet?" Mary asked, putting her kettle on.

"I think so."

"I know Mr. Woonbisiseet. He got a wife, Miss Sooxei. She be nice. She give me that basket." Mary waved toward her shelf, and Millie noticed a rough-looking basket that shimmered in the candlelight. "It coated with tree resin. Keeps me flour dry." As Mary talked, she set out tavern biscuits and tea cups.

Millie rubbed her face trying to scrub away her exhaustion and confusion. Like Dom, Mary liked Indians. Millie didn't understand.

Nanko darted forward, jumped onto the table, and snatched a biscuit. "No!" Millie grabbed for the baby goat but missed as the little animal escaped to the floor.

"Leastwise they share," said Mary, watching Nanko and her sister devour the biscuit.

Millie rubbed the bridge of her nose, feeling a headache coming on. "Do you think Dom will be okay?"

"Course. Mr. Woonbisiseet and he people come once, maybe twice a year. Visit them hot springs near town. They be friendly Arapaho." Mary placed a new tavern biscuit on Millie's plate and poured out steaming tea. She settled into her seat and looked at Millie. "You here 'cause Mr. Woonbisiseet visit?" She lifted her eyebrows. "Or something else?"

Millie scowled. Mary knew how Millie felt about childbirth and babies.

"Marriage bliss was…I mean." Millie blushed and Mary burst into laughter. Millie threw up her hands and gave up on proper decorum. "How do I make sure I don't become in a family way?"

Mary's laughter quieted, and she scratched at her thick hair. "I ain't rightly sure." She looked down at the table and added in a softer voice, "I wanted me baby."

"You had a baby, Miss Mary?" Millie asked, shocked. Last fall, while helping Millie survive, Mary had mentioned the death of her husband, but she'd never explained the circumstances. Millie had suspected something terrible had happened. Something so bad Mary fled New York City and came West.

Never, though, had Mary mentioned a child.

"When Adam die, I be in a family way." Mary's voice cracked. "I lost me baby girl. Got hurt. She come out early. Baby girl got toes, fingers, everything. Perfect, but no breath." She shook herself, as if shaking away the memory. "That be long ago."

Millie reached across the table and took Mary's hand. "I'm so sorry, Miss Mary. I didn't know."

Mary used her free hand to swipe at her tears. Shrugging her wide shoulders, she said, "It be another life." She squeezed Millie's hand and pulled away. "I heard there be ways to stop babies, but I ain't certain how." Taking a deep breath, she looked up. "How bad you want to know?"

"I don't want a baby," Millie said, shuddering at the thought. "At least not right away." Millie didn't add that she doubted she'd ever want her own children.

"Well…Seems you need an expert."

"An expert? Who'd be an expert in…" Millie's eyes widened. "Miss Mary. You aren't suggesting I…" Millie swallowed. "I couldn't possibly speak with…Or worse visit…" Millie shook her head. "Oh Lor'! You're right, Miss Tit Bit or Miss Smooth Bore would know!"

FIVE

January 4, 1864

Tit Bit

Millie took a sip of tea, set it down, and twisted her wedding ring in agitation. As an orphan growing up in New Orleans, she'd often visited the French Quarter and jealously watched proper families pass by in fancy pony traps and carriages. She'd dreamed of becoming one of those well-dressed ladies, shopping along Royal Street or attending banquets at Casa Faurie. Now she was married—as proper as it got here in Idaho Springs. Tit Bit and Smooth Bore were public women, the working kind. A real lady would never visit them—not for any reason.

Oh Lor', what would The American Lady and Florence Hartley advise? Growing up at the Annunciation and Calliope Girls House of Refuge, Millie had memorized every rule in The American Lady's book, *True Politeness: A Hand-Book of Etiquette for Ladies*. Later, on her way to the Colorado Territory after she'd answered the wife-wanted ad, she'd read Florence Hartley's *The Ladies' Book of Etiquette, and Manual of Politeness* from cover to cover. But neither book helped in this situation.

Worse, what would the town matrons—Mrs. Beebee, Mrs. Griswold, and Mrs. Gilson—say if they ever found out?

Millie's fear of childbirth overcame her worries about improper behavior, but doubts assailed her. "They won't talk to me, Miss Mary," Millie said. "I've shunned them, like all the other town ladies. The two of them, along with Mr. Turck, were the only townsfolk not invited to my wedding."

"Oh, Miss Millie!" Mary rolled her big, brown eyes. "Those two ain't expecting no invite." Her face broke into a huge grin. "Can you see 'em in the Beebee House?" She doubled over slapping her thigh. "Mrs. Beebee would die. Public women in her fine 'stablishment. And Brother Bunce…" She shook her head. "You got 'nough trouble with me and Buttercup."

Millie wanted to contradict her friend, but she too had felt the undertone of hostility toward Mary at her wedding. Millie picked up her teacup and asked, "Would Miss Tit Bit or Miss Smooth Bore help me?"

"Course. They knows Mr. Dom."

Millie's cup froze half the way to her mouth. "They know Dom? Surely, he didn't. I mean."

"Before you," Mary said quickly. "Them working girls knows all of Idaho Springs' menfolk. Married or single."

Millie took a deep breath. The past was the past, but if Dom ever…She shook her head. Tonight, she and Dom were going to have a long talk. A heart-to-heart—before any marriage bliss—about proper behavior, Indians, and working women.

An hour later they walked toward town and Mary chatted about the wedding, focusing on Mrs. Beebee's fashionable new crimson gown. "I think it be made of liberty satin. With thems full skirt, draped folds, cap pieces and epaulets over her puffed sleeves, that dress could be featured in *Godey's Lady's Book of Fashion*."

Millie nodded, but she wasn't really listening. Why had she gotten married? Nothing, not even marriage bliss, was worth this kind of embarrassment. She felt like she was walking toward her own lynching.

Sensing Millie's mood, Mary's conversation faltered as they crossed the icy Clear Creek bridge and passed the general store run by the man everyone called Old Shakespeare. Despite the cold, Millie's palms began to sweat when Mrs. Griswold and Mrs. Gilson nodded their greetings as they passed on the street. And there was Mrs. Beebee!

Grabbing Mary's arm, Millie hurried behind Blacksmith Shumate's workshop trying to hide, but instead they ran square into Widow Ferris. The mousy woman glared at them. "You got my gold nugget?" she demanded.

"No," Millie said, flustered.

"I want it tomorrow, or else." The unpleasant woman spun around and shoved open the door of the blacksmith shop. "Blacksmith Shumate, I got some chores for you. Lots of Southern sympathizers here. And bring that boy. I want a better look at his face."

"My," Millie whispered, hurrying away. "Widow Ferris has, as Blacksmith Shumate likes to say, a bee in her bonnet."

"That woman be downright nasty." Mary shook her head as they carefully skirted around the icicles hanging from the edges of the blacksmith's roof. "She likely cracked after what her husband done."

The mention of Mr. Ferris caused Millie to remember that awful afternoon just a few weeks past. She'd figured out Mr. Ferris had murdered Dom's older brother, the man who'd placed the wife-wanted ad. Setting off to warn Dom, she'd encountered the villain and in the confrontation that followed, Mr. Ferris had fallen to his death. Millie couldn't look at Widow Ferris without feeling a twang of guilt, although the unpleasant woman's behavior and sketch of Millie's wedding had reduced some of the guilt.

Reaching the edge of town without further mishap, Millie paused to catch her breath and glanced around. At least there was no one in sight now. Mary turned down a frozen path toward a lone grove of evergreens that shaded a rough building with rickety steps leading to two battered doors. Tit Bit and Smooth Bore's crib was barely noticeable from town except for the well-worn tracks in the snow. Winter was hard on prospectors, but that didn't seem to stem the girls' popularity. After last night's introduction to marriage bliss, Millie understood why.

Millie took a deep breath, steeling herself for the public women's contempt, and followed Mary toward the crib. To avoid childbirth and babies, she'd have spoken with Lucifer himself, but that didn't mean she'd enjoy the conversation. Her worries were interrupted when a woman with the soft strains of Ireland flowing through her voice demanded, "First, I want me coin. You're full rubbered and—"

The woman's words were cut off by an ugly curse and the sound of a hand striking flesh. "The pock be on ye," hollered the woman. Her scream broke the quiet morning, and the crib wall shook as something large struck it.

"Miss Nessa!" Mary lifted her skirt and rushed forward, climbing the dilapidated stairs and throwing open the door. She disappeared into the dim interior, but Millie hesitated, feeling like a coward. She'd recognized the drunken voice behind the curse.

"Wwwha…Whad'yaaa?" slurred Mr. Turck. "Youss that colored girl." His words were garbled and incoherent, worse than at the wedding. "Once I took me a ssslave, llike youu."

"I be free!" shouted Mary, her voice shaking.

"Free?" Mr. Turck's voice petered out and Millie heard a slap. Mary careened into the light, falling just inside the open door. Millie rushed to her friend's aid.

"Uuuppity colored bbitch." Mr. Turck sounded much too close as Millie knelt on the rough wood floor. Mary's eyes were open but glazed over.

Footfalls shook the floor, and Millie quickly looked up. Mr. Turck staggered past a bed covered in tangled bedclothes, his back to her and bent over a dark-haired woman dressed only in a silk chemise. The woman lay sprawled on the floor, blood smeared across her cheek.

"Yous uppity too!" Mr. Turck jerked the woman onto her feet and dragged her unsteadily to the bed, shoving her onto it. He struck her thigh, knocking her chemise indecently high above her hip. The scantily clad woman cried out in pain and curled into a ball as Mr. Turck lifted his hand for another blow.

"You leave her be!" Fear radiated through Millie's words, and her hands shook as she rose to her feet, unbuttoned her coat, and reached into her apron pocket. All she felt was her pocket watch. Like a fool, she'd forgotten to get her six-shooter back from Mary! Swallowing hard, she lifted her hand and pointed to the door. "Get out!"

Mr. Turck's beard braids were twisted together, and he looked at her stupidly, blinking his bloodshot eyes. "Yyyou!" He took two unsteady steps closer and dread shivered up Millie's spine. It took all her courage to hold her ground.

"Yyyou!" he repeated, so close he showered her with whiskey-soaked spittle. "Yyous shudda married me!"

He backhanded Millie across the face.

The blow spun her around, and she fell beside Mary, stunned. Before she could recover her senses, Mr. Turck wrapped a fist around her long braid and another about her arm, jerking her onto her feet. Millie screamed, her scalp igniting in pain, but fear surpassed all other emotions as he dragged her out the door.

In terror, she struggled against his hold and threw her weight forward. He stumbled and they both tumbled down the stairs, landing hard in the mud and slush. Blinded by pain, Millie fought to escape as Turck rolled over, staggered to his feet, and ruthlessly hauled her up beside him.

"Yyour coming wid me!" he slurred, staggering unsteadily down the path.

Millie gagged at his foul breath and redoubled her efforts, knowing what he wanted would be worse than death. Jerking backwards, she unbalanced him again and they fell, but this time she felt his hold loosen. Using nails, knees, and elbows, Millie struck him, gasping for breath as cold seeped down her neck while pain burned her scalp like fire.

Turck swore loudly and pushed himself to his knees, crying out when Millie managed to rake her nails down his cheek.

"You bitch!" he screeched, sounding almost sober. He flipped her onto her back, his beard braids slapping her, and raised his fist. Millie's teeth chattered as she stared into his dilated pupils. He paused, his eyes widening in shock and confusion, fear replacing fury. His breath billowed out, filling the air with a whiskey smelling fog.

Millie didn't wait to find out if his temporary sobriety would clear his head. She curled her body, getting her knees between them, and pushed him away with a sharp kick. He grunted, his sober expression vanishing, and knocked her legs away before roughly slapping her across the face. Millie's head spun as he dragged her back onto her feet.

A loud thump reverberated through the air.

Mr. Turck's hold loosened, and he sluggishly twisted around and dropped to his knees in front of Millie. For an instant, he looked like the suitor he'd once been. His hands fell to his sides, and he crumpled backward splattering mud all over Mary's skirt.

Mary stood over him, a cast-iron frying pan gripped in her hands. "Die!" she screamed, lifting the heavy pan above her head. She swung it toward Mr. Turck's exposed face.

SIX

January 4, 1864
Miss Mary's Past

Dazed, Millie stumbled over Turck and shoved Mary backward. The frying pan slammed into the mud with a force that would have shattered bone, the pan's edge burying one of Mr. Turck's filthy braids. Eyes wild, Mary thrust Millie aside and again lifted the cast-iron pan.

"Miss Mary, no!" Millie wrapped her arms around her friend and propelled her away. "You've done enough. I—"

Mary screamed insanely and elbowed Millie in the gut. "He just like the white man who kill my Tom!"

Millie saw murder in her friend's eyes as Mary launched herself at Turck, her frying pan swinging. The prone man scrambled onto hands and knees, his face white, his expression sober. He slipped in the muck but managed to get onto his feet. Mary swung the pan and struck his backside, knocking him into the snow. She raised the frying pan for another blow, but Turck rolled to one side, found his footing, and stumbled down the path.

With her frying pan grasped in a death grip, Mary screamed incoherently as she chased after Turck. Despite the weight of the heavy pan, she was gaining on him when her feet slipped out from beneath her. Snow flew in one direction, the frying pan in another. She landed hard and writhed facedown in the mud, hammering the slushy earth with her fists, kicking out with her feet like a temperamental child.

Cautiously Millie approached, watching her friend's violent movements gradually abate. Dropping to her knees, she gathered Mary into her arms and cradled her as Mary's sobs wracked through Millie's body.

"A white man shot me husband Tom. He laugh as he kill Tom. He kept laughing as—he hurt me…Hurt me so bad, me baby come out. He kill me babe." She groaned, babbled, and wept.

Gradually Millie understood, though she didn't want to. Mr. Turck's violence had caused Mary to relive her husband's murder. Nausea roiled through Millie's stomach. The cold and wet chilled her to the bone as she realized Mary's husband, Tom, had been murdered by a white, drunken bully like Turck. Millie didn't want to imagine anyone killing a man and then abusing his pregnant wife, but she knew better. Mary and her husband might have been free, living in a Union state, but they were still colored.

Tears tracked down Millie's face as she rocked back and forth, holding Mary like a child.

"Come, ma'am, bring Miss Mary inside." Tit Bit reached down and helped Millie lift Mary. The working girl's feet were bare, and her face was bruised and splotchy, but she lifted Mary's arm over her shoulder and helped Millie carry Mary back into her crib.

Inside, they passed the bedstead and Millie was surprised to see a door on the far wall. Tit Bit opened the door, and they entered a small back room with a tiny stove that warmed a surprisingly homey space. The strong smell of mint permeated the air and a fire crackled in the stove. Mary's legs trembled as Millie and Tit Bit lowered her onto a rough-hewn bench. Millie sat beside her, feeling helpless as Mary silently rocked back and forth, her tears dripping onto the table.

The soft clinking of china caused Millie to look up.

Near the stove, Tit Bit arranged a tea tray, adding a plate of hard tack and biscuits. She had washed the blood from her face and donned an ornate silk wrapper embroidered with bright yellow sunflowers. Millie couldn't hide her surprise as Tit Bit poured steaming tea into three dainty porcelain cups, far finer than anything Millie owned.

"Begorrah," said the working girl quietly, catching Millie's eye. "I weren't always a fancy girl. Me mam taught me good, but she died when I were twelve. Her and pa. A girl got to eat." She poured the last of the steaming kettle water into a bowl and dipped a rag into it. "There be blood on your face, ma'am."

Millie's hands shook as she took the rag and washed her face. The warmth calmed her chattering teeth. "T-thank you." Tit Bit nodded and handed Millie a cup of steaming mint tea. Thankfully, Millie sipped the hot liquid. It warmed her insides all the way down to her belly.

"My life ain't so bad," said Tit Bit, as she cleaned the rag and gently wiped Mary's face. "I got me own money and working a mining town pays." She wrapped Mary's shaking hands around another steaming teacup and picked up her own. "I can buy myself pretty things," she said, admiring the fine china.

Millie nodded, still too shaken to speak, uncertain how to respond.

"You be alright, Miss Mary?" Tit Bit reached over and gently squeezed Mary's arm. "Have bit of mint tea and a touch of belly cheer. Everything 'tis always better with a wee bit of mint tea."

Mary looked up, her eyes rimmed red, her expression so tragic Millie had to look away. "Thank you. I..." Teardrops slid down Mary's wide face, and she roughly shook her head. "You all right, Miss Nessa?"

"Nessa?" Millie looked at Tit Bit and lifted her eyebrows.

"Tit Bit be me working name," said the woman, shrugging her thin shoulders. "I be good, Miss Mary. Thanks to you." She touched her swollen lip. "When Mr. Turck be full rubbered, he can be a bad egg."

"He's hit you before?" Millie couldn't imagine.

Tit Bit shrugged. "'Tain't me first blow, but 'tain't regular. Most of me lads be looking for bit of female companionship, a bit of…" she shrugged. "You know. They be lonely young lads. Away from family and wanting a bit of warmth." She flashed a mischievous grin that made her look very, very young. "Or they be husbands, looking for something they ain't be getting at home. Me and the proper ladies have one thing in common—their husbands be buying me gowns too."

Millie swallowed. She'd definitely speak with Dom when she got home. Of course, Dom had an irrational streak and often ignored her good advice. She sat up straighter and looked earnestly at the working girl. "If Dom ever shows up at your door, Miss Nessa, I'd be obliged if you'd use the frying pan on him."

Tit Bit burst out laughing. "Aye, but you ain't be needing to worry, Mrs. Drouillard. Mr. Dom be a good husband."

Mrs. Drouillard. It was ironic that a public woman was the first townsperson to call her by her married name. She smiled. "Please, call me Miss Millie. I think after what just happened we can do away with formalities."

Tit Bit's eyes widened. "I thank you both kindly, but…" She glanced at a clock sitting on a small shelf. "One of my regulars be coming soon." She tilted her head to one side. "You and Mr. Dom be married just yesterday. Only one reason I can think why you might be calling on me."

Blushing, Millie managed to stammer out her business.

Tit Bit nodded seriously. "Aye, 'tis a problem. There ain't an easy answer, but there be options." Without any appearance of embarrassment, Tit Bit explained about sponges laced in vinegar, silver dollars, washes, silk or animal bladder sheaths, and other methods that made Millie's face heat. "There also be pennyroyal oil, but you must take care. Just a wee bit, else I hear it be fatal."

"Fatal?" Millie shuddered. "Everything you've mentioned sounds awful."

"'Tis. Worse be the doctors in Denver City. They can abort it, but that be as dangerous for a lady as birthing a babe."

Millie shook her head. She'd heard about doctors like that. In New Orleans, another orphan she'd known had visited such a doctor as soon as quickening began. The girl never returned, and Millie heard rumors she'd died on the doctor's table.

Rising, Millie wrapped an arm around Mary and helped her to her feet. "Thank you, Miss Nessa. I appreciate your advice. We'd best be going." They stepped out onto the rickety stairs just as Mr. Gilson came into view. The married man spotted Millie, spun around, and tripped over his own feet as he hurried away.

"Men," Mary said quietly. "They's all bad."

They silently retraced their steps back to town. Walking caused twinges of pain from Mr. Turck's brutal attack, but it was Mary and her past that made Millie hurt. Passing Blacksmith Shumate's shop, Millie stopped short when Sheriff Reynolds strode around the corner.

"Mrs. Drouillard. Miss Mary." He narrowed his eyes. "What happened? Who did this to you?"

"Mr. Turck," Mary spat out.

"He was drunk," Millie added quickly. "You can't tell Dom." Even before they were married, Dom was as protective as a mother grizzly. Millie knew he'd kill Mr. Turck if he heard what happened. Mr. Turck might deserve to die, but Millie didn't want Dom doing the killing. Grabbing the lawman's arm, Millie said, "You know what kind of temper Dom has. Please, don't tell him."

"Tell me what?" boomed the voice Millie knew so well. Dom stepped around several large icicles, his stride long and determined. "Millie. I've been looking everywhere for you. I wanted to explain about Woonbisiseet and—" His eyes narrowed and he hurried to her side. "Are you okay? What happened?" He glanced from Millie to Mary and his expression went flat and hard. "Who struck you?"

"Dom." Millie took his hand. "We're fine. Mr. Turck was drunk. He didn't—"

"Turck!" Dom thundered.

"Och aye the noo!" Blacksmith Shumate lumbered out of his shop. "What's all the fuss?"

"Mr. Turck's gone too far," Sheriff Reynolds said, sounding as angry as Dom looked.

"I'm going to kill him." Dom's voice was quiet, controlled like a hammer about to strike a nail. "Did Turck do anything improper?"

"No. He…" Millie shivered. Perhaps sharing Mr. Turck's actions was unwise. "We were visiting Tit Bit and—"

"Visiting Tit Bit?" Dom roared. "Why in tarnation were you visiting Tit Bit?"

"Did Turck strike Miss Nessa?" Sheriff Reynolds cursed. "Dom, you stay with your wife. I'll take care of this."

"Like hell you will!" Dom thundered. "Millie, you stay here until I come back."

"Dom, I—"

"Don't argue with me, Red!"

Dom's tone left no room for compromise, which infuriated Millie as much as the blasted nickname. "Mr. Drouillard, you will not call me Red! I—"

"Finding Turck may take a wee bit of time," interrupted Blacksmith Shumate. "Why don't I escort the lassies home, after they warm up." The big blacksmith stepped back into the doorway of his shop, pulled out a coil of rope, and tossed it to Sheriff Reynolds. "You might be needing this."

The sheriff nodded. "Let's go."

Millie watched in horror as the two men strode away, a hanging rope slung over the sheriff's shoulder.

SEVEN

January 4, 1864
Contraband

T hey won't really lynch him, will they?" Millie asked nervously, turning to Blacksmith Shumate.

"Aye lassie, they will. 'Round here, stealing a man's horse is cause for a lynching. Striking another man's wife." He shook his head and looked grim. "Mr. Turck be a dead man."

Millie felt cold. Mr. Turck was an ugly man—at least when he was drunk—but hanging him without a trial was wrong. Worse, Mr. Turck wouldn't go down without a fight. "You should join Dom and Sheriff Reynolds, Blacksmith Shumate. Mr. Turck is dangerous."

"Later, if they need me. Now come. Come warm yourself by me fire."

Millie supported Mary as the large blacksmith led them inside. The dim room smelled of smoke and was filled with rough workbenches and cluttered with tools, wood, and dirt. In the center, a large bellows hung over a blazing hearth. The air from the fire warmed Millie's frozen hands and face as she settled Mary onto a three-legged stool.

After removing her wet coat and gloves, Millie shivered and moved closer to the hearth. A man she didn't know stepped forward and took her wet clothing, laying it out so it would dry. "Thank you, sir," Millie said, eyeing the stranger.

"Yes 'um." The man's wide eyes and ebony face reflected the flickering light.

"Who that?" Mary asked, pointing at the man.

"Jake." Blacksmith Shumate put a buffalo robe over Mary's shoulders. "Jake, this is Miss Mary and Mrs. D."

"Ma'am." Jake nodded to Millie, but his eyes stayed on Mary.

"You contraband?" Mary asked, crinkling her nose like the word smelled bad.

"We free now. We—"

"Who we?" Mary interrupted. Millie didn't understand why her friend was being unnecessarily rude, but after their unpleasant morning, Millie stayed silent.

"By the bellows," answered Blacksmith Shumate, indicating with his hand. "The lad is Jake's son, little Samuel."

A small, lithe form moved cautiously in the shadows. Millie thought the boy looked to be seven or maybe eight, but he was so deep in the darkness it was difficult to tell.

"Hello, Samuel," Millie said, feeling warm and slightly light-headed.

"Samuel," Blacksmith Shumate said gently. "Come, lad. Come out and greet Mrs. D and Miss Mary."

The boy moved hesitantly, edging around until he was behind his father. He took his father's hand and huddled close to him, staying in the shadows. "Pa, she 'scape, too?"

"Naw." The man shook his head. "She ain't one ah us."

Jake stepped forward and brought his son into the fire-light. Millie gasped and the child immediately disappeared behind his father, but she'd seen enough. Samuel had black, kinky hair, and coal-dark eyes like his father, but his skin was the color of dirty honey. Except for his hair, the boy could pass for an Italian immigrant or one of the Arabs that Millie had seen in New Orleans.

"He your boy?" Mary asked.

"Samuel my son," Jake said, grasping the boy's hand.

"My wife babe." He looked away. "Slave ain't got no choice. Gotta do what massa want."

His words—along with the meaning behind them—pricked Millie's heart. A white man had killed Mary's husband and caused her to lose her baby. Another had fathered this light-skinned child. Millie didn't want to imagine that kind of cruelty, but she knew it existed. For a long moment, the only sound in the room was the crackling of the fire and the low howl of wind slicing through the slats in the walls.

"Did your wife escape too, Mr. Jake?" Millie asked.

Jake snorted. "She free. She die day Samuel born."

Another death during childbirth. Millie lowered her eyes as exhaustion crept through her. What would she do if Mr. Turck harmed Dom? The sooner they left, the sooner Blacksmith Shumate could join Dom and Sheriff Reynolds. "Miss Mary, are you warm enough to head home?"

Mary nodded wearily and Blacksmith Shumate stepped forward. "I'll escort you, lassie."

"Perhaps you should go after Dom and Sheriff Reynolds," Millie said. "Mr. Turck carries a six-shooter and—"

"They can take care of themselves, lassie." Blacksmith Shumate helped bundle Mary back into her wet clothing and took her arm. "Come now."

They passed through town as twilight lengthened their shadows and Millie's worries increased. The emptiness bore down on her, and she spoke just to break the silence. "Blacksmith Shumate, how did you come by Jake and his son?"

"Well now, that's a bit of a story. Before I come West, I be part of that underground railroad. The one that be helping many a lad and lassie cross into freedom. I ain't believe that one man should own another." He paused and gently slipped his arm around Mary's shoulder. "Just lean on me, lassie. You be looking a wee bit under the weather."

Mary's eyes were dull, flat, and her stride unsteady. Millie hurt for her friend but didn't know how to help. Mary was lost in another world. A past that would never change. Blacksmith Shumate shook his head, as if he understood. Maybe he did. Maybe stories like Mary and Jake's were common in the underground railroad.

"Jake and Samuel come last week," Blacksmith Shumate added, interrupting Millie's thoughts. "Me old mate, Silas Soule, sent them. Contraband ain't got it easy in the Colorado Territory, and Samuel's light skin makes it more difficult."

"That boy won't never belong in the white world, nor the black," Mary said quietly.

They reached Mary's cabin and Millie busied herself putting out tea and food. She offered to stay and keep Mary company—or at least leave the goats with her—but Mary flatly refused. Millie glanced at Blacksmith Shumate. He shrugged his large shoulders and reminded Mary to keep her door barred.

After escorting Millie to her cabin, he carefully checked all the rooms. "Lassie, like I told Mary, don't be opening the door for nobody but Mr. Dom. Mr. Turck be a dunderhead, but that don't mean he ain't dangerous."

Dangerous enough to kill Dom. Millie pushed away the thought and remembered her manners. "Thank you, sir, for escorting us home. Good night." After barring her door, Millie banked her fire and sank into the quilts on the floor. Buttercup crawled into her lap and Nanny and Nanko pushed up against her. Their warmth soothed her, but worries soon had her up pacing the floor, cleaning up the quilts and returning the room to order. Hours passed. Buttercup followed Millie everywhere, sensing her unease as she scrubbed the floor, washed dishes, and baked sourdough bread she didn't need.

The night was half over, and Millie was crazy with dread when footsteps finally sounded on the porch. Millie rushed to the door, slid the bar out, and jerked it open. She remembered Blacksmith Shumate's warning as she stared outside. In the icy cold, a dark figure stood before her, hunched over as if in pain. Millie's heart missed a beat before she recognized her husband.

"Oh Lor'! Dom, are you hurt?"

He stumbled inside knocking into her as he staggered toward the fire. Nanny and Nanko bounded to their feet, their eyes bulging, and backed away. Even Buttercup didn't approach as Dom sank into his rocking chair, his uncoordinated movements almost overturning the heavy furniture.

"What happened?" Millie asked, relief making her legs feel like rubber. She closed and barred the door. Hurrying to him, she took his gloved hands into hers. Blood glistened on his coat collar and sleeve. "You're hurt?"

"I'm fine." He pushed her hands away, none too gently, and unbuttoned his coat, pulling it off and dropping it in a heap on the floor. Finger by finger, he removed his gloves, exposing bruised and bloody knuckles.

"Did you fight with Mr. Turck?" *And kill him?* Millie was too frightened to voice the thought.

Dom didn't answer. Instead, he silently rocked back and forth, his head bowed.

Confused and scared, Millie picked up the pile of clothes. Whether angry or exhausted, Dom always set his boots near the fire, hung his coat on its hook, and placed his gloves and hat on the nearby shelf. It wasn't that he was neat, but wet clothes left in a pile remained wet. Millie quickly put away his things and put water on for coffee. While it heated, she returned and knelt before him. "Dom, what happened tonight?"

"Nothing. Leave me alone, Millie." His voice was flat, but she smelled whiskey on it.

"Have you been drinking, Mr. Drouillard?" Deliberately she used the formal address. She knew he hated it as much as she hated his nickname for her, Red. Right now though, his anger would be a welcome relief over his ominous mood.

"Go away, Millie. I need some time to think." His words

were harsh—hurting far more than Mr. Turck's blows this morning—and his distant, emotionless expression sent a chill down her spine.

"Dom, I—"

"Go away," he said grimly.

Tears brimmed in Millie's eyes, but she was also angry. How dare he keep her waiting and worried for hours and then treat her like this? *Killing Mr. Turck wouldn't cause this.* The thought was unwelcome, but it wouldn't go away. *He's safe.* Tonight, she'd give him time, but tomorrow...tomorrow he'd tell her what had happened, or he'd find himself sleeping in the barn with his burro for the rest of the winter.

*****

Millie awoke to an empty bed and a freezing cabin. She dressed and hurried out, finding Dom asleep just where she'd left him with Buttercup and her daughters asleep at his feet. Not so quietly, she stoked the stove's firebox and rekindled the main fire. It blazed into life just as her own temper bubbled over. Turning she found Dom staring at her.

"What happened last night, Dom?"

"Nothing happened." He rose, winced, and rubbed his hip. Millie just stared at him and tapped her foot impatiently. "I didn't find Turck," he said dismissively. Turning his back on her, he limped toward the bedroom. "I need some sleep."

Millie's temper flared like a hot ember. She charged around and blocked his path. "Don't you dare turn your back on me, Mr. Drouillard. You kept me up waiting and worrying half the night. Now what happened?"

"Nothing." He tried to move around her, but Millie just stepped in front of him. Glaring, he planted his fists on his hips and snarled, "I don't want to talk about it, Red. Move out of my way."

"Talk about what?" she demanded, ignoring the nickname.

"Nothing that concerns *you*."

His emphasis of the word you just made Millie madder. "Mr. Dominic Drouillard. You will tell me what happened last night or—"

A loud knock silenced her. Dom paled and his eyes widened slightly as he stared at the door. Oh Lor', Millie thought, what had he done? Had he lied about Mr. Turck? Did he expect the miners' court to arrest him? The knock came again, louder and more insistent.

Dom scooted around Millie and hurried into the bedroom. "I don't want to talk to nobody," he said, closing the door.

Millie stared. Dom never hid from a problem. He attacked trouble head-on, usually loudly and without thought. She'd never known him to shrink away from anything, no matter how bad. *What had happened?*

The cabin was tiny, but a third knock echoed through the stillness before Millie unbarred the door and cautiously cracked it open. She felt Buttercup peek out by her knee.

"Misah D," Jake panted, his eyes so wide the whites gleamed in the early morning light. "Mistah Shumate. He say you gotta come."

"Blacksmith Shumate?" Millie opened the door wider, despite the freezing morning air. "Come where?"

"Come to town. Mistah Shumate, he say…" Jake scrunched up his face, carefully repeating Blacksmith Shumate's message, word for word. "Find Misah D. She a detec-tive." Jake stretched out the word detective so badly Millie almost didn't recognize it. "She find the killer."

"The killer?" Millie's voice rose, and she glanced back at her closed bedroom door. "What killer?"

"Widder Ferris!" Jake threw up his arms dramatically. "She get murdered!"

EIGHT

January 5, 1864
Murder

S omeone murdered Widow Ferris?" Millie gasped. Buttercup's eyes bulged out, and her legs went stiff. She fainted; Nanny and Nanko collapsed in a heap on top of her. Jake looked down at the comatose goats, his dark pupils floating in a sea of white. "Misah D," he said mournfully. "I kill you goats."

Millie ignored the goats and stepped closer to Jake, shivering as cold air bit into her bare skin. "Widow Ferris was murdered?"

"Yes 'um," Jake whispered, his eyes still on the pile of fur and hooves at his feet. "That sheriff. He take Mistah Shumate." Reaching down, he rested a hand on Nanny's flank.

"He arrested Mr. Shumate? Why?"

"Goats ain't dead?"

Millie shook her head absently. "They just fainted." She turned and paced the floor, speaking to herself as much as to Jake. "Why would Sheriff Reynolds arrest Blacksmith Shumate?"

"Donno know. Mistah Shumate ain't done nothin'."

Stopping mid-stride, Millie's eyes turned on Dom's heavy winter coat. The bloodstains were now dry, but still visible. "She was killed last night?"

"Yes 'um." Jake gently picked up Nanny and nuzzled her soft neck. "We gotta go. You gotta start detectin'."

"I'm not a detective." Millie rubbed her head. Worry and confusion made her normally agile mind slow.

"You gotta help Mistah Shumate."

How could she help Blacksmith Shumate when she had her own problems? Millie strode toward her bedroom. It was time for Dom to answer some questions. "One minute, Mr. Jake. I need to, uh, get my…detective things."

She reached for the bedroom door latch and paused to take a deep, calming breath. Dom had spent the second night of their married life sleeping in a rocking chair. Alone. Only something truly dreadful would distract him from his marital duties. Dom would never kill a defenseless woman.

"Oh Lor'!" Millie shook her head and stepped into the bedroom, closing the door behind her. Dom sat on the bed, his face in his hands. "You heard?"

He looked up and nodded, his expression haggard. The knot in Millie's stomach tightened. "What happened last night? Did you kill Mr. Turck?"

"No, I—"

"Where'd the blood on your coat come from?"

"Sheriff Reynolds and I got in a tiff." His voice petered out, and he looked down at his bloody knuckles. "He tried to stop me from going after Turck. I was too furious for anyone to stop me."

"You beat up the sheriff?"

"I think I broke his nose."

"You broke Sheriff Reynolds' nose?" Millie felt as furious as she was scared. "Why can't you control your temper, Dom. What about Widow Ferris?"

"I didn't kill her." His tone caused the hairs on Millie's neck to rise.

"But you knew she was murdered?"

"No, I—"

"You saw someone kill her?"

"No…I didn't know she'd been killed." He lifted his head, but his shoulders remained hunched and tense.

Millie wasn't sure she believed him, and that was a first. As far as she knew, Dom had never lied to her, but if he wasn't lying now, he was evading the truth. "What happened last night, Mr. Drouillard?" She said each word slowly, deliberately. "What upset you?"

"Mr. Turck struck you. I wanted to kill—"

"Besides that. What happened between you and Widow Ferris?"

Dom blew out a long breath and ran his fingers through his hair. "I ran into her last night. As I was coming home." His words were slow, like he was carefully picking each one. Fear knifed through Millie, and she braced herself for the worst. "It was late. I'd spent hours searching for Turck. She was coming out of Old Shakespeare's store and waved me down." He paused and looked at the floor. "She showed me a letter."

"A letter? Let me see it."

"She wouldn't let me keep it." Dom rose and took Millie's hands, squeezing them gently, his expression uncertain. "I didn't know. I swear. If I had, I'd have gone back."

Gone back? Millie didn't understand, but she clearly remembered Widow Ferris' earlier threat about Dom's past. "Gone where?"

"I'm so sorry." He tightened his hold on her hands. "The letter was from my hometown in Ohio. It said, I've…I've got a daughter."

"A daughter?" For a moment, Millie was too stunned to react, but as his words sunk in, she felt a betrayal worse than anything in her life. She jerked free from his grip and stepped back. "You have another wife?" Her voice was barely above a whisper.

"No, of course not." Dom tried to retake Millie's hands,

but she crossed her arms over her chest and pressed her hands against her body, squeezing tight to keep from falling apart. "I swear, Millie. I didn't know."

"You didn't know? What kind of a fool do you think I am?" She pushed him away, unable to stop her tears. "We're married, Dom. I *now* understand marriage bliss. You had to know!" She couldn't breathe and the blood pounding through her head made it difficult to think.

"Millie, I swear, I—"

His plea died as Millie spun around and grabbed her loaded six-shooter off a rough, wooden shelf. She turned to face him, narrowing her eyes. Dom glanced uncertainly between Millie's face and the weapon.

"Misah D," came a muffled shout. "We gotta go. Help Mistah Shumate."

"I'm leaving. You best hide here. If Sheriff Reynolds hears about your daughter," she spat out the words, "he might just think you had reason to murder Widow Ferris." She jammed the gun into her apron pocket so hard she heard a seam rip. "I know I do!"

"Millie, I—"

"I can't talk to you right now. I can barely look at you. Later, I want the whole, disgusting truth, but not now." Millie fled the room, slamming the door behind her. She wiped away tears as she donned her hat, boots, and coat. Jake watched her, eyes wide, but he said nothing as they headed out into the cold morning, with Buttercup at Millie's heels.

Jake led the way down the snowy trail, but he paused to stare at the cabin on the far side of the meadow. "That where Misah Mary live?" Millie nodded and kept walking.

By the time they reached Clear Creek, Millie had her emotions under control. Or at least she'd stopped crying. She blew her nose, creating an explosion of vapor in the cold air and tried to forget Dom and his daughter. That was impossible, but she forced her mind to focus on Widow Ferris. The woman had threatened her at the wedding. Blackmailed her. There'd also been that fight between Widow Ferris and Blacksmith Shumate the following day. Had she also tried to blackmail him?

Millie knew she wasn't a detective, but if Sheriff Reynolds learned about Dom's encounter with Widow Ferris—and about his daughter—he'd assume Dom had reason to kill the woman. Millie might want to skin Dom alive, but she couldn't really believe Dom had killed Widow Ferris.

"Jake, you said Sheriff Reynolds arrested Blacksmith Shumate?"

"Yes 'um. But Mistah Shumate ain't killed nobody."

"How do you know?"

"Me and Samuel, we sleep near the fire, Misah D." He waved his hands as he talked. "Mistah Shumate bed in corner just behind us. He sleep there all night."

"But he could have gotten up in the middle of the night and left while you were sleeping."

"No 'um, Misah D. I 'scape me massa. I sleep bad." He threw up his hands. "Real bad. I hear Mistah Shumate. I wake iffin he leave he bed. He ain't kill Widder Ferris."

Millie believed him. Even if Widow Ferris had something that compromised the blacksmith, Millie couldn't see the gentle Scot killing anyone. *Now Dom…* She tried to ignore the thought, but a flicker of doubt made her tremble. If Dom lied about his other family, what else might he lie about? Did she really know the man she'd married?

"How you find Widder Ferris killer?" Jake wanted to know.

Millie had no idea, but she had to try. Whoever killed Widow Ferris would be lynched—most likely without a trial. If she had doubts about Dom, what would the townsfolk or Sheriff Reynolds think? Guilty or not, while emotions were high, he could end up hanging from a rope. Millie was furious, but despite his daughter, she still couldn't imagine life without Dom.

She had no choice but to find Widow Ferris' killer. "Jake, do you know how Widow Ferris died?"

"No 'um, Misah D."

Millie chewed her lip. Maybe if she figured out how Widow Ferris was killed, she'd know who killed her. Of course, after the nasty sketch of her wedding, Millie should add herself to the suspect list.

How had Widow Ferris learned about Dom's daughter?

The question made Millie pause. Dom said Widow Ferris showed him a letter, but how had she gotten that letter? Widow Ferris must have found it in her husband's papers. Millie could well imagine Mr. Ferris as a blackmailer, but surely Widow Ferris hadn't been stupid enough to threaten someone dangerous enough to kill her.

Deep in thought, Millie crossed Clear Creek and climbed up the slippery embankment. Dom said he'd met Widow Ferris just after she left Old Shakespeare's shop. Maybe the shopkeeper knew something. It was as good a place as any to start.

"Jake, you need to go back to the blacksmith shop and make sure your son is okay. I'll find the sheriff."

Jake bobbed his head dubiously. "Yes 'um, Misah D." He strode off glancing back at her before he disappeared into the cluster of buildings.

Millie pushed open the door to Old Shakespeare's shop, holding it as Buttercup scurried inside. By the door hung Mr. Tappan's latest quote, *"No legacy is so rich as honesty."*—The Bard.

Old Shakespeare could quote the Bard on just about any subject, but in his store, his quotes were always aimed at reminding his customers to pay their arrears. The Bard, Millie had been surprised to learn, had written liberally about honesty, honor, and the evils of debts.

"Old Shak…ah, Mr. Tappan," Millie corrected, stepping into the dim interior. The small stove near the apple barrel was cold, and his flint glass oil lamps were dark. It was midmorning, yet the shop looked deserted. Concern crept up Millie's spine. Old Shakespeare was too suspicious of his neighbors' honesty to leave his shop unattended and unguarded.

"Mr. Tappan. Are you here?"

Footfalls broke the silence and a door to the living area scraped open. "Who's there?"

Who's there? "Mr. Tappan, what is the matter? It's Mrs. Drouillard." Millie paused and shivered. It was the first time she'd called herself that, but now the name had a slightly sour taste. Shaking her head, she added, "I need to speak with you."

Old Shakespeare peeked through the door, holding a flickering candle that cast sinister shadows across his face. The storekeeper's tight-cropped mustache and small, triangular beard were uncombed and lay at an angle across his face, as if he'd rubbed them sideways with grease. Dark bags hung below his eyes, his hair was askew, and his clothes were wrinkled and stained.

He looked as worn out as Dom. And as guilty.

NINE

January 5, 1864

Reading the Walls

M r. Tappan are you unwell?" Millie hurried over and rested a hand on his shoulder. "You look poorly. I'll fetch Doc Noxon."

"N-no. No need. Just a touch of the catarrh." He leaned heavily on the door. "I've downed some bitters. I'm sure I'll be fine soon."

Millie had her doubts. In Idaho Springs, bitters—especially those concocted by the male population—were usually five parts whiskey and one-part snake oil. Not her idea of a remedy for catarrh. "I'll make you a tonic," Millie insisted. Turning to the shelves, she shooed Buttercup away from the bags of sugar and pulled out several bottles. "A base of cider vinegar, some tincture of iron, and a bit of wormwood should help." She uncorked the tincture of iron, releasing a sour, offensive metallic smell.

Old Shakespeare turned green, spun around, and stumbled back into his living area, slamming the door behind him.

"I believe your tincture is rancid," Millie said, thoughtfully recorking the bottle. In his present state, Old Shakespeare wouldn't be answering any questions, but her visit had given her something more to consider. Old Shakespeare didn't look to be suffering from catarrh. His nose and eyes weren't running, and he wasn't coughing.

No, Old Shakespeare, like Dom, appeared to be suffering from guilt and maybe a bit too much drink. Turning, she called to Buttercup, but the goat refused to leave the sugar bag. "You naughty girl." Millie swatted the goat, but Buttercup stretched her neck to get one more bite from the hole she'd chewed in the gutta-percha sack. "Indian rubber is supposed to be rat proof," Millie muttered, shaking her head. She picked up Buttercup and left, cradling the little goat in her arms.

Frigid air burned her throat as she strode outside the shop and headed in the direction of Widow Ferris' cabin. "Mrs. Drouillard," hollered a weak voice. Looking back, she found Mr. Tappan peering out his back door, squinting in the light, his complexion pasty. "Mrs. D, your package came in." He lifted a brown-paper parcel.

"My package?" Millie had ordered several things for the wedding—the canned peaches and canned oysters being the most popular—but everything had arrived before the big day. She walked back to where Mr. Tappan stood. "Why thank you, sir, I can't—"

"H-here." He dropped the slim parcel into her arms— right on top of Buttercup—and slammed the door.

"Well that was rude," Millie said, lifting the package off the goat and stroking Buttercup's floppy ears before setting her down. "But maybe he has a peek hole and saw you chew into his sugar bag."

Turning the package over, Millie couldn't imagine what it was, but when she ripped the paper off, she smiled. The night Dom proposed, they'd disagreed over proper decorum and Dom—in a fit of temper—had thrown Millie's copy of Florence Hartley's *Ladies' Book of Etiquette* into the fire. She thumbed through this new copy, feeling a twinge of sadness. Even reading Florence Hartley's excellent advice every night would hardly compensate for Dom's shameful past.

Millie shook her head, missing the days when her only worry was trying to improve Dom's manners. She squeezed the book into her apron beside her six-shooter, deciding her next apron would need a bigger pocket, wrapped her scarf around Buttercup, and led the goat through town. They passed the Beebee House and Brother Bunce's church, but as she circled around the blacksmith shop, Jake and Samuel hurried out.

"You help Mistah Shumate?" Jake asked, concern creasing his face.

"Not yet." In the sunlight, Samuel's light skin glistened like heavily creamed coffee. The boy bent to pet Buttercup, and for an instant he looked familiar. Millie tried to decide who he reminded her of, but Samuel glanced up, ducked his head, and backed up until he was hidden behind his father.

Millie knelt until her eyes were at the same height as the child. "Mr. Samuel, would you do me a favor? Can you keep track of Buttercup until I come back?" She held the goat's scarf lead out to him.

"Buttercrap?" asked the boy timidly, peeking out from behind his father.

"No, it's Buttercup." She scooted the little goat toward the boy.

Samuel reached out and took Millie's scarf. "Yes 'um, Misah D." He pulled the goat into the shop. "Come, Buttercrap."

"Don't let her play under those icicles." Millie added, eying the long, pointed ice hanging off the roof.

"Yes 'um, Misah D," repeated the boy, disappearing from sight.

"Mr. Jake, please keep track of them."

"Yes 'um, Misah D," Jake said.

The two needed language lessons, but that was a chore

for another day. Millie struck out toward the Ferris cabin, hoping the sheriff was done and gone, so she might have a moment alone to search for Dom's letter. His indiscretion mortified her, but if others didn't know, he wouldn't be a murder suspect, and she wouldn't be the talk of the town.

She followed a frozen trail down toward the end of the open valley to a lonely spot near Mr. Ferris' placer claim on Clear Creek. Rounding the edge of the cabin, she found the cabin door ajar. "Hello," she called. Silence answered her. Furtively glancing around—knowing Sheriff Reynolds would be furious if he caught her—Millie slipped inside.

The room was dark and freezing. Millie's breath formed vapor clouds as she hurried to the window and unlatched the shutters, pushing aside the skin coverings. Light poured into the small living space revealing a mess that made Millie's skin crawl. She unbuttoned her coat and removed her six-shooter, placing it in the outer pocket of her coat and within easy reach.

Taking a deep breath, Millie turned a complete circle. Papers were scattered on and under Mr. Ferris' work desk, dishes and pots had been knocked off shelves, hand-forged nails and silverware littered the floor, and Widow Ferris' paint easel lay smashed near her tiny cook stove. Even the wood from the wood box littered the floor.

Had the killer ripped the place apart in a temper, or was he searching for something—something like a blackmail letter? Millie's eyes slowly adjusted to the light in the room, and she noted a half-burned candle stuck directly to Mr. Ferris' desk. Widow Ferris had been a poor housekeeper, but no woman would stick a candle directly on a wooden surface. The drippings would make a terrible mess and probably permanently stain the wood—not to mention the fire danger.

The desk, though, would be the most likely place to find any blackmail material, including Dom's letter.

Millie stepped carefully over the wood and debris, pausing when the smell of fresh paste filled her senses. Glancing
around, she noticed new papers glued haphazardly on the
wall, the edges still dark and damp looking. Confused, Millie approached the wall and sniffed. Definitely fresh paste.

Unlike her neighbors, Millie didn't paper her walls—
she preferred the look of the wood—but that didn't stop
her from enjoying her neighbor's walls. Mrs. Gilson—the
hardworking matron who'd taught her about washtub panning—had a kitchen covered with illustrations from *Pe-
terson's Ladies' Magazine*, *Godey's Lady's Book*, and *The Eng-
lishwoman's Domestic Magazine*. Mrs. Beebee—the most
elegant and stylish matron in town—preferred *Frank Les-
lie's Illustrated Newspaper* and *Harper's Weekly* pages. During
her wagon train trip across the plains, Millie had even met
an Army wife with the inside of her tent papered.

But why had Widow Ferris papered her walls the night
she was killed? And in such haste. The papers weren't even
straight and several sagged in the center. Had Widow Ferris known she was in danger? Was it possible she'd tried to
hide her blackmail material, like Dom's letter?

A surge of excitement filled Millie as she examined one
paper more closely. The page was from the *The Deseret News*,
a Salt Lake City paper, dated July 15, 1863. Widow Ferris
had circled a story about an Indian massacre.

> FIVE MORE MEN KILLED ON THE OVERLAND ROUTE.
> AN ATTACK WAS MADE BY INDIANS ON WHAT IS KNOWN
> AS KANYON STATION, NEAR DEEP CREEK, ON WEDNES-
> DAY LAST, WHICH RESULTED IN THE KILLING OF FOUR
> SOLDIERS AND THE STATION KEEPER, WILLIAM RILEY...

Morbid curiosity had Millie scanning the paper beside
it. It was a *Rocky Mountain News* from April 9, 1863, and

again Widow Ferris had circled a story about an Indian attack.

THE WESTERN INDIANS. OUR NEVADA EXCHANGES COME TO US FILLED WITH ACCOUNTS OF INDIAN MURDERS AND OUTRAGES IN THAT TERRITORY AND WESTERN UTAH. EVERY THING INDICATES THAT THE COMING SUMMER WILL SEE MUCH TROUBLE WITH THE SHOSHONES AND OTHER TRIBES OF THE GREAT BASIN...

Millie shuddered. Papering walls with stories of death and Indian atrocities was morbid. Could Widow Ferris have circled the stories to show she was afraid of someone? Millie thought of Dom's Indian friend, Woonbi something. She hadn't seen him last night, but that didn't mean he wasn't still in the area. But what reason would an Indian have to murder Widow Ferris?

The paper in front of her sagged badly as if something behind it was pushing it out from the wall. Taking off her glove, Millie ran a frozen finger down the face of the paper. Her heartbeat jumped. Despite numb fingers, she could feel the hard edge of something underneath.

Hurrying back to the window, Millie glanced outside—no one was in sight. Scooping up a butcher knife from the floor, Millie hurried back to the paper and poked it with the knife, making a small hole, but the hole wasn't big enough to see what was underneath.

Millie paused and took a deep breath. This was wrong and not just because it was poor etiquette. Still if the sheriff found Dom's letter, he'd accuse Dom of the murder. Millie shivered. She might never forgive Dom for his daughter, but for that sin, she'd think up an appropriate punishment No way she'd let him hang for a crime he didn't commit.

Taking a deep breath, she made a ragged slit in the

newspaper. When the opening was big enough, she put her cold fingers inside and withdrew an envelope.

Millie excitedly flipped the envelope over, her heart pounding. The letter was addressed to Mr. Frank Ferris, Esq., and the postal stamp showed it had been sent from Memphis, Tennessee. Disappointment warred with curiosity as Millie fought an internal battle against the impropriety of reading another person's mail. Of course, if no one knew she'd peeked inside the envelope, it couldn't be that improper.

Plus, after she'd read it, she'd give it to the sheriff.

Her stomach fluttered—in fear and excitement—as her stiff fingers fumbled with the envelope's contents. She withdrew a single sheet of paper, but when she unfolded it, a newspaper clipping fluttered to the floor. The sender had added neither a date nor a salutation, but simply written, *Here's the article you requested about the murder. Found it in the 30 July 1861, Memphis Daily Appeal. – Franklin*

Murder? Millie's hands trembled as she picked up the clipping and read.

MURDER IN MISSISSIPPI.—WE LEARN FROM CAPTAIN HENRY JOHNSTON, OF WASHINGTON COUNTY, MISSISSIPPI, NOW IN OUR CITY, THAT, ON THE 18TH OF JULY, MR. PRESTON PICKETT, AN INFLUENTIAL PLANTER OF EGG POINT, WHILE RIDING ALONG THE LEVEE, NEAR THE POINT, WAS SHOT BY SOME PERSON CONCEALED BEHIND A CLUSTER OF COTTONWOOD BUSHES, AT A DISTANCE OF NOT MORE THAN FIFTEEN OR TWENTY PACES. THE WEAPON USED WAS A DOUBLE-BARRELED SHOT GUN. FIFTEEN SHOTS ENTERED THE CLOTHS OF MR. PICKETT, BUT FOUR TAKING EFFECT IN THE BODY...

Millie cringed. It took a cold-blooded killer to fire a shotgun point-blank at another man. But why had Mr.

Ferris asked for the article? Had the killer fled to Idaho Springs? A cold shiver ran up Millie's back as she read the rest of the article.

Surprisingly, Mr. Pickett had survived the attack. Somehow he'd managed to return to his hotel and a physician had tended his wounds. The article said he was convalescing, expected to recover completely until an unknown man entered the sickroom and shot Mr. Pickett in his bed, killing him.

Unbidden, Mr. Turck's face came into Millie's mind. He was the only person she could imagine mean and cowardly enough to shoot a man in his bedclothes.

Stuffing the letter and article back into the envelope, Millie slipped it into her apron and stepped over to the next freshly pasted paper on the wall. It was a *Weekly Commonwealth and Republican,* dated Thursday, July 2, 1863. It too had an article circled.

UTE INDIANS AND THINGS. IT HAS ALWAYS BEEN THE IMPRESSION IN THIS COUNTRY THAT THE UTE INDIANS WERE THE MOST MANLY, FRIENDLY TRIBE IN THE INTERIOR. NEITHER THE FIERCE JEALOUSY AND ANTIPATHY TO THE WHITES OF THE APACHES AND CAMANCHES...

She lost interest as she cut through the paper and removed another envelope. This one had "Paid. Central Overland Pony Express Company" printed along the top edge, Mr. Lucius Bunce beneath it.

Brother Bunce, the Baptist minister!

Millie wanted to open the letter, but she knew time was running out. Hurrying over to the first newspaper she'd seen on the wall, she cut it open, finding a letter addressed to Miss Ada LaMont. Millie didn't know Ada LaMont, but she stuffed the envelope into her apron and hurried to the last two papers. Behind them, she found a letter addressed to Mr. Batterson, another name she didn't recognize. But the last letter was addressed to someone she did know: Gene Reynolds.

"This way, Doc," Sheriff Reynolds said. "But I got to warn you. It ain't a purdy sight."

Millie dropped the letter as the Sheriff and Doc Noxon passed by the window. Bending down, she scooped up the letter, stuffed it into her apron, and spun to face the door just as the two men stepped inside.

"What in tarnation?" thundered the sheriff, his words slightly garbled. "Mrs. D, why are you here?" Millie always considered the sheriff a good-looking man, but this morning his swollen nose and puffy blue-black eye made him look grotesque. Millie cringed. Dom had called it a tussle, but Sheriff Reynolds looked like someone had beaten the living daylights out of him.

"Sheriff Reynolds, Doc Noxon. It's a pleasure to see you both. I came by, after hearing about Widow Ferris, hoping I could help." Adding a bit of penitence to her voice, she added, "And I wanted to apologize for Dom's temper."

"How long you been here, snooping around?"

"I've been, well…" Millie took a step back and stumbled when she stepped on a loose nail. *Was Sheriff Reynolds worried she'd found the letter with his name on it?* Millie had always liked the lawman. He was a stocky man with a full beard and solid, pleasant features. She'd always considered him a good lawman, but now, with the letter burning a hole in her pocket, fear made the hairs on the back of her neck rise.

Sheriff Reynolds might have killed Widow Ferris to protect his secrets.

"Mrs. D, this is no place for a lady." Doc Noxon hurried forward and took Millie's arm. "Widow Ferris' death is a terrible shock. Please, sit down." He righted a kitchen chair and offered it to Millie.

"Thank you, sir." Millie gladly accepted Doc Noxon's offer and appreciated his gentlemanly behavior. She glanced over the doctor's shoulder and decided Sheriff Reynolds looked anything but sympathetic, although his deformed face made it difficult to read his expression. "It is such a shock. I'm afraid, sir, I'm feeling quite faint." She thickened her Southern accent. Over the past year, she'd learned Northern men became downright stupid around a strong Southern drawl.

"Doc, I'll tend Mrs. D," said the sheriff, pushing the other man away. "Why don't you examine Widow Ferris."

"Widow Ferris?" Millie's pretend remorse disappeared, and her eyes widened. "Widow Ferris is still here? I assumed…I mean…" She looked at the bedroom door and felt her stomach lurch. "You left her here?"

"Blacksmith Shumate has to build the box. Plus, Doc Noxon needs to examine her." Sheriff Reynolds shook his head. "Didn't get to the bedroom yet, huh?"

The doctor patted Millie's arm. "You just sit tight. Holler if you need me." He turned and disappeared into the back room.

Sheriff Reynolds leaned over and scowled at Millie. She recoiled, both from the man's appearance and the knowledge he might be Widow Ferris' killer. Swallowing the bile that rose in her throat, she forced out a question, one slow word at a time. "How. Was. Widow. Ferris. Murdered?"

"That's no concern of yours." The lawman took Millie's arm. She jumped to her feet, backing away from him, but he easily kept hold of her. "It's time you left, Mrs. D." He led her to the door, opened it, and released her arm. "Good day, Mrs. D."

A part of Millie wanted to run away, but another side worried if she left and Sheriff Reynolds was the murderer, he would jump on any evidence that pointed toward someone else. Like Dom. "Sheriff," Millie said carefully. "Did you find Mr. Turck?"

"No." He exhaled, and a cloud of vapor momentarily blurred his expression. "I tried to stop Dom from ripping apart Mr. Turck's cabin, sort of like this one here." Millie didn't like the comparison—or where it might lead. "Dom wouldn't listen to reason." He touched his swollen nose and shrugged. "After he knocked me down, he stalked off. I assume he didn't find Turck." He lifted a thick eyebrow.

"No, Dom did not find Mr. Turck." Unless he'd lied about that too. "Which means Mr. Turck could have killed Widow Ferris."

"Might have, but I doubt it. After what he did to you, I think the rascal hightailed it out of town."

"Maybe Widow Ferris blackmailed him."

Sheriff Reynolds' good eye narrowed making him look downright mean. Millie backed out the door, but he grabbed her arm again and stopped her. "How'd you know about the blackmail?"

Millie swallowed hard and tried to keep her voice from shaking. "Widow Ferris threatened Blacksmith Shumate. The day after my wedding. I just assumed. I mean. Maybe, she'd threatened other townsfolk." *Like you.*

The sheriff glared at Millie, his tone none too friendly. "Mrs. D, you didn't remove anything from this cabin, did you?" He looked down at her bulging apron.

TEN

January 5, 1864

Proper Etiquette
at the Scene of a Murder

Millie followed Sheriff Reynolds' gaze and saw a rectangular shape clearly outlined inside her apron pocket. Glancing back up at his misshapen face, she swallowed. Sheriff Reynolds had never been one of Millie's suitors—he'd been chasing the Espinosa gang when she first arrived—but until this moment, she'd never been afraid of him.

"This?" She pulled her arm free of his grasp and carefully removed her new book, making sure the letters didn't come out with it. "This, sir, is my new etiquette book. Old Shakespeare, ah, Mr. Tappan, ordered it for me. Unfortunately, it does not offer advice on proper behavior at the scene of a murder. I'm afraid I'm uncertain how to behave."

The edges of the lawman's grim expression softened, and he took the book from her and paged through it, his rawhide gloves sticking to the paper. "Perhaps you should refer to the chapter on 'Polite Deportment and Good Habits.' I'm sure it would mention the inappropriateness of poking around the scene of a murder. Or better yet, the section on 'Morning Receptions or Calls—Etiquette for the Caller' must include the impropriety of calling on a dead woman."

"Now Sheriff Reynolds—"

"Gene, I could use your help," hollered Doc Noxon. "This icicle's a ripsnorter."

"Icicle?" Millie glanced over the sheriff's shoulder. "What icicle?"

"Goodbye, Mrs. D." Sheriff Reynolds returned her book, stepped back, and shut the door in Millie's face.

Millie didn't move for several heartbeats. Her mind churned through icicles, blackmail letters, crooked lawmen, and Dom's daughter. She needed to read the letters in her apron, but instead she circled around the cabin and stopped beside the bedroom window. Just as she had done in the main room, Doc Noxon had opened the shutters and pushed the skin aside for better lighting.

"This icicle's something." Doc Noxon's voice carried clearly through the open window. "Only Blacksmith Shumate's shop grows 'em this big."

"Between that, the soot on the wall, and the nails on the floor, I had to bring Sooty, Blacksmith Shumate, in for questioning." Sheriff Reynolds' nasally voice sounded so close Millie took a step back. "But I don't really believe he's the culprit. Sooty doesn't have the meanness—nor the temper—to thrust an icicle through a sleeping, defenseless woman."

Millie clapped a hand over her mouth to silence her gasp. Widow Ferris had been stabbed with an icicle! The horror of it made her cringe.

"Whoever did this was furious," Doc Noxon said sourly. "This icicle has pierced through her body and into the straw tick."

"Why didn't the icicle melt?" asked Sheriff Reynolds.

"It did. Leastwise the part through her did. But when it melted, the rest of it just settled lower. Cabin's as cold as an ice box."

Millie felt ill. Dom had a temper and acted impulsively, but he'd never murder a sleeping woman. That was the work of a cold-blooded killer. Someone like the murderer in the Mississippi article. Millie turned to leave, intending to read the other letters and see if they identified the killer.

"What's that?" Sheriff Reynolds sounded surprised.

"Looks like an envelope."

Millie froze as a terrible premonition settled over her.

"A letter?" Doc Noxon asked. "Under her nightcap?"

Darting forward, Millie stuck her head in the window and watched Sheriff Reynolds lean over the bed. He stood back up and turned toward the light, an envelope in his hand. He was so focused on the document that he didn't see Millie. "It's addressed to…Mr. Drouillard."

"No!" Millie hollered.

"Mrs. D?" Sheriff Reynolds looked from the letter to Millie and scowled. "What in tarnation! I told you—"

"Mrs. D!" Mrs. Beebee's high-pitched voice split the cold morning air. Millie twisted around and found the tall woman striding toward the cabin, her skirt swishing along with her swinging hips. "How kind of you to come, especially since you're just settling into married life." Her strong New England accent made the words sound as crisp as the morning air. "We'll need all the help we can get to prepare Widow Ferris for her wake."

"Prepare Widow Ferris for her wake?" Millie mumbled, still stunned by the Sheriff's discovery.

"Ladies, let's go inside. It's freezing out here." Mrs. Griswold, a round, grandmotherly matron, waddled toward the door as Mrs. Beebee took Millie's arm and jauntily escorted her back inside the cabin. Mrs. Gilson, a hardworking, practical farmer's wife who'd taught Millie how to find gold flakes while washing miners' clothing, followed them in.

"My," Mrs. Gilson said, surveying the ransacked room with raised eyebrows. "Only a man would be this messy."

Mrs. Beebee pointed at the walls and made a tsk-tsk sound. "He even destroyed her nice wall papers."

Millie was too flummoxed to blush. The sheriff found Dom's letter under Widow Ferris' nightcap! Had he planted it there and then pretended to find it? Either way, Dom's secret would soon be public. The miners' court and the rest of the townsfolk would assume Dom killed Widow Ferris. Millie had to show someone else had a better motive. She had to read the other letters, and then show them to...To whom?

"We'll need to straighten up," said Mrs. Gilson, pushing up her sleeves.

Mrs. Beebee nodded her approval and turned toward the bedroom door. "Ladies, why don't we check on Widow Ferris. Decide what we need to do to prepare her for her wake."

"Her wake?" Millie asked, unable to think clearly through her worries.

"You poor, poor dear. I can see you're shocked." Mrs. Griswold's elderly voice cracked as she gave Millie a grandmotherly hug, bumping her bonnet against Millie and knocking it askew. Millie had always found the short, older woman comforting, but even the matron couldn't calm her racing heart. "I'm sure Widow Ferris' Irish wake will help you grieve."

"T-thank you, Mrs. Griswold. I am a bit overwhelmed." Millie shook her head and rubbed her face. Who should she give the letters to?

"Widow Ferris wanted us to sit with her all night," explained Mrs. Gilson matter-of-factly, picking up two tin plates and placing them neatly on a shelf.

"And tell stories," added Mrs. Griswold, sighing. "We'll enjoy a last supper with her, and in the morning, if she hasn't woken up, we'll know she's dead. That's why it's called a wake."

"Widow Ferris planned her own wake?" Despite her own problems, Millie was shocked. "I've never heard of such a thing."

"Yes. She attended one last year in Denver City," explained Mrs. Beebee, taking off her coat and hanging it on one of Blacksmith Shumate's hand-forged nails. "She said she wanted one too, even if she wasn't Irish."

Mrs. Gilson broke off the candle stuck to Mr. Ferris' desk and used a knife to scrape off the melted wax. "Widow Ferris insisted we have a practice session, just so she wouldn't miss the experience. It was such fun. Widow Ferris dressed up in her sapphire taffeta gown and sat in her rocker, still as the dead. We told stories, laughed, and planned the menu."

"She insisted she wanted fine foods. No bear, catamount, and especially no porcupine." Mrs. Griswold sentimentally removed a handkerchief and dabbed at her tears. "Who knew she'd die so young." Her round face sagged in grief. "Poor, poor dear. I think she might have known her time was near."

Mrs. Beebee crossed the room, looking imposing in her calico dress, green flannel petticoat, and matching bonnet. The hand-carved wooden buttons down the bodice added to the costume's stylish appearance, but Mrs. Beebee, as usual, was all business. "We need everything ready by dusk. Widow Ferris is in the bedroom, isn't she?"

"Yes," Millie said, "She's with…" Her voice petered out as Mrs. Beebee swept into the bedroom, followed closely by Mrs. Griswold and Mrs. Gilson.

"Sheriff Reynolds. Doc Noxon." Mrs. Beebee's voice rose two octaves. *"What are you two doing here?"*

Millie crept to the doorway and peeked around the matrons. The faces of Sheriff Reynolds and Doc Noxon looked like two guilty boys who'd been caught stealing cookies. They backed away until they stood side by side, their backs against the wall.

Mrs. Gilson scooted around the indignant Mrs. Beebee and hurried to the bed. "Messy," she said, looking down. "It'll take some work to clean her up."

Fashion conscious Mrs. Beebee joined her and crinkled her nose. "I may have to retrieve my work apron."

"That may not be necessary, Mrs. Beebee." Mrs. Gilson squeezed the dead woman's hand. "If we keep her frozen, she won't bleed much. Maybe we can patch up that hole before we warm her. What do you think, Mrs. Griswold?"

Mrs. Griswold squashed her round frame into the tiny space. "Oh dear. We can cover up the hole, but once we warm her, she'll start leaking."

Millie felt her stomach gurgle. She'd butchered wild game, but the thought of Widow Ferris' blood made her feel queasy.

"Wonder if she's stiff yet." Mrs. Gilson lifted Widow Ferris' hand. The whole arm, stiff as a board, rose. "Well, that should make it easier to clean her up. Sort of like scrubbing a washboard."

"We'll plug the hole with rags before we warm her." Mrs. Beebee nodded decisively, resting her pointed chin on her gloved fingers and tapping a finger on her cheek. "After we warm her, she'll be pliable and we can bend her into a sitting position and place her in her chair."

"Don't you worry, dear." Mrs. Griswold leaned over and patted Widow Ferris' night bonnet. "We won't let you bleed on your lovely taffeta gown."

Millie felt bile rise in her throat again and covered her mouth.

"No time like the present to get to work." Mrs. Gilson turned and faced the men. "May I borrow your rawhide gloves, sheriff? I don't want to ruin mine."

"No." Sheriff Reynolds shook his head, as if to clear it, and stepped forward. "Ladies, please. Widow Ferris was murdered. Doc Noxon and I need to examine Widow Ferris and to search her cabin for clues."

All three matrons turned and stared, their eyes narrowing. "*Examine Widow Ferris?*" they said in unison, their voices shrill.

The sheriff shrunk back.

"Sheriff Reynolds. I thought better of you." Mrs. Beebee fisted her hands on her hips and jutted out her chin. "You know I only allow proper gentlemen into my establishment."

Sheriff Reynolds opened his mouth, but immediately shut it. Millie knew the single man took most of his meals at the Beebee House.

"Doc Noxon, does your dear wife know you're examining another woman?" Mrs. Griswold's kind, grandmotherly tone made the accusation even worse.

"The very idea!" Mrs. Gilson held out her hand. "Your gloves, sheriff. Now! Thank goodness, we arrived in time."

Millie saw Sheriff Reynolds discreetly tuck Dom's letter into his coat, and her amusement at the men's discomfort faded. Once he read that letter, he'd know about Dom's indiscretion, if he didn't already. If Sheriff Reynolds was the killer, he'd do everything in his power to make sure Dom was blamed for the crime.

"You poor, poor dear." Mrs. Griswold brushed loose strands of hair off Widow Ferris' face. "We won't let those nasty men defile you."

"Out, both of you!" Mrs. Beebee commanded.

The men shuffled by Millie, saying nothing until they were outside the room. Only then did Sheriff Reynolds make a feeble attempt to dissuade the women.

"You can take a good look at her tonight. After we've prettied her up." Mrs. Gilson hollered. Millie heard grumbling in the other room, but soon the front door slammed shut.

"Mrs. D, dear, how should we do Widow Ferris' hair?" Mrs. Griswold rubbed the dead woman's hair between her fingers. "Thank goodness she washed for your wedding. Her hair's hardly greasy."

Millie nodded absently, slipping her hand into her apron to reassure herself the letters were still there. The letters were the only thing between Dom and a hangman's noose. She needed to get out of there and go somewhere private to read them.

"Are you all right, Mrs. D?" Mrs. Griswold sounded worried.

"Um, I'm sorry. Her hair." Millie approached the bed and looked down at the wide-eyed Widow Ferris. She lay on her back, everything but her face and one arm covered by a well-worn quilt. The icicle had melted some, but it still stuck out eight inches above her body and was as thick as Dom's lower arm. Millie swallowed, glad the frigid air kept smells to a minimum. "She…Well, she was, ah, always fond of the Marie Antoinette coiffure."

"Excellent idea." Mrs. Gilson nodded her approval. "The Marie Antoinette was featured in last year's *Godey's Lady's Book*. I used that page to paper my wall."

"Mrs. D," said Mrs. Griswold kindly, "those silver combs you wore at your wedding would add a nice touch, don't you think?"

Millie cringed. Her silver combs were the only finery she owned, but her manners got the better of her. "I'd be pleased, ma'am, if you used them."

"Excellent. And when you get home, remember to invite Miss Mary." Mrs. Gilson slipped into Sheriff Reynolds' gloves as she spoke. "Mrs. Beebee, Mrs. Griswold. Shall we begin the wake at say, seven tonight?"

"That's after dusk, Mrs. Gilson, but we'll need all the time we can get." Mrs. Beebee tapped her gloved finger against her pursed lips. "We'll need food. A night's worth."

"Food's the only way we'll get the menfolk to come,"

agreed Mrs. Gilson. "Once the menfolk are inside, we'll bar the door. Else they won't stay after they've eaten."

Millie doubted even food would convince Dom to spend the night with a dead woman.

Mrs. Beebee strode to the corner of the room and lifted Widow Ferris' Sunday dress off a hook. "Widow Ferris will look good as new in this, after I press out all the wrinkles."

Millie glanced from the dress to Widow Ferris. The dead woman's open eyes and startled expression were almost life-like, but her waxy pallor, not to mention the icicle through her cold heart, meant Widow Ferris wouldn't care what she wore.

"Now," said Mrs. Gilson, wrapping her fingers around the icicle. "Let's see how stuck this is." She pulled but the icicle didn't budge. "Removing this without thawing her might be more difficult than I thought." Mrs. Gilson climbed onto the bed—planting her feet on either side of Widow Ferris—and bent down to grip the icicle.

Millie gagged.

"Are you squeamish, dear?" Mrs. Griswold patted Millie's arm.

"Mrs. Drouillard," said Mrs. Beebee in the voice of a schoolmarm. "If you're squeamish, you can leave and inform the town about the wake."

Millie opened her mouth but before she could respond, the icicle pulled free with a sickening pop. Her stomach lurched again. Millie covered her mouth and rushed from the room. Eyes lowered, she burst from the cabin and ran headlong into a man she didn't know.

ELEVEN

January 5, 1864
Blackmail Letters

Untangling her arms from the man, Millie stepped back, took several deep breaths, and rubbed the sheen of sweat from her face. The sick feeling in her stomach quieted, and she decided she wouldn't retch. Only then did she bother to examine the stranger in front of her. He was tall, maybe just an inch or two shorter than Dom, wearing fringed buckskin and a worn beaver skin top hat. She opened her mouth to apologize, but he spoke first.

"Whoa there, little lady." His vowels were drawn out in a deep Texas drawl as he surveyed Millie from head to foot with earnest, hazel-colored eyes. "You're looking a bit peaked, darlin', but I guess murder has that effect on a lady. Just take a moment and calm yourself."

"You know about Widow Ferris' murder?" Millie took another step back, her gurgling stomach forgotten, as she eyed the newcomer warily. "Who are you?"

"Name's Hunt." He swept off his top hat and bowed, causing his windblown hair to fall over his eyes. Brushing it aside, he said, "Marshal Hunt from Denver City. Rode down this morning from Georgetown and heard there'd been a murder. I'm a lawman, was born a lawman, and have dedicated my life to catching and punishing criminals. I'm looking for Sheriff Reynolds to offer him my assistance."

Millie sized up the man. Lord she wanted to read the letters in her apron, but this Marshal Hunt—assuming he really was a Denver City Marshal—was the perfect person to give them to. "Sheriff Reynolds isn't here. I was just going to find him. We—"

"Mrs. D." Mrs. Beebee swept outside, a crushed slouch hat in her hands. "We found this between the bed frame and the wall. Since Mr. Ferris always wore a stovepipe hat like President Lincoln's, we thought the killer might have dropped this."

Marshal Hunt stepped forward and took the hat. He turned it over and examined it closely. "Thank you, ma'am. This might be the clue that solves the murder."

Millie bit her lip to stop from groaning aloud. Most miners in Idaho Springs wore slouch hats. They were wide-brimmed felt hats that were used to hold a candle bracket while in a mine. The one in Marshal Hunt's hand didn't have holes for a candle bracket. It looked brand new—new like the one Dom wore at their wedding.

"Who are you?" asked Mrs. Beebee suspiciously.

Marshal Hunt repeated his introduction, but Millie ignored him, trying to remember if Dom had returned last night wearing his new hat.

"Glad you're here to solve this murder," Mrs. Beebee said admiringly. "Please come join us tonight for Widow Ferris' wake. It might help you find her killer."

"I'll come, ma'am. Thanks." He turned to Millie. "I need to share this new evidence with Sheriff Reynolds. Do you know where I can find him?"

The hat—assuming it was Dom's—was one more nail in her husband's coffin. There was no time for Millie to read the letters. "I was just going to find him, sir, and let him know about the wake." She led Marshal Hunt toward town, waiting until Mrs. Beebee disappeared into the cabin before adding, "You see, while cleaning the cabin, we found some incriminating letters."

"Incriminating letters?" Marshal Hunt's hazel eyes flashed, and his chest puffed out. "Let's see 'em."

Maybe she could use the privy outside the Sheriff's office before they went in. That would at least allow her to read Sheriff Reynolds' letter. Stalling, Millie said, "I think I need to give them to Sheriff Reynolds in person. You see… one letter is addressed to him."

"Addressed to Sheriff Reynolds?" Marshal Hunt whistled and scratched his weatherworn cheek. "That's not good, but don't you worry none little lady. I've been in numerous situations where another man less shrewd or courageous would have been shot dead. If Sheriff Reynolds is the culprit, I'll find out. Nothing I hate worse than a double-dealing lawman."

Millie rolled her eyes at the man's bravado but said nothing. She'd need all the help she could get to prove Dom's innocence. She led the way through town, and when they reached the sheriff's office, Millie did some feet shuffling and hinting about needing to visit the privy. Marshal Hunt—despite all his so-called detective skills—just ignored her. He burst into the sheriff's office and pulled Millie in beside him.

"Gentlemen," he said, once again removing his top hat and taking a quick bow. "Name's Hunt, Marshal Hunt. I'm here to solve this murder. I'm a Denver City lawman, and I always get my man." The three men—Sheriff Reynolds, Doc Noxon, and Blacksmith Shumate—rose to their feet, but Marshal Hunt didn't wait for introductions. "This slouch hat was found stuck between Widow Ferris' bed frame and the wall." He pointed at Millie. "This little lady said they found incriminating letters."

"Letters?" Sheriff Reynolds bruised and swollen face paled slightly.

Doc Noxon and Blacksmith Shumate stood in front of a big belly stove and doffed their hats politely at Millie. "Guess Dom and Blacksmith Shumate aren't the only suspects," said Doc Noxon thoughtfully.

"You have other suspects?" Marshal Hunt narrowed his eyes. "Based on what evidence?" Before anyone could answer, Marshal Hunt tossed the hat at Sheriff Reynolds and extended his hand with a flourish toward Millie. "Let's see those letters, little lady."

Millie ground her teeth. If the man called her little lady one more time, she might commit murder. Tamping down her temper, she reached into her apron pocket. "I found these letters while cleaning up. One fell out from behind a wall paper. So, I checked the other papers."

"Hidden behind wall papers?" Marshal Hunt took out a daybook and pencil from his weskit pocket and began furiously scribbling. "Ingenious!"

"Let's see 'em," scowled the sheriff. His swollen face and bruises looked worse in the harsh candlelight.

Millie fished a letter from her apron and handed it to Marshal Hunt causing Sheriff Reynolds to scowl. His expression relaxed as the Marshal read, "Mr. Lucius Bunce."

"Brother Bunce?" Blacksmith Shumate whistled. "Aye, bet the lad caused some mischief with his proslavery leanings."

"A Copperhead?" Marshal Hunt placed the letter on the wall shelf beside him. "We've had trouble in Denver City with Southern sympathizers. I'll read the content of the letter after you're gone, little lady, but I believe you mentioned you found more than one letter?"

"I found several." Millie fished out another letter, annoyed the lawman didn't read Brother Bunce's letter aloud to her.

"Miss Ada LaMont," he announced, his eyebrows lifting until they formed a thick V over his eyes.

"I wouldn't mind receiving a letter from Miss Ada," said Doc Noxon. "But my wife would toss me out."

Millie wanted to ask who Miss Ada LaMont was, but Marshal Hunt was waving his fingers, indicating he wanted another. She turned slightly so the excitable lawman couldn't snatch the next letter and glanced at the address. "I found this one first. I looked at the contents, just to see what—"

"I bet you did," said Sheriff Reynolds darkly.

"I guess we can all see it then." Marshal Hunt took the letter and removed the contents. His face darkened as he scanned the article and summarized the murder at Egg Point. "I think we've found our killer."

"I wonder how many of our lads come from Mississippi?" Blacksmith Shumate mused.

"And which of those arrived in the spring or summer of '62," added Doc Noxon.

"Half the town's male population," Sheriff Reynolds snapped. He turned to Millie and held up the slouch hat. "You recognize this?"

Millie blanched. "It…Well, it looks like the hats worn by most of the miners around here." Before the sheriff could accuse Dom, Millie added, "There are two more letters. One is addressed to a Mr. Batterson. I don't know him, but the other one I do know. It's addressed to you, Sheriff Reynolds."

The sheriff's misshapen faced turned the color of a ripe tomato.

"Sheriff Reynolds," Marshal Hunt said, frowning suspiciously, "care to explain your dealings with Widow Ferris?"

TWELVE

January 5, 1864

Dom's Daughter

Millie stumbled toward her cabin as storm clouds turned the sky black, reflecting her ill temper. She jerked open the door, unamused to find Dom and Mary whispering with their heads bent close together. Buttercup scampered over to the fire, as Millie slammed the door behind her. Millie planted her hands on her hips and glared at Dom. Anger, fear, and love warred with a single question she was afraid to ask.

"Dom, where's your new slouch hat?"

Dom stood and glanced toward the shelf by the door. Only his gloves lay on it. "I-I don't know. I guess I lost it. Maybe yesterday during my tussle with Sheriff Reynolds."

Millie had been fairly certain the hat was Dom's, but the confirmation just made her more frightened. The real killer—Sheriff Reynolds or someone else who had managed to find both his hat and the letter—had made sure Dom looked very, very guilty. Fear washed over her, but like a coward—knowing the details of Dom's past would break her heart—Millie procrastinated.

"They're having a wake for Widow Ferris." She glanced at Mary. "We'll need to make food."

"A wake for Widow Ferris?" Dom asked.

Millie removed her coat, bonnet, and gloves and hung them by the door. She turned back toward the kitchen and said, "Miss Mary, we need to start cooking food."

"What a wake?" Mary's expressive eyebrows rose.

"It's like a funeral, but instead of a preacher, friends tell stories about the departed. And it lasts all night."

"All night?" Dom rubbed his face. "We're going to spend the night with dead Widow Ferris?"

"Yes." Millie swept past him and reached for her sourdough starter. She took it down, but for once in her life, even cooking didn't appeal to her. She needed to talk with Dom, to get some answers. "The wake is to make sure Widow Ferris doesn't wake up."

"You say she dead. How she wake up?" Mary looked confused as she took the starter from Millie and pulled down Millie's egg bowl.

"She won't wake up, and I'm not sure what the matrons have planned, but I promised we'd both bring food."

"Sourdough bread okay for dead people?"

"How would I know?" Millie threw up her hands and glared at Dom. Stalling, she pulled Florence Hartley's book from her apron, and paged through it. "I'm sure Mrs. Hartley will have suggestions on proper food at a wake."

"Florence Hartley? Oh God." Dom groaned. "You got another copy of that book?"

"Sheriff know who kill Widow Ferris?" Mary asked, adding flour, sugar, and water to the sourdough. She set aside a new starter before mixing ingredients for bread.

"No. But I found some letters." Millie began recounting her morning, but Dom soon interrupted her.

"You found a blackmail letter for Sheriff Reynolds?" Dom shook his head. "And Brother Bunce?"

"I think Sheriff Reynolds is the killer," Millie said, putting voice to her suspicion.

"No way." Dom didn't hesitate. "Gene Reynolds is a

good man. He respects the law. Even if he was being black-mailed, he'd never harm a woman."

Dom's words and more importantly, his tone, made Millie pause. Dom had known Sheriff Reynolds much longer than she had.

"Maybe Bunce ain't no real preacher," Mary said thoughtfully as she kneaded the dough. "I ain't never liked how he look at me."

"You think Brother Bunce isn't a real preacher?" Millie hadn't thought of that. "He married us!"

"Wonder what Gene did?" Dom rubbed his bare chin.

Millie pushed aside her worries about Brother Bunce. It was time to quit being a coward. "Sheriff Reynolds found a letter under Widow Ferris' nightcap. It was addressed to you, Dom."

"H-he found my letter?" Dom lowered his face into his hands and whispered, "Under Widow Ferris' nightcap? Oh, God."

"What letter?" Mary asked, her head swiveling back and forth between Millie and Dom.

Dom stepped over to Millie and knelt in front of her, taking her hands in his. "I swear, Millie. I didn't know. I had no idea about…about my daughter. Not until last night. And I didn't kill Widow Ferris."

Millie swallowed and asked the question she'd been dreading. "Who's the girl's mother?"

"She was—"

The door burst open and Marshal Hunt and Sheriff Reynolds charged inside. In the stormy half-light of late afternoon, Sheriff Reynolds' swollen nose and black eye made the man look dangerous. Dom scrambled to his feet, and Millie turned to face the men, her heart racing. "Gentlemen," she said, her voice shaking. "What…a surprise."

"Mrs. D." The sheriff doffed his hat, his speech nasally. "Dom, Mary."

"You're Mr. Dominic Drouillard?" Marshal Hunt asked in a threatening tone, his hand resting on his six-shooter. "You need to come with us and answer some questions about the murder of Widow Ferris."

"Who the hell are you?" Dom asked, taking a threatening stride toward the lawman. "How dare you burst into my home."

"Calm down, Dom." Sheriff Reynolds stepped between the two men and withdrew an envelope from his weskit pocket. "We found this letter under Widow Ferris' nightcap. We know she was blackmailing you, Dom. After your wedding to Mrs. D, you had cause to kill her."

Dom's glare darted between Sheriff Reynolds and Marshal Hunt. "Widow Ferris showed me that letter last night. I didn't know nothing about it until then. And I didn't kill her."

"Mr. Ferris wasn't blackmailing you?" Sheriff Reynolds sounded surprised.

"Was he blackmailing you, Sheriff?" Millie asked.

"He was," Sheriff Reynolds said, "but I've satisfied Marshal Hunt I had nothing to do with Widow Ferris' murder."

Dom's shoulders slumped. "Ferris was probably blackmailing my older brother, Johannes. He was always protective. Treated me like a kid. If Ferris showed him that letter, he wouldn't have told me."

Marshal Hunt paced the floor, his movements a flourish of activity. "Mr. Drouillard, the sheriff mentioned you killed two men last month, a Mr. Gould and Mr. Ferris. Seems like a lot of killing in this little town. The Sheriff said the miners' court called it self-defense, but now—"

"I shot Mr. Ferris," Millie interrupted. "He tumbled to his death while trying to bury us in a landslide. Mr. Gould fell and broke his neck after drinking coffee laced with laudanum that I gave him." Not completely true, but it was the story she'd told the miners' court. "At the time,

Dom was incapacitated due to injuries from Mr. Ferris' landslide."

Stepping forward, Millie grabbed the envelope from Sheriff Reynolds' hand and pulled out the letter. "I think it's time I read this letter!" She turned her back on everyone.

Behind her, the room went silent. As she read, tears filled Millie's eyes blurring the words on the page.

> *Louisville, Kentucky*
> *February 21, 1861*
>
> *Mr. Drouillard:*
>
> *Sir: Yours of the 24th was duly received but unwelcome. As I have informed your lawyer, Mr. Ferris, I want neither money nor attention. In fact, I do not wish any further correspondence. My husband believes Rachel is his daughter. There is no need for him to know of my past imprudence. Do not write again.*
>
> *Yours,*
> *Mrs. A. L. Lane*

Dropping the letter, Millie turned to face Dom, her heart breaking. "Who...who is Mrs. Lane?"

"She's the girl I fancied before I came West." Dom's voice was barely above a whisper. "My brother and I planned to join the gold rush. I tried to talk Alice into marrying me, but she said her family was in Ohio." He shrugged helplessly. "She refused to marry me unless I stayed. So..." He shrugged. "I left."

"You left her?" Anger felt better than the pain searing her heart. "That was cowardly and unspeakable, Mr. Drouillard. An unmarried woman in a family way would be disgraced, forced into a life of destitution. How could you?"

"I didn't know!" Dom held up both hands and stepped back. "Not until last night. I didn't—"

"You'll have to continue this later," Marshal Hunt broke

in. "Based on the evidence, Mr. Drouillard, you need to come with us and answer more questions."

"Ain't got no evidence," Mary said flatly.

Despite her roiling emotions, Millie looked at Mary, confused.

"Ain't got no evidence," Mary repeated, pointing at the floor.

Millie looked down. Buttercup licked her lips and burped.

"Blast it," Marshal Hunt hollered. "That goat ate our evidence!"

Millie wanted to laugh and cry. She did neither. Later she would skin Dom alive, but no way was she allowing the lawmen to hang Widow Ferris' murder on Dom. "There were other letters." She glared at Sheriff Reynolds. "And placing Dom's letter under Widow Ferris' nightcap seems a bit obvious, like someone was trying to make him look guilty."

"True," Sheriff Reynolds said, "but I still got questions. Dom, what happened after our scuffle?"

"I spent hours searching for Turck. Didn't find him, so I went back to town. Widow Ferris was heading toward Brother Bunce's cabin and hollered at me, but I was too angry to talk. I went to see Tit Bit."

"You went to see Tit Bit?" *Could the day get any worse*, Millie wondered?

"I don't mean that way," Dom said, throwing up his hands. "I went to ask her what happened. She was busy when we stopped by earlier. After she told me, I wanted to kill Turck all over again, but I didn't know where else to look. I decided to come home. On the way, I ran into Widow Ferris outside Old Shakespeare's store. That's where she showed me that letter."

"What time was that?" Marshal Hunt asked, his pencil poised over his daybook.

Dom shrugged. "Not sure. Maybe ten, ten-thirty."

"What did you do after reading the letter?" Marshal Hunt pressed.

Dom shrugged. "Widow Ferris demanded I give her five gold nuggets—to keep her quiet. I don't think I said anything. I just stood there, dumbfounded, and she left. When I finally got my senses back, I went to Diefendorf's saloon." He looked at Sheriff Reynolds. "I saw you there."

The Sheriff nodded. "I remember. You arrived just after Old Shakespeare came in. You didn't say nothing, just took your drink and went to a corner stool."

Marshal Hunt paused in his scribbling and looked up. "Anyone else there?"

"Brother Bunce and Mr. Poor." Sheriff Reynolds scratched his nose, winced, and let his hand fall to his side. "Poor joined the boys at the gaming table for a bit of chuck-a-luck."

Any of them could have murdered Widow Ferris, Millie thought.

"Where'd you go after Diefendorf's Saloon?" Marshal Hunt asked Dom.

"I stood outside a bit, still stunned." Dom hesitated. "Then I headed home."

"You went straight home?" Marshal Hunt cocked an eyebrow at Dom.

"No." Dom hung his head, his voice barely above a whisper. "I went to Widow Ferris' cabin. Wanted to see if she had more information. About my daughter. I knocked and called out, but she wouldn't open the door."

"Was she inside?" asked Sheriff Reynolds.

"I'm not sure. I could see candlelight through the shutters, but I didn't hear nothing." He paused and frowned. "Must have been someone inside. After my knock, whoever it was blew out the candle. I waited a minute or two more, called a couple times, but no one opened the door."

Millie closed her eyes. Dom's honesty was going to get him hung.

"Is this your hat?" Sheriff Reynolds pulled a slouch hat from his coat pocket and handed it to Dom.

Dom turned it over and shrugged. "Might be. I bought a new one for the wedding. Did you pick it up after our tussle?"

"No, the matrons found it—"

"Sheriff," Millie interrupted, desperate to turn the attention away from Dom. "Did Old Shakespeare mention a visit from Widow Ferris?"

The sheriff shook his head, winced, and gently touched his swollen nose. "No, but last night he was drinking heavily. Quoting the Bard like he does when he's upset."

"And what about the letter with your name on it, Sheriff?" Millie pressed. "Why did Widow Ferris blackmail you?"

Sheriff Reynolds glared at her. "That ain't your concern, but I'll tell you this much. I've been paying Mr. Ferris for years. When he died, I thought it was over, but then Widow Ferris showed up at my cabin. Demanded I buy her a horse."

Millie lifted an eyebrow. "Did you murder her, Sheriff?"

"I did not, Mrs. D." Sheriff Reynolds angrily took the hat from Dom. "I'll need to hold onto this. We still have a few questions we'd like to ask, Dom, in private." He rested a hand on Dom's arm.

"You're just taking him to talk, right?" Millie's mouth went dry. "You won't lynch him?"

THIRTEEN

January 5, 1864

Widow Ferris' Wake

That evening, clouds blocked the stars and a cold wind blew out their candles as Millie and Mary stumbled into town. They reached the Ferris cabin and found most of the male population of Idaho Springs outside, huddled in small groups, shifting uneasily, and speaking in whispers. Everyone appeared to be there except the one face Millie wanted to see, Dom.

A shudder ran up her spine as she followed Mary toward the cabin. Had Sheriff Reynolds and Marshal Hunt lied?

Mrs. Gilson stood shivering outside the cabin door and greeted them with a chattering, "Your fingers must be frozen." The stocky matron took Millie's dish, sniffed, and nodded. "Thank goodness you brought lots. These menfolk won't set one foot inside unless we bribe them with eats." She gave the door a rather unladylike kick. "What did you make?"

"Miss Mary made this saddle of venison and several loaves of sourdough bread. I brought a couple crocks of Lemon Calf's Feet Jelly." After they'd taken Dom away, Millie had been unable to settle or focus, not even to cook.

Mrs. Beebee cracked the door and reached for Mary's sourdough loaves. "Let me take those from you, Mary. Miss

Card dropped her scones when she stepped inside. Fortunately, her scones bounce like balls, but I'd rather keep your bread off the floor. Please, come in."

Despite her worries about Dom, Millie followed Mary and the matrons inside. The view that met her eyes made her forget to shut the door, but the cold wind sucked it closed with a resounding thud. Wall candles blew out, leaving the room almost dark until the grandmotherly Mrs. Griswold relit them.

Mrs. Beebee and Mrs. Gilson carried the food to a table overflowing with roasted wild game, egg balls, scones, tapioca, boiled potatoes, and other delicacies. Normally Millie would have examined each dish and asked for recipes, but tonight she barely noticed the assortment. Even her personal woes were temporarily forgotten as she caught sight of the room's centerpiece.

"Oh Lor'!" she muttered.

"Egad!" Mary exclaimed, bumping into Millie.

Widow Ferris sat reclining in a stiff-backed horsehair chair, staring open-eyed into the room as if lording over her realm. She was dressed in her taffeta gown—looking ready for church—her arm casually resting on her husband's desk, her hand curled around the desk's lip. *The Scarlet Letter* by Nathaniel Hawthorne sat balanced in her lap, and her face looked calm and composed, albeit paler than normal.

"Oh Lor'," Millie repeated, stumbling over a rough bench. Only then did she notice benches, stools, and rough wooden planks resting on stumps had been set up in an uneven semicircle three rows deep, surrounding the dead woman.

"Her sit like that," Mary whispered in Millie's ear. "It ain't right."

"No," Millie agreed. "It isn't."

Mrs. Beebee swept back over, her features sharp in the flickering light. Proudly she motioned toward Widow Fer-

ris, beaming like she was showing off a new quilt or a nee-
dlepoint canvas. "What do you ladies think?"

"She's...I mean..." Millie didn't know what to say. "How
did you get her to pose like that?"

"We had to tie her to the chair, poor dear." Mrs. Griswold lit the candle nearest Widow Ferris and patted the
woman's dead hand. "I hid the ropes under her shawl." The
portly matron lifted a crocheted red shawl and showed the
ropes circling Widow Ferris' thin waist.

"Her hair!" Mary took a cautious step closer.

Mrs. Ferris' hair was her most shocking feature, and that
was saying something. Her normally mousy-looking locks
were wrapped into an elegant coiffure that looked remark-
ably like the Marie Antoinette featured in *Godey's Lady's
Book*. Her bangs were pulled back over her head and wo-
ven into a sophisticated knot with the ends curling down
her neck. Her long face and prominent nose could never be
made beautiful, but in death, the matrons had made Widow Ferris quite pretty.

"We didn't need your silver hairpins after all," Mrs. Gilson said, joining them.

"You didn't?" Millie had totally forgotten her hair clips.

"Ladies," Mrs. Beebee clapped her gloved hands together. "Please, sit down. It's time to let the menfolk in."

Millie sank into the nearest seat and turned toward the
door, her thoughts returning to Dom. She pulled out her
pocket watch and glanced at the time. If Dom didn't arrive
in the next five minutes, she'd go find him.

Mrs. Beebee opened the door and announced, "You may
come in." Her high-pitched voice was swept away by the
howling wind as half the candles again blew out. "Remain
respectful, like in church. No pushing or shoving."

Normally, whenever free food was involved, the miners
stampeded like oxen, but tonight there was a long pause before Doc Noxon—his wife on his arm—finally strode inside.

"Remarkable. Simply remarkable." After seating his wife, he edged through the benches for a closer look. "Ladies, you've done an amazing job. Widow Ferris looks like one of Madame Tussaud's wax masterpieces."

Mr. Poor, one of Millie's more odious former suitors, stomped into the cabin and knocked over a stool as he barged through the chairs until he stood right in front of Widow Ferris. He bent down until his face was within inches of the dead woman's placid features. "You should have 'cepted my proposal, Widow Ferris. Then you wouldn't have ended up stiff like a board." He shook his head and took the seat directly in front of her, his knees almost touching hers.

Other men filed in, quickly dropping into seats as Mrs. Griswold scurried around relighting candles each time the door opened. Minutes ticked by. Millie rose to her feet, determined to find Dom, but as she turned, he appeared in the door. The sight of him made her tense muscles go limp.

"What'd you do to her?" Dom bellowed, making Millie cringe despite her relief. The cold had given color to his bare cheeks, but they paled slightly when he spotted Millie. He rushed to her side. "You okay?"

Despite herself, Millie felt her eyes tear, and she took his cold hand in hers. "I'm fine, just worried. Sheriff Reynolds let you go?"

"Course. He knows I didn't kill her."

Millie doubted that was true, but for now she was relieved to have Dom by her side. They took their seats as Blacksmith Shumate and Jake arrived carrying a whip-sawed board coffin. They lifted it over the crowd's heads and carried the wooden box into the bedroom, returning just as Brother Bunce and a miner Millie didn't know entered the cabin.

"Them kind shouldn't be allowed to mix in proper society," muttered the miner loud enough for everyone in the room to hear.

Millie felt Dom tense up, but it was Mary she was most proud of. Her friend lifted her head and said politely, "Mr. Jake, why you not join us?"

Jake beamed and quickly took the seat beside her. "Evening, Missah Mary. You lookin' real nice."

Brother Bunce's companion swore, but a harsh glance from Mrs. Beebee caused the two men to find seats as far from Mary and Jake as possible.

When all the seats were filled, Mrs. Griswold relit all the candles, and the three matrons squeezed through the crowd and stood beside Widow Ferris, making a contrast in women's figures. Mrs. Beebee's tall, thin, dignified and fashionable frame towered over Mrs. Griswold's short, round, disorderly grandmotherly stature. Beside them, Mrs. Gilson with her callused hands and windburned face looked like the hired help.

"Thank you all for coming," Mrs. Beebee began. "Before we share a final supper with our dear friend, Widow Ferris, we'd like to remember her by telling a few stories about her." The room groaned, and several men shifted toward the food table, licking their lips as they eyed the food. Mrs. Beebee ignored them and lifted a refined eyebrow. "Is there someone who'd like to start?"

Every male head in the room ducked, as if their boots were now the most interesting thing in the room.

"Who has a shared experience?" Silence. "A fond memory?" Mrs. Beebee frowned and glanced at her cohorts. "Perhaps ladies, we should start the evening with our own memories."

Mrs. Griswold nodded, dislodging her bonnet. Mrs. Gilson said, "Why don't you start, Mrs. Beebee?"

Mrs. Beebee's polite smile tightened perceptibly. "Very well. I remember when Widow Ferris first arrived. Newly married, the poor girl could hardly boil water. Said she always had servants and asked me to teach her how to roast a wild hare." Mrs. Beebee's expression softened. "Never met a woman who could burn the outside of a roast like Widow Ferris. Still, we did enjoy berry picking every fall up Chicago Creek."

"I tried to teach her to wash miners' clothes," added Mrs. Gilson. "To earn a bit of gold dust for herself." Millie remembered her own lessons on "wash tub panning" and the tidy pile of gold flakes she'd recovered from the bottom of her wash tub. "Unfortunately, no matter how many times I reminded her, Widow Ferris always managed to toss the gold flakes out with the dirty water." Mrs. Gilson shook her head and smiled sadly.

"She told me the story of coming across the plains with Ada LaMont," Elder Griswold said in his deep, storyteller voice. Every face turned toward the older gentleman.

Elder Griswold was known for telling fine stories, but the way the miners perked up, Millie thought she was missing something. "Who's Ada LaMont?" she asked Dom, remembering the name from one of the letters.

"Denver City's first working girl."

"Widow Ferris and Miss Ada came across the plains in the summer of '59," began Elder Griswold, silencing any further questions Millie might have asked. "They were both married at the time—Miss Ada to a young minister of good standing and Widow Ferris to Mr. Ferris. Unfortunately, somewhere on that vast, sunbaked prairie, Miss Ada's youthful husband disappeared. He went missing the same night a young lady of doubtful reputation disappeared." He paused for effect and when he began again, Millie heard her neighbors—all but Widow Ferris—exhale.

"The conclusion was unfortunate, but obvious. The fledgling minister and popular lady had run off together. Widow Ferris said Miss Ada kept her grief to herself, saying nothing until the day they reached Indian Row in Denver City. That day, Miss Ada made an announcement." Elder

Griswold smiled and shook his head. "Widow Ferris used to blush—red as Indian paintbrush—as she repeated Miss Ada's words, but after talking with other fifty-niners who were there, I believe Widow Ferris repeated Miss Ada's announcement accurately.

"On her first day in Denver City, Miss Ada climbed onto a barrel and announced, 'As a God-fearing woman, you see me for the last time. Tomorrow, I start the first brothel in this settlement. Any man in need of a little fun will always find the flaps of my tent open.'"

The audience hooted appreciatively. "Her fine establishment on Arapaho Street is still open," said Mr. Poor, his face taking on an expression of pure bliss. "I visited twice, last time I was in Denver City."

There were hollers of agreement and laughter, but when Elder Griswold discretely coughed, the room instantly quieted. "Unfortunately, Miss Ada's debut was stalled when a band of friendly Arapaho visited the new settlers. The young chief was so taken by Ms. Ada's beauty, he offered five ponies for her. These new arrivals didn't know the savages' ways and thought the offer a joke. That is until the young chief returned with ponies and warriors. Poor Miss Ada was forced to hide in her wagon until the men got the Indians to leave, but once they were gone, Miss Ada kept her word. Within a week, men were visiting from far and near to enjoy her charms." He sighed. "I've never heard of a man who didn't appreciate her bagnio."

"Thank you, dear!" said Mrs. Griswold sharply, and her husband's dreamy expression vanished.

"Anyone have something else to share about Widow Ferris?" Mrs. Beebee asked, snapping her teeth together with an audible click and pressing her lips into a line thin as paper.

"She were a dreamer," said Blacksmith Shumate, his voice sad. "She loved to sketch. Would stop by me shop to get charcoal." He shook his head. "Poor lassie. Only sketch

I ever saw was the one she made of the Drouillard's wedding." He pulled a roll of paper from beneath his coat. "She finished it and gave it to me. Asked me to put a fixative over the drawing, to protect it."

Millie wanted to jump up and grab the sketch, but that would just make the situation worse. Blacksmith Shumate stood and handed the drawing to Mrs. Gilson who carefully unrolled it. Millie groaned, and several men snickered as Mrs. Gilson held the drawing up for all to admire.

"She really was quite talented," said Dom, leaning forward. "Look how cleverly the faces are drawn."

Widow Ferris had cleaned up the sketch, making each person's features recognizable, but Millie didn't appreciate the realistic details added to Dom and Mr. Turck's brawl. Blood dripped from Dom's split lip, and Mr. Turck's beard braid was wrapped like a hangman's noose around Dom's neck. Even Buttercup was accurately portrayed, devouring Kinnikinnick under Brother Bunce's scowling face.

Mrs. Gilson carefully rolled the picture and handed it to Millie. "A keepsake, Mrs. D."

"Thank you." Millie politely accepted the picture, glancing at the dead woman and forcing herself to add politely, "We will always treasure it."

"I have another one," said a voice in a refined English accent. "Here." A tall, skinny man dressed in yellow-gummed leggings took an unlit pipe from his mouth and rummaged through his bag. He knocked into Marshal Hunt as he removed a rolled-up canvas from his bag. The Denver City lawman dropped his daybook, scowled at the man, and bent to retrieve it.

"Who's that?" Millie asked.

"Billy Batterson." Dom whispered loud enough that several heads turned in their direction.

"One of the letters I found had William Batterson on it," Millie said quietly. "Who is he?"

"One of those remittance men."

The poorly dressed man with a badly cut door knocker beard didn't look like money. Remittance men were usually second or third sons of English Lords or titled English gentry. They were sent to the States with a monthly allowance—usually to get them out of the way. It was considered either a new start since they couldn't inherit the family fortune, or a way for families to remove undesirable sons from England. From the looks of Billy Batterson, Millie imagined he was in the latter category. "Why haven't I ever seen him before?"

"He's got a claim up Hukill Gulch. Doesn't come to town much, but when he does, I keep a tight hold on my hat." Dom fingered his new slouch hat.

"Why?" she asked, surprised the sheriff had returned it.

"Batterson always shows up wearing some terrible looking headpiece, like the one he's got now, but when he leaves, somebody else's fine-looking hat usually leaves too. He—"

"Why thank you, Mr. Batterson," said Mrs. Gilson taking the canvas and squeezing back through the crowd. She unrolled the window-sized sketch and admired it before turning it toward the audience. "She *was* talented."

"She was," said Mr. Batterson, the stiff English accent a stark contrast to the man's scruffy appearance. "When that skilamalink husband of hers went to Denver City for business, Widow Ferris would come visit me. She'd draw and… and do other stuff."

And do other stuff? Millie blinked. Mrs. Ferris had been a married woman!

"Wonder why she didn't sell her work," Dom commented. "She could have."

"She wanted to," Billy Batterson's grey eyes turned on Dom, "but her husband wouldn't let her. Said it wasn't proper." He snorted. "Mr. Ferris wasn't proper. He was a scoundrel and a crook who used her." The man glanced at

Mrs. Ferris and sat up straight, suddenly showing a spark of nobility. "I loved her. I want to find her killer and lynch him!"

For several heartbeats, no one spoke. Finally, Marshal Hunt asked, "Do you know where Widow Ferris met her husband?"

"Perhaps in Mississippi, near Egg Point?" Millie blurted out. Maybe Widow Ferris had known the Egg Point killer.

"No." Mrs. Beebee turned to Dom. "Widow Ferris told me she was raised near you, Mr. Drouillard, in Kentucky."

"Dom knew Widow Ferris?" Millie turned to her husband wondering what else she didn't know about the man.

"Course." Dom squirmed under Millie's scrutiny. "Her Pa was one of the wealthiest men 'round Louisville. We farmed near Harrods Creek, but she lived closer to the Ohio River. Her Pa built a sweet sorghum plant near his home. That's how he made his money."

"Sweet sorghum?" Mr. Poor said. "What's that?" Millie's former suitor was dressed in his usual striped overalls, his thick beard looking tangled and unkempt. She was glad he was sitting several rows away. Last fall, when he courted her, Millie learned Mr. Poor considered bathing optional.

"It's like molasses, but not as thick or as sweet," said Old Shakespeare with authority, fingering his tight-cropped beard. "It costs fifty to sixty cents a gallon, much less than molasses." The shopkeeper appeared recovered from his morning catarrh, although his eyes were still bloodshot.

"What was Widow Ferris like, Mr. D, before she married Mr. Ferris?" Mrs. Beebee smiled encouragingly at Dom.

"I don't remember her all that good. Always had my eye on another girl." Dom glanced at Millie, then looked away, deflating a bit. "Anyway, Widow Ferris, Miss Purity back then. She seemed happy. Had more money than the rest of us and lived in a nice house with slaves to cook and clean. Always rode a fancy horse, a gun gray stallion." He stared at the dead woman. "She was a darn good horsewoman. And well educated."

"Did Mr. Ferris live nearby?" asked Marshal Hunt, his pencil poised over his daybook.

"No." Dom scratched the stubble on his face. "I don't know where Ferris come from."

"How'd they meet?" Mrs. Gilson sighed. "I'm sure it was romantic."

"Doubt it." Dom shrugged. "After she left, I heard folks say she married the first man willing to have her."

"First man who'd have her?" Millie repeated. "But you said her family was well off."

"They were, until the accident." Dom rubbed his chin. "Don't remember the date, but we were all at a dance— Widow Ferris too. The fiddlers were in the middle of 'My Old Kentucky Home, Good Night' when the explosion happened." He shook his head and shrugged. "It sounded like a crack of thunder, but there weren't no clouds. We piled into wagons and onto horses and headed toward the sound. Ended up at the Purity homestead—Widow Ferris' home. Place was a mess. The big sorghum tank had ruptured and there was syrup everywhere. The wave of sorghum took out the house and part of the factory. Killed her whole family."

"Sticky way to go," commented Mrs. Gilson, crinkling her nose. "Smothered in a wave of molasses."

Sticky indeed, Millie thought.

"Widow Ferris lost everything that night—her family, their money, and her home," Dom shook his head. "Later, I heard she went to Louisville, still dressed in her evening finery, and married the first man who'd have her."

"Ferris married her to look more respectable," spat out Mr. Batterson bitterly. "He wasn't a solicitor. She was the educated one. I helped her write all his legal documents."

The room erupted. Men jumped to their feet and began shouting. "She wrote my mining claim?"

"What about my homestead?"

"He wrote the purchase papers for my burro."

Hollers shook the rafters until Mrs. Gilson pulled out her six-shooter and fired off a shot. Everyone stared. The matron put the gun back into her apron and said in a strict schoolmarm voice, "Everyone sit down! Mr. Batterson, please explain."

"Your documents are legal. Long as Ferris filed them proper." Mr. Batterson bit down on his pipe, speaking through the side of his mouth. "I trained as a solicitor. In England."

Had their marriage certificate been legal? Millie glanced at Dom, horrified they might not really be married. Florence Hartley had clear views, and even clearer names, for an unmarried woman sharing a bed with a man.

"I'll travel to Denver City," said Elder Griswold. "Make sure Ferris filed our claims and other documents properly. If there are any issues, I'll—"

The cabin door banged open, blowing out candles as Sheriff Reynolds strode into the room. "Sorry for the interruption, folks." He doffed his hat at the matrons as the door slammed shut behind him. "Unfortunately, we're going to need to cut this short. A winter storm's brewing. Folks need to get home while they still can."

FOURTEEN

January 5, 1864
Ice Storm

Total mayhem followed the sheriff's announcement. Men bounded to their feet, knocking over chairs as they pushed and shoved toward the food table. Mr. Poor collided with Old Shakespeare and the short shopkeeper stumbled and landed in Widow Ferris' lap. He howled and scrambled up, knocking the dead woman's chair over. Widow Ferris crashed to the floor, her head flopped sideways at an unnatural angle, and her shawl slipped off.

Millie scrambled to her feet, horrified by the mob attacking the food table. Men—including Dom—used fists, elbows, and boots to block the crowd behind them, shoveling food into their mouths with their fingers.

"Men are such animals," growled Mrs. Gilson, hurrying to Widow Ferris' side.

Millie saw Dom knock Marshal Hunt to the ground after a tug-of-war over Mary's venison. "It's like they haven't eaten in weeks," she said, eyes widening as Blacksmith Shumate jerked the roast from Dom's hands and turned into a corner, huddling there like a disciplined child as he devoured the meat.

"Poor, poor Widow Ferris," cried Mrs. Griswold mournfully. "We need to help her."

Millie hurried over, and with Jake's help they managed to right the chair, but Widow Ferris' head now drooped at an unnatural angle.

"She ain't looking so good," Mary said. "Maybe best we put her in her box." She and Jake disappeared into the bedroom. Loud scraping noises mixed with the men's shouting as the two dragged the wooden box out.

Despite the chaos and Widow Ferris' unpleasant condition, Millie couldn't help noticing Mary and Jake looked good together. He was tall, a bit too thin, but nicely featured. Mary was solidly built and had a kind, loving face. Jake was obviously interested, but Millie wasn't so sure about her friend.

"Stop woolgathering, Mrs. D," Mrs. Beebee snapped. "Help us put Widow Ferris to rest."

Mrs. Gilson untied the dead woman and as the ropes loosened, Widow Ferris slumped forward, almost falling off her chair. Everyone seized a limb—leaving Mary to hold the dangling head. On Mrs. Gilson's command, they all lifted, but Widow Ferris sagged between them. Jake hurried to help.

"Don't need your help, boy," Mary panted irritably as they edged the body over the wooden box.

So much for matchmaking, Millie thought. Widow Ferris was lowered into the coffin, but the tight spacing meant they had to release her several inches above the bottom. Widow Ferris' body settled into her resting place with a rather sickening thud. Millie cringed as she stood up and looked down.

"We should cover her up," Mrs. Gilson said, grimacing.

"Don't want to see that no more," Mary agreed, spreading a quilt over the body.

Mrs. Beebee angrily planted her hands on her bony hips and scowled as she gazed around the room. "This wasn't what Widow Ferris wanted."

"No," said Mrs. Griswold, patting her friend on the shoulder, "but Widow Ferris always did like to make an exit."

"I get our coats and boots." Mary ignored Jake as she stepped around him. "Menfolk be leaving. We best go too."

"Blast it!" Dom roared, spraying a mouthful of tapioca pudding across a rickety three-legged stool. "The mutton-head stole my hat!"

Sheriff Reynolds stopped stuffing the last of Mary's sourdough loaf into his mouth and chuckled. "Batterson always gets one. The man must have a cabin full of fine hats." He nodded to the matrons. "Thank you, ladies, and I'm sorry to disrupt your plans. I'll take care of Widow Ferris. Once the storm's over, the boys and I will thaw the ground and dig a grave. You best be getting home, while you still can."

Millie slipped Widow Ferris' wedding sketch under her coat, buttoned it up, and donned her hat and gloves. A freezing wind sucked the breath from her as she stepped outside. Dom wrapped one arm around her waist and another around Mary. Together they stumbled through the blowing snow and ice. By the time they passed old Shakespeare's store, Millie was truly worried.

This wasn't a blizzard; it was an ice storm.

Speech was impossible as they crossed Clear Creek and began the climb up Spring Gulch. With each difficult step the wind threatened to drag Millie off the mountain and sharp ice crystals battered her exposed cheeks and nose. Breathing was difficult and tiny icicles formed on Millie's eyebrows and turned the loose hair around her face into frozen strands.

After a brutal hour and several falls, they finally reached their cabin.

"Get the critters in and restock the wood boxes," Dom hollered, releasing Millie. "We'll retrieve extra supplies from Mary's." He and Mary disappeared into the whiteout.

Millie struggled to the wood pile, almost losing her way as she filled her wood box and retrieved Dom's burro, Columbine, from the barn. The burro walked into Millie's kitchen like a queen entering her throne room and immediately lifted her tail. Millie called the animal several vile names—words she'd learned from Dom—but she didn't have time to clean up. Her chickens might already be frozen.

They weren't, but they clucked unhappily as she stuffed them into a wooden box and dragged it into her kitchen. Exhaustion clawed at her. Her teeth chattered violently, and she couldn't control her shivering. Forcing herself to keep moving, she heated water and dragged quilts, skins, and blankets in front of the fire, glancing often at the door. Why hadn't Dom and Mary returned? Mary's cabin was just on the far side of the meadow, but in these conditions, it was dangerously easy to get lost.

Despite all of today's terrible revelations, Millie didn't want a life without Dom. Somehow, they'd find a way to get past Dom's daughter—and Widow Ferris' murder.

Millie hauled their rocking chairs aside and made a bed in front of the fire, putting her quilts on top of the skins. Buttercup and her daughters immediately cuddled on top, refusing to move as Millie banked the fire. Just as Millie thought she'd go crazy, the door finally burst open. Dom and Mary stumbled inside, accompanied by a bone-chilling wind and a blast of snow and ice.

"Oh Lor'!" Millie struggled to shut and bar the door before turning to help Mary and Dom. They were both hunched over, their clothing, eyebrows, and hair frozen white. Taking the supplies, they carried, Millie helped them peel off their frozen coats, boots, and gloves before placing hot drinks between their cold fingers. She herded them to the fire and soon joined them, listening as wind rattled the window shutters and howled around the cabin.

"Millie." Dom picked up Nanny and put her in his lap. "I-I want to explain."

"Dom, I don't—"

"Just listen." He placed a cold finger on her lips. "When I told Alice I was coming here, she was furious. She wouldn't consider coming with us and refused to see me to say good-bye. My brother, Johannes, was glad. He didn't like her, but I was young, in love, and my heart was broken." He lowered his hand and scooted closer to Millie. "We were packed, ready to go, but Johannes had one last thing he needed from town. Alice came by just after he left.

"I thought it meant she'd changed her mind. I immediately dropped to my knees and proposed and was thrilled when she accepted. She'd brought a bottle from her father's still and we celebrated. It was strong. One thing led to the next and when Johannes returned, he found us together." Dom shook his head. "He was furious, but finding us that way, there was nothing to be done. He said we'd stop in Louisville on our way through and get the marriage license there.

"That's when Alice announced we were getting married but would be staying in Kentucky." He shook his head. "Alice and Johannes fought, but I was too stunned to join in. Alice knew how much I wanted to go West. Now I was trapped, and when I hesitated to agree with her, Alice stormed out. She said I'd shamed her and must marry her."

Dom rubbed his forehead as if remembering the fight was giving him a headache. "I didn't know what to do. Johannes threw the last of our supplies into the wagon and said we were leaving." Dom lifted his hands. "What was I supposed to do?"

"You left her?" Millie couldn't hide her disgust.

"Yes…No…Only for a day." He ran his fingers through his hair. "We camped that first night west of Louisville, and I knew I had to go back. It took me most of the next day, but finally I reached Alice's home." He shook his head. "I arrived to find a celebration. She'd just married another man." He hung his head. "I admit I was relieved. Her hateful stare when she spotted me made it easy to go back to Johannes."

"The child could be yours," Millie said.

"Yes." Dom wrapped his arm around her. "I've no idea why Alice might have written, but if she did and Johannes got the letter, he wouldn't have told me. After what she did, he hated Alice. He would have paid blackmail money to protect me." His blue eyes glittered in the firelight. "I'm sorry, but I need to find out the truth. I need to know if Rachel is my daughter."

FIFTEEN

January 18, 1864
Too Many Suspects

T he ice storm lasted all through the night and the following day, but the devastation from it wreaked havoc for weeks. When the storm finally abated, Dom, Millie, and Mary battled freezing weather as they cleared downed trees blocking the path toward town. Unfortunately, temperatures during the day warmed to unseasonably high levels, melting the snow and ice. Every night the melt refroze, creating slick, dangerous ice patches. Dom had resorted to wearing his hobnail boots—normally worn only in his mine—whenever he went outside. Millie didn't own mining boots, and the bruises covering her hips and legs attested to the numerous times she'd fallen.

Despite these issues, Millie couldn't remember being happier. For two weeks, she ignored Widow Ferris' murder and Dom's illegitimate daughter and settled into married life. It was wonderful, but unfortunately, their supplies of tea, sugar, and flour dwindled until they were forced to attempt a trip to town. Leaving Nanny and Nanko curled up with Mary in her cabin, Dom, Millie, and Buttercup headed toward Idaho Springs.

The morning was cold and clear as they struggled through the patch of thick evergreen trees surrounding their meadow. Millie sighed with relief as they left the dark forest but froze when she saw the steep slope down Spring Gulch. The hill and switchbacks were covered by a layer of thick ice.

"We can't go down that." She took a step backward. "If we slip, we won't stop until we hit the bushes near the stream."

"Don't worry. My hobnail boots will hold." Dom wrapped his arm around Millie and stepped forward. "Just hold on to me."

"I don't think this is a good idea," Millie said.

Dom just laughed and stepped out, driving the nails in the bottom of his boots into the slick ice. Carefully, step-by-step, he began descending. Millie clung to him, slipping whenever she put weight on her own feet.

To her amazement, Dom's boots held. They reached the second switchback and Dom paused to catch his breath. Millie opened her mouth to admit she'd been wrong, but Buttercup's bleat made her look up. She'd totally forgotten Buttercup!

Above them, the little goat leaned over the ice slick and bleated again.

"Buttercup, stay there!" Millie yelled, but it was too late. Buttercup tentatively stepped onto the ice. "No!" Millie hollered as Buttercup's legs splayed, and the goat fell forward with an unpleasant thunk. Buttercup spun around and began sliding down the incline, picking up speed as she approached them.

"Dom, Butter—"

Buttercup plowed into Dom's legs, knocking his feet out from under him. Millie screamed as they both fell backward and began to slide down the hill. "Hold on!" Dom yelled. He drove his heels into the ice, spraying snow and ice over them. They slowed a bit, but a bump knocked them sideways, and they spun around backwards with their feet above them. Like an out-of-control avalanche, they slid down the hill stopping abruptly when they crashed into the bushy banks of Chicago Creek.

"You okay?" Dom asked, rubbing his knee as he gingerly stood up and lifted Millie to her feet.

"I think so." Millie tenderly probed her aching backside. She gasped when she noticed a pile of fur and hooves. "Buttercup!"

The goat lay half-buried in the snow, unmoving, her legs tangled in the brush. Dom rushed over and gently picked her up, tenderly probing her legs and neck. Buttercup bleated weakly and snuggled into his arms. "I think I better carry her."

"Maybe you should carry me," Millie muttered. New twinges of pain radiated from her backside as she carefully walked to him. He gave her a cold kiss and led the way down the trail.

Millie was sore and cold by the time they reached town, but mostly she was worried about Buttercup. The little goat hadn't lifted her head once from Dom's arm. "I think we should stop by the Beebee House. Have a piece of pie and make sure Buttercup's okay."

Dom nodded and they carefully navigated the slippery streets of Idaho Springs. The town was eerily deserted, but it was Mrs. Beebee's empty dining room that shocked Millie. With weather like this, the hall should be filled with customers. Dom gingerly set Buttercup down and the goat bleated unhappily, stood up, and took a couple of wobbly steps.

"Mrs. D!" Mrs. Beebee swept into the room. "Glad you made it. We've been worried." She eyed them critically. "You both look like a stagecoach wreck. I'll get you some hot pie, tea and coffee, and a roll for Buttercup. You rest while I retrieve Mrs. Griswold and Mrs. Gilson." She hurried into the kitchen, calling over her shoulder. "We need to talk."

Talk? They sat at the table closest to the fire, and Buttercup collapsed at Millie's feet. When Mrs. Beebee brought her a roll, she devoured it with gusto.

"Mrs. Beebee, thank you, but you know, Buttercup's just as happy eating paper," Millie said as the matron fed Buttercup a second roll.

"That may be, but the stagecoach hasn't made it here since the storm. I've got flour, but my newspapers are saved for the privy. Now sit tight. I'll get the ladies."

"Why is she getting them?" Dom asked as Mrs. Beebee swept from the room.

"I don't know," Millie said, "but it can't be good."

Millie finished the last of her pie just as the ladies returned and joined them. "Miss Millie," Mrs. Beebee began after everyone had settled into their seats with hot drinks and pie, "we need to find Widow Ferris' killer."

Millie glanced uneasily at Dom. "Did something happen?"

"Not yet, dear." Mrs. Griswold patted Millie's hand. "But rumors are running rampant and folks are acting odd."

"Lots of sneaking around after dark," explained Mrs. Beebee, "and notice how the streets are empty? I don't have a single man here buying my pies."

"It's like Widow Ferris was blackmailing the whole darn town. Everyone is suspiciously watching their neighbors." Mrs. Gilson turned to Dom. "Some say she even tried to blackmail you."

Dom opened his mouth but closed it as Brother Bunce and Old Shakespeare hurried inside, shook snow off their coats, and settled down at a table in the far corner.

"I need to tend to them." Mrs. Beebee rose. "Not another word until I get back."

In the silence that followed, Millie finished a second piece of pie, noticing Dom hadn't touched his. Mrs. Beebee returned, talking as she took her seat. "We've been helping clean up from the ice storm and—"

"And doing some detecting of our own," interrupted Mrs. Gilson, excitedly. "After all, ladies can be detectives."

Mrs. Beebee gave her friend a withering look, and Mrs. Gilson's mouth closed with an audible click. Clearing her throat, Mrs. Beebee continued in her proper, high-pitched voice. "Remember in '59. That Pinkerton agency hired Miss Kate Warne, and she solved the embezzlement problem at the Adams Express Company. We—"

"If she can be a detective, we can too!" Mrs. Gilson interrupted again, too excited to contain her enthusiasm. "We've been doing some detecting and discovered important things."

"Detecting?" Millie asked, a feeling of foreboding washing over her.

"We've made you a list of suspects. Everyone we think Widow Ferris blackmailed." Mrs. Beebee pulled a paper from her apron. "Amazing what people say when they're eating a meal. Just last night we added Old Shakespeare after Sheriff Reynolds mentioned his name."

"But now we got the list, we ain't certain how to ferret out the killer." Mrs. Gilson looked at Millie. "That's why we need you. You're an experienced detective."

Millie opened her mouth to deny this, but Dom spoke first. "Of course, we are. We've been doing some detecting ourselves. Let's see who's on your list, and we can compare it to ours."

Our list? Millie stared at her husband, but he ignored her and scanned Mrs. Beebee's list.

"We didn't add your name, Mr. D," Mrs. Gilson said quickly, "'cause we didn't believe the rumors."

He nodded absently, without looking up. "Mr. Drouillard," Millie said sharply, "please read their list aloud. After all, I'm the experienced detective."

Dom narrowed his eyes but did as she bid. "Blacksmith Shumate, Old Shakespeare, Mr. Diefendorf, the saloon owner, Mr. Batterson, and Mr. Turck."

"We aren't certain about Turck," said Mrs. Griswold in

her motherly way, "but we added him because he's not a nice man."

Millie agreed Mr. Turck was the most likely suspect, but there was another man high on her list. "You need to add Sheriff Reynolds."

All three ladies gasped.

"And Brother Bunce," Dom added quietly, glancing at the minister.

"Oh, my." Mrs. Griswold fanned herself, but Mrs. Gilson was strangely silent.

She stared stonily at the table, blushing as she whispered, "I guess...I mean...To make the list complete, we should add Mr. Gilson. But he didn't kill no one. He was home, all night, with me."

"What did he do, dear?" Mrs. Griswold patted her friend lightly on the arm and gave her an understanding smile.

"He's been visiting Tit Bit...on the sly."

Mrs. Beebee laughed. "If that's a blackmailing offense, we'd have to add all our husbands." Mrs. Gilson didn't look amused, but Millie eyed Dom speculatively. She'd forgotten to remind Dom that visiting public women was no longer acceptable. She'd explain this new rule as soon as they got their supplies and headed home.

Returning her attention to the list, Millie sighed. "That's a long list. I wonder how long Widow Ferris, or Mr. Ferris, was blackmailing folks?"

"She threatened me two days before your wedding," said Mrs. Gilson. Tears filled her eyes. "She wasn't very nice. She took my tin with all my washtub earnings. I almost had enough saved for a gown of white grenadine with a fluted flounce of green silk, just like the one pictured in the last *Godey's Magazine*."

"Don't you worry dear, we'll find your money," Mrs. Griswold said in her comforting way.

"But we didn't," wailed Mrs. Gilson. "I searched that

cabin up one side and down the other, when I cleaned it. I didn't find my tin or my gold."

"She must have a hidey hole somewhere," Dom said thoughtfully.

Mrs. Beebee perked up. "We'll search the cabin again. Once Sheriff Reynolds removes his padlock."

"There's one more suspect," Millie began, and Dom kicked her under the table. She glared at him. "It might be someone already listed, like Mr. Turck. We're not sure. I found a newspaper article from August of '61 in the Ferris' cabin. It described a killer from Egg Point, Mississippi."

Mrs. Beebee rested her sharp chin on her fist and tapped her lips in thought. "With crossing the plains and all, he probably wouldn't have reached Idaho Springs till spring of '62 or later. Sheriff Reynolds and his brothers were fifty-niners, mining in Tarryall before he came here. Mr. Diefendorf arrived in Golden City in '59 or '60."

"Mr. Gilson and I arrived in '60," added Mrs. Gilson quickly.

Brother Bunce and Old Shakespeare rose, tipped their hats politely, and left.

"Can't see either of them killing anything but a pie," said Mrs. Beebee.

Millie agreed but until she was sure, she'd leave them on the list. And she definitely wanted to know Brother Bunce's sin. If he wasn't a real preacher…Well, she didn't want to think about that.

Samuel burst through the kitchen door and hurried to the men's empty table. He loaded the dirty dishes onto a tray and carefully carried them back into the kitchen.

"Samuel's helping me out during the day," Mrs. Beebee said, "while Mr. Shumate teaches Jake blacksmithing."

"Wonder what Blacksmith Shumate did to be black-mailed," mused Dom.

"That's it!" Mrs. Beebee excitedly jumped to her feet. "If

we find out why Widow Ferris was blackmailing each person, we'll understand why someone killed her."

"That would give the killer reason to kill us," Millie said dryly.

"That's true, dear." Mrs. Griswold rose and patted Millie's arm. "Plus, no one will willingly confess their sins."

"Yes, they will!" Dom's chair scraped against the floor as he rose, "'cause I'll be the one asking."

Alarmed, Millie rose beside him. "We'll be asking." No way Dom was questioning folks alone. There was a cold-blooded killer out there, and the other miners had mean tempers and loaded six-shooters.

Mrs. Griswold, Mrs. Gilson, and Mrs. Beebee slipped into their coats. "We're coming too."

Dom's eyes widened. "I think it might be best if Mrs. Drouillard and I go alone. Folks might not be friendly."

"That's why we're coming," said Mrs. Gilson, narrowing her eyes. "You might need a bit of help if things get rough."

"And a bit of feminine persuasion," added Mrs. Beebee.

"Feminine persuasion?" Millie asked.

"Guilt and food. Any unfriendly suspect won't be welcome in the Beebee House." Mrs. Beebee nodded. "Most men will confess to just about anything for one of my pies."

"I would," Dom agreed.

"Ready?" Mrs. Griswold opened a parasol and held it over her head, looking like a proper grandmother. "Who's first?"

Dom looked at Millie, his lips twitching into a smile. "Well?"

Millie picked up Buttercup. The goat appeared miraculously recovered after two rolls and a slice of strawberry pie. "Old Shakespeare. He should be sweetened up after his pie." *And she hoped he was harmless.*

SIXTEEN

January 18, 1864

Old Shakespeare's Floating Theater Troupe

O ld Shakespeare looked pleased to see so many customers enter his shop, but his cordial behavior disappeared when instead of purchasing goods, Dom's demanding voice rattled the shelves. "So, what'd you do, Old Shakespeare? Drill out your weights? Sell rat-infested sugar? Or worse, did you misquote Shakespeare?"

"Mr. Drouillard!" Millie said sharply. "As I have explained numerous times, Florence Hartley advises, 'Be careful in conversation and avoid topics which may be supposed to have a direct reference to events or circumstances which may be painful for your companion to hear or discuss.'"

Dom rolled his eyes. "Florence Hartley never tried to find a killer."

"True, but we can still be polite." Turning to Mr. Tappan, Millie smiled and asked, "Please, Mr. Tappan, I'd like to buy some supplies—tea, coffee, sugar, and such. I'll pick out what I need after you explain why Widow Ferris was blackmailing you."

"I beg your pardon?" The small shopkeeper shrank back tugging nervously on his trim, triangular beard.

Mrs. Gilson stepped beside Dom, fisting her hands on her hips, but after a glance at Millie, she asked politely, "Was Widow Ferris blackmailing you, Mr. Tappan?"

"No, of course not." The shopkeeper retreated behind his counter.

"I saw her come out of here the night she was murdered. Later that night you were drinking at Diefendorf's saloon." Dom leaned across the counter. "Did you kill her?"

"Mr. Drouillard!" From now on, Millie would insist on a nightly reading of her *Lady's Book of Etiquette* before any marriage bliss.

Dom scowled and turned to the shopkeeper. "Well?"

The small man's face was as white as a sheet. "O-of course I didn't kill her."

"Why'd she blackmail you?" Dom struck the shop countertop for emphasis.

Buttercup fainted dead in Millie's arms. Old Shakespeare looked like he might follow suit. He stood a full head shorter than Dom and was literally shaking in his boots. "I'm not a killer. I just…" He hung his head.

"Tell us what you did, dear." Grandmotherly Mrs. Griswold walked behind the counter and patted Old Shakespeare's shoulder. "If you confess, Mrs. Beebee will make you a pie."

Old Shakespeare looked up, his eyes wide. "A pumpkin pie, Yankee fashion?"

"Of course," Mrs. Beebee said. "Just the way you like it."

Millie hoped Dom noticed that proper behavior—and calm conversation—was much more effective than pounding on the countertops.

Old Shakespeare stood up a bit straighter and narrowed his eyes, looking more like his normal self—a shrewd merchant. "Okay, but I want two pies. As the Bard said, 'Nothing will come of nothing.' And you can't tell nobody."

"I'll even bring some extra sweet cream," Mrs. Beebee promised.

"*Extra sweet cream.*" The small man sighed. "Sure, because I didn't do nothing wrong. It's just…The miners round here wouldn't understand. They'd think I was a milksop. Or a Uranian."

At the mention of a Uranian, Dom backed up and moved behind Mrs. Gilson.

Mr. Tappan frowned at him. "I'm not a Uranian. I like women. Me and Tit Bit, we have a regular night, once a month."

"*Once a month?*" Dom took another step back.

"What did Widow Ferris threaten you with?" Millie asked impatiently.

Old Shakespeare blew out a long breath. "Before I come here, I was a member of a floating theater troupe. We performed Shakespearian plays: *Othello, Hamlet, Richard III, Romeo and Juliet, The Merchant of Venice* and such. We traveled up and down the Mississippi on a barge, stopping at each port."

"Did you perform in New Orleans?" Millie asked, joining the other matrons at the counter. "I once saw *A Midsummer Night* on a floating barge."

Mr. Tappan brightened. "That might have been us. We stopped in New Orleans at least twice a year. Was it—"

"Get on with it," Dom demanded, although he didn't move any closer.

Mr. Tappan's animation faded. "As I said, our troupe performed along the Mississippi for years, but one evening, we stopped near what we thought was a settlement. They were always changing, but this settlement turned out to be a group of Inspirationalists, religious zealots migrating to their new home, Amana. I didn't know anything about Inspirationalists at the time. Neither did our troupe manager, as it turned out. We prepared to perform *Romeo and Juliet*. It used to be my favorite play."

"Did you play Romeo?" asked Mrs. Gilson enthusiastically. Millie tried to imagine the short, portly shopkeeper playing a passionate young lover, but she couldn't envision it.

"Nooo." Mr. Tappan's eyes swept over the group and he squirmed uncomfortably. "We were a traditional Shakespeare cast."

"Meaning what?" asked Dom, suspiciously.

"Meaning…we didn't allow women. I, uh, played Juliet."

"Juliet?" Mrs. Beebee's eyes widened. "What kind of dress did you wear? Was it anything like the walking costume with the Marie Antoinette Fichu shown in the February issue of *Godey's Lady's Book*?" She sighed dreamily. "I love that dress."

"That dress was nice," said Mrs. Griswold. "But Miss Godey's story on *Marrying a Fortune* was the best part of that issue. I wish my daughters had married fortunes."

"My dress was a taffeta gown," explained Mr. Tappan proudly. "It was cut in early Elizabethan style. The audience could hardly tell I was a man."

Except for the tight-cropped mustache and triangular beard, Millie thought. "So what happened Mr. Tappan?"

"We were professionals. Well received and appreciated in most towns, but…Well these Inspirationalists were fanatics. Crazy Germans. They took umbrage to a man dressed as a woman. They thought I was…Well, they assumed I was a Uranian." Old Shakespeare's face colored as he glanced uneasily at Dom. "But I'm not. Like I said. Anyway, those religious fanatics took offense. Burned our barge and tarred and feathered my fellow actors."

"Oh my," gasped Mrs. Griswold. "You poor, poor dear. What did they do to you?"

"I was ready for the next act, dressed in my gown, kirtle,

and farthingale when they caught me. But they got confused. Some of them didn't think a woman should be tarred and feathered, even though I weren't no woman. So, while they were arguing, I ran off."

"Dressed like a woman?"

Old Shakespeare nodded and puffed out his chest. "It was my most dramatic role. The barge on fire behind me, the river reflecting the red glow. My fellow actors writhing on the ground, screaming, covered in tar and feathers. And me, racing across the burning stage, my blond hair flowing behind."

"Oh dear," said Mrs. Griswold, laying a hand on her heart. "I can just picture it."

There was a reverent pause as they all considered the scene. Finally, Millie asked, "How did Widow Ferris learn about your acting?"

"Not Widow Ferris. Mr. Ferris. He blackmailed me for years."

"With what?" Dom asked.

"Our troupe were professionals, so of course we had placards. For advertising. One placard showed me in full Juliet costume. Somehow Ferris found a copy of that one. The night she was murdered, Widow Ferris came by and showed me the flier. Threatened to post it in Diefendorf's saloon if I didn't zero out her debt. Mr. Ferris hadn't paid his bill for months. I did what she wanted, 'cause if a miner like Turck saw that poster, he'd darken my daylights."

"Don't worry, dear." Mrs. Griswold patted Old Shakespeare's hand. "We won't tell anyone."

"We won't," said Mrs. Gilson, her eyes narrowing, "if you do a private reading of *Romeo and Juliet* just for us."

"A private reading?!" Mr. Tappan's eyes widened. "But who will read Romeo?"

"I will!" Mrs. Gilson clapped her hands. "I've always wanted to be Romeo."

The matrons began planning their evening entertain-
ment as Millie and Dom slipped outside. In the cold midday light, Dom shook his head. "Sometimes I wonder about
our neighbors."

Millie ignored the comment, excited their questioning
was working. Maybe everyone would confess to their sins,
and they really could uncover the killer. "Who's next?" she
asked, feeling like a real detective. "What about Billy Batterson? Surely a remittance man has something to hide."

"Maybe, but he's too far away to visit today." Dom
laughed. "Last year I heard he was selling painted nuggets to greenhorns. Probably Ferris blackmailed him over
something harmless like that. I think we should talk with
Brother Bunce or Diefendorf."

Brother Bunce was nowhere to be found, but a crowd of
miners came and went from Diefendorf's popular saloon.
Millie had been inside the establishment only once—a saloon was no place for a lady—but to track down a killer,
Millie would forgo some etiquette.

As if reading her mind, Dom turned to her. "Let me
handle this, Millie, and no more manners lessons. Fox Diefendorf can be ruthless if he feels threatened. Mr. Beebee
once told me the story of a lynching in Golden City. A man
named Vanover argued with his partners and afterwards,
started drinking and shooting bottles in local saloons. The
cuss threatened to kill anyone who got in his way. Several
Golden City townsmen, including Diefendorf, believed he
might murder someone, so they voted to hang him."

"They decided to hang a man for making threats and
shooting bottles?" Millie thought of the evidence against
Dom and shivered.

"The vote was almost unanimous. They all thought it
was safer to hang Vanover than to try and exile him. They
caught him and took away his gun before taking him to the
wooden bridge at Ford Street. Strung him up on the struc-

ture the town used for butchering oxen. Just before he was hung, Vanover yelled, 'All I've got to say is that Fox Diefendorf is a—'" Dom hesitated. "Well, he called Diefendorf a name I won't repeat."

Millie frowned. "Maybe Widow Ferris blackmailed Diefendorf about the hanging."

"I don't think so. The hanging's common knowledge."

"Still, if Mr. Diefendorf hung a man for making threats, he could be our killer. He won't be happy with us asking questions." Setting Buttercup down, Millie slipped her hand into her coat, wrapped her fingers around the butt of her six-shooter, and followed Dom into the watering hole.

Despite it being just past noon, Diefendorf's saloon was filled with a rowdy crowd. A man pounded the keys on an old piano, rough looking miners sat hunched over a gambling table, and two barkeeps kept up a lively business serving fifteen cent beers and two-bit shots of hard liquor. All business stopped and the room became eerily silent as Millie followed Dom toward the bar.

Acutely uncomfortable, Millie wondered if Mr. Diefendorf was the barkeep that looked as large as a bear or the smaller man with flaming red hair.

"Fox," Dom nodded cordially to the giant mountain man wearing hard worn buckskin. "Mrs. D and I thought we might pick up a couple of your meat pies and some drink to take home."

Fox Diefendorf made Dom look small, and the scar that ran down his right cheek caused Millie to tighten her hold on her six-shooter. "I don't allow women," said Diefendorf coldly. His eyes flicked to Buttercup, "or critters in my bar."

"Of course. We'll be on our way after we pick up our order," Dom said easily.

The barkeep shook his head but slipped into the back kitchen and soon returned with meat pies wrapped in newspaper and a bottle that sloshed out a dark liquid. "That's six bits," he said, sliding the merchandise across the sticky bar and holding out a beefy hand.

Millie wouldn't eat anything cooked in this place, much less pay six bits for it, but Dom pulled a small, tear-shaped gold nugget from his weskit pocket and extended his hand. "Afraid this is all I've got."

The barkeep grunted, pulled out his scales, and carefully measured the nugget, replacing the two pennyweight with a single pennyweight, half a pennyweight, and slowly adding grains. "This is one and a half pennyweights, six grains." Removing the nugget, he slipped it into his worn, deerskin poke and measured out one and a half pennyweights of gold dust.

Dom scowled and Millie knew something was wrong, but she wasn't sure what. "Thanks, Fox. Now if you have a moment, I'd like to ask you some questions about Widow Ferris' murder. Care to step outside?" Dom spoke calmly, quietly, but the threat in his tone was clear.

The silent barroom exploded into noise as men scrambled to leave. Millie jerked out her six-shooter and aimed it at the giant barkeep.

Diefendorf's eyes narrowed, and he made a growling noise like a Rocky Mountain lion. "Tell the lady to put away her piece. We'll talk in the back."

Dom scowled at Millie and reluctantly she put away the gun, but she kept a tight hold on the grip as they followed the barkeep toward a crowded storeroom lit by a single, ill-smelling, tallow candle. Millie hated small, dark spaces, but no way was she leaving Dom alone with this man.

The door slammed shut making Millie jump, but Dom's face remained impassive as he looked up at the barkeep. "Fox, I'm disappointed. Always thought you ran an honest saloon."

"Are you accusing me of something, Dom?" The man's

voice was so menacing Millie felt the hairs on the back of her neck rise. She wasn't sure if Dom's calm was brave or foolhardy.

"I use that nugget to calibrate my two pennyweight for my gold assays. You know how accurate the measurement of ground ore to flock must be. I know that nugget weighs exactly two pennyweights." In the silence that followed, Millie heard Buttercup bleat through the door. "You hollow out your weights, Fox? Is that why you killed Widow Ferris?"

SEVENTEEN

January 18, 1864
The Arapaho

Diefendorf scowled and Millie felt sweat trickle down her back. He folded his thick arms over his chest and leaned forward, his nose inches from Dom's. "I didn't kill Widow Ferris. Never even met the lady." His voice was harsh, threatening. "Plus, the night she was killed, I was here, working. You saw me. I was too busy to kill anyone."

Dom nodded slowly and rubbed his chin. "You saying Ferris never blackmailed you?"

"Mr. Ferris was a dishonest crook. He discovered my light weights and agreed to keep his mouth shut long as I gave him free drinks. But she never came near me." He narrowed his eyes. "Now what do I need to do to keep you and your missus quiet?"

Dom didn't flinch at the man's anger. Millie was proud of him since her own hands were shaking and slick with sweat. "Buy some honest weights, Fox, and give me back my two-pennyweight gold nugget."

The closed-in space felt even more oppressive as the two men stared each other down. Finally, Diefendorf gave a curt nod, stepped back, and unfolded his arms. He reached into his poke and withdrew Dom's gold nugget. "Done. Now get out of my saloon."

Dom tucked the nugget back into his weskit and opened the door. The smoky barroom air felt fresh and cool as Millie stumbled out into the mostly empty saloon. She hurried toward the door and called to Buttercup, but just like during the sugar incident at Old Shakespeare's store, the goat refused to come. Millie stomped toward the disobedient animal and repeated her call, but Buttercup just lowered her head and licked the rim of a glass.

"Ssshe were thhhirsssssty," slurred a drunken man. "I give her ma wissskey."

Buttercup's bulging eyes were as glassy as the drunk's. Millie muttered an expletive, picked her up, and trudged outside. She would never, ever again set foot in that awful place.

At Old Shakespeare's store, Millie was relieved the ladies were gone. She felt filthy and exhausted and was in no mood to talk with anyone. Gathering supplies, she noticed a daybook—just like Marshal Hunt's—and added it to their purchases. Tonight, she would make notes about each of their suspects.

Dom's pack was full as Millie carried Buttercup and struggled up the icy slopes of Spring Gulch. Halfway through the thick band of trees that surrounded their meadow, Millie stopped and turned in a circle, sniffing. "I smell smoke."

Dom took two long strides down the trail before turning to face her. "Millie, honey. Do you remember Woonbisi-seet?"

She spun toward him knocking Buttercup's limp head into a tree. "The Indian?"

"Yes. Ah...I've got a surprise for you." He backed another step away.

"I've had enough surprises this month, Mr. Drouillard!"

"Well...yes, but, well...Woonbisiseet's first visit. It was, uh, to let me know, that he planned to return." Dom turned and fled, hollering over his shoulder. "With his family."

With his family? Fuming, Millie blew out a long vapor trail of breath as she followed, wondering how big Woonbi-siseet's family might be. The smell of smoke grew stronger as Millie stomped out into her meadow. She froze, staring at the scene before her. "Oh Lor'!"

On the far side of her meadow, Indian boys tended a herd of mustangs. Closer to where she stood, women and girls cleared snow from the ground while others lifted long poles bound together by a rawhide rope. Stunned, she watched one group deftly spread a hide over a framework of wooden shafts.

Everywhere she looked there were Indians. One large teepee was located right in front of her cabin, its base spanning the length of two horses, its top higher than her roofline. In the middle of this disaster stood Dom, Mary, and Woonbisiseet. Mary caught sight of Millie, waved, and hurried over.

"Oh Lor'," Millie repeated.

"Ain't nothing like it, huh?" Mary grinned. "They come last spring."

"Last spring? But." Millie's eyes widened, and her voice dropped to a whisper. "How many miners did they kill and scalp?"

"Miss Millie!" Mary said derisively. "These Injuns be friendly."

"No Indians are friendly. Remember what they did to Matilda Lockhart? The military finally rescued that poor woman, but her head, arms, and face were covered in bruis-es. The brutes had tortured her and even burnt off her nose."

"Miss Millie, they good Injuns and bad Injuns, just like whites. And newspapers ain't always telling truths. South newspapers say blacks is property, like dogs."

Millie turned to her friend. "Miss Mary, you know I don't agree with the Southern papers, but Indians are dif-ferent. They're savages."

"They ain't!" Mary's eyes narrowed, and her expression turned indignant. "Injuns. Blacks. Chinese. We all the same. We want to live. Have babes. Be free. Not have husbands killed by nasty white men like Turck."

Millie blew out a breath. "But…good settlers get murdered by Indians each year."

"How many Injuns do them white soldiers kill?"

Millie wasn't sure, but the newspapers did report that the military often wiped out whole villages in retaliation for an Indian atrocity.

"These Arapaho," Mary said, gesturing toward the meadow. "They stay a week. Maybe two. Visit them hot springs. They pray, they dance." Mary's expression turned thoughtful. "You know. You ain't liking Miss Nessa's advice. Maybe Miss Sooxei, Woonbisiseet wife, might help you."

"Help me?" The Indians before her looked dirty, their clothes ragged, their expressions sad. If she was honest, they didn't look like killers at all. Instead, they reminded her of the swarms of New Orleans' immigrants living in hovels on the wrong side of Canal Street—the ones with desperate eyes and ribs protruding from hungry bodies.

"Injun ladies. They know 'bout childers. They only having one babe every five or six years. More than one babe means you can't run. Can't 'scape white soldiers."

"Miss Mary. You want me to trust some vile Indian medicine?"

"You trusting Miss Nessa."

Millie bit her lip. Could these savages offer a better solution than Tit Bit's advice on Dr. Power's French Preventatives—not that she'd gotten the courage to mention such a contraption to Dom—or a pessary coated in cocoa butter or chemical quinine? Even if the Indian women did have other solutions, was Millie desperate enough to use them? She considered confinement and babies. Oh yes, she'd use anything—even an Indian's concoction—to avoid children.

"Come," Mary said. "Meet Miss Sooxei."

Millie's head swung from side to side as they passed through the encampment. The Arapaho around them paused to watch, appearing as curious as Millie. The men wore fringed buckskin shirts, long leggings, breech cloths, and buffalo robes. Clothing like she'd seen on Woonbisiseet. The women wore buckskin dresses decorated with porcupine quills, loosely draped capes over their shoulders, and knee-high leggings. On their feet, men, women, and children wore heavy moccasins.

"They sick," Mary whispered. "Lots be pox-marked. And scrawny. Ain't no grannies, no gramps."

Mary was right. Several of the Indians had deformed skin on their faces, a trademark of smallpox, and the women set up their teepees with slow, deliberate motions like they were injured or in pain. "I don't see any babies either," Millie whispered. Maybe they *did* have methods to prevent children during hard times.

They reached Dom, and Millie gave her husband her most severe scowl. "Mr. Woonbisiseet's family is rather large."

"This here's Lawyer," Dom said sheepishly, resting a hand on an older man's shoulder. "He's their medicine man."

Unnatural gray eyes stared at her without blinking. The medicine man's wrinkled face looked as cragged as the mountains and his long, gray braids fell almost to his waist. Millie shivered. She felt like he could see right into her soul.

Woonbisiseet sauntered over, his movements both graceful and powerful, reminding Millie of the curved-horn mountain sheep that scrambled up sheer cliffs with ease. She blushed, remembering her impolite words during their first meeting.

"You met Woonbisiseet." Dom looped an arm over the Indian's shoulder. "He's their chief."

"It's a pleasure to see you again, Mr. Woonbisiseet." Millie inclined her head. As a young girl, she'd memorized every page of *True Politeness, A Hand-Book of Etiquette for Ladies*. The book instructed, "Upon a first introduction to a lady or gentleman, make a slight but gracious inclination of the head and body." When Millie had practiced the gesture, she'd never dreamed she'd be using it with Indians. She couldn't remember any advice for proper etiquette after a social faux pas, so she pretended it hadn't happened.

Woonbisiseet eyed her for a moment, grunted, and imitated her head gesture. An awkward silence ensued until Millie said uncomfortably, "I need to tend to Buttercup and start supper. It was a pleasure meeting you both."

"What's wrong with Buttercup?" Dom asked.

The goat's eyes were still glazed, and her head lolled on Millie's arm. "She's had a tough day." Millie nuzzled the goat and turned to leave, but Dom touched her arm.

"Woonbisiseet's people have had a rough year," he said in what he considered a whisper, although anyone in twenty feet could hear him. "Between disease and hunger, they're not doing well. They came here mid-winter—something they seldom do—hoping the healing power of the hot springs will help. Mostly they're just hungry. Make as much as we can spare."

As much as we can spare? Millie gazed around at the thirty or so Indians who'd invaded her meadow. "What can we make for all of them?"

"Hotcakes. They fill bellies," said Mary. She took Millie's arm and led her through the camp. They passed close to one teepee door flap, and Millie stopped and looked back. Decorating the door was something with clumps of hair hanging from it.

"Miss Millie," Mary said. "This here's Miss Sooxei, Woonbisiseet's wife."

"Those are scalps!" Millie whispered. The sight of them made her own scalp tingle.

"Yup. Now pay attention." Mary swatted Millie's arm. "This here's Miss Sooxei."

Millie turned to face the woman. A tattooed black circle on the woman's forehead marred the beauty of her round face and gentle doe-like eyes. She smiled shyly and said, "Tous, Miss Mary," flipping her long braids over her shoulder. Her soft deerskin dress was decorated with intricate quillwork, animal teeth, and colorful beads.

"Tous, Miss Sooxei." Mary turned and touched Millie's arm. "Friend, Miss Millie."

"Tous, Miss Millie." The woman pointed at herself. "Miss Sooxei."

"A pleasure to meet you," Millie said, inclining her head.

Sooxei's eyebrows drew together in obvious confusion and Mary elbowed Millie. "Tous. That how ladies say hello in Arapaho-speak."

"Tous," Millie said and Sooxei beamed.

"Miss Sooxei. You," Mary pointed at the woman, "help us." She pointed at Millie and then at herself. "Make food?" She mimicked eating.

The woman nodded and rubbed her belly. "Hungry. Me—"

A wild cry interrupted them, and a young boy astride a black and white painted pony galloped over, his horse skidding to a stop before them. The child glowered down like they'd deliberately blocked his path.

"You boy grow," Mary said, lifting her hand up high. "He big."

Sooxei nodded proudly. "Me boy. Hosa."

The child started at his name, his angry expression deepening.

Mary turned to Millie. "Take Miss Sooxei and start hotcakes. I bring the baby goats and more flour. Miss Sooxei shy. Make her welcome." Without waiting for a reply, Mary turned and strode toward her cabin, leaving Millie alone with the Indian woman and the angry boy.

"Oh Lor'!" Shifting Buttercup's lolling head back on her arm, Millie skirted around the mustang and motioned Sooxei to follow. At her cabin, Millie took a deep breath and invited the woman inside, groaning inwardly when the boy vaulted from his pony and sauntered in. Miss Sooxei stopped just inside the door, staring at Millie's cook stove with wide eyes. Even the boy seemed intimidated.

Millie set Buttercup on her quilt, rekindled the fire, and began lighting candles to brighten the dim interior. As she worked, Sooxei stood like a statue, only her eyes moving. The boy snorted, lifted his head, and strutted to the fire, settling down beside Buttercup and fingering the goat's floppy ears.

Millie kept an eye on him—not trusting he wouldn't hurt Buttercup. She pulled out ingredients for hotcakes, mixing the batter and placing her frying pan on the cookstove. The pan was sizzling when Mary, Nanny, and Nanko hurried into the cabin. The baby goats tumbled over each other, playing as they bumped into a chair and knocked it over.

The boy bound to his feet, let out a holler, and attacked them. He roughly wrestled Nanko to the ground and followed her down when Nanny butted him. Millie darted forward, but Mary stepped in her way. "He fine, Miss Millie. That boy not hurt baby goats."

"Are you sure?" Millie was going to kill Dom if she survived the afternoon.

Soon they had two hot frying pans and the sweet smell of hotcakes filled the cabin. Millie watched the boy sniff the air and desert the goats. He moved closer to the stove, his eyes hungry. Millie turned her back on him, piled hotcakes onto a plate, and handed the food to Sooxei.

"Thank you." The woman said slowly. Turning to the boy,

she said something in Arapaho and handed him the plate. He grunted, stuffed a steaming hotcake in his mouth, and rushed from the cabin. Nanny and Nanko darted after him.

"Nanny. Nanko. Come back here!" The baby goats ignored Millie and charged after the plate of food.

"They be fine," Mary said, handing Sooxei a second plate. "We need more batter."

Sooxei slipped past Millie and out the door. Millie went to close the door but paused to watch the woman offer hotcakes to the first man she met. Soon men surrounded her and moments later she headed back with an empty plate and a hopeful expression.

"Why did Miss Sooxei only feed the men?" Millie asked. "She didn't even take any for herself."

"Braves eat first. Always. They need strength, for fight and hunt."

The afternoon slowly passed, and the sky turned dusky red. Millie and Mary cooked batch after batch of hotcakes, talking with Sooxei while they worked. Mary pantomimed her words, and Millie couldn't help laughing as her friend used charades to ask Sooxei how to avoid having babies. Sooxei tilted her head in confusion, but suddenly she nodded and said something that sounded like "oo." The next time she returned with an empty plate, she also carried a tall, handwoven basket. Leaving both items on the table, she went to the stove and heated water in a pan.

Millie picked up the basket and smelled, inhaling mint and mountain sage. She poured a bit of the contents into a tin cup and poked at the mixture, recognizing dried yarrow and rose hips, but the other dried herbs and berries were unknown. Sooxei took Millie's cup, added a bit more of the mixture and poured hot water over it. She swirled the liquid until it turned murky. Taking a tiny sip, she nodded and offered it to Millie.

"Do you think it's safe?" Millie asked, sniffing the tea.

"How bad you not want a babe?"

Millie cringed and took a sip. It tasted bitter, but not bad. "You think it will work?"

"Ain't sure she understood." Mary grinned. "Either it help you get childers or help you get no childers. Guess you find out next month."

EIGHTEEN

January 24, 1864
Brother Bunce's Holy Orders

W e are going to church, Mr. Drouillard!" Millie
narrowed her eyes and stared at her husband. It
was Sunday, and she was sick to death of cooking for Miss Sooxie's family. For a few hours, she wanted
refined company, someone to cook for her, and to catch up
on news about Widow Ferris' murder.

"No," Dom said, although there was no fight in his re-
fusal.

"I'm out of flour, dried milk, eggs, and just about everything else. Plus, Mr. Jake said Brother Bunce is finally back
in Idaho Springs."

Dom stood up and stretched. "When was Jake here?"

"Yesterday. He said he was here to trade with the Arapaho, but…" Millie smiled. "Poor man. He's sweet on Miss
Mary, but she won't give him the time of day. Never seen
her so unfriendly."

"That means she's sweet on him too."

Millie shook her head. If that male logic was what Jake
believed, the poor man was in for a heartache. "Go put on
your Sunday clothes. I want to make sure Brother Bunce is
a minister."

They'd spoken little about Widow Ferris' murder since

the Arapaho's arrival—although Millie had diligently written the names of all their suspects in her new daybook. While cooking for the Arapaho, she'd had plenty of time to think about the different suspects and to note what she knew about each. Brother Bunce's disappearance after the storm seemed suspicious, even if he was a saddlebag preacher.

"Bunce didn't kill Widow Ferris," Dom grumbled, stuffing the last of his bread into his mouth. "He's a Baptist minister, for land's sakes."

Millie ignored her grumbling husband and supervised while he donned his Sunday best—the same clothes he'd worn to their wedding—and herded him out the door.

Brother Bunce, nicknamed the Arkansas Traveler, was a fine orator, but his sermon on the rights of states and the evils of the war between the North and South contained too much Southern sympathy for Millie's taste. His voice rose and fell—at times cracking like thunder—but Millie turned her attention to her neighbors.

Most men in Idaho Springs worked mining claims; their bearded faces showed the cares of hard work in a harsh environment. The women were dressed in their Sunday best, trying to make the small town respectable, or at least keep the rowdy miners from misbehaving too inappropriately. They were good people, yet one of them was a killer. Her eyes flicked from face to face. Sheriff Reynolds, Old Shakespeare, Brother Bunce, and Blacksmith Shumate. Diefendorf and Billy Batterson weren't at church, but any of them could have murdered Widow Ferris. Or maybe it was Mr. Turck or even someone not on her list.

The service ended and Dom ambushed Brother Bunce with the decorum of a bull in a china shop. "We need to talk." Dom placed his big hand on Brother Bunce's narrow shoulder.

The minister scowled, not appearing intimidated. "What can I do for you, Dom?"

"We'd like to take you to supper, Brother Bunce." Millie decided it was time to show Dom, as Poor Richard's Almanack recommended, that a spoonful of honey will catch more flies than a gallon of vinegar. "Will the Beebee House be acceptable?"

"You paying?" asked the minister, suspiciously. "Pie included?"

"Of course," Millie took Brother Bunce's arm and led him toward the Beebee House. Politely she asked, "What's the news from Denver City? I haven't seen a paper in days."

"Everyone's talking about the proposed Thirteenth Amendment, not that you'd be interested." He turned to Dom. "Can you believe Senator John Henderson of Missouri introduced a bill like that?"

Dom shrugged. "Don't remember the details of that bill."

Millie rolled her eyes. She read any newspaper she could get her hands on, but Dom preferred to spend his evenings studying his books on assays, geology, and minerals. "I'm impressed by Senator Henderson's Thirteenth Amendment," Millie said rather loudly.

"Figures." The minister shook his head in obvious disgust and pulled his arm free as they entered the Beebee House. They sat down and he turned toward Dom. "Missouri's a slave state, yet its senator submitted a proposal to permanently prohibit slavery."

"Best do it now." Dom shrugged. "Before we crush the Rebs. Once the South rejoins the states, they'll never get it through."

Mrs. Beebee arrived and set out the day's meal—salted pork and cabbage. After pouring drinks, she adjusted her skirt and settled into the seat beside Millie. She tasted her cooking, nodded, and looked over. "So, Brother Bunce, what'd you do?"

Brother Bunce choked on his coffee.

Dom whacked him on the back knocking the man half out of his chair. "W-what do you mean?" he asked uneasily, his eyes darting from face to face.

"Brother Bunce," Mrs. Beebee said casually, "if you ever want to eat at my establishment again, you'll tell Mrs. D what Widow Ferris had on you." The matron daintily cut and ate a piece of pork. "My pie today is gooseberry. You won't be getting none, unless you start talking."

The preacher's eyes narrowed, and he shook his head, his long beard jerking with the motion. "Women! God help us if they ever get the vote." He jammed food into his mouth, talking as he chewed. "Not that it's any concern of yours, but it's nothing to kill over." He used his bread to sop up his gravy and added it to his already full mouth. "Mr. Ferris found out I've never been officially ordained. Not that it matters none. I'm still a Baptist minister."

"Ordained?" Millie stared at the preacher. "What exactly does that mean?"

"It's the way the Baptist church confers holy orders, but it's not important." The minister swallowed and licked his lips. "It's just—"

"Holy orders?" Millie stood, alarmed. "Aren't you a real Baptist minister?"

"Of course, I'm a real minister!" Brother Bunce glanced around. "Sit down Mrs. D and lower your voice. Lacking holy orders just means I've never officially entered the ministerial society. I can't mediate divine grace to the laity, but I can do everything else."

"Mediate divine grace?" Dom rose and glowered down at the man. "That mean you ain't got permission to perform wedding ceremonies?"

The minister's face reddened. "Not officially, but that don't matter none. I have divine grace through obedience to my faith and—"

"Brother Bunce," Millie interrupted. "Are Dom and I legally married?"

"'Course you're married. You signed the marriage certificate. The community blessed your joining." He glanced around uneasily as other diners stared in their direction. "Ordination is bestowed by the Holy Spirit which he done. The Church's official ordination isn't required."

Millie considered. She and Dom were legally married—assuming Mr. Ferris' marriage certificate was legal—but how did God view them? Normally, Millie wasn't sure what to think about God, but marriage was marriage. A lady had to be married in the eyes of the Lord or she was a fallen woman. Oh Lor'! Millie grabbed Dom's arm, dragging him away from his half-eaten meal. "Excuse us, Mrs. Beebee."

"I'll get you some pie, Brother Bunce," Mrs. Beebee said behind her. "'Cause you told the truth. But you need to get those holy orders before the next wedding."

Dom grumbled as Millie dragged him through town. "We should have asked what Widow Ferris tried to get out of him and what he did after she left his cabin."

"Later," Millie snapped. They approached Parson Rice's small cabin. The parson was new to the community and Millie had never met him, but that didn't stop her from pounding on the door until it opened. A small, delicate man peeked out. "You ordained by your church?" Millie demanded.

"Ah, yes," he said, his eyes wide.

"I want to see your papers!" She extended her hand. "Assuming they're real, I want you to marry us!"

NINETEEN

January 28, 1864

Intruder

W oonbisiseet invited us to his teepee for stories," Dom announced as Millie put away their supper dishes. She felt a surge of pleasure. Her apprehension toward the Indians had waned as she'd learned they were neither the "noble savages" idolized in the James Fenimore Cooper books she favored nor the "red devils" described in newspapers. She didn't trust them all, but she'd come to like Sooxei and surprisingly, the angry boy, Hosa.

Hosa had made himself at home in Millie's cabin, eating anything he could find and becoming Nanny and Nanko's playmate and protector. The little boy was as bad as Dom when it came to food, but Millie appreciated how he kept the baby goats safe and out of her way, although she wasn't sure how she felt about him using the goats for target practice.

Several days before, Millie had caught Hosa astride his mustang shooting a padded arrow at Nanko. Furious, Millie had marched over to give the boy a piece of her mind, but before she reached him, Nanny charged in front of the horse and the boy's bow twanged. The padded arrow bounced off Nanny's rump and the little goat fell in a dead faint. Millie laughed till she cried, watching as Nanko excitedly ran around until she too was shot.

"What kind of stories?" Millie asked as she donned her coat.

Dom shrugged, took her hand, and led her out under a moonlit sky, skirting between smoldering campfires, shadowy faces, and tall, silent teepees. The fire inside the medicine man's lodge produced an eerie glow, and Millie shivered as low moaning—or maybe it was singing—whispered through the night. She'd gotten used to Woonbisiseet, but the silent gaze of Lawyer the medicine man still scared the living daylights out of her.

Woonbisiseet's teepee lay in the center of the makeshift camp, and Dom pushed open the flap and bent down to enter. "Shouldn't we knock or announce ourselves?" Millie asked.

"Millie, we're visiting Indians!" Dom ducked inside, drawing Millie in beside him. She immediately felt uncomfortable in the dim, closed-in, smoky space. Dom ignored her hesitation and tugged her past two Indians sitting cross-legged on the floor and around a small campfire. Millie quickly lifted her skirts above her ankles, deciding the impropriety was better than having the lace on her petticoats singed.

On the far side of the fire, Dom dropped onto a buffalo robe, crossing his legs Indian style. Millie stared at him. She hadn't considered the lack of proper seating. Awkwardly, she lowered herself down, her voluminous skirt spilling onto Dom's lap and covering the legs of the men behind them. Nervously she settled her skirt, feeling a bit more at ease when Sooxei—working quietly in the shadows on the far side of the lodge—nodded to her.

Hosa entered, spotted Millie, and hurried to her side. "Good evening, Miss Millie." He bowed and sat down beside her. Millie had taught the boy a bit of English and tried to teach him manners and personal hygiene. Thus far, she'd only been successful with the language lessons. Little boys, she decided, no matter what culture, were always dirty and sticky.

"Good evening, Mr. Hosa," Millie said slowly. "How are you doing, sir?"

He scrunched up his face in concentration. "I am wa-well, ma'am. Y-you gook prudy."

"Look pretty," Millie corrected automatically.

"Gook pretty."

Dom snorted. "He won't be attending a ball, Red. Teach him useful English."

"As I have often told you, Mr. Drouillard, it never hurts to be polite."

Dom grunted and was silent, leaving Millie to gaze around curiously. Sooxei had never invited her into her tee-pee, and Millie hadn't been sure what to expect. There was meat drying on willow racks just below the smoke flap and strange geometric symbols drawn on the inside walls, but it was the creature lying near Sooxei that gave Millie moment to pause.

"Dom, there's a baby horse in here. Are they going to roast it?"

"Of course not," Dom's voice echoed through the quiet. "Horses are critical to the Hinon'eino's survival. They—"

"Hinon eye what?" Millie asked.

"Hinon'eino. What the Arapaho call themselves. It means our people, or something like that."

"Why do we call them Arapaho?" Dom shrugged, and Millie rolled her eyes. "So, what about the foal?"

"Arapaho rely on horses. They use them to hunt, to drag their travois, and carry teepees from camp to camp. A horse gift ensures a prestigious marriage. Foals—especially one born so early in the winter—are kept in the teepee at night to keep them safe. You'd never leave the goats outside."

It was true. Buttercup, Nanny, and Nanko were part of their family, and with Hosa's training, the babies were becoming tolerably well behaved. Millie opened her mouth to ask about the geometric symbols on the walls but closed it as Woonbisiseet stepped through the flap. He strode to the fire, his back straight. Leaning over, he picked up the foal and moved it so he could sit down. His deep voice penetrated the silence.

"Welcome, woman of Kwiyágat." He spoke in accented, but understandable, English. "I thank she. She feed my people."

"You are welcome, Mr. Woonbisiseet." Millie made a slight, but gracious, inclination of her head. Despite Dom's derision, Millie would always strive for proper etiquette, even in an Indian's teepee.

Woonbisiseet mimicked Millie's head motion and the displaced foal moved on unsteady legs, sniffed the air, and wobbled over until it stood before Millie. It stuck its nose in her face and snuffed loudly, moving a step closer. Millie petted the foal's soft muzzle, amazed by its velvety feel. The foal stepped even closer and its legs buckled. It fell onto her lap, its behind landing on Dom.

"You always get the better half," Dom grumbled, stroking the foal.

The baby horse snuggled against Millie and licked her hand. Gradually the foal's tongue drew Millie's fingers into its mouth and it noisily suckled her fingers, its broomstick tail wagging and batting against Dom's side.

Woonbisiseet said something in Arapaho and Dom turned to Millie. "He wants me to translate for him. He's going to tell you some of his people's stories."

"Why does he call you Kiy-Kwiyágat?" Millie's tongue stumbled over the word.

"It's their name for me. It means Bear."

Millie barked out a rather unladylike laugh. Loud Bear

would be more appropriate, although she didn't say so. Stroking the foal's soft coat with her free hand, she turned to Woonbisiseet and gave him her full attention. He began to speak and Millie forgot about the foal, Dom's well-earned name, and even Widow Ferris' murder. In the smoky teepee, she became mesmerized by Woonbisiseet's guttural language and the shadows produced by his constantly moving hands.

Woonbisiseet told the story of the Creator, Heisonoonin, and the Sky World. He described porcupine man who fell in love with an Arapaho woman and took her to the Sky World, but the woman missed her family and returned to her world, assisted by a buzzard and a hawk. The stories were abstract, teaching life lessons and proper behavior, but it was Woonbisiseet's voice and hand movements that mesmerized Millie.

During the respectful pause after one story, Sooxei added wood to the fire, causing it to flicker to life, casting new shadows on the teepee walls and sharpening the angles of Woonbisiseet's face. "Life for us was good," he said through Dom's translation, "until the gold seeker came. Unlike the trappers and mountain men, the gold seekers were like a plague, infecting every corner of our land. They killed our buffalo, deer, beaver, and elk but only used the hides. The meat was wasted, left for the wolves. They gave us their white man's diseases, smallpox and galloping consumption. Worse, their firewater made our warriors act crazy. During our wars, the white soldiers fought like cowards, destroying our lodges and killing our women and children."

He paused and Millie glanced at the faces around her. Had the white pioneers truly taken so much from these people? Were the Indians killing settlers from cruelty or out of desperation?

When the stories were done, Dom lifted the foal off them, and Millie stood and stretched her stiff legs. She followed Dom into the fresh, cool night air and gratefully wiped the smoke from her eyes. Dom took her arm and when they reached the cabin, in an unusual act of gentlemanly behavior, he held open the door. Tired after the long evening, Millie stepped inside.

"Oh Lor'!"

"What?" Dom darted in front of her and cursed, shoving Millie back outside. He pulled out his six-shooter and disappeared into the shadowy interior. Millie did her own cursing as she unbuttoned her coat and pulled her six-shooter from her apron pocket, following Dom into the cabin.

"Whoever it was, he's gone." Dom's voice echoed from the empty bedroom. "I'm going to check the root cellar, barn, and privy."

Millie surveyed her cabin, her heart pounding. "Thank goodness Mary took the goats for the night." The mess in front of her reminded Millie of Widow Ferris' cabin. Someone had thrown dishes off shelves, pulled clothes off hooks, and even emptied the wood bins. "Why would someone do this?"

Putting her gun in her apron, Millie's hand shook as she lit a candle and went into their bedroom. The ornate box she'd inherited from Dom's brother was on the floor, its contents flung pell-mell on the floor. Millie knelt and retrieved her treasures, finding the map that had been hidden in her pocket watch, the carte de visite of Dom's brother, and the legal documents for their homestead, mining claim, and marriage. She even found the three tear-shaped gold nuggets she kept hidden in the box.

The intruder had ripped apart the cabin, but Millie didn't notice anything missing. Slowly she cleaned up the room, pausing when she found her daybook laying face up near the bed, opened to the page that included her list of suspects.

Sheriff Reynolds – opportunity, motive unknown
Old Shakespeare – doubtful, too much of a Uranian
Brother Bunce – unpleasant but a man of God
Billy Batterson – did he love Widow Ferris?
Mr. Diefendorf – nasty, busy all night
Blacksmith Shumate – too nice, but icicle from his shop
Mr. Turck – most likely suspect
The Egg Point Killer – who is he?

Millie closed her daybook and looked around her bedroom. What had the intruder been searching for? More importantly, what would he have done if he'd found Dom and Millie at home? Anyone desperate enough to search their cabin with the Indians camped just outside was a dangerous man.

Millie shivered. She had to discover Widow Ferris' murderer before someone else was killed. There might be a way to identify the killer, but it could stir up trouble. Carrying her daybook to the kitchen table, she flipped to a clean page and wrote a letter.

TWENTY

February 5, 1864
Dr. Doy

Millie's cabin was again clean and tidy, but the intruder had rattled her. She still couldn't imagine what he'd been searching for. Had she unknowingly found evidence of the killer's identity? The riskiness of the search hinted at a desperation that kept Millie up at night and on edge during the day.

This morning, tired and a bit irritable, she kneaded dough and watched Dom complete an ore assay while Hosa sat by the fire, training Nanny and Nanko to lie down on command. She jumped, knocking her dough to the floor when something struck the door with such force the leather hinges bowed out. Dom rose, his hand resting on the six-shooter he now wore at all times. Cautiously, he unbarred the door.

Woonbisiseet—a raised tomahawk in one hand—stood outside, his expression dark as a thundercloud. The Indian spoke in a sharp, unfriendly manner, gesturing at the door as he strode arrogantly inside. Millie took several deep breaths to slow her racing heart, picked up the dough, and brushed it off. "What's the problem?" she asked.

"Woonbisiseet dislikes doors." Dom shrugged. "It's an Indian thing. He believes no man should peck on wood like a jaybird. He came to tell us they're leaving."

"Leaving? But…why?"

"Lawyer says a bad storm is coming. They want to get to their winter camp before it arrives."

Would they have enough to eat in this winter camp? "I'm going to take Columbine to town and pick up supplies. You go through the root cellar. Don't let them leave until I get back."

Several hours later, Millie trudged home, amazed to find her meadow silent and empty. Trampled snow, fire rings, and travois tracks were all the tribe had left behind. Millie breathed a sigh of relief when she spotted Sooxei and Woonbisiseet near their cabin talking with Dom and Mary. She hurried over to join them.

"Good afternoon, Miss Millie," Sooxei said, a wistful expression on her face.

"Good afternoon, Miss Sooxei." Millie pointed at Columbine's bundles. "For you. Gifts."

"Thank you. Gift for you." Sooxei handed Millie a basket filled with the dried tea Millie now drank daily. After a round of polite thank-yous and bows, Sooxei helped Millie transfer packages of sugar, hard tack, beans, and salted pork from Columbine to her mustang. When they were done, Millie pulled a package of brightly colored glass beads from her coat pocket. Sooxei's face lit up. "Thank you, Miss Millie."

"We go," Woonbisiseet said, glancing at the sky. He stepped forward and enfolded Millie into his buffalo robe. The man still smelled of horse, wood, fire, leather, evergreen boughs, fresh earth and male, but Millie found his embrace almost comfortable. "Thank you, woman of Kwiyágat. You not like my people, but you feed us. Fill us with flapjacks."

Shame burned Millie's face. "You're wrong, Mr. Woonbisiseet. I've learned to appreciate your people. I'll miss you." She was going to miss them. She'd miss Sooxei's shy smile, Hosa's silly antics, and even Woonbisiseet's stern face.

"Got more problems," Mary said, glancing behind Woonbisiseet.

Millie followed her gaze and found Hosa huddled on the ground beside his mustang, a baby goat cradled in each arm. His head was bowed and his eyes downcast. A boy his age would never cry, but he was darn close. "I see."

"That boy love them babies," Mary said, staring pointedly at Dom.

Dom nodded, looking miserable.

"He'll take good care of them," Millie added.

"I know." Dom's voice sounded gruff.

"We don't need three goats," Millie added.

Dom sniffed, wiped his nose, and walked stiffly toward the boy, looking like a man heading to the gallows. Hosa peeked up when Dom rested his big hand on the boy's shoulder. "Nanny. Nanko. You gift." He used hand signals and some guttural noises to make himself clear.

Hosa's eyes widened and he looked from Dom to the goats, his face lighting with understanding. He jumped into the air, let out a death-curdling cry, and danced around the goats with wild abandon. Nanny fainted dead, but Nanko butted the boy and knocked him over. Millie laughed and even Dom smiled as Hosa bent down and spoke harshly to the naughty goat. When Nanko was properly chastised and Nanny was awake, Hosa rushed to Millie wrapping his skinny arms around her waist.

"Thank you, Noo'ohutee' Beie'ee."

"You're welcome." She patted him on the head, the way she might one of the goats, uncomfortable with his physical appreciation. His spindly arms released her, and he stepped over and solemnly shook Dom's hand.

"What did he call me?" she asked Woonbisiseet.

"He call Kwiyágat woman, Noo'ohutee Beie'ee." Nodding in obvious agreement, Woonbisiseet led his mustang toward the trees. Sooxei took the rope of the second horse and followed her husband.

Hosa vaulted onto his horse and snapped his fingers. Nanny took a running leap and landed easily on the horse, but Nanko would have slipped off if Hosa hadn't grabbed her. The boy set the goats in front of him, their legs splayed out on either side of the horse, their heads pointing in opposite directions. "Goodbye Kwiyágat. Goodbye Noo'ohutee Beie'ee."

"But Mr. Woonbisiseet," Millie called out. "What does the name mean?"

"It mean Flaming Hair," Woonbisiseet answered and disappeared into the trees.

Millie scowled and hollered, "My hair is auburn with a few red streaks!" Annoyed, Millie glanced at Dom, but her husband looked like he'd just lost his best friend. "There, there," she said, patting him on the shoulder.

"We just gave away our kids."

"There'll be other kids."

"You don't want children."

"Nanny and Nanko are better off with little Hosa." Millie hoped her words were true. Lately, it felt like every newspaper carried a story about Indian depredations and soldier retaliations. Hosa and his family would be in danger.

*****

With the Indians' departure, Millie turned her attention back to Widow Ferris' murder. She wrote notes in her daybook, made lists, and reviewed everything she could remember, but she saw nothing to indicate who the killer was or why he'd searched her cabin. After two frustrating days, Millie invited Mary to go to town with her. If she couldn't be a detective, she might as well be a matchmaker.

"Why we visit Blacksmith Shumate?" Mary asked as Millie led the way toward his workshop.

"I've got a couple more questions for him."

"Questions?" Mary scowled. "People forgetting Widow Ferris murder. Even that Denver City Marshal gone. You best leave it alone or you dig up more trouble for Mr. Dom."

Millie thought Mary was probably right, but surely asking Blacksmith Shumate a few questions would do no harm.

At the blacksmith shop, Millie knocked politely on the open door before hurrying over to the warm hearth. "Mr. Jake, Blacksmith Shumate. Hello."

"Misah D." Jake emerged from the dim interior, his expression brightening when he spotted Mary. "Misah Mary. How you?"

"I fine. We here for Blacksmith Shumate." Mary turned her back on the man.

Maybe Dom was right, Millie thought. She'd never seen Mary treat anyone so rudely.

"Och aye, lassies, what can I do for you?" The big blacksmith lumbered into the light, soot smeared across his nose and forehead.

"I was hoping, sir. I mean." Millie hesitated, not wanting to insult the man. "Would you be willing to tell me about…" She paused and blushed.

"Aye. You be wondering about Widow Ferris. To prove I ain't the killer."

"I never thought you were the killer, Mr. Shumate," Millie said quickly. "It's just…"

"I've been expecting you, Detective Drouillard." He laughed. "'Tain't a big town and word gets around. Settle yourself and I'll make some tea."

He disappeared, leaving Millie to wonder if perhaps her questions had motivated the killer to search her home. Detective Drouillard. She smiled. It had a nice ring to it.

"Misah D. I wanna ask." Jake interrupted Millie's thoughts. "Me and Samey. We wanna learn letters. Ta speak better. Mistah Shumate. He say you might could teach us?"

"I'd be happy to. And I'm sure when I'm not around, Miss Mary would be pleased to help." Millie almost laughed at Mary's sour expression.

Blacksmith Shumate lumbered back carrying a tray. "Now for a bit of tea, belly cheer, and a story." He served tea and ash cakes, appearing to enjoy himself as he settled his big frame on a thick stump. "Widow Ferris weren't really blackmailing me, she just tried a bit of coercion. See, somehow Mr. Ferris learned about Dr. Doy."

"Dr. Doy?" Millie bit into her ash cake but her teeth couldn't penetrate through the rock-hard exterior. Discreetly she set the cake back on her plate. "I don't think I've met the gentleman. Does he live nearby?"

"Course he ain't." Mary scoffed. "Dr. Doy from Kansas Territory. He part of that underground railroad. Helping slaves 'scape. I hear 'bout him 'fore I come West." Mary eyed Blacksmith Shumate. "You know that Dr. Doy?"

"Aye. Before I come here, I be part of the underground railroad. It were back in '59. Dr. Doy and his lad be captured helping thirteen slaves escape Lawrence, Kansas. Border ruffians—proslavery Missourians—caught 'em. They took the lads to Missouri, tried them, and found poor Dr. Doy guilty."

He leaned back and devoured his ash cake with gusto, licking his lips and turning them black. "They planned to send the good man to a penitentiary, so we had to do something. Mr. Soule—me mate in Denver City who sent me Jake and Samuel—convinced me to join a group of men that planned a jailbreak. 'Tweren't legal, but it were right."

"Colorado ain't Reb territory," Mary said. "Why you care if Widow Ferris tell others?"

"I didn't. Since Jake and Samuel arrived, Southern sympathizers round here know me views. But I felt sorry for poor Widow Ferris, and I'd hoped she'd give me the picture."

"Picture?" Mary set her plate down, and Jake quickly put a second cake on it. Millie decided Jake needed both letter and matchmaking lessons. He'd never win Mary's heart by following her around like an overeager puppy and feeding her disgusting ash cakes.

"Aye, after we freed Dr. Doy, we went back to Kansas and took a picture. All ten of us with Dr. Doy seated in front. I've no idea where Mr. Ferris found the photograph, but he showed it to me last year. He tried to blackmail me, but I just laughed at him." Blacksmith Shumate paused and a faraway look came into his eye. "I tried to buy the picture, but Mr. Ferris refused to sell it. I'd like to have it."

"Sheriff Reynolds didn't find it when he searched the cabin?"

"Nay, lassie. Widow Ferris must have burned it."

"Maybe." Turning to Mary she said, "I think it's time we searched that cabin."

"Miss Millie," Mary muttered, shaking her head. "You opening up a hornet's nest."

TWENTY-ONE

April 25, 1864

A Hornet's Nest

Over the next several months, Millie searched Widow Ferris' cabin with Dom, the matrons, and Mary, but she found nothing. Blacksmith Shumate's picture, Old Shakespeare's theater bill, and Mrs. Gilson's tin of gold dust were either well-hidden or Sheriff Reynolds had found and taken them. Millie tended to think the latter.

Winter passed and gossip about the murder faded. Even Millie's interest waned as she prepared for spring, fencing in a garden, turning the soil, and planting early seeds. Unfortunately, with the warming weather, the unrest between settlers and Indians worsened. Worried about Hosa and his family, Millie read every newspaper she could find.

In late March, an article in the March 19 *Daily Mining Journal* had infuriated Millie. She'd stormed home and waved the newspaper at Dom. "I can't believe this idiot wrote something like this."

THE INDIANS WANT TO BE KILLED OFF—THAT'S CERTAIN; OUR NEW MAJ. GENERALS AND BRIGADIERS WANT TO DISTINGUISH THEMSELVES, AND THERE ARE PLENTY WHO WANT THE SUPPLY AND TRANSPORTATION

CONTRACTS. ONLY GET THE THING STARTED, IT WILL WIN BY A DECIDED MAJORITY.

Millie tossed the paper into the fire. "Indians want to be killed off. How can they believe that?"

"They don't," Dom said, calmly grinding gold ore in his pestle. "Miners just want an excuse to finally own their mining claims. Even our homestead and mine legally belong to the Utes."

"Our claim belongs to the Indians?"

By early April, newspapers declared the Indian War had finally begun. This morning, anxious like always for fresh news, Millie donned her coat, determined to see if anything new had arrived with the morning stagecoach. Dom and Buttercup joined her, and they tromped through patches of snow, ice, and ankle-deep mud, but when they reached Idaho Springs, Mr. Tappan just shook his head. "I haven't gotten anything new, but the mail came in. You might check with Mrs. Griswold."

Mail—any news from friends and loved ones in the States—caused excitement throughout the town. Mrs. Griswold had been elected the acting town postmistress since her grandmotherly demeanor kept even the unruly miners in line. Millie joined the jostling crowd—leaving Buttercup and Dom just outside the door.

Mrs. Griswold spotted Millie and waved her to the front of the line, "Look dear, it's from Doctor Edwards of Egg Point, Mississippi." She handed Millie a letter. "I told Mrs. Gilson and Mrs. Beebee. They're waiting at the Beebee House. Make sure Buttercup doesn't eat the letter before I see it."

"Doctor Edwards from Egg Point?" Dom said in a voice that made everyone turn toward the door. "Blast it, Red. What have you done?" He pushed through the crowd, reached Millie, and glowered down at her. "How'd you find the doctor?"

"I didn't," she said indignantly. "I sent a letter to the editor of the *Memphis Daily Appeal* months ago. He must have forwarded it on to Egg Point."

"Goldarn it, Red." Dom plowed a path through the eavesdropping crowd. They stepped outside just as two children jumped from behind a horse, howling with delight as Buttercup fainted. Dom grumbled, picked up the comatose goat, and muttered, "Might as well get some pie out of this nonsense. I'm sure everyone's already heard about the letter."

In the Beebee House, Samuel served them pie, coffee, and hot tea under Mrs. Beebee's exacting eye. "The pie goes closer to the customer, Samuel. The tea and coffee closer to the center of the table." She nodded as he completed the chore. "I'm teaching Sam how to serve food like a proper waiter. I told him I'll increase his wage to twenty-five cents a day when he learns it right."

"Good morning, Mr. Samuel," Millie said, picking up her tea. "How do you spell cup?"

The boy rubbed his head and sounded out the word. "K, u, p."

"C, u, p, but good. Keep practicing with your father."

"Yes 'um." He disappeared into the kitchen.

"What does the letter say?" Mrs. Gilson asked, not bothering with a greeting as she took a seat at the table.

Millie removed the letter and quickly read it. "Doctor Edwards attended Mr. Pickett after he was shot. He says, despite the fifteen shots that entered Mr. Pickett and his clothes, the gentleman wasn't mortally wounded."

"Fifteen shots? Oh my!" Mrs. Gilson stabbed her fork into her pie. "Someone sure wanted him dead!"

"Indeed. But the doctor says Mr. Pickett was healing nicely until the killer returned. It was the night of July 24 and Doctor Edwards was out of town, tending another patient. Mr. Pickett's servant said the killer entered the hotel room, chased him out, and shot Mr. Pickett with a double-barreled shotgun. The discharge was so close, it burned Mr. Pickett's bedclothes."

Dom, his mouth full of pie, said something rude before adding, "It takes a cold-blooded killer to shoot a helpless man. Same kind of a killer who'd stab an icicle into a sleeping woman." He pulled out his six-shooter and checked the cylinders. All but the dead man were loaded and ready. "Don't suppose they caught him."

"No. Dr. Edwards says they searched, but the murderer simply disappeared."

Billy Batterson, Brother Bunce, and Sheriff Reynolds followed Mrs. Griswold into the room.

"What'd I miss?" asked Mrs. Griswold, settling down into a chair.

Sheriff Reynolds touched his hat by way of greeting. "Mrs. D, I heard you got a letter concerning the Egg Point killer."

"Egg Point?" Billy Batterson's refined accent was again at odds with his scruffy appearance. "This have to do with Widow Ferris' murder?"

"One of Widow Ferris' blackmail letters included information about a killer from Egg Point," explained Sheriff Reynolds. He extended his hand. "May I read it?"

Millie considered refusing his request, but manners kept her civil. She glanced at Billy Batterson. They had never managed to question him, but for now Millie was more curious about Brother Bunce and his Southern past. "Sir, many call you the Arkansas Traveler. Were you a traveling pulpiteer before you came West? Did you ever go to Mississippi?"

"Millie, you're as subtle as a kick in the head," Dom grumbled. He pushed his empty pie plate aside and helped himself to Millie's.

The minister eyed Millie distastefully. Since she'd accused him of not being ordained, the man of God tended to avoid her. "Of course, I traveled throughout the South. I shared the gospel with all my Southern brethren in Arkansas, Mississippi, Louisiana, and Alabama. I even attended the Augusta, Georgia Southern Baptist Convention in '45. I—"

"The Southern Baptist Convention in '45?" Mrs. Beebee interrupted. "Wasn't that where Southern Baptists separated from Northern Baptists because of slavery?"

"Not because of slavery, ma'am," Brother Bunce said sharply. "For differences of opinion in foreign missions."

Mrs. Beebee arched an eyebrow at the minister. "I heard the Southern Baptists defended slavery with scriptures."

"Baptists, both Northern and Southern, use scripture to define their beliefs. As Reverend Ross clearly explained in his 1857 book, *Slavery Ordained of God*, the Holy Scriptures, both by precept and example, establishes—"

"This is a Union territory, Brother Bunce," Millie interrupted. "Slavery is not—".

"The Bible is the word of God, Mrs. D." Brother Bunce's voice thundered. "In the Old Testament, God instructed the Israelites to purchase bondmen and bondmaids and these persons were an inheritance for them and their children. In the New Testament—" His sermon died and his eyes widened as Samuel stepped into the room carrying three servings of pies.

The boy approached their table and looked up at Mrs. Beebee. "Where I put these, Misah Beebee?"

"Thank you, Samuel." Mrs. Beebee rose and took the pies from the child. "Gentlemen, why don't you sit at this table." She led them to a corner table and set the pies out. Sheriff Reynolds—Millie's letter in hand—followed her, trailed by Billy Batterson. Brother Bunce, his face white as a sheet, spun around and left, his footfalls rattling the floorboards.

Sheriff Reynolds watched him go and shook his head. "If not for the war in the States, I think he'd head back to Arkansas." He turned to Millie and held up the letter. "Mrs. D, may I keep this?"

"Of course," Millie said politely, but she couldn't help adding, "but it would help my investigation if I could read your letter."

Sheriff Reynolds stuffed a piece of pie into his mouth, talking as he chewed. "I can assure you I had nothing to do with Widow Ferris' death." He glanced at Dom and added, "You should encourage your wife to focus on fashion, cooking, and other feminine wiles. Murder and investigations, like voting, should be left to men."

"Look here," said Billy Batterson excitedly, holding up Millie's letter. "The servant, the one the killer forced from the room, said the murderer had a distinctive red birthmark on his forearm. Said the birthmark looked like the horns of a bull."

"Wonder if Turck has a birthmark like that?" Dom leaned back and sipped his coffee.

"I doubt we'll ever know." Sheriff Reynolds took the letter and tucked it into his weskit pocket. "Turck's gone. He won't come back."

Turck was gone, but Millie knew one person who might know. At least she assumed men removed coats and shirts when they visited Tit Bit, although that wasn't, strictly speaking, necessary. She'd ask—about the birthmark, not the clothing—later. No need to encourage Dom to visit the girl.

Later as they headed home, Dom scowled at Millie. "Widow Ferris' death was all but forgotten. If her murderer really is this Egg Point killer, he'll hear about your letter." He shook his head. "You've stirred up trouble, Red. You mark my words."

TWENTY-TWO

May 2, 1864

Arrested

Aweek after receiving the Egg Point letter, Millie was cleaning her cookstove—covered from head to foot in soot when a loud pounding on her door made her start. She stepped back and kicked over her ash pail as Jake burst into the cabin.

"Misah D!" Jake's eyes were wide and his hands were bound together with rope. "Misah D, you gotta help. Marshal Hunt here. He bring a de-tec-tive from Denver City. They come ta arrest me. Say I kill Widder Ferris."

"They came to arrest you?"

"They tried," Mrs. Beebee gasped sweeping into the cabin, her fashionable skirt dotted with mud. "I needed Samuel early today and got there just as Marshal Hunt and Detective Cook arrived. They said they got a letter. Someone saw Jake leave Widow Ferris' cabin the night she was murdered."

"That ain't true," wailed Jake. "I ain't killed nobody!"

"We know that." Mrs. Beebee brushed dirt off her skirt, not looking at Millie. "That's why Dom got involved."

"Dom?" Millie's stomach clenched into a knot. Dom was in town doing an assay for Mr. Poor. "What'd he do?"

"He told them Jake was innocent." Mrs. Beebee nodded

her head in agreement. "When they insisted on arresting Jake, Dom wouldn't let them." Mrs. Beebee shook her head. "Your husband has an impressive temper."

"Oh Lor'!" Millie hurried over and grabbed her coat, spreading the soot throughout the room. "I need to find them. Did Dom hurt anyone?"

"He knocked Marshal Hunt to the ground and started pounding on him." Mrs. Beebee picked up one of Millie's knives and cut the ropes from Jake's wrists as she spoke. "Detective Cook pulled out his six-shooter and made Dom stop."

Millie froze as fear washed over her. "Did…did he shoot Dom?"

"No. Detective Cook covered Dom while Marshal Hunt tied him up. The coach came by and they flagged it down. Said they were taking him to Denver City."

"Denver City?" Millie pulled on her braid, unsure what to do. "Why take him to Denver City?"

"Marshal Hunt arrested Dom, saying he attacked a lawman. He also indicated Dom had a motive to kill Widow Ferris and a temper to match." Mrs. Beebee shook her head. "Tomorrow Elder Griswold can escort you to Denver City and get this straightened out." She turned to Jake. "You best make yourself scarce. Like Dom said, as contraband, you wouldn't even get a trial. I'll move Samuel into the Beebee House for now."

"Yes 'um." Jake headed toward the door. "I get Miss Mary."

"Tomorrow's too late!" Millie cried. "Dom's lying on the floor of some filthy stagecoach or, or…" She couldn't voice the alternative.

"Can't do nothing until tomorrow's stagecoach, Mrs. D." Mrs. Beebee took Millie's broom and began sweeping up the ash. "Dom should be fine unless he causes more trouble."

"Dom always causes trouble!" A new thought made Millie freeze. "They won't lynch him, will they?"

"Probably not. Attacking Marshal Hunt was bad. Course Widow Ferris' murder is worse." Mrs. Beebee shook her head. "With so few women in the territory, her murder is unusual."

"But Dom didn't kill Widow Ferris!" Millie cried.

"We know that, but Marshal Hunt don't." Mrs. Beebee swept soot onto a newspaper and used it to dump the ash back into the pail. "But if Denver City folks believe he killed her, it could get bad."

"Bad?" Millie repeated dumbly.

"You've got to understand, Mrs. D, during Denver City's first few years, gold seekers were joined by thieves, con men, hustlers, and crooks. By Christmas of '59, the city had hordes of thieves roaming the town, stealing from clothes lines, refusing to pay for their drinks, and causing trouble just because they could.

"The troublemakers called themselves Bummers, and the townsfolk put up with their antics until a rancher from the Picketwire River brought a wagon full of wild turkeys to town. Would you believe them greedy Bummers stole the whole wagonload? That was the last straw. The honest folk in Denver City resorted to frontier justice to save the town."

Momentarily distracted, Millie asked, "Stealing turkeys started lynch law?"

"It did. Editor Byers of *The Rocky Mountain News* called it 'The Turkey War of 1860.'" She chuckled. "Respectable citizens, including my husband, organized themselves into a militia and issued an ultimatum. The Bummers had to leave Denver City or be lynched." She opened the door and brushed soot outside. "The turkey thieves were led by Tom Clemo, Chuck-a-Luck Harvey, William Todd, and Buckskin Bill Karl. We thought there'd be a gunfight or worse— they might burn down the town. We—"

"The Bummers were led by a guy named Chuck-a-Luck? Burn Denver City over stolen turkeys?" The Colorado Territory was crazy. Dom had been arrested and might be lynched.

"I kill if someone steal my turkey!" Mary hurried inside and wrapped an arm around Millie.

Jake quickly followed Mary inside. "Me too," he added. "Ain't never eat turkey. Hear them good."

Buttercup shook herself, producing a cloud of soot. Ignoring the filth, Millie buried her head in Mary's ample bosom. Denver City vigilantes might lynch Dom before she got there.

"Were there a real turkey war?" Jake asked.

"No." Mrs. Beebee used the broom to brush off Buttercup and then Millie. "Shots were fired, and one Bummer made the mistake of threatening Marshall Noisy Tom Pollock. He went after the ruffians, and when a Bummer waved his bowie knife in the marshal's face, old Noisy Tom just walked over and smacked the scoundrel on the head with his Hawkins rifle. That rascal dropped like a sack of potatoes, his skull split open. The rest of the Bummers turned tail and skedaddled. That's when the honest citizens of Denver City learned the importance of frontier justice."

"But that was back in '59," Millie moaned. "It's 1864. Surely Denver City has trials, lawyers, and real justice now."

"It does. It's just when folks get riled…" Mrs. Beebee shrugged. "A woman killer will inflame the good citizens."

TWENTY-THREE

May 3, 1864

Editor Byers

The next morning—after a sleepless night filled with visions of Dom swinging from a hangman's noose—Millie hugged Mary and Buttercup goodbye and hurried to town. She stumbled down the trail, her exhausted mind a jumble of worries.

She had to discover Widow Ferris' killer. It was the only way to save Dom.

The killer must have heard about the letter from Egg Point, felt threatened, and sent Marshal Hunt the letter about Jake. If Dom hadn't interfered, Jake would be dead, and the murder solved. It was a nasty plan, as ugly as killing a sleeping woman, but it meant the killer was still in Idaho Springs.

Mr. Turck hadn't been seen in months.

Leaving her carpet bag outside the Beebee House, Millie hurried across town and followed the well-worn path toward Tit Bit's crib. She rounded the corner just as Mr. Poor stepped outside, buckling up a strap on his black and white coveralls. He spotted Millie and shook his head. "Iffen you'd married me, Mrs. D, you'd have a husband at home, and I'd be saving my gold dust for the saloon and other important stuff." He tilted his head sideways. "After they lynch Mr. D, how 'bout we tie the knot?"

"They will not lynch Dom!" Millie said. *Unless they already had.* Fear knotted in her belly and caused her heart to race, but it also solidified her determination.

Mr. Poor shrugged. "Just letting you know you got options." He passed her on the trail and headed toward town.

Tit Bit stepped outside wearing a low-cut night jacket that barely covered an indecent red silk chemise. On her head was a proper lace nightcap with frills around the face—just like the one Millie wore. "Mrs. D, I be sorry to hear about Mr. D. Can I be helping you?" Her Irish lilt made the words almost song-like.

"Miss Nessa. I, ah, I was hoping you could identify a man."

"A man?" Tit Bit's expressive eyebrows rose.

"Dom didn't kill Widow Ferris. He—"

"Begorrah! Course Dom ain't killed her, but I wouldn't be blaming him if he did." Miss Nessa fisted her hands and planted them on her hips, making her chemise hem rise to an even more indecorous height. "But I ain't got no idea who killed the woman."

Millie nodded and hesitated. "Yes, well. The real killer. I think he has a birthmark on his forearm. It looks like matching bull horns."

"A birthmark?" Her fists dropped from her hips, and she absently picked at the sleeve of her night jacket. "Matching bull horns. Aye, I remember such a mark. Someone. But I ain't certain who." She looked at Millie and shrugged. "Me lads usually be a wee bit excited. Ain't often time to remove anything else, once them trousers hit me floor."

Millie blushed all the way to her toes. "I'm leaving today. To Denver City. If you remember anything, can you write…" Millie belatedly realized the fancy girl was probably illiterate. "Have Miss Mary write and send word to me. It's very important."

"Aye." The girl shook her head. "I know I've set me piercers on such a mark, but I ain't certain who."

"Thank you."

"Mrs. D, what be your plan if the Denver City folk insist Dom be guilty?"

Millie shuddered. "I don't have a plan. Not unless I can discover the real killer."

"That's the law's job," said a familiar voice. Millie spun around to find Sheriff Reynolds striding up the path. "Sheriff? Mrs. Beebee said you were in Empire." And conveniently not around when they arrested Dom.

"I was but that remittance man, Billy Batterson, came up and told me about Dom. I'm heading to Denver City today to see what can be done." He rested a big hand on Millie's shoulder, holding her like a rat in a trap. "You should stay here, Mrs. D. Let me handle things."

"No." She jerked free of his grip and backed away. "How did you know I was here?"

"I didn't." He strode past her and climbed up beside Tit Bit. "How are you, Ness?"

Tit Bit snuggled against him, her movements both comfortable and suggestive. "'Tis good to see you, Gene."

"Hold the coach for me, will you? I'll only be a few minutes." Sheriff Reynolds took Nessa's hand and led her inside.

Ness? Gene? A few minutes. Millie blushed but her mind churned as she retraced her steps. Why had Billy Batterson hiked all the way to Empire to get the sheriff? Dom said Batterson seldom came to Idaho Springs, so how had he known about the trouble? What about Sheriff Reynolds? Was he heading to Denver City to help Dom or to make sure Dom was lynched?

She shivered and hurried through town, halting as she

spotted a crowd clustered around her carpet bag. The Griswolds, Beebees, Brother Bunce, Old Shakespeare, and even Mr. Batterson. They all appeared to be waiting for her.

"There you are, dear," said grandmotherly Mrs. Griswold, her bonnet slightly awry. "I saw your bag and was concerned."

"Mrs. Griswold." Millie raised her voice as a stagecoach rumbled toward them. "Can Mr. Griswold escort me?"

"Of course, dear. Now you listen to him. Denver City is a big, dangerous town." The older woman patted Millie's arm while her husband hefted Millie's carpet bag into the coach's boot. He returned for her just as Brother Bunce climbed into the stagecoach, followed by Billy Batterson and Old Shakespeare.

All three men on her suspect list were heading to Denver City. Millie wanted to ask why, but her questions got stuck in her throat as Elder Griswold offered her his arm and led her to the door of the stagecoach. Millie took one look at the dark, crowded interior and backed away. She hated closed in spaces and the last time she had ridden inside a stagecoach the motion had made her sick.

"I'll ride in the shotgun seat." She scrambled up onto the open-air seat beside the driver.

"Are you sure, dear?" Mrs. Griswold gave her a concerned look. "A storm's brewing and it's cold this morning. You'll freeze once the coach starts moving."

"I'll be fine," Millie said, wrapping her scarf tightly around her neck.

"You'll be frozen by the time we reach Central City," said Sheriff Reynolds, approaching with a definite bounce in his stride. He leaned into the coach and pulled out a buffalo robe. "Put this around you."

Millie wrapped the buffalo robe around her, feeling the stagecoach shift as the sheriff and Elder Griswold climbed inside. A rough looking driver swung up beside her, wearing heavy skins, a beaver fur hat, thick gloves, and warm moccasins. He nodded to Millie, picked up his whip, and snapped it over the horses' flanks.

Frigid air bit into Millie's skin as they galloped through town. She pulled the buffalo robe tighter, but the cold whipped over her face and fingers. By the time they reached Central City, her fingers were stiff and numb, her teeth chattered, and she felt as cold as the dead—but not cold enough to join the men in the crowded confines of the coach.

Hours later, the horses labored to drag the coach up Big Hill and wearily pulled into the Guy House. Millie was so cold she wouldn't have been able to climb from the coach if Sheriff Reynolds hadn't lifted her down and carried her inside.

"Sit by the fire, Mrs. D, and I'll order you some tea." Elder Griswold looked concerned as he served Millie a bowl of Mr. Guy's steaming turnip soup.

"B-Brother B-Bunce, why are you off to D-Denver City?" Millie asked, her teeth chattering.

"I've a meeting with Col. Chivington," he said, puffing up a bit.

"Col. Chivington?" Elder Griswold nodded his approval. "The Fighting Parson is one of Denver's most distinguished citizens."

"Can anyone recommend a place to stay?" asked Mr. Batterson, cutting into his mountain mutton, a local novelty from the nearby herds of big horn sheep. "Outside of Miss Ada's place, I don't know Denver City all that well."

"Staying at her fine establishment a couple nights might kill you," said Sheriff Reynolds, laughing.

"But what a way to go," added Elder Griswold.

"I always stay at the Tremont House on Front Street," explained Old Shakespeare. Turning to Millie he added, "It's near Cherry Creek. Close to the shops."

"Mrs. D and I won't need a hotel," said Elder Griswold.

"We'll be staying with William Byers, the editor of the *Rocky Mountain News*."

"Editor Byers?" Slowly warming up, Millie was surprised by Elder Griswold's choice of lodging. The *Rocky Mountain News* was Denver City's main newspaper, although Millie sometimes questioned the biased opinions expressed in its articles. "How do you know Editor Byers, Elder Griswold?"

"Byers has been in Denver City since '59." The older man helped himself to more soup and refilled Millie's bowl. "I helped him out of a tussle once. Since then, Mrs. Griswold and I always stay with his family."

"What kind of a tussle?" Sheriff Reynolds stretched out his long legs and leaned back.

"Shouldn't we be on our way?" Millie asked, knowing Elder Griswold tended to draw out his stories.

"The driver isn't ready," said Old Shakespeare. "Hush up and let Elder Griswold talk."

Elder Griswold cleared his throat, and Millie scooted closer to the fire, giving in to the inevitable.

"Back in '60, while Mrs. Byers was trying to gentrify Denver City, her husband's newspaper was riling it right up. Editor Byers has a way with words, but all too often he don't know when to hold his tongue, or his pen as it were. One day he wrote a scathing article about one of Denver's fancy gamblers, a man named Charley Harrison."

"Fancy gambler?" asked Mr. Batterson, lifting a brow.

"A man who makes his living at the tables," explained Sheriff Reynolds.

"That's right." Elder Griswold sipped his beer. "Charley Harrison was one of Denver City's best. He wore a fancy frock coat, silk shirt, and of course twin pearl-handled Colts on his hips. Folks called him a fine gentleman."

"Gentlemen," Millie huffed, "do not make their living gambling."

"Perhaps not, but a skilled gambler can do well. Charley earned enough to buy into the Criterion Saloon, best gaming house in Denver City. He also acted like a gentleman, at least toward the ladies. But one night, Charley shot and killed the Professor, a well-liked giant with a preference for white starched shirts and black tailored broadcloth. Charley, a Southerner, claimed self-defense, but everyone knew it was murder. The Professor was a colored man who'd bought his freedom from his Missouri master."

"Did Editor Byers write against slavery, gambling, or murder?" Millie couldn't decide which vice was worse.

"The killing of course." Elder Griswold lifted his cup and the proprietor quickly refilled it. "Byers wrote a scathing editorial about the lack of legal action against Harrison."

"The gambler wasn't lynched for the killing?" asked Sheriff Reynolds.

Millie winced. How often did Denver City lynch folks? And how fast? "Shouldn't we be on our—"

"Charley wasn't punished at all for killing the Professor," interrupted Elder Griswold. "That's why Byers wrote the article."

"Why? Colorado's a Union territory. This Professor was free, even if colored." Billy Batterson sounded indignant.

"True, but Charley Harrison had friends on both sides of the law." Elder Griswold shrugged. "Even today, Denver City officials aren't all honest gents."

Was Marshal Hunt honest? What about this Detective Cook? Millie stood up, willing the driver to come as Elder Griswold continued his story.

"The Professor's killing happened back in '60, when tensions between the North and South were just starting to run high. Editor Byers was the only one who dared attack Charley. He criticized not only Charley, but all of Denver City's rowdies, ruffians, and bullies." Elder Griswold yawned. "The Bummers took insult and came after the editor."

"As the Bard once said." Old Shakespeare solemnly nodded his head. "'Hell is empty, and all the devils are here.' Or in Denver City."

"Right." Mr. Griswold gave Old Shakespeare an annoyed look and scooted his chair away from the man. "Anyway, the *News* building sits on stilts over Cherry Creek. Byers attempted to placate both Denver City and Auraria when he built his office."

"Never mind the office." Sheriff Reynolds waved his hand. "What did the Bummers do to Byers?"

Elder Griswold took another long sip of his beer. "Editor Byers wrote many unpopular editorials and the man ain't no fool, but..." He shrugged. "I guess he got complacent. Several Bummers jumped him, right there in his office. They seized his arms and shoved a cocked revolver into his ear." Mr. Griswold's face took on a faraway expression. "I was there but couldn't do nothing but admire the man's audacity. Byers is surrounded by angry ruffians and has a revolver pressed to his head, and guess what the man says?"

Utter silence answered him. The fire crackled and outside a cold wind made the trees groan.

"Just as cool as a cucumber, Editor Byers asks, 'What can I do for you gentlemen?'"

The door burst open and a blast of air made Millie shiver. "Let's go," said the driver. "New horses are hitched up and weather's looking bad."

Millie hurried toward the door, but Sheriff Reynolds' demanding voice made her stop. "Wait one minute. I want to hear what happened." He looked at Elder Griswold. "Did they shoot him?"

Elder Griswold stood and stretched. "Nope, they kidnapped him. Took him to the Criterion Saloon, to Charley Harrison, but despite the article, Charley didn't appear to hold a grudge. He snuck Byers out the back door and the editor hightailed it back to his office. The ruffians came after him again." Elder Griswold offered his arm to Millie. "We had quite the shoot-out before the hoodlums finally left town."

"A shoot-out?" Millie stared at the older gentleman. "You were in a shoot-out?"

"Of course."

Millie headed outside. If the upright Elder Griswold had taken part in a shoot-out, Denver City was truly lawless.

Dom didn't stand a chance.

TWENTY-FOUR

May 3, 1864
Golden City,
Territorial Capital of Colorado

R ain began to fall as the coach topped a rise and the wide, open Eastern Plains came into view. The plains were as flat as a lumpy hotcake and spread out as far as Millie could see, but black clouds churning over the immense landscape made it look dangerous, menacing. The coach descended the perilous trail as lightning lit up the sky and thunder shook the ground. By the time they reached Golden City, the horses were jostling and bumping into each other, their eyes wide, their nostrils flared.

Millie—soaked to the skin and shivering badly—thankfully climbed off the stagecoach and stumbled into a room lit by a blazing fire. Despite her worries and fears, Millie felt bone-weary and dreaded the last leg of their journey. She crowded as close to the fire as she dared, rubbing her frozen hands and watching steam rise off her skirt.

"Have to spend the night here," said the coach driver, eying the group warily. "Lightning's making the horses skittish. Mud's deep enough to swallow a cow."

"But," Millie said, her lips numb. "I have to get to Denver City. Today!"

"Find yourself a horse," said the driver, slamming the door.

Elder Griswold touched Millie's arm. "I'm sorry, Mrs. D, but we'll have to stay here. Nothing for it."

"I hope they haven't hung Dom yet," said Old Shakespeare, placing a hand over his heart. "But as the Bard said, 'Thou know'st 'tis common; all that lives must die.'"

Millie glared at him. "At least the Bard's dead and not saying anything new."

Old Shakespeare looked horrified, but Sheriff Reynolds laughed aloud. "Don't worry none, Mrs. D. They don't lynch folk in weather like this."

"Here's the *Rocky Mountain News* from today." Billy Batterson held up a ragged newspaper. "Found it in the privy. Nothing about a lynching in *Last Night's Report*."

"What about the Indian war?" Elder Griswold asked. "Last I read, Governor Evans was enlisting Captain Butterfield to raise a company of mounted men. At last they'll exterminate the red devils."

Exterminate the Indians and lynch Dom. Oh Lor'! thought Millie.

Sheriff Reynolds pulled open the door and glanced outside. "Looks like the rain is letting up a bit. A friend cooks for the Overland House." He glanced at Millie. "Bet they'll even have a bath for you."

Fear gnawed through Millie, but she couldn't help asking, "A hot bath?"

The lawman led the way into town on a rickety wooden sidewalk. Millie cautiously stepped over holes left by missing planks, as she curiously glanced around. She had traveled through Golden City when she'd first arrived in the Colorado Territory. At the time she'd thought the territorial capital a rough town lined with saloons. Living in Idaho Springs had changed her perspective.

Saloons still dominated the landscape, but now Millie noticed dry good stores, a bakery smelling of yeast and bread, boarding houses that almost looked respectable, and even a few neatly made homes with real glass windows. The town felt downright civilized.

The Overland House was a two-story building with a mercantile sign on one side, an eatery on the other. Inside, the dining tables were rough, but the interior was reasonably clean, almost respectable looking except for a corner packed with unsavory men playing backgammon and reading yellow-kivered literature.

Millie looked around the dim interior and jumped when Sheriff Reynolds hollered, "Presley, you scoundrel, come on out!" Her eyes widened as a large man wearing a filthy apron burst through the door, his beefy fist wrapped around a bloody knife. The sheriff grinned. "Poisoned anyone today, Presley?"

"Gene, you no-count thieving rascal. Last time I saw you, you were hurrying into the hills, shepherding away a miner I'd grubstaked." Millie sucked down a breath as the huge man pointed his knife at the sheriff. "Never saw that rascal again. Did you steal my provisions?"

"Course. Man was as green as grass." Sheriff Reynolds casually pushed the knife aside and stepped forward, smacking the cook's shoulder. "That greenhorn wouldn't have spotted color if it rained down on him. I left him in Central City working at a dry goods store."

Presley wiped the knife on his apron, leaving a streak of blood on the filthy material. "You still pretending to be a sheriff? Bet that works well with your feet on both sides of the law."

Both sides of the law? Millie inched closer, hoping to learn more about the sheriff's less than honest endeavors. Her movements caught the attention of the giant cook.

"What in tarnation did you bring in?" The cook eyed

Millie dubiously. "She looks like a waterlogged whore, though I like the flaming red hair."

Millie jerked her six-shooter from her coat pocket and aimed at the cook's greasy forehead. "Your manners, sir, need improvement."

"Improve my manners?" The cook tilted his head back and roared with laughter, not looking the least concerned. "From the looks of you, darlin', your powder's too wet to fire."

"I wouldn't recommend riling Presley, Mrs. D." Sheriff Reynolds pushed her gun hand down. "Presley's the cook here. If you get on his wrong side, you'll spend the night hurling in the privy." He turned back to his friend. "Now, who do we need to see about rooms?"

"Talk to Mr. Anderson, the Overland House proprietor. And tonight, I'll make you all something special. How do you feel about—" He paused and cocked his head as the blare of a trumpet sounded.

The tavern's male patronage was suddenly galvanized into action, jumping from their seats and knocking chairs over in their haste. Like a buffalo stampede, men charged toward the door, led by Presley, Sheriff Reynolds, and Old Shakespeare.

Presley and the sheriff reached the door together, getting stuck as they tried to force their way through. Men, including Elder Griswold, shoved from behind and the dam broke. Sheriff Reynolds tumbled outside, and through the chaos Millie heard Elder Griswold yell, "I'll be back in a bit. Get yourself some food, a bath, or whatever."

An instant later, Millie stood alone in an empty tavern, listening to the thud of footfalls outside. "What in heaven's name?" She went outside and watched men tumble from every establishment lining the street. They splashed, slipped, and slid down the muddy road like their life depended on it.

"Is it a fire?" Millie asked as a rotund serving woman stepped outside.

"Humph!" the woman said, her eyes narrowing. "They act like it's a fire, but it ain't. It's old man Hill blowing his blasted trumpet." Her strong New York accent emphasized each word.

"Why?" The last of the men disappeared into a building.

"Means business is slow in Jack Hill's place." The woman shook her head. "He blows that blasted trumpet like a military call to arms. Any man who reaches his saloon within three minutes gets a whiskey on the house."

"A free drink?" Elder Griswold had abandoned her for a free whiskey!

"I best go check the kitchen and make sure nothing's going to burn or bubble over." The woman sighed. "One moment and I'll show you to your room."

*****

That night, after a hot bath and a surprisingly good meal, Millie crawled into a real bed covered by a warm quilt. Despite the comfortable bed and her own exhaustion, she couldn't sleep. Worries about Dom made her thrash about as drunken laughter filtered through her window.

Gradually, exhaustion took over, but she jerked awake when gunshots disrupted the night. Bolting from her bed, Millie pushed her feet into slippers and donned her night jacket. She grabbed her six-shooter, ignoring propriety, and rushed from her room, following Sheriff Reynolds out onto the wooden walkway. Near the building that housed Jack Hill's saloon, a group of men shouted for a doctor.

"Stay here, Mrs. D." Sheriff Reynolds stepped into the street, his stockinged feet sinking up to his ankles.

"Why'd you shoot him, Detective Cook?" shouted a voice. "Miles weren't no crook."

Detective Cook? Millie edged down the wooden walkway, straining to see what had happened. The cold night air bit her exposed skin as men lifted a limp body and carried it into another building.

Sheriff Reynolds returned, climbing onto the walkway and looking down at his ruined stockings. "Knew I should have brought an extra pair."

"What happened?" Millie asked.

"That Denver detective, Cook, was hunting a horse thief. Shot Jack Hill's brother by mistake." Sheriff Reynolds peeled off his filthy socks. "Townsfolk are in an uproar. From what I saw, Miles Hill won't make it." Barefoot, he carefully tiptoed toward the Overland House, cursing each splinter. "Folks are angry enough to lynch the detective. Best if we go back to our rooms, unless you plan to stand outside in your nightclothes all night."

Even embarrassment couldn't dampen the profound sense of dread mixed with hope that filled Millie. If Detective Cook was here killing innocent people, he wasn't lynching Dom.

Back in her room, Millie laid her revolver on the table, crawled back onto the bed, and pulled her legs up against her chest. Dom had to be alive. Oh Lor' she missed him! Resting her head on her knees, she listened as the street outside grew quiet. Cold air seeped in through the window, so she crawled under her bedding. Just as she got comfortable, she heard whispering in the hallway. The scuffing of boots on wood made her grab her six-shooter and silently rise from her bed.

"Franklin, we want you," yelled a man, so close it sounded like he was in Millie's bedroom. She jumped and the back of her knees struck the tin washtub. With neither grace nor dignity, she tumbled into the tub, dropping her gun on the way down.

"The hell you do!" whistled a man with a lisp. Millie thrashed about, but her legs were tangled over the rim while her derrière was jammed into the narrow metal basin.

"Oh, it's irons you have, is it?" The man's lisp worsened as he yelled. "If that's what you're up to, I have some myself!"

Millie managed to drag herself from the tub and fell to her knees on the floor as the man shouted, "I'll fight your whole gang, if you will give me a fair show. I won't be arrested. I won't go. I'll die first—but I'll die hard. Ed Franklin does not sell out on a song."

Something slammed into the wall, causing it to bow while grunts from a skirmish in the room next door filled the silence. Millie dove back into the tub when a gunshot reverberated in the small space. The thin metal wouldn't stop a lead ball, but it might slow one.

The smell of burnt powder permeated the room and a man panted, "Don't worry Detective Cook. Franklin's dead and harmless. He sowed the wild oats of a reckless and useless life and now he's reaped the full harvest."

Detective Cook, again? Millie clambered from the tub and crept into the hall, determined to ask about Dom. She stumbled over a form crouched just outside her door and fell against the opposite wall.

"Who's out there?" A man peeked out, a candle in one hand, a cocked revolver in the other.

"Sheriff Reynolds from Idaho Springs," said the form, rising and using his body to shield Millie.

"Go back to bed, sir. I'm Detective Cook. The outlaw, Ed Franklin, resisted arrest and I was forced to kill him."

"Detective Cook, sir, you sure are in a killing mood," Sheriff Reynolds said sourly. "Is Miles Hill also dead?" Millie was surprised at the sheriff's bravado and obvious anger.

"Miles Hill was aiding a horse thief. If he dies, it was an accident."

"What about my husband? Mr. Drouillard?" Millie shook as she squeezed around the sheriff. "You didn't kill him too, did you?"

TWENTY-FIVE

May 4, 1864

Lynch Law

They caught the morning stagecoach and passed an angry mob near Jack Hill's saloon. Miles Hill had not survived. The slain man had been well liked and many were demanding an inquiry—or a lynching—for his unjustified killing. The crowd's angry demands went unanswered. Detective Cook had slunk away under the cover of night, but before he'd left, he'd assured Millie that Dom was in the Denver City jail, alive.

Fresh air chilled Millie's face as they followed the muddy trail toward Denver City, skirting around a flat-topped mountain. Millie chafed at their slow progress. It felt like she hadn't seen Dom in years, and she could barely contain her impatience. Trying to make the time pass more quickly as Denver City came into view, she asked the driver about the stream that split the town in half.

"That's Cherry Creek." The coach driver pointed with his whip. "We'll be crossing the other, the Platte, 'fore long."

"Those buildings seem much too close to the creek." Millie shaded her eyes from the morning sun. "And look, there are a couple built right over the creek."

"The big one's Byers' *Rocky Mountain News* office. A good flood will wipe him out, but he ain't had no problems yet."

An hour later, the horses splashed across the Platte, and Millie saw a cluster of Indian teepees, reminding her of Hosa and his family. Were her friends safe or embroiled in this escalating Indian war? The road became even muddier as they passed saloons, boarding houses, and shops. The number of horses, wagons, and oxcarts increased until the coach finally stopped in front of a building with the sign, "The Overland Stage Line—Ben Holladay Proprietor," over the doorway.

The men tumbled from the coach and without a backward glance, everyone except Elder Griswold scurried away.

"The sheriff's gone on ahead to let the jail know a lady's coming," Elder Griswold said, offering Millie his arm. "A boy will deliver our luggage to the Byers' home."

Millie was impatient to see Dom, but each shop they passed revealed goods she hadn't seen since leaving New Orleans. A milliner shop displayed a fetching hat and a chandlery displayed real beeswax candles and elegant scented soaps. The next store had a whole shelf of books—even a couple cookbooks!

"This isn't looking good," muttered Elder Griswold, gripping Millie's arm tighter.

"What?" Millie tore her eyes from a well-stocked dry goods shop and looked around, feeling the hairs on the back of her neck rise. All around them, groups of men were dodging wagons and hurrying up the street, looking flushed and excited. They clustered together, spoke in harsh whispers, and glanced furtively up the road. They reminded Millie of the angry mob they'd left in Golden. "What's going on?"

"Gonna be a hanging," said a voice that made Millie cringe.

She whirled around to find a man leaning against a building, half hidden by shadows. "Mr. Turck?" The former Idaho Springs scoundrel wore a military uniform and almost looked respectable, except for his ugly scowl and ratty beard braids.

"Mrs. Drouillard." He drew out the name as he stepped into the light, his fists wrapped around his beard braids, squeezing them in a rhythmic motion. "Come to see the lynching?"

"Lynching?" Millie repeated, her heart pounding. "W-who?"

"Who do you think?"

"Dom!" Millie spun around, jerked free of Elder Griswold, and raced toward the growing crowd outside the jail. Her boots sank deep into the mud as she threaded through the thickening horde, gagging at the smell of unwashed bodies. Her muddy skirt was heavy by the time she reached the mob outside the jailhouse.

"Hang him!"

"Murderer!"

Millie pushed forward, but the crowd was so thick she couldn't get through.

"Show him how Denver City deals with killers."

"Thief!"

She jumped up and down, straining to see over the sea of heads. Two men dragged a third man from the jailhouse, but Millie couldn't see his face.

"That ain't Mr. D," said Elder Griswold, breathing hard as he grabbed Millie's upper arm. "Just wait one darn moment and we'll find Dom after they're gone."

Millie gulped down a sob as she caught a glimpse of the condemned man. The prisoner was as tall as Dom, but slimly built. They dragged him down the road and the crowd surged forward, carrying Millie and Elder Griswold in their flow. Step-by-step, they were marched, just like the prisoner, away from the jail. Everyone stopped when they reached the Larimer Street Bridge.

"Who is he?" Millie asked breathlessly, clearly able to see the unfortunate man as he climbed onto a wagon.

"That's Musgrove. He's part of a mule-thieving gang."

A man with bloodshot eyes leaned into Millie, spraying whiskey-smelling breath down on her. "His boys planned to break him out, but Detective Cook foiled them. Yesterday, Cook tracked the hoodlums to Golden City and killed one. We're making sure Musgrove don't escape, permanent like, before the rest of his gang tries anything else."

"Marshal Hunt let them take him?" Millie leaned as far away from Whiskey Breath as possible. "What about a trial?"

"Don't need no trial. Not after the *Rocky Mountain News* printed the stories of James Torrence, Alex Delap, and Judge Brooks. Thems were Musgrove's victims. Last week, Musgrove's lieutenant, Franklin, robbed Judge Brooks and threatened to 'Plant the damned old snoozer.' Detective Cook killed Franklin and now we're gonna plant Musgrove."

Millie covered her mouth as a rope was lowered from the bridge and a noose placed around the prisoner's neck. Too clearly could she envision it around Dom's neck. The crowd quieted, and Elder Griswold wrapped an arm protectively around Millie. "You might want to look away, Mrs. D."

Millie looked down at her mud caked skirt, but she immediately glanced up when she heard Marshal Hunt's distinctive drawl. He stood on the bridge above the prisoner and insisted justice wouldn't be served by an unlawful hanging.

Hollers from the crowd drowned out his words, and he was forced out of sight. In the quiet that followed, the condemned man hollered, "If you're bent upon murdering me, you will at least be men enough to permit me to write to my friends and tell them the shameful story of your conduct."

The crowd murmured.

"I've a pencil and paper." Elder Griswold kept Millie by his side and pushed through the crowd until they reached the condemned man. Musgrove wrote a quick note and handed it to Elder Griswold. Dragging Millie away, Elder Griswold thrust the man's letter into Millie's hand. "Hold on to this. I want my gun hand free."

Millie looked down, unable to help reading the man's final words.

Denver C.J.

May 4

  My Dear Wife — Before this reaches you I will be no more Mary I am as you know innocent of the charges made against me I do not know what they are agoing to hang me for unless it is because I am acquainted with Ed Franklin — godd will protect you I hope Good by forever as ever yours sell what I have and keep it.

  L. H. Musgrove

Millie felt a tear slide down her cheek. Musgrove was probably guilty of many crimes, but somewhere a woman named Mary was about to lose her husband. Had she loved him the way Millie loved Dom? Millie didn't want to watch, but she couldn't help looking up when the crowd began to roar.

Musgrove stood passively as a slouch hat was pulled low over his eyes. The wagon lumbered forward, and the condemned man sprang into the air, landing on the wagon bed. He swore loudly, and his second leap left him hanging.

Millie buried her face against Elder Griswold's shoulder, but not before the gruesome image of Musgrove dangling from a rope was forever burned in her memory.

"We've got to free Dom," she whispered.

TWENTY-SIX

May 4, 1864

The Denver City Jail

Millie kept her eyes averted as Elder Griswold forced their way through the crowd and back toward the jail, but she couldn't stop hearing the yelling around her. The lynching had galvanized the mob, and their angry voices cried out for more. More hangings. Millie trembled. Were there other prisoners, besides Dom, in the jail?

"Elder Griswold!" A well-dressed man with a strong face and receding hairline dashed toward them, bumping off the crowd like a billiard ball. "Elder Griswold," he repeated breathlessly, "what a pleasure to see you." He glanced at Millie, his eyes taking her in as he added smoothly, "And in such pleasant company."

"Editor Byers. I'm surprised to see you. Shouldn't you be at the office preparing copy on the hanging." Elder Griswold rested a fatherly hand on Millie's arm. "May I introduce Mrs. Drouillard, one of Idaho Springs most respectable matrons."

Millie had never been called a respectable matron and from the editor's reaction, she suspected the title communicated far more than the simple words.

"I see." He shrugged. "A pleasure, Mrs. Drouillard." He

grabbed Mr. Griswold's hand and shook it enthusiastically. "I am in a hurry. The *News* always prints a story first." He turned to Millie and his chest puffed out. "We were the first paper published in the Cherry Creek area. On April 23, 1859, we beat Jack Merrick's *Cherry Creek Pioneer* by twenty minutes."

Elder Griswold lifted bushy eyebrows. "What do you want, Editor?"

"Timing is everything, but unpublished details are important." He extended his hand, palm up. "The *News* will be happy to post Musgrove's letter. It's our civic duty."

"Civic duty," Elder Griswold scoffed. "You'll post it after you print what's inside." He looked down at Millie. "What do you think, Mrs. D?"

Printing the dead man's letter appalled Millie, but she needed help keeping Dom from the hangman's noose. She held up the letter, noticing how Editor Byers eyes followed her movements like a famished man dying for a morsel.

"It would be a kindness, Editor Byers, for the *News* to post this. Musgrove's poor, poor wife will want to know his unhappy fate." She spoke in a strong Southern accent and batted her eyes. "I understand completely. We're here because my husband has been falsely accused of a terrible crime. I'm so worried." Unbidden tears welled in her eyes.

"That is awful," the editor said, snatching the letter. "I'll post this and tonight we'll discuss your husband. I'm sure Denver City will want to know the truth about this dreadful mistake."

"Thank you," Millie said.

The newspaper man strode away but paused. "Elder Griswold, we've moved to a farm on the South Platte, just outside of Denver. There's a room for both of you there. Ask anyone and they'll know where it is." He doffed his hat and dashed away.

They found Sheriff Reynolds and Marshall Hunt inside the jailhouse, standing beside a short, squat man seated at a desk. The sheriff stepped forward. "Mrs. D, this is Jailer—"

"Where's Dom?" Millie demanded.

"Ma'am," the jailkeeper said, standing. "As I have told Sheriff Reynolds, we don't allow women—"

There was an open door to Millie's right, and she charged through it, finding two small cells lining the walls. Dom—looking filthy and with two days growth of a beard—stumbled to his feet.

"Dom!" Millie rushed to him, tears blurring her vision. Bruises covered his face and his shirt was torn. "Oh Lor', Dom!" She grabbed his hands through the bars.

"Millie!" Dom pressed his face between the narrow bars and tried to kiss her. His lips, like the rest of him, were filthy. "I told Sheriff Reynolds not to let you come in here. This is a foul place. After they took Musgrove from my cell, I worried they might…" He lifted an eyebrow, his expression grim. "Did they lynch him?"

Millie nodded. "We'll get you out of here, Dom. I promise. Editor Byers offered to write a story about you." She gagged on the foul air as tears streamed down her face.

"Editor Byers," Dom's face darkened. "Watch out for that man, Millie. It was his reporting that riled the town up against Musgrove. Not that villain didn't have it coming, but he deserved a fair trial."

"Why did—"

"Little lady," Marshal Hunt said in his strong Texas drawl. "This is no place for you. I'll protect Mr. Drouillard, until—"

"The way you protected Mr. Musgrove?" Millie spun around and faced the marshal, narrowing her eyes. "Dom didn't kill Widow Ferris. You had no right arresting him. Free him immediately!"

Marshal Hunt frowned. "Based on the evidence found,

your husband had motive and opportunity to kill Widow Ferris. He also—"

"Marshal Hunt? Lola got brought in again." The short, squat jailer led a disheveled, homely woman into the jail room. "It's vagrancy again. What are we gonna do with her? Hate to put Joe in with the woman killer."

"My husband is not—"

"Don't put me in with him," cried a mousy-looking man with buckteeth. He stood in the opposite cell and pointed at Dom. "I were arrested for disorderly conduct and drunkenness. That ain't nothing to murdering a woman. He shoulda been lynched with Musgrove."

"Dom is not a killer!" Millie insisted although no one was listening to her.

"Marry me an we can share a cell," said the vagrant woman, taking an unsteady step toward the disorderly conduct man.

"I don't think—" began Marshal Hunt.

"I don't got no money for a marriage license," said Disorderly, grinning stupidly. "But if I do, I'd marry you."

"I'll provide money for the license," offered Elder Griswold. "I'm sure Judge Brooks won't charge to perform the ceremony."

"Okay," said the two, giggling.

Marshal Hunt threw up his hands. "Why not? We even got a proper lady for a witness." He unlocked the cell door and the vagrant woman shuffled inside. The disorderly conduct man grinned at his future wife, showing a mouth with only three teeth. "Guess we'll celebrate our honeymoon here. Maybe they'll give us clean hay."

"What's my name gonna be?" asked the woman.

"Montez." The man tentatively wrapped his arm around his future wife. "I'm Joe Montez."

"Lola Montez. Like the spider dancer." She did a little jig and kissed him.

Millie shook her head, stunned. The world had gone crazy. Elder Griswold soon returned with Judge Brooks who nodded amiably before taking his place outside the cell. Without preamble he asked, "You have him?"

Lola nodded, "Yes."

"You have her?"

"Kinder," Joe answered.

Millie didn't even know what kinder meant, but the response satisfied the judge.

"Done." Judge Brooks turned to Elder Griswold. "One dollar. You and the lady will need to sign as witnesses."

TWENTY-SEVEN

May 4, 1864

Toughen Up, Buttercup

Mrs. Byers did not appear overly pleased at the arrival of guests, but the well-bred matron graciously invited Millie and Elder Griswold into her two-story farmhouse. Soon they were chatting amiably as Millie cooked a bouilli soup, garnishing it with thin slices of pickle and toasted bread. Editor Byers arrived and as they ate, Millie told the Byers about Widow Ferris' murder, the blackmail, and Dom's innocence.

"That's quite the tale," said Editor Byers. "I'll put it on the front-page tomorrow."

The story, unfortunately, only brought attention to Dom's plight and seemed to divide Denver City. Judge Brooks set a trial date for a week from Monday. Millie worried that Dom wouldn't live to his trial.

Saturday morning, Millie was so distraught after her visit with Dom, she retrieved her Florence Hartley book and called to the two Byers children to sit at her feet. The little girl and boy sullenly obeyed—this was not Millie's first etiquette lesson. "While your mother is meeting with the Ladies Union Aid Society, we'll read about proper behavior for a young lady and soon-to-be gentleman."

The children groaned, and Millie gave them a severe look. "Mrs. Hartley says, 'To be truly polite, remember you must be polite at *all* times and under *all* circumstances.'"

"Even when someone's not being polite to you?" the little girl wanted to know.

"Of course." Millie felt a twinge of guilt. She hadn't been polite to Marshal Hunt this morning.

"Boys aren't polite," said the little boy. "That's a book for girls or milksop boys."

Millie scowled. "This is a *ladies'* book of etiquette, but it also applies to gentlemen." She raised her voice over the child's impolite snort. "For example, Mrs. Hartley says, 'If nature has not invested you with all the virtues which may be desirable in a...'" She paused and made substitutions, "'desirable in a man, do not make your faults more conspicuous by thrusting them forward upon your cultured wife. And if—'"

Editor Byers burst through the door, followed by his wife. "Mrs. D. There's talk of another lynching."

"*Another lynching?*" Millie's book fell to the floor.

"Even the ladies at my meeting said your husband's as guilty as Musgrove," said Mrs. Byers. "They think he should be hung."

Millie rose unsteadily, fear gripping her like a vice. "The killer is spreading these rumors. Mr. Turck, Mr. Batterson, Old Shakespeare, and Sheriff Reynolds are all still here. Widow Ferris tried to blackmail each of them. One of them is spreading lies about Dom."

"Don't forget Brother Bunce," said a grandmotherly voice. "We just passed him near the Methodist Church. Mrs. Byers, why don't you look nice."

Mrs. Griswold strode into the room, followed by Mrs. Beebee. Mrs. Gilson peeked over one of Mrs. Beebee's shoulders and Mary peeked over the other.

"Mrs. Beebee. Mrs. Gilson, Mrs. Griswold. Miss Mary."

The ladies filed into the small room and Millie spotted a fifth woman. Her jaw dropped. "Tit, ah. Miss Nessa."

Mrs. Griswold and Mrs. Gilson were dressed in calico dresses and matching bonnets, looking rather unstylish compared to Mrs. Beebee's flounces and lace. Mary wore homespun, but all four looked like country paupers beside Tit Bit. The working girl was bedecked in the latest style— a hoop skirt, silk blouse, matching bonnet with intricate lace, and a dainty umbrella held in gloved hands.

Buttercup, wearing a new braided ribbon collar, charged through the women's skirts and enthusiastically butted Millie. "*Buttercup?*"

"'Tis a pleasure to see you again, Mrs. Drouillard." Tit Bit inclined her head like she'd been raised in Irish high society.

"You do keep interesting company, Mrs. D." Editor Byers bowed as he greeted each lady. "Mrs. Griswold, your husband will be pleased to see you. Mrs. Beebee, Mrs. Gilson, so pleasant to see each of you again. I don't believe I've had the pleasure of meeting you." His eyes lighted on Tit Bit, passing over Mary like she didn't exist.

"This is Miss Mary, my friend." Millie hurried over and took Mary's arm. "And this is Miss…" Millie hesitated, not knowing Tit Bit's surname.

"Miss Kavanagh," Tit Bit finished smoothly, curtsying to the Byers. "My apology, ma'am. We're here unannounced and uninvited, but there be nothing for it. We're concerned about Mr. D."

"Mr. D must indeed be a special man to garner so much support. Please, have a seat. I'll make tea." Mrs. Byers glanced at Buttercup. "Children, why don't you take the uh, goat, outside."

Buttercup nosed open Florence Hartley's book and ripped out the front page, devouring it happily as the children pulled her from the room.

"Editor Byers." Millie picked up her book and clutched it to her chest. "Is Dom safe?"

"Might be best if I round up Elder Griswold and Sheriff Reynolds. We'll keep an eye on him today. Maybe we can discover who's been spreading those rumors." The editor bowed to the ladies and turned to Tit Bit. "I hope to have the pleasure of seeing you again, Miss Kavanagh." He bent low and kissed her hand.

"Aye," Tit Bit glanced toward the kitchen and said quietly, "I be staying at the Washington House, if you have a mind to visit."

Millie rubbed her face as Editor Byers nodded and left. She'd come to like Mrs. Byers, but the editor was a mixture of bravado, determination, and snake oil salesman. He was Denver City's biggest promoter, and there was much about him Millie could admire, but she wouldn't want to be married to him. Turning to the matrons, she said, "It's wonderful to see you all, but…Why are you here?"

"To free Mr. D," chorused the women.

"Free Dom?"

"After you left, I visited Miss Nessa," explained Mrs. Gilson. "I needed to discuss a personal problem. After Miss Nessa and I came to an agreement, she mentioned her concerns about Mr. D. I spoke with Mrs. Beebee and Mrs. Griswold, and we decided we best come to Denver City. Miss Nessa invited Mary."

"That Jake were driving me crazy," Mary grumbled. "Why you ask that man to live in you cabin?"

Before Millie could answer, Tit Bit spoke. "We decided you needed assistance,"

Mrs. Gilson's face lit up. "We're planning a jailbreak!"

"A jailbreak?" Millie asked.

"A jailbreak?" echoed Mrs. Byers, her eyebrows raised as she carried a tray laden with tea and decorative cakes into the room. "Please ladies, sit." She set her tea tray on the table and began pouring. "My Ladies Union Aid Society helps the poor and less fortunate, but we've never done anything unlawful." She turned to Millie and offered her a delicate china cup on a saucer. "You're sure your husband is innocent?"

"Of course, he is," answered Mrs. Beebee.

"Mr. D would kill to protect Mrs. D," explained Mrs. Griswold in her grandmotherly tone, "but he wouldn't murder a defenseless woman."

Mrs. Byers handed out fine porcelain teacups on matching saucers and plates adorned with fancy cakes before taking her own seat. "Very well. So, how do we break him out?"

Millie choked on her tea. "*We?*"

"We have a plan," said Mrs. Gilson excitedly.

"Miss Nessa will distract the guard while we release Mr. D." Mrs. Griswold beamed at Tit Bit like a proud mother.

"*Distract the guard?*" Millie's eyes widened.

"Ah," said Mrs. Byers nodding. "Miss LaMont's girls are the only women who can afford the kind of dress you're wearing."

Tit Bit rose from her chair. "I'll see myself out."

"No, please sit." Mrs. Byers offered Nessa another cake. "Perhaps after we plan the jailbreak, we can discuss how to help women like yourself. My Ladies Aid Society has discussed opening a home, but we're unsure about the type of training to offer."

Tit Bit tilted her head to one side, nodded, and returned to her seat. Mrs. Beebee stood and explained their plan.

"It might work," Mrs. Byers said thoughtfully. "Tomorrow's Sunday. After a rowdy Saturday night, the town's quiet and empty before church."

"We told Brother Bunce we'd attend his service tomorrow," Mrs. Gilson explained. "No one will suspect us if we are attending church right after we break Mr. D out."

A feeling of unreality settled over Millie as Mrs. Beebee

added conversationally, "Mrs. Byers, may I compliment you on these excellent cakes."

"Why thank you, Mrs. Beebee. Since the jailbreak's tomorrow, do you ladies have plans for today?"

"Shopping, I should think," said Mrs. Beebee.

"And a show tonight," added Mrs. Gilson.

"Excellent." Mrs. Byers dusted crumbs off her skirt. "Please, allow me to accompany you. Toole and Leach just received a new shipment from the States and Flormann's Old Stand has an excellent Ice Cream Saloon."

"We should get a disguise for Mr. D," Mrs. Gilson said thoughtfully. "We can dress him like a woman, so he won't be recognized when he sneaks out of town."

"Mr. D ain't gonna sneak away like a coward." The other ladies ignored Mary's comment, but Millie knew her friend was right. Dom would never run away. He was as proud as he was loud. Somehow, she'd have to convince him to leave, or maybe to hide.

"It's settled," Mrs. Byers said, gathering up the dishes. "We'll plan lunch at the Denver House and tonight an opera at the Apollo. Or maybe a show at the People's Theater. In between, I'll take you to the best shops Denver has to offer."

"Mama, mama!" Mrs. Byers' son launched into the room, a horrified expression on his face. "We didn't do hardly nothing but the lady's goat fell over dead." The boy burst into tears.

TWENTY-EIGHT

May 15, 1864
Jailbreak

After a sleepless night, Millie climbed into Mrs. Byers' wagon as the sun peaked over the Eastern Plains. Few other people were out, but after experiencing Denver City last night, Millie wasn't surprised. Mrs. Byers had shown off her growing town by taking the ladies to a concert at the People's Theatre on Larimer Street. Afterwards they all strolled along the crowded streets, seeing firsthand how Denver celebrated Saturday night. To Millie, it seemed the entire male population was spending their paychecks and gold dust on drink, games of chance, billiards, and fancy women.

Mary waved as they passed the Washington House and climbed into the wagon. "Them matrons help Miss Nessa dress." Her eyes widened. "That girl corset so tight she not barely breathe. I—" A familiar bleat sounded behind them.

"Buttercup?" Millie moaned. Yesterday, after assuring the children Buttercup had just fainted, Millie had settled the goat in the barn with the Byers' animals. Buttercup had not taken the demotion well, and her cries echoed late into the night. This morning, Millie had deliberately not entered the barn trying not to disturb the little goat. The last thing she wanted was Buttercup causing trouble during the jailbreak.

Buttercup jumped into the wagon and butted Millie none too gently.

"That goat is spoiled rotten," Mrs. Byers said, shaking her head. "But it's too late to take her back."

Mary took off her scarf and tied it to Buttercup's ribbon collar. "Leastwise we hold onto her."

They reached Cherry Creek and left the wagon and horses tied out of sight. Staying in the shadows, they crept closer to the jail and waited.

"Here she comes," Mrs. Byers whispered excitedly.

Indeed, Tit Bit had arrived. The working girl sauntered down the rickety walkway like she owned it, dressed in a deep red gown with a neckline so low her cleavage threatened to bounce out with each rhythmic step. Her waist was unnaturally narrow, but the flaring of her hips and how she moved that portion of her anatomy was as eye-popping as the colorful paint on her face.

"Oh Lor'!" Millie whispered.

Tit Bit sashayed into the jail without knocking and a moment later, Mrs. Beebee, Mrs. Griswold, and Mrs. Gilson arrived, each carrying a bundle.

"Miss Nessa said she would need two or three minutes to distract the guard," explained Mrs. Beebee.

"Not in that getup," Mary muttered.

"Ladies." Mrs. Gilson glanced at Buttercup and shook her head. "Just as we discussed, Miss Mary will wait outside and keep watch."

Millie hadn't wanted to insult her friend, but Mary couldn't be part of the jailbreak. If they got caught, the white ladies would be chastised, but Mary's punishment might be severe.

"We'll go in, release Mr. D, put him in his disguise, and bring him out to the Byers' wagon." Mrs. Beebee said, her voice shriller than normal. "As we discussed, he'll leave the wagon south of town along the Cherokee Trail."

Millie nodded. The matrons thought Dom would flee south, but Mary had suggested an alternative plan. Millie hadn't shared this with the matrons—the fewer people who knew where Dom was, the better.

"I put a few treats behind the seat, dear." Mrs. Griswold patted Millie's arm. "You know how Mr. D is always hungry. And I found an extra-large chemise and shift."

The disguise was one of many aspects of this plan that worried Millie, but it was too late to argue. "Let's go," Millie said, not even attempting to leave Buttercup with Mary. If the goat threw a fit, she'd attract attention. Millie hurried to the jail and opened the door. Tit Bit was nowhere to be seen, but the room wasn't empty. "Marshal Hunt. What are you doing here?"

"We felt two men should guard Mr. D at all times." His eyes widened as the other ladies followed Millie into the room. "L-little Ladies." He politely doffed his beaver skin cap, his eyes flicking uncertainly toward the closed door behind him. "I'm sorry, it's too early to visit the prisoner."

"We were hoping," Millie said uncertainly. "I mean…" A loud groan and thud sounded from behind the closed door. "Oh my. What's that?"

Marshal Hunt colored. "W-we're punishing a prisoner."

"We can do that?" hollered an excited male voice.

Marshal Hunt's face turned bright red and he strode toward the ladies. In a husky voice, he said, "You must leave. We're rather busy."

Mrs. Byers shoved Millie aside, as if she'd just rushed in. "Marshal Hunt. Thank goodness I found you. There's been an emergency."

"Mrs. Byers. What—"

"No time for questions. Quick. I've got my wagon." She grabbed the marshal's arm—looking small and very feminine beside his unusually large frame—and dragged him toward the door.

Millie and the other women quickly moved aside.

Marshal Hunt's eyes darted between Mrs. Byers, Millie, and the closed door. "Y-you ladies need to leave too."

"Of course." Millie herded the matrons and Buttercup from the jail, shutting the door behind them. They stood on the wooden sidewalk and waved until Mrs. Byers and Marshal Hunt were out of sight.

"That was brilliant," whispered Mrs. Gilson.

"Wonder where she'll take him?" muttered Mrs. Beebee.

"Wonder what Miss Nessa's doing with the other guard." Mrs. Griswold sighed. "Me and Elder Griswold been married so long we haven't tried anything new in years."

"Come on," Millie said, hurrying back inside, ignoring the noises behind the closed door. She reached for a key ring hanging on the wall and rushed into the cell room.

"My, it smells dreadful in here." Mrs. Beebee covered her mouth with a fashionable handkerchief that showed her initials in fine silk embroidery in the corner.

"Dom says they only empty the slop buckets once a day," said Millie through her hand.

"Millie? What in tarnation are you doing here?" Dom's eyes widened as the other ladies squeezed in, filling the narrow space between the two cells. Straw clung to his filthy clothes, but it was his gaunt frame that worried Millie. "Ladies, w-what's going on?"

"We're breaking you out." Mrs. Gilson choked and waved to Millie. "Mrs. D unlock the door. Mr. D, remove your clothes."

"*Remove my clothes?*" Dom backed away, his eyes darting from one woman to the next. "Millie, what—"

"They're talking about lynching you." Millie gave Dom a hard stare. "Do as the ladies say. We don't have much time." Millie didn't know if it was her words or the desperation she felt, but Dom stripped down to his woolens.

"Lord it stinks in here." Mrs. Griswold handed Dom her

bundle. "Put these on and be right quick. Tit Bit won't be able to distract the guard much longer."

"Tit Bit?" Dom lifted his bushy eyebrows in confusion. Millie shook her head and pulled the largest petticoat she'd ever seen over his head.

"Would you ladies be so kind as to unlock my door?" asked a scruffy man with a beard so long it almost reached his knees. "I'd be much obliged."

His drunk cellmate hiccupped and squinted at them. "Iss ttthat aaa goat?"

"What happened to the married couple?" Mrs. Griswold asked. "Elder Griswold told me about the wedding."

"They left, thank God." Dom pulled the petticoat down over his hips. "Two nights of listening to their marriage bliss almost killed me."

Mrs. Beebee crept closer to the mens' cell. "We couldn't possibly release you. You're criminals, but…" Her words were muffled behind her handkerchief. "If you gentlemen agree not to, uh, mention you saw anyone helping Mr. D escape. Well, I make the best fruit pies in the territory. Would you prefer apple or strawberry?"

Mr. Scruffy gripped the bars, his face transforming into an expression of lonesome yearning. "I haven't had a home baked pie since I left mama's kitchen." In a rapturous whisper he added, "Strawberry's my favorite."

The drunk stood up unsteadily, stumbled, and landed face down in the straw, tipping over his very full slop bucket. "Aaapple."

Mrs. Beebee gagged and backed up. "I'll bring apple later today, strawberry tomorrow. You never saw us, right?"

"We ain't seen nothing, ma'am."

"Ccept aa goat."

"I can't wear this," moaned Dom.

Millie didn't laugh, she was too scared, but she doubted Mrs. Griswold's voluminous calico skirt would fit over

Dom's broad shoulders. Mrs. Gilson pushed Millie aside and using the skills of a mother with several children, settled the skirt into place. She spun Dom around and forced a loose Garibaldi blouse over his head, arranging the clothing and stepping back to survey her work. "Drat," she said, fisting her hands on her hips and staring at the eight inches of woolens showing beneath the skirt.

Mrs. Beebee stepped forward and jerked the skirt down low on Dom's hips. "Good thing we brought a long apron."

Dom groaned. "I thought lynching was the worst that could happen to me."

"Compared to this stink, a hanging might be merciful," said Mrs. Beebee, adding the apron to Dom's ensemble. Mrs. Gilson placed a matching shawl on his shoulders while Mrs. Griswold carefully set a frilly pink bonnet on his head and neatly tied a bow under his chin.

The ladies stepped back to admire their work, but Millie just shook her head. Dom, his face now covered with a week-old beard, looked ridiculous.

"I think we best wrap the shawl around his face," Mrs. Beebee said, scowling.

They rearranged the shawl and hurried Dom from the jail. Buttercup followed them, dirty straw sticking out of her mouth.

"Where's the jailer? Or Marshal Hunt?" Dom asked.

"Busy," whispered Mrs. Beebee, glancing at the still closed door.

"This way." Mrs. Gilson hurried outside. "Come on."

"Mr. D." Mrs. Beebee sounded exasperated. "Bend over and hobble like an old woman."

"I can't hobble. I keep tripping over this blasted skirt. How do you ladies walk?"

"Where are you going to take him?" Mrs. Gilson looked grim as they joined Mary in the shadows. "Mrs. Byers took her wagon."

"I'm not running away!" Dom bellowed.

"You shush, Mr. D, and come with us," Mrs. Beebee said sternly. "Mrs. Byers and that very good-looking Marshal Hunt may be back any moment."

She led them down Front Street, passing quiet shops and businesses, but as they turned on Third Street, Millie stopped. "Ladies, Dom and I appreciate all you have done, but we need to go on alone. All of us will draw attention." She paused and glanced at Dom. He was hunched over, but his big hands and feet protruded unnaturally from the blouse and skirt. If anyone looked at him—not to mention Buttercup—they'd take a second look.

"Mrs. D is right, although I don't know where you'll go." Mrs. Griswold wrung her hands.

"We'll be fine, ladies. You all go on to church. I'll get Dom off and join you if I can." Without waiting for a response, Millie grabbed Dom's arm and pulled him down the street. Several blocks later, Millie led him into a filthy alley and gave him a heartfelt hug. "Dom, I know you don't want to hide, but if they find you, they'll lynch you."

"I'm not running." His expression was grim under the pink bonnet.

"Just hide, for a few days." She kissed his filthy face. "Please, for me." He wavered, and Millie knew she'd almost won. "Miss Mary is staying with a free colored family, a Mr. and Mrs. Smith. Blacksmith Shumate told her about them. They're part of the underground railroad and have a human hidey-hole under their cabin. You can stay there, for a couple days, until things simmer down."

Dom hesitated, and Millie took his hands. "Please, just for a few days."

"Fine," he said wearily, rubbing his forehead. "But then we both leave, right?"

Millie nodded, relieved. They circled back toward Cherry Creek, taking empty roads populated by passed out drunks.

After several more turns, they reached Cherry Creek and followed it down to a rough log cabin. Glancing around uncertainly, Millie knocked on the door, relieved to see Mary hurrying toward them.

A colored woman immediately opened the door and pulled them inside. Millie's eyes widened as she glanced around. Five children sat huddled against the far wall, silently watching as their mother rolled back a rag rug and opened a trapdoor. Hand-carved dirt steps led down into a damp root cellar so small Dom would have to sleep in a sitting position.

Millie shuddered at the underground hiding place, but Dom climbed down without comment, looking worn and tired. "Millie, there's a killer on the loose. I'm afraid—"

"I know. I'll be careful. Promise me you'll stay here until I come for you."

"I will," Dom sighed. "If you promise not to do anything stupid."

Millie gave him a weak smile. "Me?! Do anything stupid?"

TWENTY-NINE

May 15, 1864
Mount Pleasant Cemetery

From the back pew, Millie kept Buttercup hidden under her skirt, wincing each time a muffled bleat interrupted the fire and brimstone sermons of Brother Bunce and the Fighting Parson, Col. Chivington. Brother Bunce's small stature and snowy white beard contrasted strongly with Col. Chivington's ox-like build, round face, short-cropped beard, and dark, intense eyes, but both men's loud voices shook the walls. Millie ignored them; bigger worries filled her thoughts.

She had to find Widow Ferris' murderer before Dom came out of hiding. Either that, or she had to find someplace where she and Dom could hide indefinitely.

Just the thought of not going home made Millie pull out her daybook and look at her suspect list—Sheriff Reynolds, Billy Batterson, Fox Diefendorf, Old Shakespeare, Brother Bunce, and Mr. Turck. Which one was the killer? Or was it someone she didn't know?

She glanced at Brother Bunce, trying to imagine the older man killing Widow Ferris. He had passion, at least while preaching, but enough to murder a woman? Her thoughts were interrupted as Billy Batterson strode down the aisle and took a seat beside a well-dressed man holding a black slouch hat.

Millie knew nothing about Mr. Batterson—except he was a remittance man and said he loved Widow Ferris. Why had Mr. Ferris blackmailed him? Maybe he'd loved Widow Ferris, but she spurned him. He wasn't much to look at and he—

"Get that goat out of here!" hollered Brother Bunce.

Millie started and looked up. Buttercup, her eyes bulging, stared up at Brother Bunce, the altar flowers dangling from her mouth. She tumbled over in a dead faint.

"The goat kicked the bucket," shrieked an altar boy. A child screamed, and the church erupted into chaos as the congregation poured from their pews like they were rushing to communion.

By the time Millie pushed her way through the crowd, Buttercup lay crumpled in a bed of flowers, surrounded by adoring children, looking like the Christ child in the manger. Mortified, Millie apologized to Brother Bunce and Col. Chivington, picked up Buttercup, and made a hasty retreat. Just as she reached the door, she heard a man yell, "Where's my hat?"

Mr. Batterson was already outside the church. He glanced back at Millie, winked, and darted away.

"You really must teach that goat some manners." Mrs. Beebee said crossly when she joined Millie outside.

"Now, now, dear." Mrs. Griswold patted Millie's hand. "She didn't cause too much trouble."

"She cut Reverend Chivington's sermon short," said Mrs. Byers, patting Buttercup. "The man is a windbag."

"An incensed windbag," added Mrs. Gilson. "But Brother Bunce wasn't much better. They were carrying on about Indians like the world was about to end."

"Never mind their sermon." Mrs. Beebee turned to Millie. "Where's Mr. D?"

"He's left town," Millie lied. "We decided it would be

best if I stayed here. He stole a horse, and I…I don't know how to ride."

"Will he be okay, dear? The lawmen will certainly form a posse to find him." Mrs. Griswold looked so worried Millie took her hand and patted it.

"He knows this country. He'll find a hiding spot and hunker down until the trouble blows over." Feeling guilty with her lie, Millie turned to Mrs. Byers. "Thank you for distracting Marshal Hunt. Where in the world did you take him?"

"He's awfully good looking," said Mrs. Beebee, fanning her face. "Your husband will be jealous if he hears of your morning jaunt together."

"Marshal Hunt is quite good-looking, but don't introduce him to your daughters." Mrs. Byers led the way down a rough walkway. "Man's a born showman. He favors cards, drink, and a good joke. His homestead is near Camp Weld, east of the Platte."

"Was Miss Nessa there when you returned?" Millie asked.

"No, and Marshal Hunt was none too pleased. I guess I should add fancy women to his list of transgressions." Mrs. Byers stepped into a restaurant and turned to Millie. "Please, keep a tight hold on Buttercup. Being kicked out of church is unfortunate but missing a meal at the People's Restaurant and Saloon would be dreadful."

They settled at a table and Millie firmly knotted Buttercup's scarf lead around one of the table's legs, admonishing the little goat to behave. The proprietor brought plates of baked apples, buckwheat cakes, honey, sausages, and hot drinks. As they settled down to their meal, Mrs. Beebee asked excitedly, "Now tell us about Marshal Hunt."

"I took him to Mount Pleasant Cemetery," Mrs. Byers said, taking a sip of tea. "The cemetery is located east of town."

"How in the world did you explain going out there?" Millie asked as she cut into a sausage. It smelled delicious, but the innards spilled out in a rather gelatinous glob. Millie gagged and discreetly set the plate down beside Buttercup.

"After we were on our way, I explained about Mr. McGavron's shameful sign. I've been wanting to do something about it for weeks. Mr. McGavron's Denver City's undertaker and he's an uncouth, avaricious man. Right in front of the cemetery, he put up a sign that read: *Not dead yet? I'm always on hand. I insure all my work. As an undertaker, I am prepared to respond to any call without delay, as I have coffins ready-made, and a new and fashionable hearse and pledge myself to give satisfaction.*"

"Oh my." Mrs. Griswold fanned her face. "How dreadful. Did Marshal Hunt remove the sign?"

"He did. He was so furious I'd taken him away from Miss Nessa, he ripped the sign down with his bare hands."

"Speaking of Miss Nessa..." Mrs. Gilson nodded her head.

Tit Bit sauntered into the room. Her face was clean of paint and her dress was modestly cut, but her figure and movements still caused every male eye to turn and watch as she crossed to their table.

Without makeup, Tit Bit looked young as she glanced uncertainly at the matrons. Millie quickly patted the seat beside her. "Please come join us, Miss Nessa. I can't thank you enough for all you've done."

"That be kind of you, Mrs. D, but I be thinking it be best if we were not seen together. Both the jailer and Marshal Hunt be recognizing me. They surely know I be helping whoever freed Mr. D."

"Marshal Hunt knows we broke Mr. D out. Please join us Miss Nessa." Mrs. Byers casually took a bite of her hotcake, not appearing to notice Mrs. Beebee, Mrs. Griswold, and Mrs. Gilson's widening eyes.

"Surely he doesn't know it was us?" Mrs. Beebee gasped. Her baked apple rolled off her fork and bounced down her bodice, leaving a dark stain.

Mrs. Byers laughed. "Of course, he knows. Marshal Hunt and the jailer will be the brunt of jokes for weeks to come. They were outsmarted by a bunch of women and a goat. Not only that, they lost a prisoner."

"Will they put us in that awful jail?" asked Millie. She'd been so worried about Dom that she hadn't considered the consequences of their actions.

In answer, Marshal Hunt charged into the restaurant, trailed by Sheriff Reynolds and Mr. Byers.

THIRTY

May 15, 1864

Mr. Turck

Marshal Hunt's angry strides rattled dishes, but he stopped short when he caught sight of Tit Bit. Sheriff Reynolds circled the stunned marshal and stopped behind Nessa, resting a hand on her shoulder. "Ladies." He tried but failed to hide his grin. "There's been a problem at the jail."

"What kind of problem?" Millie was unable to even pretend to be surprised.

"An escaped prisoner." Marshal Hunt scowled angrily. "Your husband, Little Lady, Widow Ferris' murderer has escaped."

"My husband is not—"

"The woman killer escaped?" hollered a man at a nearby table. He jumped to his feet. "We need to form a posse." Chairs scraped against the floor as men rose and drew their weapons.

"Should have lynched him yesterday!" another man yelled as he headed out the door. "But today will work just fine."

Fear for Dom replaced concern for her own wellbeing. If those men found Dom, he wouldn't have a chance. Marshal Hunt didn't know about Mary, but Sheriff Reynolds and Editor Byers did.

"How careless of you, Marshal Hunt." Mrs. Byers sounded confident and insolent. "When did you misplace this prisoner?"

The lawman's expression darkened. "We did not misplace the killer, ma'am. You ladies busted him out."

"That is a dangerous accusation, Marshal Hunt." Mr. Byers moved behind his wife and pulled out pencil and paper. "Do you have proof?"

"You needn't write a story, Editor Byers." The lawman's voice had an uncomfortable edge. "We'll recapture the killer, but maybe not before the mob lynches him." He stared at Millie. "Little Lady, care to tell me where he is, so I get to him first?"

"That might not be best," said Sheriff Reynolds, frowning. "Musgrove was supposedly safe in your jail, but he was lynched before his trial. Maybe the ladies did you a favor."

"If the ladies had anything to do with his escape," said Editor Byers.

"These ladies visited the jail this morning." Marshal Hunt scowled at them. "They freed the prisoner after Mrs. Byers and I left."

"Marshal Hunt," said Mrs. Beebee. "We left the jail with you. After all, it wouldn't be proper for us to visit the jail without an escort."

"Especially while you were disciplining a prisoner," Millie added.

Marshal Hunt's face reddened, but he stubbornly pressed on. "And your goat left with you?"

Millie nodded uncertainly.

"You and the goat never went back to Mr. D's cell?"

"Of course, they didn't," Editor Byers said. "Mrs. D is a proper matron."

Marshal Hunt grimaced, but there was resignation in his expression. "I wonder how fresh goat droppings ended up by the empty cell. They look just like those."

Millie looked down and sure enough, there was a small pile of fresh droppings on the floor. "Buttercup, you bad, bad girl."

The goat's eyes bulged out and she fainted at Millie's feet.

Marshal Hunt shook his head. "You got a story here Editor, but I don't expect you'll print it."

The restaurant's door banged open and several men hurried inside. Col. Chivington rushed toward them, followed by three soldiers, including Mr. Turck dressed in the uniform of the First Colorado Cavalry. Col. Chivington's dark eyes burned with intensity, but Mr. Turck stopped short when he spotted the group. "I heard the woman killer's escaped," said the Fighting Parson. "I'll organize my men. Any idea where he went?"

"Mr. Turck." Sheriff Reynolds removed his six-shooter and pointed it at the man. "I've been looking for you."

Turck narrowed his eyes and wrapped his big fists around his beard braids, squeezing them rhythmically. "I didn't do nothing," he snarled.

"What's the meaning of this?" Col. Chivington's eyes flashed at Sheriff Reynolds.

Editor Byers pointed his pencil at Mr. Turck. "I've been told that Mr. Turck disappeared the night Widow Ferris was murdered."

"I didn't kill nobody."

"You struck Mrs. Drouillard and Miss Nessa," Sheriff Reynolds pressed. "Later that evening, Widow Ferris was killed."

Col. Chivington's forehead creased in confusion. "I thought the escaped prisoner, Mr. Drouillard, killed Widow Ferris? Explain yourself, Private Turck."

"I was visiting Tit Bit, the town working girl." Turck pointed at Miss Nessa. "Mrs. D showed up and insulted me, so I backhanded her to teach her a lesson. I'd been drinking a bit, but I didn't do her no harm. She was s'pose to marry me, but her worthless husband—the woman killer—jumped my claim."

"My husband did not kill Widow Ferris," Millie said indignantly. "And you didn't just backhand me, Mr. Turck. You dragged me through the mud and threatened me with unmentionable horrors."

"Private Turck." Col. Chivington's commanding voice cut through the room. "Drunkenness is no excuse for striking a woman. Go back to the barracks immediately; I'll deal with you there."

"One minute," Sheriff Reynolds holstered his gun. "Turck, where'd you go after assaulting Mrs. D?"

Mr. Turck scowled, his eyes darting uneasily between his commanding officer and Sheriff Reynolds. "Tell him the truth," Col. Chivington commanded.

"I run," Mr. Turck muttered. "Grabbed what I could and skedaddled." He glared at Millie. "I knew her murdering husband would kill me if he found me, so I took off. Spent several days making my way to Denver City. Then I joined the First Colorado Cavalry."

Millie disliked the man but surprisingly, she believed him.

"Since joining my men, Private Turck's been fighting Indians with the First Colorado Cavalry. He distinguished himself at Fremont's Orchard under Lt. Dunn where he fought twenty-five Cheyenne Dog soldiers. After Fremont's Orchard, he joined Lt. Eayer's troops hunting down the savages that stole government stock near the headwaters of Sand Creek. He returned last week bringing news of the four Cheyenne camps our soldiers burned."

"Fools," said Sheriff Reynolds hotly. "If you keep destroying their camps and killing their women and children, you'll get us into an all-out war."

"We're already in a war, sir." Col. Chivington narrowed his eyes and rested a hand on his own gun.

"Gentlemen, gentlemen. The Indians are not at issue
right now." Mr. Byers glanced at Mr. Turck. "He's the issue."

"Go back to Camp Weld, Private." Chivington turned to
Sheriff Reynolds. "If he's guilty, we'll have a military tribu-
nal, but from the sounds of it, the escaped prisoner is your
woman killer. I'll get some of my men, and we'll hunt him
down."

Marshal Hunt nodded. "I'll help you!" He glared at Millie. "I won't give up until Mr. D is back in my jail or hanging
from a noose."

THIRTY-ONE

May 18, 1864

Miss Ada LaMont

Three days later, Col. Chivington and Marshal Hunt were still searching for Dom, thankfully with no success. Furious over the whole affair, Marshal Hunt had assigned a deputy to follow Millie wherever she went, making it impossible for her to visit Dom or Mary. Millie had smuggled a note and a change of clothes to him, using Tit Bit as a courier, but she didn't dare do more. She prayed he'd stay hidden until tomorrow night.

"Mrs. D, you really shouldn't be staying at the Washington House without an escort," said Elder Griswold for the third time. They were waiting for the stagecoach that would take Elder Griswold and the matrons back to Idaho Springs. "At the very least, accept Mrs. Byers' invitation to stay with her."

"Thank you for your kindness, Elder Griswold, but Buttercup and I are comfortable in our room." Buttercup had shown her displeasure at being put back into the barn by chewing on the tails of Mrs. Byer's horses—leaving each horse with a tail that ended two feet off the ground. Millie was quite certain Mrs. Byers was relieved to have them both gone.

"And why are Miss Nessa and Miss Mary staying?" asked Mrs. Beebee suspiciously.

Millie had asked Tit Bit to stay—she needed an introduction to Ada LaMont—but no way was she mentioning that to the matrons. They'd all want to come, which was why she'd encouraged them to leave. "I'm gonna miss you all," she said, giving each woman a hug. "I can't thank you enough for all you've done."

Mrs. Gilson pulled Millie close and whispered, "Is Mary with Dom? We've noticed she hasn't been around since the jailbreak."

Millie blanched. "I think it's best—"

"Sheriff Reynolds," said Mrs. Beebee loudly. "What are you doing here?"

The sheriff strode over, carrying a bag. "Deputy Whitlatch sent a message by last night's coach. Seems someone broke into Blacksmith Shumate's shop and caused some trouble."

"Is Blacksmith Shumate okay?" Millie asked. "And Jake and his son?"

"They're all fine. Blacksmith Shumate was at your place having supper with Jake and his son." The sheriff shook his head. "Haven't seen this much lawlessness in Idaho Springs in years. It's starting to feel as troublesome as Denver City."

*****

The next morning rain and dark clouds kept the streets empty as Millie slunk from the back of the Washington House with Tit Bit—avoiding Marshal Hunt's guard. They hurried down muddy thoroughfares toward McGaa Street, finding the infamous street empty and quiet. There were no shops, churches, or respectable businesses to draw customers early in the morning.

"Were you able to speak with Miss Mary yesterday?"

Millie asked, stepping around a muddy puddle. "How's Dom?"

"Mary said he be as grumpy as a spring bear. We made plans for tonight, and he be expecting you. I be told the Cheyenne attacked settlements in Kansas, and there was another attack near Fort Larned. Me customers say Dogmen and Sioux have declared war on all whites. Col. Chivington and his soldiers ain't got time to search for Mr. D right now."

Millie suspected Tit Bit was getting her news directly from Editor Byers, but she didn't ask. "Were you able to buy a horse?"

"Aye. It be in the livery east of town. Yesterday, I apologized to Marshal Hunt and invited him over. Tonight, I be seeing to it he be out of your way. Do you—"

"Miss Nessa, that isn't necessary. I don't want you—"

"Begorrah, Mrs. D. I be a fancy girl. 'Tis me work. Now, do you have a safe place to hide?"

"I think so." There was no place in the Colorado Territory entirely safe right now, but the girl's concern touched Millie. Tit Bit lived a life Millie couldn't imagine or respect, yet the girl was kind and had done all she could to help Dom. "Miss Nessa, I can't thank you enough. After this is over, I want to find you a proper—"

"This be Madam LaMont's place," Tit Bit said, interrupting Millie and pointing at a building on their left.

Millie suspected the girl had deliberately cut her off. Perhaps Tit Bit didn't believe she could have any other life. After Dom was no longer a fugitive, Millie would address Tit Bit's future, but for now, she focused on her present chore.

Ada LaMont lived in a well-built, two-story brick building with glass windows and drawn curtains, looking nicer than any of the Denver City homes Millie had visited with Mrs. Byers. Finer than anything else in town.

"Miss Millie, be careful," Tit Bit warned. "Madam LaMont be dangerous."

Millie nodded, and Tit Bit stepped forward and knocked on the door. A beautiful woman dressed in a fine Parisian silk gown with matching green gloves, a tasteful hat, and soft leather boots opened the door. Her amber eyes examined Millie the way a spider examines a fly.

"Won't you come in, Mrs. Drouillard. Miss Nessa." Her voice was throaty, her movements arrogant. "I'm Madam LaMont."

Madam LaMont was poised and obviously educated, but there was an edge to her that made the hairs on the back of Millie's neck rise, even without Tit Bit's warning. "Thank you kindly, Ma'am. I appreciate you meeting with us, especially so early in the morning."

The woman gave a husky laugh. "I'm sure you wouldn't want to visit any other time." The Madam moved from the doorway, and for an instant candlelight illuminated her face. Beneath the powder, Millie saw lines crossing the woman's forehead and crow's feet extending out from her eyes. Ada LaMont was beautiful, but five years as a fancy woman had left its mark.

How long, Millie wondered, would it take for Tit Bit to lose her youth?

Inside, the brothel was warm and dry, but the strong smell of perfume and alcohol turned Millie's stomach. She removed her wet garments, glancing around curiously. A candle chandelier illuminated an elaborate sitting area and dance hall. Flashy red and gray wallpaper covered the walls, and matching Victorian furniture was arranged off to the side in an area resembling a proper parlor. A beautiful grand piano sat beside a full bar, but it was the ceiling-to-floor mirrors surrounding the huge fireplace that made the room look garish.

"Your home is…I mean, it's…" Millie paused, unable to think of anything polite.

"The gentlemen like it," said Madam LaMont, sweeping by Millie and pausing by an open door. "Dom was particularly fond of the dance floor. He'd grab Big Swede and swing her around when 'The Swedish Nightingale' and 'The Girl I Left Behind Me' played." She said it casually, but her eyes held Millie's. "Course, if memory serves, your husband enjoyed dancing almost as much as…Well, you know."

Millie narrowed her eyes but caught herself before she said something indelicate. She needed this woman and the information she could provide. Plus, Madam LaMont was only taunting her, just to see how she'd respond. "My husband is a remarkable man. One most ladies have trouble forgetting." Millie smiled, showing teeth. "He sends his regards."

Madam LaMont tipped her head back and laughed. "Touché, Mrs. D. Please, this way. I've made tea."

They moved into a smaller, less ornate room and settled around a parlor table topped with rose-colored marble. Millie admired the intricate, hand carved divan as Madam LaMont set out porcelain teacups. After taking her seat and settling her skirts, the madam lifted one eyebrow at Millie. "Miss Nessa said you wanted information about Mr. Ferris. Said you were the one who killed him."

"He fell to his death," Millie responded, but noting Madam LaMont didn't seem grieved by Mr. Ferris' death, she added, "although my bullet may have helped his demise."

Madam LaMont nodded. "I owe you my thanks. Mr. Ferris was becoming a bore and unpleasantly possessive." The woman casually sipped her tea, never taking her eyes off Millie. "What do you want to know?"

"Did you know Mr. Ferris was blackmailing several Idaho Springs men?"

Madam LaMont raised both of her expressive eyebrows. "Mr. Ferris had several money-making occupations. Why would I know anything about them?"

"I was told Widow Ferris wrote his legal papers. I thought perhaps you might have helped him with his blackmail business."

"And if I did?"

"I don't care," Millie said, tiring of the polite game. "I just want information to prove Dom didn't murder Widow Ferris. I found an article about a killer in Egg Point, Mississippi."

"Yes, I remember reading it." Ada LaMont gave Millie a hard look. "Why should I help you, Mrs. D?"

Why indeed. At the wake, Elder Griswold had said Ada LaMont had once been married to a minister. Maybe she still felt some compassion. Allowing her desperation to show, Millie reached across and touched the woman's hand. "Please. Dom didn't kill Widow Ferris. I need to find the killer, or they'll lynch him."

"Dom had reason to kill Widow Ferris."

"He wouldn't kill to hide the fact he'd fathered an illegitimate daughter."

"I believe you're right, Mrs. D." Ada LaMont pulled her hand away and leaned back.

"Miss LaMont, do you know who the Egg Point killer is?"

"No. He was a Southerner that Mr. Ferris knew before he came West."

"Do you know who killed Widow Ferris?"

"No." She yawned. "Mr. Ferris blackmailed many men. Several of them might kill to protect their secrets."

Millie leaned forward. "Who?"

Ada LaMont shrugged and rose gracefully to her feet. "I'm sure the good people of Idaho Springs might have an issue if they knew about Brother Bunce's past or Sheriff Reynolds' Confederate brothers."

Tit Bit sprang to her feet and grabbed Ada LaMont's arm, jerking the woman toward her. "My Gene didn't kill Widow Ferris!"

THIRTY-TWO

May 19, 1864

Disaster

Madam LaMont knocked away Tit Bit's hand and pulled out a derringer. Her face twisted in an ugly mask of rage. "I was trying to help, but I think you should leave. Now!"

Millie rose and attempted to calm the angry woman, but Ada LaMont would have none of it. She kept her gun aimed at Tit Bit and herded them to the door. They stepped outside, almost blown over by the wind, the rain pouring down on them.

"I be sorry, Mrs. D," Tit Bit said as they made their way back down McGaa Street. "But Gene, Sheriff Reynolds, ain't killed Widow Ferris."

"Do you know what she meant by his Confederate brothers?"

"Nay, but—"

"Well looky here," snarled a man. "The town harlot walking with the oh-so-proper Southern belle." Mr. Turck leaned indolently against a saloon doorway, rain dripping from his beard braids. "Slipped away from Marshal Hunt's guard, did you? Looks like I'll have to do my duty and take his place."

They hurried back to the Washington House with Mr.

Turck following so close, Millie could smell the alcohol on him. She slammed and locked the door of her room, listening to Turck pacing outside. Picking up Buttercup, she cradled the goat in her arms and buried her head in the goat's fur. "Oh Lor'! I miss Dom so much. What ever will we do if we're caught?"

Much later, Millie peeked out of her room, relieved to see Turck was gone. She went shopping, buying the last of the supplies she hoped they'd need. The rest of the evening she waited, chafing as the hours slowly ticked by. Finally, when the noises from the bars began to quiet, she patted Buttercup and left. The unhappy animal bleated loudly.

"You behave, Miss Buttercup," Millie said through the door. "Miss Mary will be back here shortly."

Rain poured down and clouds hid the stars as Millie stole from the shadows of one building to the next, working her way toward Cherry Creek. The bleak darkness made Denver City feel dangerous and forbidding, but at least the foul weather kept most men off the streets. Still, Millie glanced around uncertainly, feeling like she was being followed.

After circling a block twice and spotting no one, she made her way to the Smith's house, shocked to find Cherry Creek threatening to spill over its banks. It flowed so close to the Smith's cabin that Millie had to splash through inch-deep water to reach the door. Candlelight flickered through cracks as Millie lightly knocked. Mrs. Smith immediately opened the door and ushered Millie inside.

"Dom," Millie cried, rushing into his arms and kissing him. "Oh Lor', I've missed you. Are you okay? Why aren't you hiding?"

"Hidey-hole fill up with water," Mary explained. "He stay here, with us."

"Thank you. This rain's something terrible." Millie nodded at Mrs. Smith and Mary. With her arm wrapped around

Dom's waist, she felt how much weight he had lost, but his blue eyes were steady. "We're leaving, tonight."

"'Bout time. I hate to run, but…" He shook his head. "Miss Mary says Marshal Hunt's knickers are in a knot over my escape."

"He's upset, but he won't bother us tonight. We should go." Keeping her arm tightly wrapped around Dom, Millie thanked the Smiths, wishing she had more than a single tear-shaped gold nugget to offer the family for all they'd done. "Miss Mary, Buttercup's waiting in my room at the Washington House. Hopefully she hasn't caused too much trouble. Tomorrow, Miss Nessa will accompany you both back to Idaho Springs."

Mary nodded. "Okay. Here, we make sourdough bread."

Millie thankfully added the two loaves to her bag and tearfully hugged Mary goodbye. Huddling together against the wind and rain, Millie and Dom left the cabin and cautiously made their way up Front Street, pausing in the shadows before crossing Third and Blake.

"Rain's let up a bit," Millie said thankfully.

"Never seen Cherry Creek so high." Dom eyed the river.

"I thought we'd follow Front—"

"Shush!" Dom pulled her deeper into the shadows as shouting filled the air. A couple men stood across the street, yelling and pointing toward Cherry Creek.

"There's men in the Rocky Mountain News office!" Millie gripped Dom's arm as three men tumbled out an open window and dropped into the roiling waters of Cherry Creek.

"It's Mr. Daily and his boys." Dom released Millie and rushed toward the river's muddy banks, joined by the other men. "They're trying to swim to shore but the current is too strong." Millie watched three heads bob in the turbid waters, praying each time they disappeared that they'd come back up.

The man beside Dom threw a rope out, and they pulled one drowning man to shore. Inching closer, Millie caught sight of the man working beside Dom.

It was Marshal Hunt!

She backed away, knowing he'd recognize her. Hopefully the lawman was too busy to look closely at Dom.

An unimaginable roar caused Millie to look upstream. The roaring grew louder, and Millie saw a towering wave rushing toward them, ripping out trees like twigs. It pulled several buildings off their foundations and demolished each bridge it encountered.

Dom grabbed the arm of the last newspaper man, dragged him from the water, and then stumbled toward Millie, hiding behind a brick building as the wall of water washed by them.

The wave ripped the huge Methodist Church away like it was a toy. The Rocky Mountain News tumbled into the turbulence of surging water, taking its Union flag with it. Downstream from them, the tempestuous flow washed away Charles and Hunt's law offices, Metz's saddlery shop, and the City Hall building. Each building tumbled into the churning water and disappeared.

"Oh Lor'," Millie said. "Look!" A child flailed helplessly in the roiling current, swept downstream so quickly Dom didn't have time to throw his rope. Millie covered her face as a huge cottonwood, uprooted and twisting through the floodwater like an oversized twig, swept over the child, burying him in the maelstrom.

"Mary!" Millie grabbed Dom and splashed down the street. "The Smiths and their children."

They passed Marshal Hunt and a newspaper man as they hurried downstream. For an instant the Marshal stared at Millie and then glanced at Dom. He pointed and yelled "That's—" but his voice was drowned out by the calls of a man yelling for help.

Stumbling along Front Street, Millie and Dom passed the two-story Tremont House and were almost swept away by the raging river that now ran down Third street. Finally, they reached the block where the Smiths' house stood.

The small log cabin—along with Mary and the Smiths—was completely gone.

THIRTY-THREE

May 19, 1864
A Miracle

Dom and Millie spent a miserable night huddled with other trapped townsfolk on the second floor of the Tremont House, only daring to go outside when dawn broke over the Eastern Plains. Millie's anguish over Mary was tempered as they stepped outside to a transformed Denver City. Entire brick buildings were gone, and dangerous muddy rivers flowed down several streets.

Just trying to reach the Washington House was treacherous. Streets free from flowing water were still muddy like a hog wallow and harmless puddles turned out to be holes deep enough to drown in. Millie and Dom worked their way across town, one block at a time, Dom struggling with the exertion. After more than two weeks of incarceration and hiding—and not enough decent food—his stamina was poor.

Fortunately, he was too stubborn to give up.

"I'm sure Miss Mary left right after we did," Dom said, breathing hard as they entered the Washington House. He didn't mention the Smiths and their five children. There was no question about the family's fate. They slogged through the muddy interior, climbing to Millie's former room but found it empty. "You stay here," Millie said. "It's best if you're not seen. I'll check to see if Miss Mary's with Tit Bit or up on the roof with the crowd we saw."

"Nobody's looking for me right now," Dom grumbled, but he sat down on the bed to wait. Millie said nothing, but she knew he was wrong. Marshal Hunt had recognized Dom. Once he'd dealt with emergencies from the flood, Millie was certain the marshal would resume his search for Dom.

Millie made her way to Tit Bit's room, but no one answered her knock. She hesitated at the door of the girl's working room. If Tit Bit was there, she wouldn't be alone. Deciding to check the roof first, Millie trudged up wooden steps, spotting Tit Bit and Buttercup in the crowd on the edge of the roof.

Mary wasn't with her. Millie couldn't stop her tears as she approached the girl.

"You ain't drowned!" Tit Bit hugged Millie. "I be worried sick. What about Miss Mary and Dom?"

"Miss Mary isn't here?"

"He can't cross in that!" someone hollered.

Tit Bit shook her head, her own eyes filling. "Dom?"

Millie took several deep breaths, her voice trembling as she answered. "He's waiting in my room."

"You best move into mine. Come, I be—"

"They're putting it in the water." The crowd suddenly went silent.

"What's going on?" Millie looked around, wiping the tears from her face. Everyone on the roof was watching something below.

"They be trying to rescue the Byers." Tit Bit led Millie to the edge of the roof. The Platte River had overflowed its banks, flooding the entire area. In the distance, the Byers and their two children huddled on top of their home, the floodwater surrounding them.

"Oh Lor'," Millie whispered, "they'll be lost."

"Col. Chivington and his men be trying to rescue them."
Tit Bit pointed toward a brick building upstream. "He
fashioned a boat from a covered wagon base."

Millie held her breath as Col. Chivington climbed into
the makeshift craft and oared out into the floodwater. His
soldiers struggled to keep hold of the rope that kept him
from being swept downstream. Twice Col. Chivington
almost capsized, but somehow, he managed to reach the
Byers farmhouse. The return journey—with the craft laden
with five people—was even more harrowing. Millie sagged
against Tit Bit when they finally reached the shore.

*****

Millie, Dom, and Buttercup moved into Tit Bit's room,
forced to remain hidden until the roads became passable.
Millie spent her days missing Mary and her nights tossing
and turning, worried Marshal Hunt would find them. Her
fears escalated when Tit Bit announced Marshal Hunt had
searched their former room and questioned her. Fortunately, he only knew about Tit Bit's working room.

Millie and Dom would have to chance the roads. They
had no choice. First, though, they needed to replace their
diminished food supplies.

The flood had left a third of Denver underwater, killed
numerous townsfolk, and destroyed several properties,
but as the water traveled downstream, it ruined farms and
drowned livestock. It took Tit Bit two days to gather a
single carpetbag of food and a new six-shooter for Dom.
Amazingly, the horse she'd acquired for them was still alive
and waiting in the livery.

Sharing a tin of sardines as they waited for darkness,
Millie jumped to her feet when the door burst open. Dom
drew his six-shooter and Buttercup fainted.

"They be alive. It be a miracle!" Tit Bit charged into the

room and shoved a *Weekly Commonwealth* at Millie. "Me customer say it be written right here."

"Who's alive?" Dom asked, quickly shutting the door and putting away his gun.

"The Smiths and their wee children."

"What? What about Miss Mary?" Millie grabbed the paper and scanned the print.

"I had me a visitor, a fancy-dressed dandy by the name of Professor O.J. Goldrick," Tit Bit said breathlessly. "He got all puffed up, said he wrote about the flood, waved this newspaper at me like a fan. Told me all about it as he strutted about. He mentioned a family named Smith had miraculously survived. Poor lad must've thought me mad. I grabbed his paper and left." She giggled. "I ran out just as his britches hit the floor."

Millie scanned the article, reading bits of it aloud. "Great Flood in Denver. SEVERAL LIVES LOST!…Thursday night, the 19th…women wading waist deep in ice-cold water with children in their arms…J. M. Veasey was carried off in his house which, strange to say, traveled a mile or more right side up…eleven persons have been drowned… There were no prisoners in the City Hall Jail, so of course none were lost…" Millie stopped to breathe and swallowed hard. If they hadn't freed Dom, he'd have drowned.

"What about the Smiths?" Dom pressed, trying to read over Millie's shoulder.

"One minute. Here it is." She read, "'A Negro named Smith along with his wife and five children were carried away, but through the heroic management and cool courage of Mrs. Smith, the entire family were saved. All honor to the brave hearted woman!'" She scanned further down the page. "Nothing about Miss Mary." Millie jumped to her feet and rushed to the door. "I've got to find them and find out what happened to her." She jerked the door open and froze.

Jake and Samuel crept toward her.

"Slaver try an take my Sammy," Jake said, his eyes wide, his voice shrill. "We gotta hide."

THIRTY-FOUR

May 26, 1864
Escape from Denver City

After hearing Jake's story, Millie, Jake, Samuel, and Buttercup headed out to find the Smiths, leaving Dom to make his way out of town alone. Millie hated to leave Dom, but she knew he'd blend into the night-life easier without her. Plus, she had to find out if Mary was alive and safe. Unfortunately, a lady walking though Denver City with a black man and child—not to mention a goat—was far from inconspicuous. She wasn't surprised when Marshal Hunt strode toward them.

"Little lady, I thought you'd left town." Marshal Hunt eyed Jake and Samuel. "You do keep interesting company. Who's the boy and where are you going?"

"Marshal Hunt, what a pleasure, sir." Millie had prepared for this encounter and answered smoothly. "Of course, I didn't leave town. I've been busy helping my fellow townsmen recover from this awful flood. Right now, I'm helping this gentleman, Mr. Jake, find his friends, the Smiths. Today's *Weekly Commonwealth* reported the family had miraculously survived." Batting her eyes innocently, she asked, "Do you happen to know where they are?"

He scowled. "Where have you and your husband been hiding, little lady?"

"Marshal Hunt, as I have said before, my husband did not kill Widow Ferris. By accusing him you have let a killer run free." Lifting her eyebrows, she added coldly, "Unless you can tell us where to find the Smith family, we'll be on our way."

"I can take you." He turned and waved them along. "What about the boy?"

"The boy?" Belatedly she realized Marshal Hunt was referring to Samuel. "This is Samuel, he's Mr. Jake's son."

"His son?" The lawman shook his head, his expression a mixture of understanding and pity.

They reached a cabin, and when Millie spotted Mary, she rushed forward falling to her knees beside her friend. Even under Marshal Hunt's watchful gaze, she couldn't pretend not to know Mary nor hide her joy.

After their tearful reunion, Mary described her miraculous survival, although a wracking cough often interrupted her tale. Mary and the Smith family had been swept into Cherry Creek along with the cabin, but as the roughly-built building tipped and began coming apart, Mrs. Smith urged all to climb onto the roof. Fortunately, it was a log roof, not sod. It separated from the walls and remained in one piece as the current tossed and churned, carrying them far downstream.

"Why you here?" Mary asked Jake, her body shuddering with a new bout of coughing.

"Jake and Samuel are here because someone in Idaho Springs tried to kidnap the boy." Millie glanced at Marshal Hunt. The lawman stood nearby, listening. "I'm sure it was Widow Ferris' killer."

"Why would Widow Ferris' killer try to kidnap the boy?" Marshal Hunt wanted to know.

Millie had been asking the same question and had no answer, but she was sure the two events were related. Maybe the lawman would see a connection if he heard Samuel's story. "Samuel, please tell Marshal Hunt and Miss Mary what happened to you."

"Yes 'um," the boy mumbled. Trembling, he again described being grabbed from behind as he walked toward the Beebee House. A man with a strong Southern accent had stuffed a croker sack over his head and slapped a hand over his mouth. He'd carried the boy out of Idaho Springs and up Russel Gulch.

The whites of Samuel's eyes glistened as he described how his captor had cursed while hauling him away. Too frightened to even struggle, Samuel stood passively when his kidnapper stopped to bind his wrists, but when the Southerner explained how he would sell the boy in Texas, Samuel knew he had to escape. He was terrified as his captor lifted him onto a horse, but when he felt the man's hands release him, Samuel slid off the opposite side of the horse, stumbled to his feet and ran, ripping the croker sack off his head. "I run and run, never stop." He'd stumbled breathlessly into the blacksmith shop, his hands still bound in front of him.

Marshal Hunt scratched his head. "You say Sheriff Reynolds formed a posse but found no one?"

"Yes 'um," Jake said.

Millie added that Blacksmith Shumate had sent Jake and Samuel to Denver City, fearing for the boy's safety. He'd told them to find his abolitionist friend, Silas Soule.

Jake decided to find Mary instead.

"This is highly irregular," said Marshal Hunt as he turned toward the door. "I'll look into it." He stopped and glared at Millie. "Little lady, don't leave town."

After he'd gone, Millie waited several long heartbeats before whispering, "I'm to meet Dom at the livery east of town where we have a horse. Samuel can you and the Smith children look around outside and make sure Marshal Hunt's gone. I don't want to lead him to Dom."

"You ain't go alone," Mary said. "We's coming with you."

"Miss Mary, I don't think—"

"We all come," Jake interrupted. "Ain't safe here."

"But Miss Mary is sick. She couldn't possibly travel. Jake, you and Samuel can—"

"We come," Mary insisted, hacking out each word.

Millie sighed. She'd planned to take Dom to Sarah Ouellette's farm. Sarah and her husband had brought Millie across the Great Plains in their covered wagon and had homesteaded on a potato farm some thirty-five miles southeast of Denver City. Sarah and her husband were good people, but Millie doubted they'd welcome an extended visit from a fugitive, contraband, and several more mouths to feed.

THIRTY-FIVE

May 27, 1864
Lost

It was well after midnight by the time they finally met up with Dom and headed out of town. Although the night was relatively warm, Millie worried about Mary. They'd had to help her walk to the livery, and every time she coughed, it wracked her whole body. Now, as a partial moon illuminated a muddy trail heading East, Mary rode slumped over on the horse, Dom holding onto her from one side and Jake on the other.

"How we find this place, Miss Millie?" Jake sounded as concerned as Millie felt.

"My friend said her farm was along a creek. Box Creek, or maybe Box Elder Creek. She said to get to Denver City, they follow the creek downstream until they hit a freighter's road to Denver City. We'll do that, just backwards."

"But we don't know which freighter road and which river." Dom had objected to Millie's plan from the start. "Who knows how many creeks there are out here, Red. We should just head back to Idaho Springs."

"We've already been through this, Dom. It's not safe for you in Idaho Springs. We need to—"

"When Buttercup start eatin' horsey tails?" interrupted Samuel. "She like this one."

Millie huffed out a not so silent curse and brought Buttercup up beside her. In silence, they trudged through puddles and ankle-deep mud until the sun began peaking over the Eastern Plains.

"We've got to get off this road, Millie. From the look of the wheel ruts, freighters pass by here often. They'll be coming as soon as the sun comes up." Dom added quietly, "Miss Mary's breathing is bad. She needs to rest."

Millie glanced back. Her friend lay still, her eyes closed, her color gray. Bringing her had been a mistake, but it was too late now. "There's a line of bushes up there. I'm hoping they line a creek."

"Yous Box Creek?" Jake asked.

"I'm not sure. Maybe. I think I see a trail heading upstream."

"Then we take it," Dom insisted.

The bushes did line a small creek—Millie prayed it was Sarah's stream. She led Buttercup and the horse off the rutted road and along a narrow path beside the tiny stream. Mary groaned and would have toppled off if Dom and Jake hadn't held her.

The trail became little more than a deer track, so narrow thistles, briers, and sandburs caught in Millie's skirt, making it difficult to walk. The further they got from the freighter road, the rougher the trail became. After an hour, Millie was certain they were lost.

"See those trees up ahead," Dom's voice broke the silence. "We'll make camp there." Millie nodded, too weary to look up. In the early dawn, a meadowlark called out, answered by another, and a bee buzzed near her face. Exhausted, she rounded a corner, stumbling when Dom whispered, "Millie stop!"

She looked up to see an Indian camp with eight or nine lodges nestled amongst the cottonwood grove. They were close enough to see the faces of the women working near the river. "Oh Lor'!"

"Turn the horse around," Dom whispered. "Let's get out of here."

Bushes on either side of the trail made turning the horse impossible so Millie jerked on its halter, getting it to back up. Two, three, four steps. No one in the camp set off an alarm, but suddenly Buttercup let out a loud bleat and bounded forward. Millie grabbed for the goat, but Buttercup was too quick. Jumping over a fallen branch, the little goat rushed headlong through the green, swaying grass, bleating at the top of her little lungs.

The horse sidestepped nervously, and Mary began sliding off. Dom grabbed her, but she slid down, her weight knocking Dom off balance. Together they tumbled to the ground.

Torn between helping Dom and going after Buttercup, Millie froze when two creatures charged from the Indian encampment, bounding through deep grass as they headed toward Buttercup.

"Buttercup!" Millie cried, pulling out her gun.

"No, Misah Millie!" Jake knocked her arm down just as she pulled the trigger. Her ball ripped a hole in the grass and the echo of the blast pierced the quiet morning air.

"Ahyee!!!" A skinny Indian boy rushed around a teepee, jerked out a thigh-length bowie knife, and ran toward them.

Millie cried out as the animals attacked Buttercup, knocking her to the ground. Screams erupted from the village and four or five braves dashed out, howling in rage, carrying rifles, bows, and knives. From behind, Millie heard the beat of horses' hooves and turned to find two braves astride mustang ponies, galloping toward them, tomahawks and guns raised.

"Oh Lor'!" Millie rushed to Dom. He was struggling out from under Mary's inert body, trying not to hurt her. Millie bent over and grabbed Mary's arm, pulling her off

Dom. She stopped moving when the cries of the Indians went eerily silent.

"Miss Millie?"

Turning, Millie looked up. The skinny Indian boy dropped his ugly bowie knife and flung himself at her. "Miss Millie!"

"H-hosa?" The little boy had grown taller, and there were yellow and red circles painted around his eyes. "Little Hosa, are you wearing war paint?"

"No war. Celebration." Hosa pressed his face into her and smeared the colored paint on her dress.

"Niibeeseitit Wox?" said a deep voice.

"Mr. Woonbisiseet?" Millie swallowed. Hosa's father stood in front of her, his feathered tomahawk raised, his face painted. Hanging from his belt was a horrible object. "Is that a scalp?"

He lowered the weapon and fingered the scalp's black hair. "Creek person."

"Woonbisiseet you scoundrel," Dom scrambled to his feet and enveloped his friend in a bear hug. "It is good to see you."

Nanny and Nanko darted through the men's legs and charged Millie, skidding to a stop and prancing excitedly around her. Buttercup butted Woonbisiseet and wrapped her tongue around a leather fringe on his legging. She bit down, jerked her head, and ripped it free.

The fierce-looking Indian shook his head and turned his attention to Mary. In his deep voice, Woonbisiseet spoke several sharp commands. Hosa quickly snapped his fingers, and Nanny and Nanko shot to his side, sitting down like well-trained dogs. Two men stepped forward, lifted Mary from the ground, and carried her toward the encampment.

"She need medicine man," Woonbisiseet said, spinning around. "Come."

THIRTY-SIX

May 29, 1864
Lawyer the Medicine Man

Millie's first two days living in Woonbisiseet's village were filled with anguish. Mary got progressively worse as a raging fever left her skin hot to the touch, and her putrid throat swelled until she could barely swallow. Millie did what she could, applying wet rags—previously one of her petticoats—to Mary's face and chest, but even after the fever broke, her friend's throat and breathing only got worse. Unable to get food or drink into her, Millie finally gave in and allowed Lawyer the medicine man into the teepee.

"He's an Indian doctor," Dom insisted. "He can help."

"Medicine man bring strong medicine." Hosa snapped his fingers, and Nanny rose and moved out of the medicine man's way.

Millie watched nervously as Lawyer mumbled and shook his head, blowing smoke into Mary's face. The smoke masked the smell of unwashed bodies and sickness, but it made Millie cough. Mary didn't react at all. Finally, Lawyer rose, said something to Dom and hobbled out.

"W-what'd he say?" Millie asked. She knelt beside Mary and grasped her withered hand. Jake didn't move from where he stood. He looked too stricken for words.

"He's going to get something," Dom said. "He'll be back."

Hosa slipped out and returned with odd-shaped bowls made from wood knots. He handed them to Millie, Dom, and Jake. "Eat." In the bowl, chunks of unknown meat, fat, and vegetables floated in a steamy liquid.

Millie wasn't hungry but she ate, knowing if she didn't Dom would pester her until she finished the bowl. She left a bit of broth on the bottom, and after it cooled, she dribbled it into Mary's mouth. Most of the greasy liquid trickled down Mary's chin, but Millie hoped a little made it past her inflamed throat.

Lawyer returned and reluctantly Millie moved to stand beside Dom and Jake. The medicine man sat at Mary's head and removed a flat board from an ornately beaded bag. He balanced the board in his lap and sprinkled several sharp sandburs onto it. Warily Millie watched, unaware of any medicinal value in sandburs. Her confusion deepened when Lawyer removed an awl and poked a hole in each sandbur.

The medicine man chanted as he worked, stringing the sandburs onto a strip of sinew, producing what looked like a sandbur necklace. He pointed at Hosa and spoke, causing the boy to hurry outside followed by Nanny and Nanko.

"Do you think he's going to burn it?" Millie asked as Lawyer took his sandbur necklace and wrapped it around a stick.

"Millie, honey, I know this is hard, but you have to trust him." Dom wrapped his arm around her.

Hosa returned, a lump of grease in his hand. He scraped the substance onto Lawyer's board, and the medicine man rubbed his stick and sandbur necklace through the grease until it covered all the sandburs. Setting the board aside, the old man rose to his knees, hovering like an evil spirit above Mary.

Millie's heart raced. "No!" She stepped forward but was

unable to reach Mary or Lawyer because Dom kept her by his side. "I don't want his help. Tell him to leave."

The old man scowled at Millie and barked something at Dom.

"Millie, we have to trust him." Dom pulled her tighter against him, backing away as two young men entered the teepee, one kneeling at Mary's head, the other at her side.

Millie watched in horror as Lawyer bent over Mary and forced her mouth open. "No!" she screamed as one brave tilted Mary's head back while the other gripped Mary's shoulders.

Lawyer lifted his sandbur stick and lowered it into Mary's mouth.

"No!" Millie struggled against Dom's hold. "Jake stop him. He's killing her!"

Jake looked terrified, but he didn't move to interfere. "Mistah Lawyer help Mary," He whispered. "Else ma Mary die."

Millie shuddered as Lawyer forced the sandbur stick down Mary's inflamed throat. Tears blurred Millie's vision as Mary gagged and convulsed. Millie's knees turned weak, and she sank against Dom as Lawyer rubbed the sandburs up and down, pulling mucus and bloody secretions out as he withdrew the stick.

The medicine man leaned over Mary, listened, grunted, and used Millie's wet rags to wipe the awful secretions from Mary's face. He gave Millie a disgusted look as he rose and walked out followed by the two braves.

Dom released Millie and she sank to her knees and crawled to Mary. She took her friend's hand and sobbed quietly as she waited for Mary to die.

Hours passed. Dom lit a fire, and the flames illuminated Mary's still form and Jake's tortured profile. "She's breathing better," Dom said quietly. "Try giving her some water."

Millie looked down and realized Dom was right. Overcome, she dribbled water into Mary's mouth, and her friend weakly swallowed.

Jake gasped and moaned. When Millie sat back, he moved forward, his hands shaking as he dribbled more water into Mary's mouth. "She gonna live. She gonna live," he mumbled over and over again.

Through the long night and following day, Mary weakly swallowed tiny spoonfuls of warm broth. With each passing hour, her breathing smoothed and her color improved.

Mary would live. The medicine man had saved her life.

Several days later, while washing her face and hands in the creek, Mollie spotted Lawyer upstream, grinding dried leaves into a powder. Hesitantly she approached him. "Thank you," as she stumbled over the Arapaho word, "hahou." She removed a pocket watch from her apron pocket. "Thank you, for saving Mary's life." The silver pocket watch was the only possession she had from the family she'd never known. Bending down, she placed it in front of the old man.

Lawyer picked up the gift, grinned, and tied it around his neck with a leather thong.

*****

"The first rule with regard to paying a visit is: Never accept a general invitation." Dom groaned, and Millie's small audience looked confused.

"Why not 'cept a invitation." Samuel asked.

"Why doesn't one accept an invitation," Millie corrected automatically. Samuel, Hosa, and Jake obediently repeated the sentence. With Mary on the mend, Millie had begun filling their free time by resuming her lessons with Samuel and Jake. Hosa had joined them and proved to be an apt student, but all three struggled to understand *The Ladies Book of Etiquette*.

"You're confusing the hell out of them, Red." Dom rose and stretched. "I speak English, and even I don't understand. Let's leave poor Miss Mary to rest and go for a walk."

"I stay," Jake said, defiantly glaring at Mary. She scowled back at him.

"We walk wid you," said Hosa slowly.

"We will walk with you," Millie corrected.

They stepped outside, and Millie heard Jake ask, "When we gonna jump da broom?"

"Jump the broom. Boy, I hit yous with a broom," Mary replied hotly.

Dom laughed and kissed Millie. "Poor Miss Mary doesn't have a chance!"

"No, but Jake's got his work cut out for him. Mary's scared of getting hurt again." She took Dom's hand, and they walked through the teepees. "Let's follow the trail upstream." Last night, Woonbisiseet had mentioned there were white settlers a couple miles upstream. Millie hoped it might be Sarah Ouellette's farm.

They walked for several hours, discussing everything they knew about Widow Ferris' murder, how Dom had been set up, and the attempted abduction of Samuel. They argued about one suspect after another, but none of them made sense. They had to be missing something.

Across from them, Samuel and Hosa galloped Hosa's horse along the river, chased by Nanny and Nanko. Suddenly the boys leapt off the moving animal and wrestled each other to the ground. Samuel stole Hosa's bow and arrows and darted away. The two boys had become fast friends, and Millie found that together, they were more mischievous than Nanny and Nanko.

Hosa chased after Samuel and tackled him, taking back his bow and arrows as Samuel rolled into the stream. Hosa let out a victorious cry, took aim, and shot a padded arrow at Buttercup. Millie knew she should reprimand the boy, but she and Dom laughed when Buttercup fainted and disappeared into the soft grass.

Hosa slipped a second arrow into the bow, aimed at Nanny, but the boy suddenly froze and sniffed the air. Fast as a jackrabbit, he charged up the embankment. Near the top, he dropped to his stomach and squirmed forward. Nanny and Nanko bounded after him, dropping to their bellies and wiggling their little tails as they crawled to his side.

"Something's wrong," Dom said. He splashed across the stream and followed Hosa. Millie followed, soaking the hem of her skirt in the water. Hurrying up the hill, she felt a bit ridiculous as she crawled forward to peek over the embankment. The landscape was unusually green from the heavy spring rains, and the rolling hills made a picturesque view, but across from them, heavy smoke curled up from a burning cabin, blackening the deep blue sky.

Oh Lor'! Was that Sarah Ouellette's potato farm?

THIRTY-SEVEN

June 11, 1864

Hungate Massacre

D om rose up and hurried down the hill, his six-shooter in his hand. "They might still be here," Millie whispered loudly. "We need to go warn Woonbisiseet! Boys, you..." The boys dashed after Dom. Cursing them all, Millie pulled out her six-shooter and scrambled after them. When she finally caught up, she saw why they'd moved forward.

A man lay sprawled in the green grass, his body horribly mutilated, his scalp ripped off.

Millie gagged and looked away, but she'd seen enough to know the man was too heavy and large to be Sarah's husband. Again, Hosa lifted his head and sniffed as he cautiously turned in a slow circle. His expression made the hairs on the back of Millie's neck rise.

"See anything?" Samuel asked, his wide eyes glued on the mutilated body.

Dom ignored them all and started jogging in the direction of the smoke. The boys hurried after him. Millie took a final look at the dead man, said a silent prayer, and followed them. Over the next rise, she approached the smoldering cabin, edging around an outhouse to find the boys and Dom standing over another body.

Samuel stared at a tiny form, turned, and was sick. Millie looked around and felt her stomach roil. Closer to the cabin lay the bodies of a woman and another small child. The woman had been stabbed, scalped, and abused. The children—a little girl and an infant—had their throats cut so brutally their heads were nearly severed from their bodies.

"Oh Lor'!" Millie's eyes stung from the smoke. "Dom, I—" Hosa darted away, whistling to his mustang and mounting the horse without slowing his pace. He lay low on the animal's neck and galloped toward the river, Nanny and Nanko following as best they could.

"We need to leave too," Dom said quietly. "Come on."

Hosa could have only beat them back by a half hour, yet when they reached the Arapaho camp, all the teepees were down. Mary stood tottering near a cottonwood while Jake held her steady. Within five minutes, everything was packed onto travois and the entire camp except Hosa, Woonbisiseet, and Sooxei followed Lawyer out onto the plains.

"Soldiers come," Woonbisiseet said, scowling. "They kill bad Indians." He used gestures to punctuate his words. "Woonbisiseet family not bad, but soldiers kill good Indians too. We go." He looked from Dom to Millie. "You come?"

"No," Millie shook her head, but doubts assailed her. "We'll find my friend. Thank you for all your kindness."

Woonbisiseet nodded, Sooxei gave Millie a hug, and the two turned and left.

"You come?" Hosa asked Samuel.

"No," Samuel said, obviously unhappy. "I stay with Pa. And Misah Mary." Hosa nodded, climbed onto his mustang, and caught Nanny and Nanko as Samuel tossed them to him. Without another word, he turned and followed his mother and father. Millie wondered if she'd ever see them again. Where could they go to be safe from the soldiers?

"What you find that make them leave?" Mary asked. "That Hosa arrive, say something, and the whole camp go crazy."

"We found a family, massacred. Scalped and mutilated. Even the baby." Dom shook his head, helping Mary onto the horse.

"Woonbisiseet is right," Millie said. "When Governor Evans hears about that family, he'll want revenge. He won't care which Indian tribe killed them."

"None of them will." Dom shook his head. "Byers, Evans, and Chivington. They've all been waiting for an excuse to exterminate all Indians. The killing of a whole family will fuel the settlers' hatred." He looked at Millie. "It'll also bring them here."

"Then we best get going." She turned and led the way back upstream, hoping Sarah's farm was well beyond the massacre site. But even if this was the right stream and they found Sarah, would her farm be a safe hiding place? Soldiers would soon swarm across the entire Eastern Plains. Like Woonbisiseet's family, there might be no place safe for Dom to hide. Maybe they should have stayed with the Arapaho.

THIRTY-EIGHT

June 11, 1864

Sarah Ouellette

The sun turned the clouds a deep red as it dropped behind the mountains. Footsore and tired, Millie rounded a bend in the stream, looking for a camping spot, but stopped when she spotted a petite woman hanging clothes on a clothesline. A dog-sized goat grazed nearby. Buttercup bleated and dashed forward. Millie picked up her skirts and followed, calling out a greeting.

Sarah spun around, her face alarmed, and Millie stumbled to a stop. Sarah had been a small thing—a slight girl with a stick figure. Now that figure looked like a pear on legs, her huge belly extending out so far it dwarfed the rest of her. "Miss Sarah, what happened?"

"Miss Millie!" Sarah squealed and waddled forward, looking like an overweight duck. "You got ma letter!"

Millie rushed to greet her, afraid Sarah's distended belly would cause her to tip over. Buttercup galloped to her former mistress, bleating excitedly.

"Buttercup!" Unsteadily, Sarah bent over and gave Buttercup a strangling hug. Millie wrapped her arms around Sarah's thick waist to stop a tumble, and after greeting the little goat, Sarah awkwardly hugged Millie.

"Miss Sarah, you're…ah, going to have a baby." Millie

didn't dare hug her friend too tightly. Even a gentle squeeze might cause the baby to pop out.

"I knowed you'd come, Miss Millie." Sarah's strong east Kentucky accent thickened with emotion. "I just knowed it. Mr. O said no, but I knowed. You come ta do the birthin'."

"Birthing?" Millie released Sarah with enough force that the girl stumbled backward. "Miss Sarah, I don't know the first thing about birthing babies."

"But you knowed cookin' and readin'." Sarah's expression became alarmed. "Ain't no grannies out here ta help. I need you ta birth ma babe."

"I'm sure Millie will do everything she can." Dom wrapped his arm around Millie and smiled. "It's a pleasure to meet you, Mrs. Ouellette. Millie's told me so much about you."

Sarah looked Dom up and down and whistled. "You ain't writ he was as big as a bear. Nice ta meet you, Mr. D." She bobbed her head. "Tham you servants?"

"These are my friends, Miss Sarah. I'd like to introduce you to Miss Mary, Mr. Jake, and Jake's son, Samuel."

"His boy? But tha boy's white."

"I knows about birthing babes," Mary said, climbing unsteadily from the horse. Jake was immediately at her side, and she reluctantly took his arm. "I birth lots of babes in New York."

"You can help?" Sarah's smile brightened and Samuel's skin color appeared forgotten. "Thank goodness. Come." She turned and waddled toward her cabin. Beside her, Buttercup and the other goat excitedly butted each other. "This is ma house. Ain't much, but Mr. O and I am happy. Just a bit afeard of the birthin'."

"You're not afraid of the Indians?" Millie asked.

"What them Injuns done now?" Sarah folded her arms and rested them on her belly.

"They killed your neighbors." Millie pointed. "Several miles downstream."

"Ma neighbors? Mean that Hungate family?"

Millie explained what they'd found, and Sarah shook her head. "That ain't right. Poor Hungate family only been there three, maybe four months. Mr. Hungate work for that mean Van Wormer man. He fightin' with Injuns, stealin' their ponies, and treatin' em bad."

"The Indians don't bother you?" Dom asked.

"Nah. They come beggin' eats. We give 'em taters." Sarah smiled. "Once, I churn ma butter and a buck come visit. That buck don't know butter and wants et. I made 'im a butter ball and put et in cabbage, but the buck don't know cabbage neither. He take ma butter ball and wrap et inside his buffalo robe." She shook her head and laughed merrily. "Bet he were confused when he look and ma butter ball were nothin' but a spot on his robe."

Instead of taking them into her tiny cabin, Sarah led them to her barn and corral. Buttercup charged ahead; the other goat forgotten at the sight of the he-goat. Millie hurried to separate Buttercup and the male goat, glad there was a fence between the two. Sarah stepped into the pen and proudly introduced each goat, including the six babies, belatedly introducing her husband who'd joined them.

Dom shook Mr. Ouellette's hand. "This here's a mighty fine setup you have."

"We're happy," said Mr. Ouellette. "Dirt's rich, leastwise near the river. Enough water and cottonwoods to keep the wind at bay. Only problem is those blasted goats. They breed like rabbits." He gestured toward the goats, and one of the young ones looked up, hopped on stiff legs, and fell over in a dead faint. He scoffed and shook his head. "She won't even let me roast one."

"Now, now, Mr. O," Sarah said, patting her husband.

"You knows how I feel about ma goats. How about some antelope stew 'stead?"

They sat outside—there were too many of them to fit inside the cabin—and enjoyed Sarah's stew. Millie had taught the girl to cook when they crossed the plains, and it appeared her lessons had been well learned. After supper, Dom, Jake, and Mr. Ouellette settled back with glasses of whiskey. Millie enjoyed a cup of hot tea as she explained about Widow Ferris' murder, the other murder suspects, and Dom's jailbreak. As laughter died over Millie's description of Dom dressed as a woman, everyone piped in with their thoughts about the murder.

"I think it Sheriff Reynolds," Jake said. "He sound most guilty."

"No way Sheriff Reynolds killed her," Dom argued. "It's got to be Mr. Turck."

"Don't know," said Mr. Ouellette. "From the sounds of it, that queer shopkeeper who quotes Shakespeare could be the killer."

"I think little Sammy's kidnappin' got somethin' ta do with tha murder," Sarah said thoughtfully. Millie thought Sarah was right, but after noting everything about the attempted abduction in her daybook, she still couldn't imagine how.

*****

Mounted men rode toward Mr. Ouellette's potato field two days later. As they'd planned, Jake—who was on watch that afternoon—whistled a warning and Millie, Mary, Dom, and Samuel disappeared into the root cellar. Heart racing, Millie waited to be discovered, hating the suspense as much as the dark, dank underground room. Bits of conversation drifted through the cracks in the trapdoor, and Millie sucked in a deep breath when she heard Marshal Hunt's distinctive Texas drawl.

Marshal Hunt questioned Mr. Ouellette about the Hungate family, recommending he and Mrs. Ouellette take refuge in Denver until the baby was born. Millie felt sweat trickle down her back as the two men argued, but finally Marshal Hunt thanked Mr. Ouellette and wished Sarah a safe confinement.

"These folks got fainting goats, just like Mrs. D." Of all the people Millie hadn't wanted to hear, Mr. Turck was at the top of her list. What was the man doing with Marshal Hunt? "Maybe these folks know where the woman-killer's hiding," Turck snarled.

Millie felt Dom tense. He released her hand and despite the darkness, she knew he'd pulled out his six-shooter. She held her breath as Mr. Ouellette asked who Mrs. D was, but Mr. Turck spoke over him. "I think the killer's here, Marshal Hunt. We should search this place."

The lawman gave the order and Millie pulled out her own six-shooter, her hand shaking. Mr. Turck's loud voice filtered into their tense silence. "They ain't in the cabin nor the barn, but I bet there's a root cellar or Indian hidey-hole somewhere."

"In back," Sarah said breathlessly. She groaned loudly and cried, "Mr. O! I think ma babe want out."

"Do you have a doctor with you?" Mr. Ouellette asked, sounding alarmed.

Sarah groaned again and Millie heard Marshal Hunt stutter. "N-no. It's just me and my military guard."

"Then search the place another day," Mr. Ouellette hollered. "We're busy."

"Mount up," shouted Marshal Hunt. "On the double. Good luck sir, ma'am."

The ground shook with pounding hoofbeats. In the silence that followed, Millie swallowed hard and said, "I-I best go check on Miss Sarah."

Dom removed the bar he'd installed. Because of the Indian threat, he'd put locking slats both inside and outside the root cellar. He pushed open the door, and Millie climbed out just as Sarah rounded the corner, a huge grin on her face.

"Birthin' sure scare 'em soldiers off."

*****

Weeks passed and despite Millie's worries, the military men twice more stopped by the homestead, but they never searched the place. Feeling a bit more secure, Dom built them a tiny sod house near the river, giving them a bit of privacy, although Millie hated the mud dripping through the roof every time it rained.

Mary—adamantly refusing Jake's assistance—took up residence in the barn with the goats and used her magic on Sarah's garden. Jake and Samuel moved into the blacksmith hut he'd built. The hut was filled with blackened tools scavenged from the Hungate homestead.

They all settled into a routine, but Millie couldn't relax. Her worries about Dom were soon overshadowed by Sarah's extended belly. It grew larger until the poor girl looked like she'd swallowed a watermelon.

Sweat from the morning heat and humidity poured off Millie as she prepared their afternoon supper, a Mock Turtle soup. Dom's booming yell caused her to spill half the jar of salt into the soup. "Indians," he cried, running down from their watch point. Millie grabbed Sarah's hand and turned her toward the root cellar as a line of Indians formed on the hill overlooking the crops, their tomahawks, rifles, and knives held high.

A savage cry split the air. Millie hurried her waddling friend around the cabin, catching sight of Buttercup as she and several of the goats fainted. Mary and Samuel joined them, and Jake jerked open the heavy trapdoor and helped Sarah climb down. Millie hesitated. How could she climb down to safety without Dom?

Dom and Mr. O sprinted around the cabin. The Indians were halfway across the potato field, so close Millie could see the red, yellow, and black paint covering their faces. The closest brave had red circling his eyes and a black hand covering his mouth. Even his horse's eyes were circled with paint.

"Go," Dom hollered, pushing Millie down the earthen stairs.

She stumbled into the dark room and shuddered as the heavy wooden door closed with a muffled thud. Streaks of light cut through the cracks between the door slats, but when Dom slammed the bar into its slot, Millie felt like she was locked in a coffin. Taking several deep breaths, she tried to calm her racing heart.

"C-can, can them get in here?" asked Sarah.

"We're safe," Mr. Ouellette said. "Unless they burn us out." He lit a candle and carried it to the back of the root cellar, pushing aside a wooden board. "If we smell smoke, we'll have to go out and fight. That's why I built and stocked this hidey-hole." Beneath the board, he removed two rifles, shot, powder, and balls.

Despite her beating heart and sweaty palms, Millie started—they'd never thought to search Widow Ferris' root cellar. The thought disappeared when the Indians' wild war cry suddenly died. Sarah's eyes became as big as her belly. "They gonna burn ma house?"

"We'll build another one, if they do." Mr. O handed Jake a rifle. "But if they destroy my crops, I don't know what we'll do."

"Ma goats!" Sarah cried. The candlelight flickered as she cried, "Ma poor, poor goats."

"Buttercup," Millie whispered.

They waited several tense minutes until Dom quietly crawled up the steps and put his ear to a crack. "I don't hear them." Dom frowned. "Something strange is going on."

Sarah moaned, just as she had with the soldiers. "Ma babe." She hugged her belly. "Ma babe comin'."

Millie turned and stared. "Wha-what do you mean?"

"Ma pains. The birthin' ones. They startin' for real."

"H-how? I mean." She swallowed and her voice sounded shrill. "They can't. Not now."

"You just fine," Mary said calmly, stepping to the girl's side. "Birthin' take time. Sometimes a day, maybe two." Mary took Sarah's hand.

"The pains ain't bad. I—"

"The baby has to wait," said Dom. "Something's going on. I'm going to take a look." He quietly removed the wooden slat and pushed up on the door, peering outside, his six-shooter drawn. "I don't see them."

"Dom. Be careful!" Millie was so scared she couldn't decide which terrified her more: the savages, Sarah's impending travail, the closed-in root cellar, or Dom sticking his head out where it could be scalped.

"I think they're gone." Dom lifted the door higher and climbed out. "Mr. O, close the door and replace the wooden bar."

"No!" Millie clambered up beside Dom. No way was she staying underground with a woman in travail.

"I'm coming too," said Mr. O. He and Jake climbed out.

"Me too!"

"You're having a baby!" Mr. O said. "Miss Mary, you stay here. Take care of her."

"Ma goats are out there!"

"Sarah, I…"

Millie ignored them and followed Dom, creeping along the side of Sarah's cabin, unnerved by the utter quiet.

Had the Indians really left, or were they waiting to ambush them? At the edge of the cabin, Millie peeked around Dom's shoulder and saw the goat pen, barn, and Mr. Ouellette's fields.

Buttercup stood with her head through the fence, nuzzling the he-goat. Everything looked fine. Millie let out a long, slow breath then gasped. The Indian mustangs stood clustered in the shade of the cottonwood grove.

The savages were nowhere in sight.

Millie yelped and bumped into Dom when a chilling war whoop split the silence. Braves charged into view, whooping and hollering, looking savage and unearthly. They wore scalp locks and eagle feathers in their hair and bear claw necklaces around their necks. Every goat in the pen tumbled over in a dead faint. Buttercup fainted, almost strangling herself as her limp head momentarily got caught in the fence.

Millie might have followed the goat's example, but the noise died, replaced by hoots of mirth. The Indians circled the goat pen, slapped their thighs, and pointed. Millie couldn't believe it. These were the scariest savages she'd ever seen, but their laughter transformed them into something more human, more comfortable. One man dropped his tomahawk. A rifle tumbled to the ground followed by its owner, tears smearing his war paint.

"They like ma goats," Sarah whispered.

The goats slowly woke up, their bulging eyes fixed on their amused audience. Buttercup rose and sniffed at the man laughing on the ground, biting off one of his buckskin fringes. The leader—the man with the black hand painted over his face—signaled and the laughter quieted.

Like smoke, the warriors noiselessly withdrew.

The leader passed by them, close enough Millie could see his battle scars. He glanced their way, walking with the haughty arrogance of a man who granted favors but never asked for them. Tied around him was a tanned skin sash with what looked like a picket-pin on the end.

"Did you see the horse picket?" choked out Mr. Ouellette.

"They're Cheyenne Dog Soldiers," Dom said, awe in his voice. "That's his dog rope. Only the bravest warriors receive pickets."

"Pickets?" Millie had to swallow. Her mouth was so dry she could barely whisper. "Why wear a dog rope?"

"A brave will stake himself to the ground during a battle. To give the women and children time to escape. He'll die before he pulls the stake out. It's—"

Another wild cry interrupted him, and the braves charged the goat pen. Just like before, the goats hopped on stiff legs and tumbled over, several landing on top of each other. Not a single one remained standing. In the ringing laughter that followed, Millie heard Sarah groan. Turning, she found Sarah gripping the wall, her face scrunched in pain.

"Ma pains. They gettin' worse," she gasped. "Them Dog Soldiers got ta go." Sarah waddled past Millie and headed toward the laughing Cheyenne.

"Sarah," gasped Mr. Ouellette. He moved to follow but Dom grabbed his arm.

Surely these braves wouldn't harm a woman in travail. The thought passed through Millie's mind followed by an image of the Hungate children with their severed heads. Millie covered her mouth as Sarah waddled past the Indians, opened the goat pen, and wobbled inside. The goats rose from their faint and flocked to her, surrounding her like a living hoop skirt.

Sarah patted each floppy-eared head before turning to face the Indian leader. "You got childers?"

He tilted his painted face sideways, his dark eyes curious. "Papooses? Whippersnappers? Ankle biters?" His expression deepened, confused. Sarah pointed at her belly and then at the man. "You? Boy? Girl?"

The Indian's face brightened, and he pointed at himself. "Me." He held up two fingers. "Two boy."

Sarah lovingly selected one of the baby goats. She led it from the pen and approached the tall warrior. Millie held her breath. Sarah looked tiny and very fragile in front of his powerful frame. Awkwardly Sarah bent down and struggled as she picked up the goat. Swaying unsteadily, her body tensed as a birthing pain washed over her.

"For." She took several panting breaths. "For you. Boy. Gift." She lifted the little goat toward the large warrior.

His painted face split in a terrifying grin and he accepted Sarah's gift, but as he took the goat, Sarah's face turned as red as his war paint. She looked from the warrior to the ground at her feet. "Lawd all mighty!" A puddle of liquid spread from underneath her skirts.

The Indian stepped back with the baby goat clutched under one arm. He said something sharp and without another word, he and his warriors fled to their horses.

It appeared men from all cultures—even proud Cheyenne Dog Soldiers—wanted nothing to do with travail. Millie understood the sentiment. The braves vaulted onto their mounts, their leader protectively cradling his goat, and galloped away.

"Sarah," gasped Mr. Ouellette, running to his wife. "Y-you're the bravest woman there ever was."

"See Mr. O. Ma goats be good for somethin'."

"They saved our lives! And my crops." He helped her into their cabin and carefully laid her on their bed. "While you birth our baby, I'll enlarge the goat pen. Maybe make them a pasture." He kissed her perspiring head. "You can raise as many goats as you want. We'll sell them as peacemakers."

Sarah groaned loudly as a pain struck, and Mr. Ouel-

lette's face turned white. He backed away, looking as terrified as Millie felt. "I-I'll leave you ladies to it." He fled
outside.

"Men," Millie muttered, wishing she could follow him.

"Ma pains bad." Sarah clutched the bed frame. "Them
Injuns scare ma baby out." Her eyes widened. "Am I gonna
die?"

"Y-you'll be fine, Miss Sarah," Millie said, trying to
sound confident.

"You not worry none, Mrs. O." Mary rested a calming
hand on Sarah's arm. "Now, you and me got to take this
dress off. Miss Millie, boil water. I needs a knife, string, and
clean rags."

Relieved by Mary's calm direction, Millie set to work,
cringing every time Sarah cried out.

"Ma knife," Sarah shouted between the pains. "Where
ma knife?"

"This one?" Millie asked, taking the knife from the boil-
ing water.

"No. The big one." Sarah pointed and Millie pulled a
cleaver from a shelf. "For under ma bed. Ta cut ma pain."

Mary shrugged and Millie slipped the knife under the
bed. It couldn't do any harm. Several long hours later, Millie was drenched in sweat and gripping Sarah's hand, sure
her friend would soon die. Sarah's screams shook the cabin
during her pains, but the silence between them was worse.
Sarah suddenly shrieked, crushing Millie's hand.

"Push, Mrs. O. Push!" Mary yelled.

In awe, Millie watched a baby's head appear, followed
by a pink body and legs with tiny toes. Mary caught the
baby, calmly cut the cord, and handed the squalling infant
to Millie. "Clean him up. I care for Mrs. O."

"Miss Sarah," Millie said breathlessly. "You've got a son!"
Sarah's eyes were glazed but she smiled.

"Miss Sarah, we almost done," Mary explained calmly. "You got to push for me one more time."

Millie wiped the baby clean, amused by its hungry cries, and wrapped the newborn in a warm blanket. She turned to hand the baby to Sarah, but almost dropped the infant when Sarah screamed again.

"Push, Mrs. O. Push!" Mary no longer sounded calm. Millie's eyes widened as a second head appeared. Amazed, Millie watched a second baby slip out into the world.

"Miss Sarah," Mary said breathlessly, her hands shaking as she cut the cord. "You got twins."

When both babes were settled in their mother's arms, Millie went outside and found Mr. O, Dom, Jake, and Samuel pacing near the goat pen. They stopped and stared at Millie, looking both terrified and excited.

"Mr. O. I'm happy to say you have a son," Millie paused. "And a daughter."

"A son and a daughter? Like the goats?" His eyes rolled up and he fainted, knocking over Buttercup as he dropped.

THIRTY-NINE

September 28, 1864

Letter from Home

Jake it turned out, loved babies. Not only did he adore Sarah's twins, he was good with them. Better in fact than anyone else at the homestead. Millie had to hide her amusement whenever the twins fussed and instead of handing an infant to Mary, Sarah sought out Jake. Millie couldn't imagine how the sight of Jake cuddling and cooing the infants didn't soften Mary's resolve; it seemed to have the opposite effect. Every time she saw Jake ask Mary to "jump da broom" with him, her friend's refusals seemed more adamant.

Even Jake appeared to be losing hope. Today he carried his broom past Millie, his shoulders hunched, his face dejected. "Dat woman scared o' being hurt. I ain't sure she ever 'cept me." Buttercup meandered over and butted him in the leg, making him stop. The goat stretched out her neck and broke off several of the broom's straw bristles. Munching contentedly, she looked up at him. He shook his head and muttered, "Maybe I let you eat da broom."

He returned to his blacksmith shed and placed the broom on nails above the door—out of Buttercup's reach—and disappeared into the shady interior. Millie turned her attention back to her leg of pork and pease pudding, fearful he was right. Mary might never risk loving another man. Millie understood. She wasn't sure what she would do if anything happened to Dom. Kneeling down, she added wood to her fire, eyeing the bubbling pot. Lor' she missed her cookstove. And her cabin.

"Miss Millie." Sarah hurried over with a baby clasped in each arm. "Miss Millie, we needin' ta talk."

Millie rose, hearing the distress in her friend's voice. Sarah's eyes were wide and scared, her face pale. "What happened? Did someone follow you back from Denver?" Four days ago, Sarah, Jake, and the twins had accompanied Mr. O to Denver to sell his potatoes and her garden produce. They'd returned last night, and Millie hadn't yet gotten a chance to speak with them. "Are they still hunting for Dom?"

"I ain't sure, but…" She glanced around, handed Millie her son, and tugged on Millie's arm. "Come." She led Millie away from her cooking and down toward a private area near the river. "After I done ma shoppin', I got ma mail. You mostly tha one who writ me, but last year ma other friend writ." Glancing around suspiciously, she pulled a letter from her apron pocket. "This was thar." She held out an envelope addressed in flowing script to *Mrs. Ouellette, Denver City.* "But it ain't ta me. It's ta you!"

"Me?" Excitedly Millie took the envelope and fumbled with it and the infant, finally managing to pull out the sheet inside.

"I donno understand. No one knows ya here."

"I don't know how they knew, but hopefully this letter is a response to my note."

"Your note?" boomed Dom, stomping toward them with Buttercup following. "What in tarnation did you do now, Red?"

"I sent the matrons a letter," Millie said, too excited to be annoyed by Dom's blasted nickname. She handed the infant to Dom and unfolded the letter. "I asked them to search Widow Ferris' root cellar. I thought she might have a hidey-hole, like Mr. O's. Jake gave my letter to those freighters to mail. Remember the ones with the broken wheel who came by in early July."

Millie quickly glanced through Mrs. Beebee's letter. "They found it," she said excitedly. "They found Mrs. Gilson's tin of gold flakes beside a leather pouch hidden under one of the step slats."

"So who's the killer?" Dom asked, bouncing on his toes to keep the squirming infant quiet. "Did Sheriff Reynolds arrest him?"

"No." Millie's excitement faded as she read more carefully. "They say the pouch included a carte de visite of Sheriff Reynolds and his brothers, Blacksmith Shumate's picture, Old Shakespeare's flier, another newspaper clipping about the Egg Point killing, and two of Widow Ferris' sketches: Billy Batterson wearing an odd square hat and Brother Bunce beside Samuel." She looked at Dom and shook her head. "Nothing inside the pouch identified the killer."

"She say how she knows ta send ya letter here?" Sarah asked again.

Millie read the postscript after the signature. "Mrs. Beebee said they weren't sure we were here, but Mrs. Griswold is the postmistress and she got your letter. The one you sent asking me to help with the birthing. They guessed we might have come here, but they also left a letter for me at the Denver Post Office." She looked at Dom. "They're coming to Denver City on November 15 and bringing the pouch. They showed the contents to Sheriff Reynolds but refused to give any of it to him. They want me to look at the papers."

"Sheriff Reynolds has a good eye. If he didn't see anything, I'm not sure we will either, but we have to try." Dom shook his head. "Guess we plan a trip to Denver."

"I'll go to Denver City. You'll stay here. You're still a fugitive."

The infant began to mewl and made a noise that would have caused an adult to blush. Buttercup came over to investigate, sniffed at the bundle in Dom's arms, and fainted. Dom made a face and handed the child back to Millie. "He's yours." Stepping over the comatose goat, he waved a hand in front of his face. "We'll both go to Denver."

Millie rolled her eyes, got a whiff of the little boy, and gagged. She'd never known breastfeeding infants to smell, but since Jake introduced Sarah to his favorite treat—roasted locust dipped in honey—the babies' poop had become nasty.

Days passed but despite Millie's best efforts, Dom was adamant: he would go to Denver City with Millie and see for himself what was in the pouch. Worse, Mary decided to accompany them, and of course, Jake insisted he and Samuel would be coming. Mary objected to his plan and the fight that ensued was loud and way worse than Millie and Dom's squabble. After a week of listening to Mary and Jake, Millie was ready to break the broom over both their heads!

November 13 dawned cold and cloudy, but at least Jake and Mary were too busy to argue. While Jake was shoeing their horse, Millie noticed the poor animal's tail was so short it almost looked cropped. She turned to ask Dom if he had any idea how to make Buttercup stop chewing on the horse's tail when a yowl made her spin back around.

The glowing red horseshoe Jake had been hammering lay on the ground, and Jake was wildly ripping his shirt off. He threw the garment to the ground and splashed water on a spot on his chest. Millie sucked in a breath when he turned his back to them.

"My God!" Dom shook his head. "How can one man do that to another?"

"I don't know," Millie whispered. She had never seen Jake without a shirt, and now she understood why. His back was covered with a painful, web-like pattern of raised scars. "O Lor'! How many lashes did they give him for trying to escape?" She'd never seen anything like the scars on his back. Instead of healing, it looked like each whiplash had thickened and grown out from his back into lumpy, thick lines.

"Them Injuns come back?" Mary hurried to Millie's side carrying Sarah's daughter.

"N-no. It's...I've never seen scars like that."

"Wot?" Mary turned and sucked in her breath. "Dat man. He...he never say nothing." Tears welled in her eyes. "Here, take the babe. I got salve in me apron." Handing Millie the baby, Mary walked over. Jake spun around and warily watched her apply salve to his burn. She finished, and they eyed each other, neither saying a word.

Mary looked down at the dirt, digging into it with her big toe, and then finally looked back up at him. Scowling, she said, "Okay, I do it."

"Do what?" Jake asked suspiciously.

"Marry you."

"You marry me?"

"Yes. I marry you."

Jake let out a wild whoop and grabbed Mary, swinging her around until her feet lifted off the ground. Samuel, holding the horse's halter, grinned broadly as his father set Mary down, wrapped his arms around her, and gave her a kiss that made even Millie's toes curl.

"Lawd almighty!" Mary said when he lifted his head. Looking slightly dazed, she added, "They's childers watching."

Jake just bent down and kissed her again. He lifted his head and raised an eyebrow. "You not change your mind?"

"I say I marry you and I do," Mary huffed.

"I not trust you." He let go of her and reached above the door. Taking down the broom, he dropped it at their feet and took her hand. "Jump da broom wid me."

"No. I want me a church wedding. Front of a preacher."

Jake considered this for a moment and nodded. "We have a church wedding in Denver City, but we jump da broom now."

"We jump da broom in church!"

They started arguing, and Millie watched Buttercup sneak toward them. The goat reached down and nibbled on the broom's straw bristles.

"Okay, we jump da broom in church," Jake said, "but we practice jumping now. So I know you do it."

Mary huffed out a breath and pursed her lips, but her look softened after Jake leaned over and kissed her again. "Okay, we practice. Just once."

Jake beamed and turned to face the broom. "Ready?" Mary nodded and Jake said, "One, two..."

Buttercup bit down on a bristle and began backing up, dragging the broom away from them.

"You bring me broom back, goat!" Jake pulled Mary forward and Buttercup backed more quickly away, dragging the broom with her.

"Come here, Buttercrap," Samuel yelled, dropping the horse's lead and darting forward.

Buttercup turned and took off, the broom banging along beside her, while Samuel, Jake, and Mary chased after her.

Millie doubled over, tears streaming down her face as Mary yelled, "Bring dat back. We gotta jump over da damn broom."

FORTY

November 15, 1864
A Denver City Wedding

With Mrs. Smith's glowing recommendation, Reverend William Norrid agreed Jake and Mary would be the first couple to marry in Denver's Zion Baptist Church. It was the first and only colored church in Denver. Millie and Dom took their seats in the front pew on one side, the Smith family filled the opposite pew. Jake had insisted Buttercup be left at the livery, locked in a stall with their tailless horse.

Mary walked down the aisle, and when she reached Jake, he took a firm hold of her hand—looking worried that she might bolt. Samuel hurried out and laid the battered broom across the aisle—cutting off that path of retreat—as if he shared his father's fears. Mary just smiled at both and looked up at the minister. Reverend Norrid cleared his throat and began, speaking about love and marriage, but he paused when the church door opened.

Millie looked back and gasped.

Mrs. Beebee swept into the small church, followed by Mrs. Griswold, her bonnet knocked astray, and Mrs. Gilson clutching a worn leather bag. The matrons spotted Millie, waved, and hurried to join them.

"Here," Mrs. Gilson whispered, shoving the leather bag into Millie's arm.

"Sorry we're late," murmured Mrs. Griswold, patting Millie's arm. "Tit Bit didn't mention the wedding until we were at breakfast."

"Tit Bit?" Millie asked.

As if on cue, the church door swung open again, and Tit Bit and Sheriff Reynolds sauntered in. Mrs. Smith greeted the working girl with a hug and led her and the sheriff to their pew. They sat down side by side, Mrs. Smith on one side and the five children on the other. Tit Bit settled her skirts and demurely nodded a greeting to Millie.

"She and Sheriff Reynolds make a good match," commented Mrs. Beebee.

Millie itched to open the leather pouch but didn't dare as Reverend Norrid cleared his throat and continued his sermon. He was just regaining his rhythm when Blacksmith Shumate, Old Shakespeare, and Billie Batterson hurried inside and took a seat in the back pew.

"How did they know about the wedding?" Millie gasped.

"I had to tell Mr. Griswold where we were going." Mrs. Griswold squirmed uncomfortably. "He might have said something to the other gentlemen."

"They know about the leather pouch and have been itching to get at what's inside," Mrs. Beebee explained.

"Why is Mr. Batterson in a military uniform?" Dom asked.

"Colonel Chivington caught him stealing his military hat and gave him the option of enlisting or getting lynched," Mrs. Beebee explained. "He chose enlistment."

"Hush up," whispered Mrs. Gilson. "Let the minister marry 'em."

Had Marshal Hunt heard about the wedding? Millie prayed he hadn't.

Reverend Norrid spoke quickly, looking relieved when

he reached the vows without any more interruptions. Smiling, Jake promised to love and protect Mary for as long as they lived. Mary's voice shook as she repeated her vow, but she beamed as Jake slipped a ring he'd forged onto her finger. Holding hands, they turned to face the broom.

"After jumping the broom, I declare Mr. Jake and Miss Mary to be Mr. and Mrs. Randolph." Jake had no last name, so he and Samuel had decided to take Mary's.

Jake and Mary's hand swung back, and the church's door banged open.

"Mr. Dominic Drouillard, you're under arrest. Come peaceably and they'll be no trouble." Marshal Hunt strode into the church, his gun drawn, followed by Brother Bunce.

Dom's face darkened but he rose and walked down the aisle with his back straight and his head held high. As the door clanged shut, Mary dragged Jake over the broom and hurried to Millie's side. "That pouch got to tell the killer."

"As I told you before, you should have given me the evidence." Sheriff Reynolds rushed over and extended his hand.

Millie glared at the lawman and shook her head. After this summer's news, she knew Sheriff Reynolds' secret and no longer believed he was the killer, but with Dom's arrest she now had to find something. Hands shaking slightly, she opened the leather flap.

"As the Bard said in *Much Ado About Nothing*," old Shakespeare said, joining the group. "'Sigh no more, ladies, sigh no more. Men were deceivers ever.'"

"'I would challenge you to a battle of wits,'" said Reverend Norrid from the pulpit, "but as the Bard said in *As You Like It*, 'I see you are unarmed.'"

Laying a hand over his heart, Old Shakespeare turned to face the preacher. "'The fool doth think he is wise, but the wise man knows himself to be a fool.' *As You Like It*."

Reverend Norrid laughed. "'We know what we are but know not what we may be.' *Hamlet.*"

Old Shakespeare walked toward the reverend looking like an ecstatic groom approaching his bride. "To be, or not to be, that is the question. Whether 'tis nobler—"

"Hush," Jake interrupted. "We got to find a killer. What in that pouch?"

Millie removed the stack of papers, finding Sheriff Reynolds' carte de visite on top.

"You and your brothers are all very handsome," Mrs. Beebee said, glancing at the photo.

"Which one is James and which John?" Millie asked, offering the photo to the sheriff.

He started and eyed Millie warily. "James is on my left," he said, slipping the photo into his weskit.

Despite their isolation this summer, Millie had managed to obtain the occasional newspaper, and she'd read about a group of Confederate soldiers who'd been encouraged by their Confederate captain to cause havoc in the Colorado Territory. The group leader, James Reynolds, and his gang plundered several South Park mining towns and robbed a number of stagecoaches before most were captured and killed. Newspapers had dubbed them the Reynolds Gang. In one article, Millie read the Reynolds brothers had lived in Tarryall before the war began. Millie remembered Sheriff Reynolds mentioning he'd mined in South Park and lived in Tarryall with his brothers before coming to Idaho Springs.

"Mr. Batterson," said Mrs. Griswold kindly. "I'm sure you would like this." She reached over and took the next paper off the stack and handed it to Billie Batterson. "That's quite an interesting square hat Widow Ferris sketched."

He glanced at the picture and laughed. "She did have a twisted sense of humor."

"I don't remember that," said Mrs. Gilson crankily. "What's so funny about the picture?"

"The biretta, or Canterbury cap. It's why I'm here. It belonged to our village canon. I appropriated it while he was preparing for the Easter Sunday service. My family was not amused, and since it was not my first offence, they sent me here, permanently."

"You a remittance man 'cause you steal a hat?" Mary shook her head.

He shrugged. "I was the third son of a lord and a disappointing solicitor."

"This picture of Brother Bunce and Samuel is well done." Millie looked around but Brother Bunce had left with Dom and Marshal Hunt. Probably best since she doubted the minister would be pleased to be pictured with the boy. She shuffled the sketch to the bottom of the pile.

"Blacksmith Shumate, that one Dr. Doy?" Mary pointed at a seated man surrounded by other men.

"Aye, 'tis and look beneath it. Old Shakespeare's flyer." He coughed into his hand and glanced at the short shopkeeper. Old Shakespeare and Reverend Norrid were engrossed in an animated conversation near the altar. "The dress be fine, but his beard, 'tis grotesque."

Millie couldn't have expressed it better and handed both the flier and the picture to the blacksmith.

"Ain't nothing useful in there," Jake said, disgusted.

Millie scanned another article about the Egg Point killer, desperate for a clue, but there was no new information. "There's got to be more!" Millie handed the papers to Mrs. Gilson and turned the leather pouch upside down. Nothing came out.

Pulling on her braid, Millie began to pace. "What am I going to do?"

"You know…" Mrs. Gilson said slowly. "Widow Ferris sketched Mr. Batterson with his stolen hat." She held up the second sketch. "Why sketch Brother Bunce with little Samuel?"

Millie stared at the picture. The likenesses were good but...

"Oh Lawd," Mary whispered. "That awful. Them eyes is the same."

Millie looked at the eyes and saw it. "He couldn't be."

"Widow Ferris with her artist eye saw the likeness. I never imagined." Sheriff Reynolds shook his head. "She must have blackmailed him with the sketch."

"Aye!" Tit Bit struck her forehead and then lifted the sleeve of her dress. "It be Brother Bunce with the birthmark. The one you described, Mrs. D. Matching bulls horns, here." She pointed to her arm.

"Brother Bunce is the Egg Point killer?" Millie's head swam.

"Dat awful man. He give me Sammy?" Jake spun around, his eyes wide. "Sammy. Where me Sammy?"

FORTY-ONE

November 15, 1864

Sins of the Father

"We need to find them. Brother Bunce has killed twice. He's got nothing to lose." Sheriff Reynolds took the sketch from Mrs. Gilson. "I'll get Dom released and form a posse." He strode from the room.

"Dat man kill me Sammy," wailed Jake.

"No." Mary shook her head. "He take our boy and sell him. We gotta find him." Hand in hand they ran toward the door.

"Jake, Mary. He'll head South, toward Texas. He'll need horses." Millie thought of Buttercup and her own tailless horse. "We should search the liveries."

Jake nodded and Mary said, "We check 'em close to here."

"Be careful. He's probably armed." Millie removed her six-shooter and after checking that it was loaded, slipped it into her coat pocket.

"We'll visit liveries on the west side of town," said Mrs. Gilson. "The ones along the Platte River." Mrs. Gilson, Mrs. Beebee, and Mrs. Griswold hurried out the door.

"Blacksmith Shumate and I will check the liveries on the south edge of town." Billie Batterson took out a pearl-handled derringer and headed toward the door. "They're closest to where he wants to go. I want the privilege of putting a bullet in my love's killer."

The Smith family said they'd search the liveries east of town and Old Shakespeare and Reverend Norrid—still exchanging Shakespeare quotes—headed to the north side of Cherry Creek. As they left, Old Shakespeare laid a hand on his heart and said, "Let me say, 'Before I strike this bloody stroke, farewell.' *Antony and Cleopatra*."

Not to be outdone by his rival, Reverend Norrid said, "'What heaven more will, That thee may furnish, and my prayers pluck down, Fall on thy head! Farewell!' *All's Well that Ends Well*."

Millie looked at Tit Bit and shook her head. "Fall on thy head? How about we search the liveries near where the Methodist Church used to be? Brother Bunce spent a lot of time at that church." They set off and Millie glanced at the jail as they passed it. Surely Marshal Hunt had released Dom. She was worried sick about Samuel, but she also felt guilty feeling so relieved that Dom was no longer a fugitive.

The two liveries closest to where the church had been were crowded with horses and customers, but no Brother Bunce. Millie glanced around the second stable and pulled on her braid, unsure where to go next.

"There be a small livery near the Washington House, where I be buying your horse," Tit Bit said. "I be thinking Brother Bunce stayed at the Washington. I saw him there after the flood."

"Let's take a look." With each passing minute, Millie knew their chances of finding Samuel were getting worse. She followed Tit Bit down the crowded walkways, bumping into men who stopped to stare at the working girl. Tit Bit was walking quickly, not trying to attract attention, but even so, her narrow waist, well-endowed bust, and swinging walk was eye catching. They left the busy downtown area, and Millie followed the girl down a dirt road. Passing two log cabins, they rounded a corner and Tit Bit's rolling motion came to an abrupt halt.

Millie looked over her shoulder and saw Brother Bunce leading a saddle horse and pack horse from a dimly lit barn. She reached into her pocket and wrapped her fingers around her six-shooter, but he was faster.

"Take it out, slowly, Mrs. D." The minister pointed his revolver at them. His gun hand was steady, but his eyes were wild and crazy. "I've already killed Widow Ferris. Since they can't lynch me twice, I've got nothing to lose." He laughed and Millie realized the man was truly crazy. "Toss the gun aside Mrs. D and come here."

Millie removed the weapon and tossed it, forcing her feet to move around Tit Bit and closer to the crazy man. "W-where's Samuel?" In answer, the bundle on the pack horse wiggled and grunted. Millie glanced around. The main streets had been busy with people, but this little side street was empty.

"Sheriff Reynolds already go after Marshal Hunt to form a posse?" The man of God shook his head. "I guess I'll have to take you with me Mrs. D. As security."

Millie stared at him. She'd been terrified for Samuel, but she never imagined Brother Bunce would be crazy enough to threaten her. "If you hurt me, Dom will track you down. He won't ever give up."

"True, so here's what we're going to do. Mrs. D climb up on my horse or I'll gut shoot you. I've been told a gut shot is the worst way to die." His soft Southern accent was incongruous with his ugly words. "Tit, you tell Dom and the lawmen what I'll do to her if anyone gets too close."

"Won't you kill me anyway?" Millie asked, her voice shaking.

"Maybe." He waved his gun wildly. "But maybe if you behave, I'll turn you loose once I'm clear." He laughed crazily. "Maybe not. Get on out of here, Tit."

Tit Bit glanced at Millie. Fearful the girl might try something stupid, Millie nodded with more confidence than she felt. "I'll be okay. Go find Sheriff Reynolds and Dom."

Tit Bit lifted her skirt and disappeared down the ally.

Brother Bunce roughly grabbed Millie's arm and dragged her toward the horse. "Climb into the saddle, Mrs. D, or you're dead."

During their stay with Sarah, Millie had tried to learn how to ride, but she didn't like being so high off the ground and disliked the feel of the horse moving beneath her. Knowing her life depended on it, Millie managed to climb into the saddle, but her skirt forced her to sit sidesaddle. Unfortunately, the saddle wasn't a sidesaddle. Millie balanced precariously, both legs dangling on one side, fearful she would fall off if the animal moved.

Brother Bunce climbed onto the horse, shoved Millie forward and pressed the barrel of his gun into her side. "Let's go on a trip, Mrs. D." He kicked the horse and Millie grabbed for the saddle leather, almost tipping off backwards. "You do anything stupid like falling off the horse, and I'll put a hole in that pretty bodice." He giggled. "Now stay quiet. Wouldn't want to alarm anyone."

Millie focused on the animal's movements, trying to stay balanced. She tensed as they rode out into the busy street and headed south. Occasionally she looked up, but each time she'd lose her balance and feel Brother Bunce's muzzle dig deeper into her side. The crowds thinned, and Millie jumped when Brother Bunce yelled, "Stay back, Dom, or I'll shoot her."

Millie dared a glance and saw Dom on the side of the road, his face twisted in rage. "You hurt her Bunce, and I won't stop looking until you're dead. I'll follow you into Hell."

Brother Bunce giggled. "The gatekeeper's a friend. He won't let you in!"

Dom's expression transformed from fury to fear. Millie knew he'd seen Brother Bunce's madness.

"I love you," she cried, as they passed by and left Denver City behind.

FORTY-TWO

November 24, 1864

Surprise

"M isah Millie. Wake up, Misah Millie." Samuel's voice penetrated through the throbbing in Millie's brain. She felt his small hands touch her face, his whimpered words repeated over and over. "Wake up, Misah Millie. Please donno be dead. Wake up."

Millie carefully opened her eyes, squinting into the red of sunset reflecting off the boy's tear-streaked face. "I'm... okay," she whispered trying to calm Samuel despite the pain pounding through every inch of her body. Her headache was like nothing she'd ever experienced, and her whole body felt weak and numb, but Samuel looked even worse. His cheeks were sunken, his light skin sallow and sickly, and his bound wrists were caked in blood, scabs, and filth.

He gently dabbed at her forehead with a filthy rag that reeked of stale horse and fresh blood. The odor made her stomach roil, but Millie didn't say a word.

The clouds in the sky gradually lost their red glow and the heavens turned black. The moon was high in the sky before Millie decided to try and sit up. She took slow, deep breaths, closing her eyes as waves of nausea and dizziness washed over. As the feeling passed, she opened her eyes and turned toward Samuel, spotting Brother Bunce behind him. The preacher sat hunched over a small fire, eating from a pot with his fingers. His movements were jerky. The glow of the fire made his features demonic.

"W-where are we?" Millie whispered. The last thing she remembered was Brother Bunce knocking her off the horse. He'd done the same thing every night since taking her captive, but this time he'd knocked her off backwards, onto her head, not her feet.

"You alive?" The preacher's eyes glowed red, reflecting firelight. "Too bad." He laughed. "Hungry?" He giggled. "Got to go find it yourself. Fried grubs with a bit of prairie grass ain't bad, but this grounds too froze to dig up worms." He shook his head and went back to using filthy fingers to shove black bits into his mouth.

Millie turned away, lifted her bound wrists over Samuel, and enclosed him in an awkward embrace. For the past week they'd eaten less each day as their food supply dwindled. Worse, they'd watched Brother Bunce change from crazy to totally insane. Samuel snuggled against Millie, his bony shoulders and hips pressing into her. Lying back down and rolling onto her side, Millie pulled the boy close and rested her chin in his greasy hair. Samuel's tense body relaxed, and his breathing slowed. As he slept, Millie closed her eyes, trying to clear her throbbing head. She knew they wouldn't survive much longer.

By now, she'd given up hope they'd be rescued.

The cold woke her. The night sky glistened with stars and a half-moon illuminated a shadowed, endless landscape. The icy ground penetrated through Millie's thick coat and she squirmed, waking Samuel. His eyes reflected the moonlight, but he didn't make a sound as Millie sat up and lifted her arms from around him.

Near the dying fire embers, Brother Bunce lay with his back to them, snoring and sputtering erratically. They had to escape now while they still had the strength to run. Millie quietly pushed herself to her feet, swaying unsteadily, her head still not quite right. Ignoring a wave of dizziness, she turned in a circle, the swishing of her skirts sounding loud in the prairie silence.

Behind them, the picketed horses grazed quietly on the poor winter grass. Millie took Samuel's hand and together they inched soundlessly toward them.

"No," Brother Bunce grunted.

Millie froze, expecting—as she had all week—a bullet in the back. When only silence met her ears, she carefully turned and looked. Brother Bunce hadn't moved, and Samuel whispered quietly, "He talk in he sleep."

Her legs shook as they crept toward Samuel's mount. The animal lifted its head and snorted, backing to the end of its tether.

"Samuel, can you ride without a saddle?" The cold, still air made Millie's whisper sound hollow.

"Yes 'um."

Millie squatted and tried to untie the tether rope, but her numb, bloodless fingers were stiff and uncoordinated. She fumbled awkwardly, each moment expecting Brother Bunce to wake and kill them. The tether rope knot finally gave, and Millie stood up, grasping the rope in her bound hands. She found Samuel standing by the horse, rubbing the animal's neck to keep it calm.

Millie approached and the horse allowed her to lift Samuel onto its back. Looping the rope over its neck so it wouldn't drag on the ground, Millie led them into the dark landscape.

"How you get up?" Samuel whispered.

Even if her hands had been free, Millie doubted she could have mounted the horse, much less stay on it without a saddle. Still, she didn't want to alarm Samuel. "I'll walk until I find something to climb up on." The boy didn't answer as Millie led the horse into the night, away from the insane Brother Bunce.

Samuel's mount came willingly, but not silently. At first it nickered quietly to the animal they'd left behind, but as the distance grew, so did the loudness of the animal's whinnies.

"Samuel," Millie whispered urgently. "Can you control this horse? Keep him from going back to camp?"

"I ain't sure," Samuel replied, "but—"

A gunshot shattered the night. Brother Bunce screamed crazily and fired again. "Go, Samuel. Find help!" Millie released the lead and struck the animal's flank.

FORTY-THREE

November 25, 1864

Escape on the Plains

Millie ran after Samuel and the horse, her numb feet unsteady, her head spinning. She tried to put the glowing fire and Brother Bunce's crazy screams as far behind as possible, but her bound hands restricted her ability to lift her skirts, and in her haste, she tripped, landing hard. She scrambled to her feet, ignoring the pain shooting up from her knee, and kept moving. Finally, unable to breathe, she bent over and gasped. In the distance, she could hear Brother Bunce's insane curses, but the sounds of Samuel's horse had faded.

What if the boy couldn't control the horse? Would the animal take Samuel back to the irate minister? Brother Bunce wouldn't hesitate to kill the boy. Or Samuel might fall off. If he got hurt, he might never be found.

Millie cursed her own stupidity. She should have freed the second horse and found a way to mount Samuel's horse and remain with the child. Glancing back, she could see the faint glow of Brother Bunce's fire and hear the echo of his yells. She could also hear the shrill whinny of the horse they'd left behind.

There was nothing she could do now. Tomorrow, when dawn broke, Brother Bunce would be able to see for miles across this flat, desolate land. She had to get away from him.

The sun broke over the Eastern Plains, and Brother Bunce's fire and his crazy screams were gone, but the landscape the morning light revealed was desolate, empty, and cold. Millie had once read the story of Private Garber of the 1st Cavalry Regiment who'd become separated from his regiment while fighting the Cheyenne somewhere in this vast emptiness. He'd been fully equipped with horse, saddle, and weapons. For seven days he remained lost, but finally the mail coach from Santa Fe found him. They'd spotted him running about aimlessly, dressed only in his hat, shirt, drawers, and shoes, catching grasshoppers and stuffing them into his mouth. The vast, open prairie had taken his mind.

As thirst, hunger, and exhaustion warred with each other, Millie wondered if that would be her fate.

The sun warmed the air, and Millie's shivering subsided although her bound hands remained stiff and cold. Thoughts of Dom and Samuel caused tears to blur her vision, but they also kept her moving. To never again see Dom, to never feel his strong arms around her was too terrible to imagine. Worse would be leaving him to wonder if she were alive or dead.

By late afternoon, even Dom's image failed to keep her on her feet. Millie sank to the ground. The dry prairie air scorched her throat and caused her cracked lips to bleed. She rested her head on the cold ground, closed her eyes, and waited for death.

Death did come, but Millie was surprised it smelled like goat and tasted like fouled water. At least Dom was kissing her cracked, dry lips, but why was he licking her face? Irritated at his lack of manners, Millie opened one eye, planning to complain to whoever oversaw death, but it wasn't Dom kissing her.

A goat's tongue lapped into her open mouth while another licked her eyes. Weakly, she flung her bound hands at the animals. Their eyes bulged out and they fainted, landing on her with a painful thud. Wondering if she was hallucinating, Millie squinted into the dying light. A shadow ran toward her carrying a raised knife. It was all too much. Like the proper lady she was, Millie swooned.

*****

Millie opened her eyes to darkness, felt something pressed against her, and tasted greasy fur in her mouth. She spat out the fur, but the stale smell of unwashed bodies tickled her nose and loud noises irritated her. This was not what she'd expected in heaven. Tomorrow she'd complain to God, but tonight her heavy eyelids fell closed and darkness overtook her.

A foul-tasting liquid caused Millie to wake and turn her head, but a hand covered her mouth and forced her to swallow. Indignant, she opened her mouth to tell God what she thought about her poor treatment in heaven and a long, greasy ear flopped against her cheek. A sharp command caused the greasy ear to be removed. Turning her head, Millie saw the face of a boy beside the wrinkled countenance of an old man. "Hosa?" Millie thought she must be hallucinating. "Lawyer?"

"Miss Millie." Hosa hugged her.

The medicine man crouched above her face, Millie's pocket watch and his medicine bundle hanging from his neck. He dripped foul-tasting liquid into Millie's mouth, grunted when she swallowed it, and disappeared, his face replaced with that of a young white man Millie didn't recognize.

"Morning, ma'am." The man looked to be in his early twenties with a neat mustache and long braided hair. "Name's Charles Bent. Hosa said you're Mrs. Dominic Drouillard. Black Kettle and White Antelope have sent a scout to Fort Lyon, to let them know you're here."

"Bent? From Bent's Fort?" Millie had heard stories about Bent's Fort and its unusual owner, William Bent. The man had run a successful trading post for over twenty years, connecting Santa Fe with Council Grove and Independence.

"Yes ma'am. My father's William Bent. My mother's Yellow Woman."

Millie rubbed her face. Perhaps she wasn't dead. "Where am I?" she whispered.

"You're at the Big Sandy Camp. With the Cheyenne and Arapaho. Fort Lyon's about forty miles south of here, although by the way you were bound, I don't assume that's where you come from."

Millie lifted her hands. The ropes were gone, but bloody abrasions circled her wrists. She imagined her scars would be mild compared to Samuel's young wrists. She sat up, almost knocking into Charles Bent, and her head spun. "Did you find a little boy? His hands were bound too."

The man scowled and asked more questions. After hearing Millie's story, he shook his head, muttered "and whites call us savages," and promised to send out searchers.

Two days later, feeling stiff but more like herself, Millie accompanied Hosa, Sooxei, and Charles Bent toward the lodges of Black Kettle and White Antelope. They walked downstream, passing clusters of teepees as they followed the twisting path of Sand Creek.

"Why are there only women and children here?" Millie asked, realizing she hadn't seen Woonbisiseet.

"Most braves are hunting buffalo, trying to keep their families from starving." Charles shook his head angrily.

"After he replaced General Wynkoop, General Anthony refused to hand out the government's promised provisions."

Before Millie could respond, they rounded a bend, and Millie saw two large lodges located under an American flag and a white flag of peace. "That American flag," Charles Bent pointed, "was a gift from President Lincoln."

"Black Kettle and White Antelope visited President Lincoln?"

"Yes ma'am. They also accompanied General Wynkoop to Denver City in October. They attended the Fort Weld council and made peace with Governor Evans; although along with peace, he promised supplies. He's the one who told them to come here, to their reservation on the Big Sandy Creek. He promised they'd be safe here."

FORTY-FOUR

November 29, 1864
The Sand Creek Massacre

Millie rose before the sun peeked over the plains, feeling all her aches and pains as she slipped outside. With so many lodges and families camped nearby, she'd had an audience during her daily ablutions, and last night she'd almost gotten lost trying to find a bit of seclusion for more private activities. Climbing the steep embankment, Millie went all the way over the bluff to complete her morning constitutional.

Afterward, she paused as she topped the rise, adjusted her bonnet and coat, and watched the sun turn the clouds blood red as it illuminated the waking camp. Quiet gray teepees stretched for miles along the curving riverbank, smoke curling up from their pointed tips. East of the encampment, a herd of horses grazed contentedly, but south, in the direction of Fort Lyon, Millie noticed a strange dust cloud.

Watching it, she finally realized it was a body of men riding toward them. Surely, they hadn't sent half the cavalry to retrieve her. The foolish thought passed as below her a heavily blanketed woman sounded an alarm.

The sleepy Indian camp came to life and fear gripped Millie as hundreds of mounted soldiers drew near, their horses' hooves pounding against the frozen prairie. Millie stared. The soldiers looked like they were preparing to attack. Lifting her skirt, she ran down the hill, pausing when a group of soldiers broke off from the main body and herded the Indian ponies away. Angry cries filled the air, and the few braves in camp brought out bows, arrows, and guns. The men urged their women and children to flee as they prepared to protect them.

Millie was stunned. This was a peaceful Indian camp. Most of the men, like Woonbisiseet, were away hunting. Governor Evans had told the Indians to camp here on their reservation.

A line of mounted soldiers formed on the ridge overlooking Black Kettle and White Antelope's lodges. Someone shouted a command and the soldiers galloped toward the lodges. Dawn's early light glinted off the soldiers' drawn weapons. A light breeze caused the American flag hanging over the chiefs' lodges to flap.

Millie covered her mouth as one chief—his headdress flowing down his back—walked toward the charging men, his weaponless hands held out. Under the flagpole, beneath their white flag of peace, Millie saw numerous women and children clustered around another chief.

Gunfire rent the still morning; smoke from the black powder darkened the clear air. The advancing chief stopped. His hands slowly dropped, and he crumpled to the ground, his flowing headdress covering him.

The Indian camp erupted into chaos.

Tears streamed down Millie's face as she watched soldiers reach the American flag and indiscriminately slaughter women, children, and elderly too frail to run. "No!" she screamed, spotting a woman kneeling before a charging soldier, her child hugged to her chest and her hand held up piteously.

The soldier ruthlessly plunged his bayonet through them both.

"Miss Millie, run!" Below her, Sooxei fled upstream, followed by Hosa, Nanny, and Nanko. Most of the soldiers were downstream, perhaps a half-mile away, focusing their attack around Black Kettle and White Antelope's lodges, but Millie could see soldiers heading her way, chasing desperate women and children.

She dashed down the hill, splashed across the stream, but came to a stop when she spotted a soldier watching the massacre. As if feeling her eyes, the man turned, his two beard braids flapped against his coat.

Mr. Turck's cold eyes bore into her.

Millie gasped, turned, and ran, the screams and gunfire drowning out the wild beating of her own heart. She crashed through underbrush as thistles and branches grabbed at her long skirt. Charging into a clearing, she found a foot soldier kneeling like a suitor as he took aim at a crying infant toddling around the body of a woman. Millie cried out, too far away to stop the soldier from firing.

Millie screamed but the noise died in her throat as the solider turned his rifle on her. His long, curling mustache quivered and his eyebrows lifted in confusion as he lowered the gun. "Ma'am?"

Millie didn't answer as she ran past. She stumbled over her wet skirts and joined other desperate women and children scrambling along the river. The pounding of horse hooves momentarily distracted her, and she looked up. Why were mounted troops herding Indian ponies toward the river valley? The loose ponies disrupted and scattered the attacking soldiers, causing confusion and giving the fleeing women and children a bit more time.

The soldiers driving the horses stopped their mounts and came no closer. *Not all the soldiers supported this slaughter.* The thought passed through Millie's mind as her foot struck a branch and she went flying. She landed in the mud beside the creek. A rifle cracked, and a body fell beside her. Millie stared into the old, worn face of Lawyer.

"I'm so sorry," she said, sitting up and gathering the old man into her arms.

He groaned weakly and lifted his hand, setting it on Millie's. Mumbling something incoherent, he dropped her pocket watch and his medicine bundle into her hand as the light in his eyes died.

Millie sobbed and gently closed his eyes before setting his still form on the ground. She crawled to her feet, his treasures clutched in her hand, and scrambled on. Despite the cool of morning, sweat pooled down her back and coated her dirty face. She fought through a patch of thick willows, feeling nothing as the branches cut her skin, emerging to a sight too horrible for words.

Hosa and the goats lay slumped in the grass. A soldier nearby grimly reloaded his rifle.

"No!" Millie screamed, rushing toward them. "No!" she choked out when she recognized Sooxei's still face. Her friend lay unmoving in a pool of blood. Hosa lay over his mother's still form, protecting her. Turning toward the soldier, using her body to shield the boy, Millie cried, "Why are you killing these people?"

The soldier's eyes widened. "You's a white lady? Whatcha doing with these savages?"

"Why are you killing these people?" Millie repeated numbly.

The soldier scratched his head. "Col. Chivington toll us to kill every last one. Squaws, bucks, and babes. These are the redskins who kill Hungate and his missus."

Millie shook her head. Col. Chivington had attended the Fort Weld council. He met and spoke with Black Kettle, White Antelope, and the other chiefs. He knew they sought peace. President Lincoln had given them the American flag, told them this land was their reservation. Governor Evans sent the Arapaho and Cheyenne here.

The soldier suddenly looked excited. "These savages kidnapped you." He grinned brightly. "I rescued you."

"No," Millie choked out. "No. These are my friends."

His smile faded. "Ma'am, you confused. Captivity softened you brain." He suddenly lifted his gun. "Move. The young buck's alive. I do him in and take you to safety."

Millie took a deep breath and stood up straight. Her voice no longer shook although she felt an overwhelming sense of sadness. So many deaths, including her own. *I'm so sorry Dom*, she thought, knowing her death would devastate him. Looking the soldier in the eye, she said, "You'll have to kill me, sir, to get to the boy."

Turning, she stepped over Sooxei, not looking at her friend as she pulled Hosa to his feet and held him close. Nanny and Nanko rose on unsteady legs, their eyes bulging.

"Come," she told them quietly. She began walking, keeping Hosa's bony shoulders tight against her, making sure her body shielded him from the soldier. With each tense step, she expected to hear the crack of gunfire, to feel a bullet rip into her back. She took four unsteady steps before she dared to glance back. The soldier stood watching, uncertain, but his rifle hung limp in his hands.

Millie pushed Hosa in front of her, half carrying him around another curve and out of the soldier's sight. "We've got to keep moving," she whispered, urging the child into a stumbling trot. They went on like that, for a minute, five minutes, a quarter hour. Noise of the battle grew dimmer. At one steep embankment, women and children burrowed into the loose soil, crawling into hidey-holes, but Millie refused to stop. The memory of Mr. Turck kept her moving.

Other soldiers might hesitate to kill her, but not Mr. Turck.

They kept walking, memories of the battle and death

driving them beyond exhaustion, but finally Millie could go no further. She sank down on a gravel sandbar, gasping as she caught her breath and quenched her thirst. Nanny, Nanko, and Hosa dropped down beside her. Around them, the world was unnaturally silent, but in the distance, the echo of gunfire and cannons still filled the air.

Hosa looked over, his face ravaged with grief. "Why?" His voice choked on the word.

Millie touched his face. "I don't know." She shook her head. "I just don't know."

Wearily, Hosa rose and used his knife to cut down two willow branches, trimming off the outer bark. He offered one willow to Millie before he began chewing on the other. Millie cringed at the bitter taste, but the cramps in her belly abated slightly. The boy moved like in a trance, his movements jerky. Millie longed to comfort him, but she knew she couldn't. How did one comfort a child after what they'd just experienced?

"I find food," Hosa said, turning away. Millie rose to join him, but he stonily shook his head. "Me alone." He trudged unsteadily into the marshland, disappearing in the thick willows. Nanny and Nanko close on his heels.

Millie hated to let him go, but she suspected he needed time to mourn in private. Stumbling away from the water, she climbed up the embankment and sat down, exhaustion washing over her. Closing her eyes, she saw Col. Chivington and his soldiers massacring a camp of peaceful Indians. Women, children, old men, and babies. Tears rolled down her cheeks.

"Feeling a bit sorry for yourself, are you?"

Millie jumped and looked up, unable to believe her eyes. Brother Bunce strode out from a clump of cottonwoods, giggling as he approached her. Millie struggled to her feet; her legs rubbery as he leveled his six-shooter at her chest. The former minister looked only partially human. Tufts of hair from his beard and head were missing—as if he'd jerk-ed them out—and the hand holding his six-shooter shook badly.

"Surprise! Didn't think I could track you, did you?" He laughed uproariously. "Almost had you this morning, but the Fighting Parson and his army arrived." He jumped up and down like a child. "What a glorious sight." His amused expression faded and he stopped moving, his eyes darting around nervously. "What'd you do with the boy?"

"I don't know," she said, unsure which boy he meant, Samuel or Hosa.

"Meddling old biddy!" Without pretense, Brother Bunce fired his six-shooter.

FORTY-FIVE

November 29, 1864
Showdown

Millie cried out and stumbled backward, grabbing her shoulder. The pain was sharp, a burning sensation, and warm blood flowed between her fingers. Brother Bunce giggled, and Millie knew she should flee, but she couldn't. Her rubbery legs wouldn't move. Her mind couldn't grasp that the man had shot her.

"Oops, guess I missed." He took two steps closer. "Let's try again."

Millie closed her eyes, hating that his crazy face would be the last thing she saw. She pressed Lawyer's sacred bundle and her pocket watch against her chest and waited. The crack of a gun broke the tense stillness, and Millie's legs gave out. She landed on the ground, smelling burnt black powder. Pain radiated out in waves from her arm, but Millie didn't feel dead. Carefully she opened her eyes and gingerly sat up.

Brother Bunce lay on the ground, unmoving, a red stain expanding on his weather-worn coat.

Not quite believing her eyes, she glanced around. Mr. Turck stood near Sand Creek, his rifle smoking. "I didn't murder Widow Ferris, and I don't kill women and children." Mr. Turck's eyes were bloodshot, his beard braids shiny with grease. He approached Brother Bunce and nudged him with his toe. The minister didn't move. "I'm a mean drunk," he snarled, "but now Dom and me are even." He turned and walked away.

Millie's whole body began to shake, making it difficult to stand, but she couldn't bear to be this close to Brother Bunce, dead or not. Struggling, she staggered toward the riverbed, catching sight of Hosa and the goats crouching in the willows. The sound of a horse made her turn around.

"You ain't looking too good." Mr. Turck led Brother Bunce's horse toward her. "You'd best ride."

"W-where are y-you t-taking me?" Millie clenched her jaw to stop her chattering teeth.

"Back. Fighting should be over. I'll turn you over to Captain Soule. He disobeyed Col. Chivington and none of his Company D fired a shot. He'll know what to do with you."

"I have an Indian child with me." Millie shook her head, trying to regain control, but the movement just made her light-headed. "They'll k-kill him."

"I don't kill children." With no further promise, he led the horse beside Millie and lifted her on. "Call him."

Clutching the saddle, Millie called Hosa. The child hurried to her and crawled onto the horse, huddling in her arms. Turning toward the bushes he called out.

"What's he doing?" Mr. Turck drew his weapon.

Before Millie could answer, Nanny bounded forward and leaped into the boy's arms. He carefully laid her over the horse's neck, her belly pressed into the mount's mane, her legs hanging off on both sides. He repeated the procedure with Nanko, and soon the two goats were snuggled in front of them, their heads pointed in opposite directions.

"Looks like an aberration." Mr. Turck shook his head, grabbed the horse's reins, and led them back toward the massacre.

Millie felt warm blood trickle down her arm as she fumbled with her coat, slipping her pocket watch and Lawyer's bundle into her pocket. Her shaking hands had trouble with the buttons, but with Hosa's help, she managed to wrap the coat around the boy, hiding him. They rode in silence, the number of scalped and mutilated bodies increasing the closer they got to the former camp. Millie looked away, unable to imagine civilized white men taking trophies of Indian's ears, fingers, and private parts.

Mr. Turck said nothing as he led the horse toward a supply train, flagging down a young man who introduced himself as Captain Soule.

"You're Silas Soule? Blacksmith Shumate's friend?" Millie asked.

"Yes ma'am." He glanced around warily. "Best get you and that boy hidden." He turned and called out, "Private Batterson."

Billie Batterson, looking rather haggard, emerged from behind the wagon. Captain Soule issued a curt command, and the Englishman took the horse's reins and led Millie's horse toward a wagon piled high with pilfered buffalo robes and other belongings from the camp.

"Thank you, Mr. Turck," Millie said, looking back.

"You tell Dom we're even," he said, squeezing his filthy beard braids as he turned and walked away.

"You need to stay quiet, Mrs. D, and hide the boy," Billie Batterson said as Hosa scrambled onto the wagon and helped the goats off the horse. Millie stiffly climbed off the horse and into the wagon bed. She crawled over beside Hosa and wrapped her uninjured arm around him, feeling him lean into her.

"Mrs. D, your husband's back at Fort Lyon. Col. Chivington threw him in jail after he tried to leave the Fort without permission." Billie Batterson shook his head. "When that boy showed up—Sam or Samuel I think—your husband bellowed like a buffalo stuck in a mud slick."

"You've seen Samuel? Is he okay?" Millie felt dizzy with relief.

"He's beat up, but them Idaho Springs matrons are taking care of him." He shook his head. "This here's bad business. Captain Soule and I have been ordered to return to Fort Lyon for the supply train. We can take *you* without trouble, but if they find that boy," he nodded at Hosa, "they'll kill him."

Millie shuddered and awkwardly covered Hosa with buffalo robes. "Stay quiet Hosa and keep the goats still."

"I want to try and save Charles Bent's life," Captain Soule said, climbing onto the wagon and taking the horse's ribbons. "No matter your feelings, ma'am, you must remain quiet." Billie Batterson climbed up beside his commander and the wagon creaked into motion.

Millie pulled a buffalo robe over her, making sure Hosa and the goats were completely hidden as they drew close to a group of mounted men. She recognized the Fighting Parson and was sickened by his exhilarated expression. She pressed her mouth closed as Captain Soule drew the wagon to a stop beside him. "Col. Chivington. Per orders, sir, I'm returning to Fort Lyon to escort the supply train back. I'd like to take Charles Bent back with me."

Millie tensed when Col. Chivington glanced her way. "That Mrs. Drouillard?"

"Yes, sir."

"When you get to Fort Lyon, tell her husband that if he and those bossy women are still in my fort when I return, I'll arrest them all." He scowled at Captain Soule and added darkly, "Later, I'll determine the disciplinary actions for your blatant disregard of my orders."

"Yes, sir." Millie was impressed by the young captain. Whatever he was feeling, Captain Soule's face didn't betray him.

"Carry this letter back to Fort Lyon." Chivington handed a folded paper to Billie Batterson. "Make sure it's sent immediately by courier to Editor Byers of the *Rocky Mountain News*. Denver City will want to know about our glorious victory."

Millie bit her tongue and held Hosa tightly. The boy's life depended on her self-control, but oh Lor' she wanted to tell this horrible man what she thought about his senseless slaughter.

"Dismissed," said Col. Chivington, glaring at Millie. She might not have said a word, but her face had obviously betrayed her.

"Sir. May I retrieve Charles Bent?"

"If his brother doesn't care, I don't either." Col. Chivington waved them away.

Captain Soule handed the ribbons to Billie Batterson and climbed from the wagon. He strode quickly toward a group of teepees. Another soldier hurried past him and stopped in front of the Fighting Parson, saluting sharply. "Col. Chivington, they've taken the half-breed, Jack Smith. He's the Squaw man's son. There's talk of killing him."

"The translator, John Smith's bastard?"

"Yes, sir."

Col. Chivington turned and rode toward the American flag that still hung over the remains of Black Kettle's camp. "I gave orders to take no prisoners," Col. Chivington said coldly. "I have no new instructions."

Millie closed her eyes, feeling tears slide down her filthy face. She opened her eyes when the wagon creaked as Captain Soule and another man lifted a badly injured Charles Bent into the wagon and wrapped buffalo robes around him. The polite young man looked to be in terrible pain, but he didn't make a sound as the wagon left the massacre. Millie scooted over and awkwardly tore strips from her petticoat and wrapped the young man's injuries the best she could.

Only when they could no longer see soldiers did Millie uncover Hosa and pull him into her lap. He clung to her, his face stony. His expression broke Millie's heart. She'd never wanted a child, but Hosa was now hers. She'd do anything to keep him safe.

*****

In Millie's dream, Dom was calling to her, his voice distant and fearful. Millie reached out, trying to wave, and pain shot from her injured shoulder, waking her. Fresh blood darkened the bandage Hosa had wrapped around her injury, but Millie ignored it and checked the boy. His bony shoulder pressed into her side; Nanny and Nanko cuddled beside him, their heads on his lap. On her other side, Charles Bent lay sprawled in the wagon, bloody and unresponsive.

Hearing Dom's voice, even in a dream, made Millie ache to see him. How long had it been since she'd last held him? Whatever the future held, she could manage as long as Dom was beside her.

"Mmmiiilllliiieeee."

Millie twisted around. In the distance, a man ran toward the wagon. Hatless and coatless, he waved his arms wildly.

"Dom," she whispered. "Dom!" Scrambling to her feet, ignoring the pain the movement ignited in her shoulder, she jumped from the slow-moving wagon and ran. Nothing, not even her beaten and exhausted body, could stop her.

"Dom," she cried, as his arms crushed her against his warm body. "Oh Lor'. Dom."

FORTY-SIX

December 19, 1864

Rachel

S heriff Reynolds arrived at Millie's cabin with Tit Bit on his arm, offering Millie a newspaper as he stepped inside. "Thought you might want to see Editor Byers' report of the business at the Big Sandy Camp." He sat down beside Dom and sliced himself a chunk of fresh sour-dough bread. They'd been back in Idaho Springs almost a week, but Millie had refused to look at the news, not yet ready to see Denver City's reaction to the massacre. Now, as her guests arrived and made themselves comfortable, Millie glanced at the December seventh paper.

BIG INDIAN FIGHT!

THE 1ST AND 3RD REGIMENTS HAVE HAD A BATTLE WITH THE INDIANS ON SAND CREEK, A SHORT DISTANCE NORTHEAST OF FORT LYON. FIVE HUNDRED INDIANS ARE REPORTED KILLED AND SIX HUNDRED HORSES CAP-TURED. CAPTAIN BAXTER, AND LIEUTENANT PIERCE ARE REPORTED KILLED. NO FURTHER PARTICULARS. A MESSENGER IS HOURLY EXPECTED WITH FULL DETAILS. BULLY FOR THE COLORADO BOYS...

Millie dropped the paper into her firebox. She didn't need to read any further. Not now, not ever. Trying to ignore the ache in her shoulder and heart, she turned her attention to her guests, noticing Tit Bit still standing awkwardly near the door. "Miss Nessa, it's ever so good to see you."

"Thank ye kindly, Mrs. Drouillard. I ain't used to such finery nor a proper invitation, but I made me Ma's favorite dish: bacon and cabbage cooked with onions, carrots, and potatoes."

"Thank you. I'm sure we'll all enjoy it. Please, have a seat." Turning, Millie lifted the lid off the dish and an unpleasant smell wafted up. Discreetly, she set it at the boy's end of the table. Since their return, Hosa and Samuel ate anything and everything.

After all their guests had arrived and were seated, Millie glanced around her overflowing table and smiled sadly. She'd invited the matrons and their families, Mary, Jake, Samuel, Sheriff Reynolds, Billie Batterson, Blacksmith Shumate, Old Shakespeare, and Tit Bit to a midday meal. She wanted to thank everyone for all they'd done during this long and eventful year.

"Here's to a quiet Christmas and an uneventful 1865," Dom said, lifting his glass of whiskey as Millie took her seat.

"Here, here," shouted everyone. "To 1865."

Beside Millie, Sheriff Reynolds added quietly, "And no more murders."

Millie glanced at Tit Bit, and her smile became a real one. Unable to help herself, she added, "And to another wedding."

Tit Bit and Sheriff Reynolds both blushed, but it was the reaction from the matrons that made Millie smile. Mrs. Beebee eyes lit up. Mrs. Gilson examined the girl's figure like she was planning the wedding dress, and grandmotherly Mrs. Griswold just clapped her hands and said excitedly, "Another Christmas wedding."

Sheriff Reynolds didn't have a chance.

"Yuck," said Samuel.

"Ugh," grunted Hosa.

Millie noticed the two boys sat close to the other children, but they remained apart. They had become inseparable. Perhaps the cruel suffering they'd both experienced formed a unique bond. Whatever it was, she knew their friendship would last a lifetime when she saw Hosa gift Nanny to Samuel. The two goats now sat beside their masters, like well-trained dogs, although while she watched, Nanko stretched out her neck and stole Hosa's bread.

Maybe not so well trained.

Millie filled her plate and the room was soon noisy with the sounds of dishes being scraped clean. Rising to bring Mrs. Beebee's pies to the table, Millie froze when someone knocked on the door. After all that had happened this past year, unexpected guests were no longer welcome.

Everyone grew quiet as Dom rose and opened the door.

Mr. Poor hurried inside, bringing snow and icy air with him. He carried a tiny girl, somewhere between four and six years old, with wispy black hair and a thumb in her mouth. She wore a coat entirely inadequate for the bitter cold, her big eyes widening as Mr. Poor dumped her into Dom's arms. "This come for you on the morning coach."

"Came for me? B-but..." Dom held the child away from him, glancing at Millie. "I don't..."

Millie sucked down a breath. It didn't take a trained artist to see the resemblance between the child and Dom. Their blue eyes, both matching colors of a clear mountain sky, said it all. "Did she come with a letter?'

"Yup. Here." Mr. Poor shoved an envelope into Millie's hand and scooted around her, settling into her chair. "Don't mind if I do," he said, filling a plate with food.

The envelope was addressed to Mrs. Dominic Drouillard and had Denver City stamped on the envelope. Inside were two sheets of paper, the first dated October 3, 1864, and addressed to Mr. Ferris.

Harrods Creek,
October 3, 1864

Honorable Ferris:

Sir: It has come to my attention, through correspondences found at the residence of Mrs. A.L. Lane, that Mr. Drouillard, of your acquaintance, is the father of Rachel, the daughter of Mrs. Lane. Regrettably, Mr. and Mrs. Lane, along with their infant son, were killed by Confederate guerrillas allegedly led by Captain Marcellus Clarke. The daughter, Rachel, survived by climbing into the cabin's chimney.

If your client, Mr. Drouillard, chooses to claim his daughter, he will find her in St. Joseph's Orphan Asylum at the corner of Green and Jackson Streets.

Yours,
Robert Nicholas

A wave of pity washed through Millie. She'd been raised in New Orleans' Annunciation and Calliope Girls' House of Refuge. She understood what it meant to be an orphan with no family, no name, no dowry. She'd spent the first twenty-three years of her life that way—until she'd answered a wife-wanted advertisement to come West. She wouldn't wish that life on anyone.

Flipping to the next page, Millie read:

Denver City,
December 13, 1864

Mrs. Drouillard,

I ordered this for you. She was delivered to my establishment, but she's a bit young for my customers. You can send her back in ten years, if you wish.

Yours,
Madam LaMont

Millie glanced at the frightened child and did the only thing she could. She lifted the girl from Dom's arms and hugged her tightly. "Hello, Rachel. I'm Millie, your new Mamma. This is your Daddy." She touched Dom's arm. "And you've got two brothers over there." She waved toward Samuel and Hosa, but the little girl's blue eyes were glued on Dom, her mouth working furiously, sucking her thumb.

"D-daddy?" Dom stuttered. His shocked expression slowly faded, and his face turned soft. "Rachel...I'm your, your...Pa." His voice broke and he wiped his eyes. Taking his seat, he held out his arms.

Dom hugged his daughter protectively, and Millie returned to serving Mrs. Beebee's fruit pies, trying to ignore the quiet whispering around her. Her neighbors were shocked, but also polite. It was one thing to have an illegitimate daughter and quite another for her to arrive in person. Millie was relieved when Mr. Poor interrupted the uncomfortable still by burping and asking, "Dom. Why didn't you ever come up and question me? I heard you interrogated every other durn person Mr. Ferris blackmailed."

"Didn't know he had something on you, Asa." Dom carefully patted the girl's head, the way he did Buttercup. "Doesn't matter now."

"I think I should explain, just to clear my name." Mr. Poor laughed, obviously enjoying the attention. The devilment in his eyes caused Millie to sit down between Samuel and Hosa and wrap an arm around each boy. Rachel removed her thumb from her mouth and started chewing on Dom's shirt.

Mr. Poor burped and cleared his throat. "That scoundrel, Ferris, tried to blackmail me a year or so ago, but I just laughed at him. The good solicitor had somehow ferreted out information about a prank old Ned Wynkoop and I pulled on a certain important military man back in '60."

He helped himself to a slice of pie. "Ferris threatened to publish details in the *Rocky Mountain News*." He shook his head. "Like anyone cared. I told him to do what he wanted, and of course, he did nothing. Man was a coward at heart."

"Did Widow Ferris know?" Mr. Griswold asked with interest. He was the town's storyteller and was always interested in all the details of a new story.

"'Bout me? Donno. When she refused my proposal, she told me she'd found a bunch of letters and papers. Was gonna use them to get some money and didn't need to marry me." He shook his head. "I figured they were other people's secrets, but never thought she'd be murdered over them. Fool woman."

Rachel squirmed and chewed her way higher up Dom's shirt. Dom watched her; his eyes filled with concern. Millie sighed and looked at Hosa and Samuel. So much for a quiet, uneventful 1865.

"Poor Widow Ferris," Mrs. Griswold crooned. "She didn't have it easy."

"What kind of prank," Mr. Griswold asked eagerly.

"Well…When I lived in Denver City, I used to stay with old Ned Wynkoop. That was before he became a proper military man. It was fall of '60 and he was living with Louise, before they were married. Times—"

"Living with him before she was married?" Mrs. Beebee turned hard eyes on Sheriff Reynolds. "Sir, despite Miss

Nessa's former profession, you will not live with her before your marriage." She frowned and turned to Tit Bit. "In fact, Miss Nessa, we'll have you live with Mr. Beebee and me at the Beebee House until Christmas. We'll celebrate your wedding before the Christmas feast."

"I best get working on a dress," Mrs. Gilson said. "You'll look just fine in forest green."

"And food. I'll start working on food," added Mrs. Griswold. She turned to Sheriff Reynolds. "Is there a favorite food you want at your wedding, Sheriff?"

"I—"

"He'll eat anything," interrupted Mr. Griswold. "Heard he roasted squirrel one night during the search for the little boy. Any man who eats squirrel ain't gonna care what you serve at his wedding feast."

Millie cringed. Since she'd come to Colorado, she'd cooked bear, beaver, and even porcupine, but squirrel? She shook her head and asked, "Mr. Poor, you're talking about Major Wynkoop, the former commander of Fort Lyon, right?"

"Yep. Ned and I were young. Not as respectable as now, even though he'd been commissioned by Kansas Governor Denver as Sheriff of Arapahoe County at the time." Mr. Poor burped again, discovered a crumb stuck in his thick beard, and popped it into his mouth. "Anyway, times were tight. Most of us were staying just one step ahead of our creditors. Anyway, Louise wanted milk." He shook his head. "Ned, that man was in love. He'd give Louise anything she wanted, so out we went. Found a good milk cow at the military post. A distinctive looking critter with a stub-tail."

"What do you mean, a stub-tail?" Mrs. Gilson asked. She had the only milk cows in Idaho Springs.

"Somebody cut the critter's tail off," Mr. Poor explained. "No idea why, but it gave Ned and me an idea. I went to Smith and Chubbuck's meat market and Uncle Jake let me cut off the tail of one of his carcasses. That night, Ned and I went out and appropriated that cow. We attached its new tail on the way to its new home."

"How'd you attach the tail?" Mrs. Gilson asked.

"Hide glue. Worked great. The next morning, Louise was so pleased with her fresh milk, she made us a breakfast of hotcakes with real syrup." He looked at Buttercup and licked his lips. "Wasn't as good as roasted goat, but they tasted mighty fine."

Millie knew if Buttercup or her daughters ever disappeared, Mr. Poor would be the culprit. Trying to divert any thoughts the miner might have of stealing a goat, Millie asked, "Mr. Poor, wasn't it easy to tell the cow had a tail glued on?"

"Guess not, since the post's commanding officer come by, searching for his lost cow. He saw our new animal and immediately accused us of stealing. Ned, slick as a greased pig, says, 'But she hasn't a stub-tail, has she?' The officer looked at our cow for a long time before he finally agreed. 'Well, she isn't your cow, then,' Ned insisted, and that fool officer believed him."

"As the Bard would say," said Old Shakespeare, "'The robbed that smiles, steals something from the thief.' *Othello*."

FORTY-SEVEN

December 25, 1864

Christmas

Christmas afternoon, Millie had each of the boys carry dishes of food to the Beebee house. Dom, of course, carried Rachel. The little girl had lived with them for almost a week, never saying a word, and almost always attached to Dom. Her constant chewing had ruined two of Dom's shirts and even at night she refused to release Dom. Millie was losing patience with the child and even Dom was showing signs of missing wedded bliss.

The Beebee house was ablaze in candles and activity as a nervous Sheriff Reynolds stood in front of a Kinnikinnick altar, pacing as he pulled on the uncomfortable horsehair stock he'd borrowed from Dom. The scene was reminiscent of Millie's wedding, except behind the altar stood Parson Rice, and when Tit Bit arrived, there wasn't a brawl.

The former fancy girl beamed as Parson Rice married her to Sheriff Reynolds. The lawman hadn't really proposed, but he also hadn't put up much of a fight. "I now pronounce you man and wife," said Parson Rice. "You may kiss your bride."

Tit Bit let out a whoop of joy and threw herself into her husband's arms. Their kiss made Millie's face warm.

"It's Kissing Day," hollered Mr. Poor. "We get to kiss all

the women." He grabbed Millie's braid and pulled her over, his foul breath making the kiss rather unpleasant.

"Aye," hollered Blacksmith Shumate, pushing Mr. Poor aside and taking his turn with Millie.

Turning to Dom, Millie received a less than adequate kiss as Dom tried not to crush Rachel between them. Millie eyed the child and decided it was time to start some new rules. Taking Rachel from Dom's arm, Millie put her on the floor beside Samuel and Hosa. "Miss Rachel, you need to wish the boys a happy Kissing Day."

Rachel looked at Millie, gave her a petulant look that reminded Millie of Dom, and turned to Hosa. Without a word, the child leaned over and pecked him on the cheek. Repeating the procedure on Samuel, the child placed her hands on her hips and looked back up at Millie.

"Very good. Mr. Payne has begun to play his violin and I hear Doc Noxon accompanying him with a washboard. Hosa, Samuel, take Rachel and go dance." To Millie's surprise, the little girl allowed her brothers to lead her away.

"I can't believe she let you do that," Dom said, wiping at a soggy spot on his shirt. He pulled Millie to him and gave her a kiss that made her toes curl. "Red, what do you say we rent a room from Mrs. Beebee?" Before she could answer, he was dragging her through the dancers toward the lodging rooms.

"Mr. Drouillard, we cannot rent a room." Millie said it louder than she intended, and the matrons standing nearby all gasped. Blushing and a tad regretful, she pushed Dom away before helping the matrons put out food. "Check on the children."

Once the table was loaded with food, Mrs. Beebee warned, "Best move out of the way." They all stepped back, and she hollered, "sup's up." The men stampeded to the table, filling their plates before finding seats.

Mr. Griswold cleaned most of his plate before he rose

and took the stage. "To begin our Christmas celebration, I'll start with a story about the first Christmas celebrated in the Colorado Territory. It was told to me by William Larimer, son of General Larimer. It seems back in '58, just after gold had been discovered in Dry Creek, the early gold seekers decided to celebrate Christmas. Now you got to understand, at that time Denver City contained only a few rough cabins with canvas roofs and some tents. Nothing like today. The early gold diggers were struggling just to survive."

"But they were still celebrating Kissing Day," hollered Dom, giving Millie an exuberant kiss.

"Yes, but times were hard. Still, the men at the Spooner camp were determined to celebrate Christmas and invited several special guests including Samuel Curtis who'd platted out Denver City, and of course General Larimer." He paused, took a sip of his drink and smacked his lips.

"Fox Diefendorf makes a fine whiskey," Mr. Griswold said, "but for that first Christmas, we'd all be enjoying the Taos lightening brought by Uncle Dick Wootton. Everyone brought something. There were prickly pear preserves, buffalo, venison, prairie chicken, rice, bean soup, and a corn pudding. Now it's that corn dish I'll tell you about." Deliberately he paused, stepped from the stage to his plate, and spooned some of Mrs. Griswold's corn pudding into his mouth. "Mrs. Griswold, your corn pudding is awfully good."

"Why thank you, Mr. Griswold. I wonder if it's as good as the corn dish you just mentioned."

"Better. Much better." Dramatically he returned to the stage. "See, corn was real scarce that first Christmas, and General Larimer used the last of his rations to make a corn dish. The night before Christmas he put the dried corn in a cast-iron kettle to soak, and the next morning he brought his corn dish to the festivity. Guests gathered round and sat on buffalo robes as they ate, but young William Larimer noticed his father never ate any of his corn dish."

"I'd eat it," hollered Mr. Poor, scraping the last of Mrs. Griswold's corn onto his plate.

Elder Griswold scowled at Mr. Poor and continued. "After eating, the festivities began. Charlie Gilmore started a game of chuck-a-luck, 'Con' Orem amused the group with wrestling and boxing, and others told jokes and stories. Only after the festivities were over did young William ask his father why he hadn't touched his corn dish."

"Why he not eat it?" Jake asked, looking down at his own corn with distrust.

"Young William said his father hemmed and hawed, but eventually he admitted the truth. He said that morning, when he started cooking the corn, he'd discovered a large, dark object in the pot. The corn bubbled up, and with it came a fat field mouse."

The crowd of rowdy miners gasped.

"Yes," repeated Elder Griswold, "General Larimer was perplexed. He didn't have more dried corn, so he removed the mouse, rinsed the corn, and finished cooking it. Young William said his father slapped him on the back and said it was an example of 'double economy.' He'd saved the corn and abstained from eating any himself."

Mr. Griswold laughed and returned to the table, scooping up another spoonful of corn pudding. Millie looked down at her own plate and pushed it away, no longer hungry.

"Were there a mouse in my corn pudding?" asked a high, childlike voice.

Every head swiveled toward the fire.

"Rachel, did you say something?" Dom looked dumbfounded.

"Were there a mouse in my corn pudding?" repeated the little girl, looking down at her plate.

"You talk!" said Samuel.

"Not matter," Hosa said, licking his plate. "Mice taste good."

"You eat mice?" The girl looked at Hosa like he was a monster.

"When hungry, mice good. Just little bones." He glanced around uncomfortably as the room exploded into laughter.

Hours later, Millie, Dom, Mary, and Jake laid three sleeping children on quilts beside the goats in front of the fire. Dom and Jake, who'd carried the children, dropped into the rocking chairs with a groan. Millie and Mary pulled up chairs and joined them around the fireplace.

"Miss Millie," Mary said, yawning. "It sure funny."

"What's funny, Miss Mary?"

"You married, bound and determined not to have childers, yet looky here. One year and you got three!" She turned and grinned. "How many come next year?"

Millie shook her head. After this year, she didn't want to imagine what 1865 might bring.

Author's Note

Denver City Justice is a work of fiction, but as an author and researcher, I strive to include accurate details about actual historical events and historical figures. Many of the historical events, people, and stories included are historically accurate, but I have taken some artistic license, especially in three areas. First, the details about the Musgrove lynching are accurate, but the lynching actually took place in 1868 not 1864. Musgrove was captured by David Cook, the chief of the Rocky Mountain Detective Association, and I've used the description of Ed Franklin's death and Musgrove's hanging from Cook's biography, *Hands Up: Or, Twenty Years of Detective Life in the Mountains and on the Plains* (1882).

Next, when planning Jake and Mary's wedding, I wanted it to be in a church. The Zion Baptist Church wasn't founded until November 15, 1865, but I placed their wedding there since it was, as far as I can determine, the first African-American church in Denver.

I have also taken artistic license with Mrs. Byers, the wife of the well-known editor of the *Rocky Mountain News*. Mrs. Byers was known for her philanthropic work in founding both the Ladies' Union Aid Society and the Denver Children's Home. She was a remarkable woman, but she did not, as far as I know, assist in any jailbreaks.

Finally, in both *The Lucky Hat Mine* and *Denver City Justice*, I have put pockets in Millie's aprons and her coats, although pockets didn't really show up in womens' clothing until the early 1900s. What can I say? Where else could I have put her six-shooter?

I'm always happy to answer questions about my books or the history in them, so please send me questions at Julie@JvLBell.com. I hope you enjoyed *Denver City Justice*.

—Julie

Acknowledgements

As with my first novel, *The Lucky Hat Mine*, this book went through numerous revisions, thanks to many beta readers, various critiques, and my editors, Jon and Jody Hansen. I must give a special thanks to my critique group, the members of the 30th Street Fiction: Kate, Rick, Ian, Lezly, Tim, Mike, Juli, Jessica, Evan, Maggie, and Caitlin. They all spent many hours reviewing chapters and suggesting improvements. I also want to give special thanks to my editors at the Hansen Publishing Group. They've given me so much of their time as we worked on rewrites and improvements.

My first beta readers were my daughters, Tess and Corrie, who helped me find weaknesses in the first draft before beta readers, Tim Stephenson and HL Miller, provided valuable feedback about story flow and plot. I will forever be thankful for HL Miller's twisted sense of humor and his recommendation to have a tussle in the middle of Millie's wedding. My nieces, Kara and Nicole, provided feedback on story structure and grammar, and my final beta readers and editors, Sarah-Finch Rollins, Kristin Yodock, Peggy Howell, Helen Matterson, June Hahl, David Springfield, Joyce Bell, and Mary George, helped me to polish the final manuscript.

Denver City Justice wouldn't be a published book without the hard work, historical checking, and editing of the employees at the Hansen Publishing Group. I can't thank them enough. Finally, photographer extraordinaire Cliff Conklin took some amazing pictures of models Theresa VanLaanen and Keita Linden, and Nikki Rasmussen turned them into an amazing cover that I love.

The best part of writing, as far as I'm concerned, is the research. The stories in *Denver City Justice* came from several references, but my favorites were *The Gentle Tamers: Women of the Old Wild West* by Dee Brown, *The 59ers: Roaring Denver in the Gold Rush Days* by Stanley W. Zamonski and Teddy Keller, *Hands Up: Or, Twenty Years of Detective Life in the Mountains and on the Plains* by Detective Cook, and *Rocky Mountain Medicine: Doctors, Drugs, and Disease in Early Colorado* by Robert H. Shikes, MD. Of course, the cookbooks and etiquette books from the 1800s are some of my favorite reading.

As with *The Lucky Hat Mine*, I must thank all the wonderful people who have helped me and apologize for anyone I missed. I also apologize for any historical errors I have made.

Thanks for reading Denver City Justice.

—Julie

About the Author

J.v.L. BELL is a Colorado native who was raised climbing Colorado's 14,000 foot mountains, exploring old ghost towns, and reading stories about life in the early frontier days. She enjoys hiking with friends and family, visiting new places and meeting new people, rafting the rivers of Utah and Colorado, and reading great historical fiction. She lives in Louisville, Colorado with her two daughters and her husband.

Curious what is fact versus fiction in *Denver City Justice?* Visit the author's web page at www.JvLBell.com and read her blogs about the historical topics she researched while writing *Denver City Justice.*

ALSO BY J.V.L. BELL
THE LUCKY HAT MINE

The Lucky Hat Mine, filled with period detail and real-life pioneers such as Mountain Charley, Green Russell and the Tabors, is a spirited…tale.
—Sandra Dallas, *The Denver Post*

The inclusion of strong female characters, such as a freedwoman, adds to the appeal of the story…The novel is an entertaining read.
—Waheed Rabbani, *Historical Novel Review*

What's a Southern belle to do in 1863? Wife-wanted ads are always risky business, but Millie Virginia never imagined she'd survive the perilous trip across the Great Plains to find her intended husband in a pine box. Was he killed in an accident? Or murdered for his gold mine? Stuck in the mining town of Idaho Springs, Colorado territory, without friends or means, Millie is beleaguered by undesirable suitors and threatened by an unknown assailant. Her troubles escalate when the brother of her dead fiancé, Dominic Drouillard, unexpectedly turns up.

Available in paperback, ebook, and audiobook.

www.ingramcontent.com/pod-product-compliance
Lightning Source LLC
Chambersburg PA
CBHW071529260626
47170CB00002B/562